Praise for *MATTEO: Wild Fire*

The second book in her Raging Fire spinoff series, Matteo: Wild Fire, features more of her trademark relatable characters… They are strong but not infallible, and their experiences are believable. One of Masters's strengths is her dedication to "getting it right"—and her research pays off in delivering a story that, while containing fictional people and places, could easily be people and places we know. As an added bonus, some of the Rescue Me characters made appearances and gave us a little bit of an update on their lives. By the end of the story, Matt and Dakota felt like good friends, and I was cheering them on to their happy ending. Another job well-done for Kally, and I can't wait for the next book!

~ Erin3, a BookBub reviewer

~ ~ ~

Wow! You, Ms Kally have done it again! Matteo and Dakota's story was so touching, loving and amazing I really don't have words. I tip my cowboy, cowgirl hat to you.

~ ronib, an Amazon reviewer

~ ~ ~

I just loved this couple! … Their chemistry was amazing and the fun they have carries over into their steamy times too. It wasn't all lightness, there are some serious issues these two need to work through, and there is tenderness and caring as well. They made me smile, tear up, and squirm, and that is the best recommendation I can give

~ Dar, a Goodreads reviewer

~ ~ ~

If you want a story that has heart and soul, then Matteo: Wild Fire is the book for you. … I loved the connection between Matteo and Dakota; it was built on a solid friendship. These two could not be more different, Matteo is carefree whilst Dakota keeps her own counsel, but the chemistry that sizzles between them is impossible to ignore. Matteo is totally swoon worthy, such a kind, caring, protective man that I fell for hard and fast. It is obvious that Dakota has trust issues and that she has spent most of her life looking over her shoulder. I enjoyed the playfulness of their relationship but having said that there were serious issues that needed to be addressed, and they were handled well. … Matteo: Wild Fire was well written, with characters whose story you cannot help but become invested in. There were numerous layers to Matteo and Dakota, and it was fascinating as they were peeled back layer by layer until all was revealed in this emotional story.

~ **Erin Lewis, a Goodreads reviewer**

~ ~ ~

Matteo:Wild Fire I think is one of the best books Kallypso Masters has written. This is the story of Matteo and Dakota. Matteo doesn't realize he's missing something in his life until he sees Dakota. Dakota ends up injured riding a bull and goes to Matteo's to heal. She starts to remember things from her past that she has blocked out. I just love these two!

~ **Annette, a Goodreads reviewer**

Beth,
Thanks for the tour of your camper. You helped me with those scenes so much!

MATTEO: Wild Fire

(Second in Raging Fire Series)

Kallypso Masters

Kallypso Masters

Ka-thunk! Publishing

MATTEO: Wild Fire
Second in Raging Fire Series
Kallypso Masters

Ka-thunk! Publishing
Print Edition
E-book ISBN: 978-1941060384
Print ISBN: 978-1941060391

Serial published on Patreon: December 2019 to October 2021
Original e-book and print novel published: October 28, 2021
Last revised for e-book and print: November 10, 2021

MATTEO: WILD FIRE
Content edited by Meredith Bowery
Line edited by Christine Sullivan Mulcair
Cover design by Syneca Featherstone of Original Syn
Cover images licensed through Adobe Stock
and graphically altered by Syneca Featherstone
Formatted by BB eBooks

This book contains content that is not suitable for readers 17 and under.

To discover more about the books in this series, see the Books by Kallypso Masters page at the end of this book. For more about Kallypso Masters, please go to the About the Author section.

Dedication

To **Patryce Cornett**, **Margie Dees**, **Annette Elens**, **Barb Jack**, **Lisa Simo-Kinzer**, and **Elaine Swinney,** who have been with me as alpha readers from start to finish on this book. Your input and suggestions on ways to make my story better are invaluable. And having your honest feedback and reader reactions gave me the confidence to release my book to my other readers.

My utmost thanks to all who serve in or who have served in the fire services in their communities, including those serving with state and federal Forest Service entities. The sacrifices you make—physical, emotional, and financial—to do your best every day inspire me. You're true American heroes, and we civilians owe you so much for your dedication.

Acknowledgements

My eternal gratitude and thanks go out to…

my content editor, **Meredith Bowery**, whose uncanny insights into my characters and their motivations and psychological makeup help me take them through the growth and realization we all wish we could figure out in real life.

Duffy Counsell, one of the organizers of the Leadville Ski Joring Festival who helped me bring those scenes to life and called Dakota "Bodacious!" for what she does in her first-ever Ski Joring Festival competition. Your enthusiasm for the story line were welcome too. And I'm grateful for your being available to talk over the phone and via email as I continued to ask "just one more question." I appreciated your praise for my existing knowledge base coming into our first conversation (in large part due to the next person I'll be thanking here). Getting the research right is a hallmark of a "Kally Book" and something my readers have come to expect! Several of my team and I are planning to visit Leadville for an upcoming festival in 2023 or beyond and look forward to meeting you and some of the legendaries in the sport.

my proofreader and line editor, **Christine Mulcair**, whose keen eye and superb knowledge of spelling, punctuation, and grammar give me confidence that my book is as perfect as it can be when I publish, but the way you helped me whip the skijoring chapters into shape at the last minute by sorting through the information about skijoring in general and the Leadville Ski Joring Festival in particular went above and beyond! Both before and after we connected with Duffy (who you guided me to via Facebook), you helped me by finding research sources.

Patryce and **Michael Cornett,** FF/NRP/FP-C, for providing their expertise from a fire and rescue perspective. And bull riding. And how to survive in extreme cold! You always seem to have just the right knowledge to help me with whatever scenario I throw at you in my Raging Fire series!

Lisa Simo-Kinzer for helping me with the scenes leading up to and at the fictitious Grand Junction rodeo after Meredith said I just didn't get it right in the first draft. You channeled the characters for me and made the scenes much more emotional and realistic given where they were in their relationship.

TeraLe Jaques and **Gina Marcantonio** for their input as alpha readers before life intruded. And, Gina, as always, thanks for helping me get the Giardanos spot-on from an Italian's perspective, right up to the day I sent this one to the formatter. And thank you to the alpha readers named in my dedication for all you've done to help me perfect this story.

Patreon fan club members for providing me with two more celestial name suggestions to go with Twinkle Littlestar for Matt's two other horses—**Regina Peppers** for Streaking Comet and **Shannon O'Malley** for Big Dipper. And **Hollie** for catching a couple things I missed while revising!

Beth Curlin Weber, thanks for the tour of your Shasta "canned ham" camper/trailer! You helped me envision some of my scenes in a whole new way!

all my Patreon fan club members who read along as I post installments and encourage me with your comments. I love that you can read the rough drafts and then notice and appreciate the changes that come with the final version.

and to all my loyal fans everywhere who have stuck by me through thick and thin. I just celebrated ten years of publishing and I know many of you have been there right from the start! I appreciate you!

Author's Note

The **Raging Fire** series builds upon characters and relationships where the **Rescue Me Saga** and **Rescue Me Saga Extras** series left off. Matteo and Dakota don't have a history together there, but you did get to know Matteo/Matt a little better in *Nobody's Dream.* In this book, Matteo and Dakota burn up the pages with their passionate personalities! And "Mama Giardano" has stolen the hearts of so many readers with her straight talk and her devotion to family.

As readers have come to expect realism in my books, Raging Fire will deal with a lot of the stresses and tragedies associated with the firefighting community, but also the camaraderie and celebrations. I try to portray some of the lesser-known aspects of being a firefighter in this series, from Tony's water rescue and dive team to Matteo's work with the forest service and so many motor vehicle accidents.

Some invaluable resources I'll be making use of regularly while writing about these four firefighters and their spouses will be:

Challenges of the Firefighter Marriage, by **Anne and Mike Gagliano**.

I also listen to a number of podcasts hosted by firefighters or focusing on the fire service that have helped me gain a better understanding of the firefighting brotherhood and sisterhood. The ones that have helped immeasurably are: **Code 3: The Firefighters Podcast**, **Firefighter Training Podcast**, **Fire Engineering**, and **Firefighters Toolbox**. Hearing firefighters talking about their experiences and offering ideas to improve training and experiences on the fire ground have also sparked ideas for scenes in this series.

And for those in the fire service or wanting to know more, Patryce Cornett recommends:

Honor and Commitment: Standard Life Operating Guidelines for Firefighters and their Families, by **Lori Mercer** (honorandcommitment.com)

Firefighter Wife—Because your Heart Belongs to a Hero (firefighter-wife.com)

Fire Dept. Family (firedeptfamily.com) has a number of helpful articles and tips for fire service families.

Fully Involved Life (fullyinvolvedlife.com) offers all first responders and their families crisis intervention, critical debriefings, classes, and other resources for PTSD, EMDR, Peer Support, and Education & Training.

Chapter One

Matt Giardano tipped his head back and poured beer down his parched throat. He'd forgotten how dusty and hot it could be in the Texas Panhandle, even this late in October. Glancing around the raucous Amarillo bar, he wondered if the rodeo crowd was mostly local, or people like him who just happened to be in town and went to the rodeo.

No matter. He didn't feel like engaging tonight. This morning's wildland fire control training exercises had been grueling, and Matt needed time and space to process it all before he was ever put into a position of needing to use what he'd learned. He hoped his county wouldn't get hit with fires like his brothers Rafe and Tony's department in Aspen Corners had two years ago.

This evening, he'd attended the Saturday rodeo hoping to take his mind off work for a while. He planned on enjoying a few beers tonight before returning to his motel room. Most likely alone, but he'd keep his options open.

A loud whoop went up, and everyone turned toward the door where a woman in a tan-colored suede Western jacket stood smiling as she accepted their accolades. She must have competed today and won, judging by the pats on the back and bear hugs given as she made her way to the bar to order a longneck. Any number of cowboys—real and wannabe—offered to pay, but she waved them off.

The cowgirl's ginger curls spilled out from under her Stetson and more than halfway down her back. He didn't remember any redheads in the barrel-racing competition at today's rodeo. *That* he would have remembered.

When she turned to the guy standing near Matt and flashed him a fun-loving smile, Matt's cock stirred to life. God didn't make anything sexier than a playful woman with long red hair.

Why did something about her look so familiar? He didn't know any of the barrel racers competing this weekend. He'd checked his program before the performances in case he might recognize a name, but none had jumped out at him.

Then she looked beyond the cowboy straight at Matt, and he felt gut-punched. Her eyes widened—eyes he'd *definitely* seen before—and her smile faded before she forced it back onto her face.

Alison Parker?

No way. Her hair had been short and blonde in high school. But those emerald-green eyes were unmistakable and unforgettable. They'd been in 4-H together during their junior and senior years. She'd loved horses too, which apparently hadn't changed for either of them. But they'd never dated; they'd just been friends and fellow competitors.

Too bad for him.

She excused herself, picked up her beer bottle, and approached Matt. With each step, his heart ramped up a little more, but the stiffness in her gait told him she might be preparing herself for some kind of confrontation.

With him? Why?

"Long time, no see, Matteo."

"I could say the same, Alison. And I go by Matt now."

She cocked her head, a bit of a twinkle finally reentering her eyes. "Matteo suits you better." *What was that supposed to mean?* "And I go by Dakota Mathison these days, so I guess we both have new names to learn."

Dakota Mathison? The Dakota Mathison Matt had watched ride this afternoon—curious to find a woman riding broncs. He'd marveled at how well the rider had stacked up against the men in the competition. After a quick Google search while sitting in the stands, he'd discovered Mathison had been riding broncs for quite a while now. Things sure had changed since he'd been interested in rodeoing.

Would he have recognized her if he'd found a decent photo of her? Mathison usually wore a helmet while competing and he wouldn't have remembered Alison as a redhead.

Funny how he'd always had a thing for redheads and now Alison-turned-Dakota was ginger.

But he couldn't reconcile that his former high-school classmate Alison had become a rodeo star under a completely different name and appearance.

Remembering his manners, he vacated his barstool. "Here, have a seat."

"After the ride I had today, don't mind if I do."

Matt tamped down the thoughts running through his head about riding *her.* Mama had taught him to behave better than that around women, especially ones as sweet as Alison. However, her new name and persona gave him fantasies that were anything but sweet.

Dakota. Damn, the name was as hot as she was.

"If you want to keep calling me Matteo, I'm good with that." His full first name coming from her lips sounded pretty damned sexy—and special.

He stood next to her only a few moments before the cowboy she'd been flirting with earlier walked off to find someone else to take home tonight. Matt grabbed the vacant stool, pulled it closer, and sat down next to her. Now they sat face-to-face.

"I didn't see your name in the events program," she said.

She'd looked for it? *Nah.* Everybody in the rodeo knew who else was participating, so she probably was just saying she hadn't seen him around. "Not competing anymore." He hadn't done so since college. "Just came to watch tonight before I head home to Colorado tomorrow."

There had been a time he'd fancied himself doing the national or regional rodeo circuit, but life didn't always turn out the way you planned it as a kid.

"I saw you riding that bronc today. You're damned good."

She shrugged and took a swallow of her beer. "Thanks. It'll do for now." Had what he'd first read in her response as being modesty actually been dissatisfaction?

"Until what?"

Her face lit up. "I'm attending bull-riding school in January with a group of women who also want to compete in the sport next year."

Was she insane? Women didn't ride bulls. They rarely even rode broncs. "Those animals will get you killed."

She came the closest he'd ever seen to someone imitating a cartoon character with steam pouring out of her ears. "Would you say that to a male bull rider?"

Probably not. He shrugged rather than answer directly. "It's an insane sport for *anyone* who doesn't have a death wish."

She narrowed her eyes. Had he crossed the line and ruined any chance of getting to spend more time with her? Clearly, she loved the idea of bull riding. Maybe after a few falls, she'd reevaluate.

If she survived.

"I assure you, Matteo," she began with measured words, "I take more precautions than the men do and have no wish to end my life anytime soon. No matter what I ride—broncs or bulls—I wear a helmet and vest." She glanced away to order them both another beer. He made a mental note to ask the bartender to give him the check at the end of the night.

He looked at her profile and became distracted by that glorious head of red hair. Time for a change of subject. "You used to be a blonde."

"Actually, my hair was dyed in high school, but it's natural now." She glanced away before explaining.

That response surprised him. He had no clue. She'd moved into Aspen Corners halfway into their junior year and had already been a blonde on day one. What other secrets did she have tucked away?

"Well, for what it's worth, I like it better red," Matt said. *A lot better.* Ginger suited her. He curbed the urge to touch it.

She raised her eyebrow and met his gaze again before smiling enigmatically. Did she have any idea how many men found redheads sexy?

They spent the next hour or so reminiscing about their time together in 4-H showing horses at county and state fairgrounds. She'd been a barrel racer then.

After a few more beers, Matt's buzzed mind returned to their earlier conversation.

"Why bulls?"

"Same reasons men choose to ride them. The adrenaline rush. Accomplishing the impossible. Trying to tame the beast, if only for eight-second intervals. Haven't you ever done anything a little risky just for the thrill?" She held up her hand with a smile. "Don't answer that. Of course you have. I remember any number of Matteo Giardano stunts during high school."

Yeah, I definitely like how my name sounds on her lips.

Speaking of lips, he zeroed in on hers and wondered what it would be like to kiss her. Pulling himself back into their discussion, Matt shrugged. "Adrenaline rushes I can understand." That was probably what he enjoyed most about skijoring and firefighting. "But getting on the back of a pissed-off, two-thousand-pound angry bull goes way beyond adrenaline. What are you trying to prove?"

She drew herself up while remaining perched on the stool, narrowed her eyes, and took a deep breath. "Matteo, it's been nice seeing you again, but I don't need to explain my career choices to you or anyone else." Disappointment clearly shone in her expression now. Disappointment aimed at him.

"I saw you take precautions while riding broncs and am sure you'd wear protective gear on bulls too, but I'd have to be crazy or drunk to get on the back of a bull and try to ride for two seconds, much less eight. It's simple self-preservation."

No helmet or vest would protect her from a neck or back injury.

She rolled her eyes and asked the bartender for a shot of whiskey. After downing it in one gulp, she chased it with the rest of her beer before facing him again. "I guess that's where we differ, Matteo, and also where we'll have to part company. I'm going to bed so I'll be ready for my ride tomorrow afternoon."

Combining the words "bed" and "riding" sent his brain off into an area he didn't need to be going and made him hard. He hadn't experienced this strong an instantaneous response to a woman in a long time, if ever.

Alison—*Dakota* now—stood abruptly and swayed.

"Whoa!" Matt grabbed her by both biceps, surprised at the muscles he wrapped his fingers around. When she steadied herself, he let her go with great reluctance. "I'll walk you back to wherever you're staying tonight." He wanted to make sure she made it there safely.

"You don't need to do that. The rodeo grounds are only a few blocks away."

No way was she walking back alone at night and with this much alcohol in her system. Matt pulled out his wallet. "Bartender!" He handed over a fifty and when she returned with the change, he dropped a twenty in the tip jar.

Dakota seemed to be zoning out on her feet. Between the adrenaline drop after her bronc ride and the consumption of alcohol, her body definitely needed a bed.

He was ready for one too, even if his only option was the one at his motel. He'd switched shifts with another firefighter so he could attend this five-day wildfire training but would have to start making it up by working Monday's red shift. He'd make up the other shift day next week because he wasn't allowed to work four days straight.

He'd need to head home by midafternoon tomorrow to give him time to catch a little sleep before reporting in at the fire station in Leadville. The drive wasn't all that long when not pulling a horse trailer behind him, though after that intensive training he might have trouble staying awake. He never slept well at the station—or in motels—and was ready to be back in his own bed.

Before leaving town, though, he planned to catch Alison's—no, *Dakota's*—ride tomorrow. Matt texted the teenage boy who was looking after his two horses and asked if he could take care of them Sunday night too. The response was almost immediate that he'd love to.

Great! That bought him a few extra hours.

"Ready?" he asked her, releasing one arm but not the other until he was certain she'd be steady on her feet.

"You don't have to take me back to the rodeo grounds. I can take care of myself," she insisted. She'd been doing that for a long time. But Matteo didn't let her go. The heat from his hand did weird things to her insides. She'd had the worst crush on him in high school, but he hadn't been interested in her in that way. He saw her more as a friend or a second sister.

Why'd he come back into her life again now? There'd been a time when she'd have welcomed him as a love interest—

Whoa, Nellie! He wasn't going to be anything of the sort. He just wanted to make sure she made it safely back to her truck.

"Where are you staying?" he asked as they exited the bar. The sun had set while they were inside.

"My truck and camper are parked beyond the barns." Dakota pointed in the general direction of the rodeo grounds. A few years ago, she'd purchased a vintage Shasta camper/trailer and restored it to near-mint condition on her months off between competitions. With the camper hitched to her truck, she always had a familiar bed to lay her bone-weary body on each night, which sure beat flopping in a fleabag hotel or sleeping on a cot in the barns. And this one had water and electricity hookups, a kitchenette, fridge, and dining area to give her more of the comforts of home than she'd had in, well, a lifetime.

Something about the camper made her feel safe and secure as if snuggled in a cocoon. A home on wheels. Well, enough home for her. Nothing more than a microwave for cooking, but there were plenty of cafés and concession stands nearby to supply all the coffee and rodeo grub she needed.

Determined to show him she didn't need any further assistance, halfway down the block she eased away from his hold on her elbow. Not in a "don't touch me" way, because his hand felt kind of nice there, but she didn't lean on any man.

Matteo remained close enough that he could catch her if she stumbled, but she was determined to show him she hadn't had too many beers, even if she might have overdone it in her nervousness about meeting someone from the past. Being with him again stirred up all the sadness she'd felt growing up. She didn't like experiencing those feelings again.

Dakota usually stopped at one or two drinks the night before an event, but seeing Matteo had rattled her. Whether he realized it or not, this man knew things she'd buried long ago. Dakota had worked hard since high school to reinvent herself. New name. New personality. New hair color. Okay, so the hair color wasn't new to her, but it was to those who had known her back then.

Like Matteo.

Dakota couldn't help but notice how fascinated Matteo had been with her hair at the bar; he hadn't been able to take his eyes off it. He'd surprised her by remembering the color from back in school. Heck, she'd been blown away that he'd remembered her at all.

Nowadays, her long, natural ginger tresses were one of her trademarks when she rode without a helmet, and he wasn't the only man to appreciate them.

"Where do you call home these days?" he asked as they ambled along.

"Wherever I lay my head at night."

"I mean, where's home base?"

"Don't have one. I ride my own circuit of unsanctioned rodeos from March until the end of the season, then I travel around the country for a few months until it's time to start it all over again. I've made it to forty-two states so far. Where I go depends on how good the winnings have been that season." This year, she might need to pick up a few extra events during the off months; her winnings had been subpar lately. Maybe this weekend would be the turning point, and she'd have more rides like this one.

"How do you get your mail?"

Leave it to Matteo to be concerned about the practicalities of it all. "A box at a post office in Pueblo. I don't get much more than tax and insurance information by snail mail anymore. Most things I can do online at public libraries."

Matteo remained silent as they walked nearly another block before saying, "You don't get lonely?"

She'd have to want to be with people to miss them.

"I have plenty of people around me during the rodeo season. In my downtime, I look forward to the quiet of the wind blowing over the mesas, deserts, or prairies and the snow hitting my face while on a mountain trail ride. Or dipping my toes in the Gulf while walking along a Texas beach."

People would only spoil those moments for her. She'd been alone most of her adult life and preferred it that way now.

And yet, thoughts of traveling around with this man beside her didn't exactly repulse her.

"I used to sleep in the back of my truck or in a stall at the rodeo grounds before buying myself a camper."

Before he asked any more personal questions, she decided to turn the tables. "We spent so much time talking about me and high school at the bar that you didn't say what you're doing these days. Still interested in horses?"

"Sure am. On the ranch I purchased last year, I settled the two mustangs I rescued over the past few years. Only sixty acres, but it's perfect for them and me."

"I can remember you talking about having a ranch back in school."

He nodded. "Got tired of boarding them at a friend's ranch in Fairchance and having to drive almost ninety minutes one way to see them."

"Sounds nice. So, you've stopped doing rodeo?"

"Yeah, but the town where I work has an annual skijoring festival that I compete in."

"Skijoring?" She gave him a sideways glance, and he grinned.

"Picture horseback riding at breakneck speed while pulling a skier through an obstacle course of ice and packed snow. Leadville sets up their course down Harrison Street, the main drag. That's also where my fire station is located. We help convert the street into the skijoring course for the festival every year."

"Why'd you settle in Leadville and not Aspen Corners?"

"My brother Franco was hired on by the fire department there, so when I graduated from college, he encouraged me to apply for an opening they had."

"So you're a fireman now?"

He nodded, and they entered the main gate to the rodeo grounds.

"Wasn't your dad a firefighter?"

"Actually, no. He did search and rescue on a team out of our local fire department, but he worked as a pipe fitter."

Matteo had often talked about how proud he was of his papa's heroics, which was all she remembered. The few times she'd seen the man at their competitions, he seemed nice and clearly loved his son.

Had Dakota ever known her own father? She shook off the irrelevant question.

"All of my brothers are firefighters now, actually. It's become the family business. And my sister, Angelina—I don't know if you remember her—married an EMT who works the same shift as my brother Tony at the Aspen Corners station."

"I vaguely remember your sister, but I definitely remember one of your brothers showing up at the fair during the summer between junior and senior years." But she'd hightailed it out of Aspen Corners the night they'd graduated and hadn't looked back.

"That was Rafe. He rides some too, not to mention that he's always liked to be supportive of whatever the rest of us were doing."

"Must be nice. I was an only child." *Well, as far as I know.*

"Maybe that's why you don't mind being alone so much. I'd go stir-crazy after a week. Being one of five, I'm just used to having lots of people in close proximity at all times."

"Do you live alone?" *Way to hint at whether there was a woman waiting for him back at his ranch, Dakota.*

"Just me, my horses, and a few barn cats. It gets a little lonely, but I work forty-eight-hour shifts and that gives me plenty of social interactions to fill the void."

Having one place to go to, day in and day out, would bore her to death. *To each his own.*

Dakota stopped and pointed at her camper a few yards away. "This is home for me." With the life she led, she didn't want to be limited to a sixty-acre ranch—or a six-hundred-acre one, for that matter. She had the whole world at her feet and preferred it that way.

"You're a regular tumbling tumbleweed, Alis—*Dakota.* Sorry. It's going to take me some time to get used to a new name for you."

Not that she expected to see him again. Their paths certainly hadn't crossed since graduation day more than fourteen years ago.

"Anyway, sounds like you just blow wherever the wind takes you."

Dakota gave a shrug. She'd been so happy to shed everything from the past.

"Not so much the wind as the rodeo circuit schedule."

"You sure this is safe?" he asked, pointing to the camper.

"I haven't had any problems so far, but I'd shoot the balls off any man who enters my camper without an invitation."

He grinned. "I'll be sure to remember that."

She chuckled. Would she have invited Matteo inside under different circumstances? Probably not. She used to do the one-night stands with cowboys riding the circuit but hadn't been interested in recent years so she hadn't invited any man inside her camper. If she and Matteo embarked on any kind of relationship, he'd become a complication that would interfere with her way of life.

"Thanks for walking me back from the bar. I appreciate it." No one had looked out for her safety in a long, long time.

"I'll be watching for you in the saddle broncs tomorrow."

He planned to stay?

"I think they have us down for shortly after noon."

He nodded. "Good luck, Dakota. Stay safe."

"I'm sure your job is a lot more dangerous than mine."

She wasn't sure what else to say or do, so she held out her hand to shake his. He just looked at it, then said, "I'm a hugger. You okay with that?"

No. She valued her personal space. But she'd get rid of him quicker if she hugged him, so she closed the gap. His arms wrapped around her, and something in the gesture made tears sting her eyes. She shouldn't have had that shot of whiskey. Her defenses were down.

Blinking rapidly so as not to give away how emotionally fragile she felt at the moment, Dakota didn't make eye contact with Matteo before she turned toward the camper.

"Night, Dakota. I'll just wait until you're tucked safely inside," Matteo said.

"I can tell you aren't leaving until I'm inside." She put the key in the lock and opened the side door.

"Sweet dreams. Have a great ride tomorrow."

"I'll do my best." She wasn't as worried about the draw for broncs as she would be if riding a bull. Saddle broncs were a piece of cake. "Goodnight, Matteo."

She went inside and locked the door behind her. After opening the louver windows at both ends of her bed to let in the fall breeze, she stretched out on the mattress, staring up at the ceiling. Not that she could see much in the dark interior, because she'd intentionally parked away from the lights.

Dakota closed her eyes.

And all she could see now was the sexy smile of a handsome Italian fireman on a horse.

Chapter Two

Dakota hadn't dreamed this vividly in years, but that horseman in fireman's gear lit a fire inside her that burned long after she awoke at dawn. Voices outside her camper told her the rodeo grounds were gearing up for another busy day which would culminate for her with a ride in the saddle bronc finals at noon.

She rolled over, not quite ready to let go of that smoking-hot dream. Unfortunately, her head ached from too much booze, and her shoulders and leg muscles had grown stiff and sore from the aftereffects of the bronc she'd ridden yesterday. At least the horse had earned her extra points for being a bucking son of a bitch.

The aroma of coffee wrestled her from her bed. Caffeine always helped. She dressed for the day as quickly as her body and the cramped space would allow and opened the door.

"Good morning." The deep voice startled her at first, then she saw Matteo sitting on the ground nearby with two lidded cups beside him. Must be the coffee she'd just smelled.

"Wow. Delivery? How long have you been sitting out here?"

"Not long." He stood up and held out a hand to help her exit the camper. While she stretched to get the kinks out, he picked up one of the cups and extended it to her. "Coffee's still hot." He then retrieved his own.

Without uttering another word, she removed the lid and inhaled deeply. After testing its hotness, she blew on it and took a sip. Then another. After half a cup, she began to feel human again and smiled at him.

"You're my angel of mercy."

His laugh came from his chest. "I've been called a lot of things, but you're probably the first person who's ever called me that." His broad shoulders and chiseled pecs filled out the denim shirt wonderfully, making her wonder what lay underneath it.

Not that she had any intention of finding out.

"One of the local fire stations has a tent set up with an all-you-can-eat pancake breakfast a few minutes' walk from here. Wanna join me?"

Her stomach growled at the mental image of stacks of pancakes dripping in butter and syrup. He grinned.

"I'll take that as a *yes*."

"Definitely! You sure know how to take care of a gal." Not that she needed or wanted any man taking care of her, but she had to admit having curbside caffeine service and company for breakfast wasn't bad.

They walked slowly through the camping area, with her being greeted by others in the rodeo community and saying hello back to them. One big happy family. She'd never known a time when she'd been part of a family—until the rodeo.

At the huge white tent, they stood in line; the smell of pancakes and sausage nearly did her in. "I didn't know how hungry I was until you mentioned food."

Matteo engaged in conversation with one of the firefighters on duty, comparing departments and apparatus while Dakota accepted the congratulations of several well-wishers for her ride yesterday. When she tried to pay for her breakfast, he insisted it was all part of the coffee service.

"Thanks. I'll get the next meal." Not that she expected there to be one. She'd be hitting the road tonight for her next rodeo and Matteo would probably be heading back home this afternoon.

"Tell me about your horses and your ranch," she said after sitting down at one of the long tables with their plates and coffee refills.

"I moved my two mustangs from Fairchance this past spring." He took a bite, swallowed, and continued. "My ranch is about fifteen minutes outside Leadville. Mixture of pasture and evergreen woods on an old miner's claim that borders some Bureau of Land Management property. I get some seasonal runoff from one of the mountains, not that I need it as a water supply. My well is pretty deep. But I have a million-dollar view of the Collegiate peaks."

"I don't think I've ever been to Leadville."

"Consider yourself invited anytime you want to visit."

She nodded noncommittally but had no intention of making *that* trip anytime soon.

"Where to after today?" he asked.

"A rodeo in Utah, then it's back to Texas just before Thanksgiving. It's hard to find top-paying events that allow women to ride broncs with the men." She refused to risk her neck on the lower-paying women-only competitions. When she started on the bull-riding circuit, it would be even harder.

"There might be a reason for that."

Dakota glared at him. "Yeah, it's a good ol' boys' sport. But we girls are changing that one rodeo fan at a time. We're already getting the loudest cheers wherever we compete."

While the money had improved for women over the last few years in sanctioned events, she didn't want to go back to barrel racing. But with unsanctioned exhibitions and jackpot rodeos, sometimes women were allowed to ride saddle broncs and even bulls. That's where the money was for her in rodeo. These payouts more than covered travel costs and helped her gain more saddle-bronc experience. Dakota hoped she'd still be competing when things finally opened up for women in the sanctioned events.

"I guess it'll take time for us to change the rodeo world. It's pretty traditional. Maybe it will be the next generation that reaps the rewards and we're paving the way for future cowgirls. But I think we're making inroads."

"This seems almost like a life mission to you. Why?"

She glanced away. She didn't like to think about why she did things. She just did them. "I'm a trailblazer, I suppose." Her gaze returned to him in a pointed stare. "I also don't like having anyone tell me what I can and cannot do."

"Any *one* or any *man*?"

"Any*body*."

"I don't remember you being such a rebel back in high school."

She wondered how much he knew about her life back then. She'd never confided in anyone.

Best to change the subject. "I went to the National Cowgirl Hall of Fame in Fort Worth once. I was surprised to see women in the early 1900s competed neck and neck with the men. We're just trying to regain the ground we've lost."

Too bad it had taken her so long to figure out what she wanted to do with her life. Instead of wasting two years working as a ranch hand right out of high school, she should have started her career on the rodeo circuit. She was getting too old to keep up with the younger women coming up in the sport. But this was the only way she knew how to make a living and it suited her personality better than ranching had.

Perhaps if the cow*girls* hadn't been barred from competing in the events that interested her, she could have advanced farther in the sport. Instead, she'd been forced to waste several years barrel-racing with the other women.

But Dakota still had something to prove—to herself, to men, and to the asshole who'd stolen her childhood.

Alison had been such a quiet girl back in school. He had no clue where she'd come from; she'd just shown up at 4-H one day in junior year. While they probably had a few classes together, he mostly remembered her love for and affinity with horses in their after-school activities. She didn't have a horse of her own but always wanted to help him with his.

Matt had been the only one of his brothers who did 4-H and was still the only one who owned an animal—well, unless you counted Franco's exotic fish. Rafe had been down to Matt's ranch a few times since spring to ride, but Franco and Tony weren't interested at all. Tony preferred scuba diving with his water-rescue squad or his new bride of almost a year, and Franco could seldom be persuaded to leave Denver now that he was settling in with the arson squad.

Being with someone who understood horses excited him. He hated that their time together was coming to an end, but he couldn't hold onto her after they finished breakfast. She'd be competing in a few hours, and, while he planned to watch her ride, he probably would be leaving soon after.

"Thanks for the grub. I'd better head over to the arena to prepare for today's finals."

Sounded like he'd have to let her go sooner than anticipated. "I'll walk you over." They picked up and discarded their trash before falling into step beside each other on their way to the arena. He wanted to learn more about her. "Where'd you live before you moved to Aspen Corners?"

"All over."

That's a lot of territory. "All over Colorado?"

"Colorado, Wyoming, Texas. My…folks followed the pipeline jobs."

Strange. There hadn't been any pipeline jobs in or around Aspen Corners when they were in high school. Had she lived with both parents? He didn't remember either of them ever showing up for any of the competitions, although he did remember a sullen guy staring out the windows when he picked her up for school. Matt could see that she played things close to the vest, so he left it there. None of his business unless she wanted him to know.

"I guess that's where some of your wanderlust comes from."

She shrugged. He couldn't imagine being so rootless. He needed to thank his mama next time he saw her for giving him a strong foundation and a solid home base while allowing him to explore his world.

Dakota stopped. He looked up to see they'd arrived at the outdoor arena where the saddle bronc finals would take place.

"Thanks for the company, Matteo. If I don't see you after my event, be careful driving home."

If he left soon after bronc-riding finals this afternoon, he'd get home a little after midnight. He didn't like the thought of never seeing her again, because she intrigued the hell out of him, but they led vastly different lives.

"I'll be in the stands cheering you on."

She beamed a smile at him. "That means a lot to me."

Given her vagabond lifestyle, without any mention of family or roots, he wondered if anyone who knew her personally showed up to cheer her on at these rodeos. If not, how sad was that? He loved when his family turned up at his skijoring competitions, and that was only a hobby of his.

"Well, I guess I'd better go." Even so, she seemed as reluctant to part as he was to watch her leave.

"See ya after your ride." He wasn't ready to say a final goodbye to Alison Parker—or Dakota Mathison—just yet.

Dakota held onto the hack rein, nervously adjusted her butt in the saddle, and waited for the gate to open. The bronc she'd drawn seemed too calm for any hope of a top prize. Dakota's mind wandered to Matteo. Did he stick around like he said he would? Was he watching her now?

Focus on your ride, or you're going to be eating dirt!

To beat the person in the lead, she needed to hold onto this ride for the full eight seconds and give it all she had for added style points. The difference between first and second place would be a substantial amount of money. With the dead winter months coming up, she'd need that extra money.

Dakota took a deep breath, let it out, filled her lungs again, and gave the nod. The gate opened, and the bronc exploded out of the chute. Dakota bounced into the air and crashed into the saddle, jarring her spine as she fought to keep her grip on the hack rein. Spurring the horse with both feet while keeping her free arm raised to earn as many points as possible for the ride, she groaned as the rein slipped faster than she'd like. Just a few seconds more, or she wasn't going to make the points she needed.

Hold on long enough to cover, Dakota.

Suddenly, the beast between her legs twisted sharply before kicking its legs out behind itself, yanking the rest of the hack rein out of her hand. Dakota flew off and landed facedown. Her hands kept her face from planting itself in the dirt, but her already sore shoulder joints were painfully jarred.

How long had she stayed on? Her mount had certainly bucked and rolled enough and she'd spurred enough for a good score. Hopefully, she'd at least managed to cover.

Picking herself up off the ground, she made her way to the chute, feeling every one of her thirty-two years. Slowly the cheers of the crowd filtered into her consciousness, and she looked up at the scoreboard.

Elation flooded through her. *Ninety-six!* She must have been given points for drawing such an ornery bronc! Only one more rider, then she'd know if she'd placed first or second.

Sitting on a bench behind the chutes, she drank a bottle of Gatorade and rode the adrenaline high while ignoring the aches in her body. Fighting to catch her breath, she wondered how she'd be able to drive to Utah tomorrow. Her neck and shoulders already hurt like a son of a bitch. But she only had a week to recover before the next ride and would rather get to where she was going and rest up a bit.

The roar of the crowd died down. Then cheers erupted throughout the arena. *Craptastic.* Did that mean she'd lost the title to the last rider? Unable to see the scoreboard from where she sat, she stretched out her tightening back and leg muscles in an effort not to show her disappointment.

"There you are," She glanced up to find Matteo standing nearby. "Nice ride. Are you okay after that buck-off?"

Other than that stray thought just before her ride, she hadn't thought about him since. A distraction like Matteo could have cost her everything she'd worked so hard for.

"Thanks. I'll be fine."

"I wanted to be the first to congratulate you."

She still couldn't see the scoreboard. "I won?"

"No, but you took second place."

Her chest fell. *Then I lost.*

"You should be proud of that ride, given the bronc you drew. Quite an accomplishment."

Was there an unspoken "for a woman" hanging in the air between them?

"If you say so." She started to stand, and he stretched out his hand to help her up, but she rose under her own power, wincing as she tossed the empty bottle into the trash barrel. "It was nice seeing you again, Matteo. Be careful going home." She started to turn around, but his words stopped her when he continued.

"If you're ever in the Leadville area—or looking to branch out into skijoring during the winter months," he said with a lopsided grin, "give me a call." He handed her a piece of paper she assumed had his phone number and maybe an address on it.

"Thanks." She tucked it into her jeans without looking at it. She'd so wanted to show him what she could do but couldn't even make eye contact with him at the moment after that sorry performance.

Don't leave him this way. He's just trying to be nice.

When she forced herself to meet his gaze, the intensity in his brown eyes gut-punched her. "Bye" was all she could think to say before turning and walking away, never expecting to see him again.

Chapter Three

Two months later, Christmas Eve

After a disastrous shift at the station, Matt breathed a sigh of relief as he pulled his pickup into the long dirt lane at his small ranch midmorning on Christmas Eve. He planned to spend as much time as possible with his horses. They always helped settle his nerves after a bad call.

Matt hadn't been looking forward to spending Christmas Eve in Mama's new home eating a shit-ton of fish. But tonight, being with his family was all he wanted, no matter where they gathered or what they ate.

Last night out on Highway 24, a father and his two sons had died, leaving a wife and mother as well as her daughter to grieve during the holidays this year and probably for many to come. At least they'd managed to pull the mother and her daughter from the fiery wreckage in time. It had been the worst call he'd ever been a part of, reminding him how unpredictable, precarious, and precious life could be.

Yeah, family was exactly what Matt needed and wanted right now.

At least the Giardanos still had each other, except for Papa of course. Mama had moved on after a long period of bereavement, marrying Paul Janowski and moving to his condo in Breckenridge just before Thanksgiving last year.

Matt hadn't liked the idea of Mama leaving the house she'd lived in with Papa, and where the five Giardano kids had grown up, but seeing her happy and in love again with Paul convinced him it was the right thing for her to do. That house had been filled with too many memories of Papa, and it wasn't right for the newlyweds to start married life with another man's ghost lingering around them.

Luckily, Rafe had a sentimental side, too, and now owned and continued to live in the house, so they could always go "home." Rafe certainly wouldn't be one to entertain the family much, unless it was for a potluck cookout or something. Mama's Sunday dinners had become monthly rather than weekly with everyone spreading out and having their own lives, including Mama. It was rare for everyone to be off on the same day, but that had been the case even before Mama remarried.

Inside the barn, a quick glance told him that Jason had done a great job the past two days. The teenage son of one of the engineers at Matt's firehouse, Jason had been working for him since he bought this place last year. Matt remembered what it had been like in his late teens when he couldn't afford his own horse. If he hadn't done the same type of work for a rancher outside Aspen Corners, who'd waived Dipper's boarding fees in exchange for Matt taking care of the few horses at his ranch before and after school, he wouldn't have been in 4-H at all. It was more than a fair trade, and Matt had learned a lot about horses and ranching from that experience. The rancher had given Matt his first horse, Dipper, as a graduation present.

Jason was saving up for a horse of his own, but Matt let him work with Comet and Twinkle at his 4-H events.

Stepping into his routine, Matt fed Twinkle and Comet their oats and hay, poured them buckets of clean water, mucked out their stalls, and laid down fresh straw for bedding. The mundane but necessary chores helped ground him and gave him the sense that he was able to be of help to *them* at least.

"Hey, girl," he said, rubbing Twinkle's nose before pressing his forehead against the horse and filling his senses with barn and horse smells to help rid himself of the scent of burning flesh.

Don't go there.

"How about a ride?" His voice sounded gravelly, but Twinkle gave a quiet nicker and nod in response. Comet had enjoyed an early-morning ride two days ago before Matt started the shift he'd like to forget. Today, it was Twinkle's turn.

Of course, neither was neglected while he'd been at work. Jason gave both of them their workouts and maintained their stalls. The high-school senior eagerly helped out when Matt was working or training, but both horses vied for Matt's affection and attention whenever he was around.

Now, more than ever, though, it was Matt who needed these horses to help him decompress after those grisly fatalities. He shook off the lingering memory and compartmentalized last night as best he could.

"Comet, you get to run around in the pasture today, because I'll have to stable you two earlier than usual today." He patted the gelding who had been his most recent mustang rescue. Comet loved to blow off steam in the pasture every chance he got, but because of the wildlife dangers, Matt kept them safe inside overnight. "Going to Mama's for the Feast of the Seven Fishes. It's how we Italians celebrate Christmas Eve. I don't think you guys would care much for seafood. Tell you the truth, it's not my favorite, either. So count yourselves lucky to stay home and eat your oats."

Matt often had no one to talk to around here, so his horses took the brunt of his ramblings. After turning Comet loose, he returned to Twinkle's stall. He'd rescued the mare almost four years ago; she'd been the first horse he'd bonded with after losing his beloved Big Dipper while in college. He'd trained Dipper for almost five years, ever since he'd been a junior in high school. He'd like to get more horses, but with Jason about to graduate and go off to college, he'd have to make sure he could take care of the ones he had first.

Matt holstered his .45 pistol, which he carried with him whenever he ventured out on the property, mainly in case he encountered any mountain lions that might try to attack him or his horse.

"This'll have to be a quick one, though, Twink," he said as he saddled the horse. "I have to head out by four to get to Mama's on time, and I need to catch some sleep first." Sleep had been nonexistent for him after last night's call.

The weather should give them a small break with sunshine and double-digit temps for the next couple of hours. Both horses would be ready to return to the barn when the temps started to drop this afternoon, although the worst of the wintry weather hadn't arrived yet.

After the ride, Matt planned to heat up the lunch he'd brought home, nap, then hit the road. He wouldn't be back until tomorrow evening after all the family festivities were over at Mama's and Angelina's. Jason would be taking care of the horses Christmas morning. Great kid.

But Matt wasn't in the mood to celebrate anything. They'd understand if he was subdued this year, once he told them what had happened. Hell, knowing his family grapevine and Franco's former ties to the Leadville station, they'd probably already heard. He'd have to check his phone when he got back to the house. No sense taking it with him to the remote parts of his property because he wouldn't get a signal anyway.

Mama had a sixth sense about these things and always treated the tragedies her boys suffered on the job as if they were her own. However, Matt didn't plan on telling her any of the gory details he might share with his brothers or Marc. She didn't need to hear about the two little boys who'd lost their lives along with their dad.

Mounting Twinkle, Matt headed straight toward the government lands adjacent to his acreage. Not for the first time since seeing her in October, he wondered where Alison-turned-Dakota was today. For two months, thoughts of her had invaded Matt's mind on a daily basis—more often than they should have, given how brief their encounter in Amarillo had been.

Where had she been competing since Thanksgiving when she'd said she'd be in Texas? Had she been injured? Broncs were dangerous enough, but the woman planned to train to ride bulls now. Talk about some crazy shit! Watching Dakota flopping around like a rag doll on the back of that bronc had made him cringe with every jolt. He didn't think he'd be able to watch her fly off another horse—much less a bull. Getting thrown from either animal usually resulted in hitting the ground hard. At least with bronc riding, if you covered, there was a chance of catching the pickup man to break your fall a little. The bullfighters did their best to distract the bulls while you scrambled to safety, but getting stepped on by a bull was a lot worse than by a bronc.

While Matt hoped to see her again someday, chances were pretty slim that would happen. She hadn't given him her number and hadn't used the one he'd given her. Neither of the rodeos she'd mentioned had been in Colorado, although he did get four days off between each shift if he wanted to chase after Dakota Mathison someday.

Nothing could come of a relationship with a rodeo circuit star, though. Matt needed his roots, and he got the impression Dakota would feel too tied down if she sat in one place for long.

After almost ninety minutes of riding along the stream and stopping at some of his favorite vistas on the national forest land, he headed back to his own property and passed the rustic cabin once inhabited by the miner who'd originally owned this place. The one-room log building with a loft was structurally sound but needed a lot of work on the interior. He'd like to fix it up someday but hadn't had time yet, instead focusing his time and resources on the corrals, barn, and house. But he planned to be here for years, so he'd get around to it eventually.

When the wind started to kick up, a shiver went down Matt's back. Having achieved the sense of peace he'd come for, he and Twinkle started back to the barn.

As he approached his modest little ranch house, he reined in Twinkle. Just beyond the barn sat a dusty blue Dodge Ram with some serious miles on it. He didn't recognize it, but as he rounded the barn, he saw a familiar blue-and-white Shasta camper hitched to the back. Gently nudging his heels into Twinkle's flanks, Matt closed the gap in double time.

A woman appeared to be sleeping in the driver's seat. With that long ginger hair fanning out from underneath the cowboy hat covering her face, it had to be Dakota. Matt decided not to disturb her immediately. He returned Twinkle to her stall and gave her a quick rubdown. Comet was nowhere to be seen but would show up as the temperature continued to drop.

Exiting the barn twenty minutes later, he approached the truck slowly and rapped gently on the window. Dakota jumped from her semi-reclined position then removed the hat from her face and peered at him in momentary confusion. She winced in pain. Was she injured or just not all that thrilled to see him?

He opened the truck's door slowly, careful to make sure she wasn't leaning against it. "Hey, what brings you out here?" He flashed her a grin, but after all the times he'd fantasized about meeting her again, when it became reality he'd used the lamest greeting he ever could have come up with.

She winced again as she lifted the seatback to a vertical position. Matt sobered and held out his hand. "Here, let me help."

"Thanks." That she accepted his assistance told him she must be in a world of hurt. "Got a little banged up in a jackpot rodeo this past weekend near Golden."

That was only about two hours away. Where had she been staying the days since then? Had she received medical treatment?

"Want me to carry you inside?" The thought of holding her in his arms despite the circumstances appealed to him.

"No. I can walk."

"Okay, but lean on me." Matt wrapped his arm around her lower back, but she jerked away as if he'd punched her. It was too cold for further examination outside, so he moved his arm higher and led her toward the house.

What if she needed to be seen at the hospital, though? He'd only trained as an EMT-Basic. Rafe had insisted they all be trained EMTs, even though Matt's county had an Emergency Medical Service separate from the fire department and he rarely had to use it.

Would he be in over his head? As they walked, he remembered how to do his initial assessment. "Where does it hurt?"

"Might be quicker…to tell you…where it doesn't hurt." She drew shallow breaths in between each short string of words. Had her lungs been injured? Her ribs?

"On a scale of one to ten, what's your pain level right now?" He pulled the storm door toward them as the wind whipped down the porch. Pushing the kitchen door open, he let her precede him inside.

"Five…headin' toward six…now that I'm moving." From the outward signs, he'd have thought it a much higher number.

In the kitchen, she glanced around the room, taking in what he hoped she'd find to be a cozy place. Nothing fancy, but he wasn't that kind of guy. "Nice and warm in here," she remarked.

"How long were you sitting in your truck?"

"Since I got here, you mean?"

"Yeah." Coming from Golden, she must have been in the truck for hours. Given how stiffly she moved, had she been able to crawl inside her camper since being injured or had she been sleeping in her truck?

"An hour, give or take."

Damn. While he'd been enjoying his horseback ride, she'd been freezing her ass off in her truck. He didn't ask why she hadn't turned on the motor occasionally to keep warm. Maybe she was low on gas.

"I knocked. No answer…so I decided to take a nap."

"You should have tried the door. It's never locked when I'm around."

Yesterday had been in the single digits, so today's twenties felt almost balmy to Matt. But he hadn't been sleeping in a pickup, either. Even the barn would have been warmer than her truck.

And what if he had been in the middle of a two-day shift. But no sense worrying about that. She was safe and warm in his house now at least.

"Sit here." He helped ease her into a kitchen chair. "I need to check out your injuries."

She waved him away. "Nothing's broken. Rodeo medics cleared me Sunday."

"Yeah, but you might have some internal injuries that didn't show up the day you were thrown."

"Nah. Just…sore muscles. The cold weather…hasn't helped, though." Her breathing continued to be labored.

"If you aren't going to let me examine you, then we're going back outside and getting into my truck so I can take you to the hospital." He doubted her pickup would get them very far and wondered what had happened to the newer model she'd been driving in October. He'd ask those questions later, but now wasn't the time. He waited for her reply, but none came.

"Listen, if we're going to town, I'd like to get going soon. I have a horse to get back in the barn. What's it going to be? Examined by me or in the hospital emergency department?"

Her eyes opened wider. "Don't worry about me. Get out there and take care of your horse!"

She obviously had more concern about his horse than her own well-being. "He'll be okay a while longer. Now, are you going to cooperate here, or do we make Comet wait longer while we head into Leadville?"

She glared at him for a long moment. "I'm starting to wonder if maybe I should have kept driving toward Albuquerque."

Was she serious? That was a long-ass drive given her condition. "What's in Albuquerque?"

"An open rodeo…this weekend…I intend to compete in." She tried to find a comfortable place in the chair.

Over my dead body!

She must have suffered a concussion or become delusional. "How are you going to mount a bronc"—he wouldn't even bring up bulls, "when you can barely get out of your truck and walk into my house without assistance?"

Squeezing her eyes shut, she held onto her right side while sitting up straighter, then tilted her head back with defiance. "I managed to…get to your door…on my own steam. I just…accepted your help…since you were here." Her breathing worried him.

"It's Christmas Eve. You wouldn't find much open for hundreds of miles for the next two days."

Sparks flew from her eyes. "Look, Matteo…all I need…is a cot to sleep on in the barn. I'll be on my way…come morning."

Knowing Dakota wouldn't take to strong-arm tactics, he tried a different tack. "You're here now. I'd like you to stay, Dakota. You need some rest and a warm bed."

She raised her eyebrows as if he'd just invited her into his bed. Not a bad idea, but he didn't believe in *Babbo Natale* anymore. Besides, she wasn't in any shape for what he'd like to do with her if he ever did get her into his bed.

"I have a perfectly good guest room that hasn't been used in over a year." *I'd better put fresh linens on the bed.* "It's yours for as long as you'd like. But first, sit tight. I'll be right back with what I need." He started toward his bathroom but stopped in the hallway to adjust the thermostat. "I'm turning up the heat, but this is already the warmest room in the house." He'd need to get her out of that shirt in order to evaluate her fully but didn't want to take time to start a fire.

"I see you aren't much…on Christmas decorations."

He turned around to see her pointing at the ceramic Christmas tree in the center of the table.

"My mom made one for each of us kids in one of her art classes." Otherwise, Mama knew none of her boys would have put up a tree. "With it being just me here, I never saw the point in decorating for holidays. I did put an evergreen wreath with a big red bow above the barn doors for my horses, though."

"I saw it."

Matt smiled at her grin and hurried into his bedroom to grab a warm blanket, then into his bathroom for the medical supplies he kept on hand for emergencies. When he came back into the kitchen, he saw her looking longingly at the to-go sacks on the counter. Had she eaten lately? He'd ordered enough for two, because he'd planned to fill up before heading to Mama's for his least-favorite holiday meal. Give him pasta or meat and potatoes any day, but he could pass on seafood and fish. It didn't seem likely he'd make it to Breckenridge tonight for Christmas Eve dinner. Mama wouldn't be happy and he'd miss being with family, but that couldn't be helped. Dakota needed him and that took precedence.

He'd share his to-go food after completing his examination—unless he determined she needed further medical care. The hearty meal from the café near work would taste better than anything he could whip up for her.

"I'll fix you a plate as soon as we finish checking you over. To do that, I'll need you to undress above the waist—you can leave your bra on." His authoritative tone made it more an order than a request, and he hoped Dakota would follow through without argument.

Chapter Four

No way in hell was she stripping for Matteo Giardano!

The man needed to get that fact straight and fast.

"If this is your idea for getting into my jeans, you're going to be mighty disappointed."

Matteo's hand stopped sorting out his supplies on the kitchen table, and he stared at her as if she'd grown another head. Then he laughed out loud, and Dakota wasn't sure if she should be angry or hurt.

"I can see you're going to be a fun patient. But I didn't ask you to take off your jeans, only your shirt."

More than ever before, Dakota regretted the decision to come here. Maybe if she'd taken the faster I-25 route to Albuquerque rather than I-70 west out of Denver she wouldn't be here.

She'd been holed up for two days in a cheap motel outside Golden. All she'd wanted was to take daily soaking baths and hot showers since her bone-crunching bull ride. That had actually been the second of two bad spills that weekend—first from a bronc and then a bull. Maybe she should have gotten in more training before trying to tackle a bull, but she'd wanted to see what she needed to concentrate on when she went to bull-riding school in January. Obviously, she still had a lot to learn.

Unable to move without extreme pain, nothing she'd tried had helped loosen up her sore muscles or ease the discomfort from the cracked rib.

The doctors in the emergency department had told her not to ride again for at least six weeks, but she had to eat and wasn't about to show up at some soup kitchen. This morning, she'd started driving toward her next event, hoping by the time she reached New Mexico that she'd be ready to ride Friday night. She had never let an injury get the best of her before and didn't plan to start now. But the longer route she'd chosen would have taken her the rest of the week at the rate she'd been driving, what with all the frequent stops she'd needed to make to stretch her aching muscles.

After ninety minutes' driving time—hurting so bad she couldn't breathe sometimes—she'd accepted the fact she wouldn't make it much farther. It had gotten too cold to sleep in her camper, if she could even contort herself into the thing right now. Running low on funds after a series of bad rides over the last few weekends, she'd opened her map app to see what was nearby and had seen she wasn't too far from Aspen Corners. But no way was she going back there ever again in case *he* had moved back there to find her.

Then she'd remembered Matteo Giardano and saw that the route to Leadville took an entirely different highway bypassing her former home altogether. Best of all, he was only thirty-five minutes from Frisco where she'd pulled off the road to consider her options. Scrolling through her contacts for someone to call, she'd seen his listing.

Was it fate or had her subconscious led her here? She hoped this wouldn't turn out to be the worst mistake she'd made in her string of bad choices lately. Rekindling ties with her past wasn't a good idea, but her need for a safe place to land and lick her wounds had won out.

Matteo had been the best part of her two years in Aspen Corners.

Dakota had put his address and phone number into her phone two months ago and hadn't once been tempted to reach out to him. Seeing him in October had definitely left her wanting more, but they led such different lives.

However, today, knowing she wasn't going to be able to drive the four hours she needed to make it to the halfway point in her trip, she'd programmed his address into her map app and set off on this detour.

Now she wished she'd kept on driving. She probably ought to give up on the Albuquerque event, but it would be her last one of the year, and she needed the money. Assuming she'd even win any.

And the choice to compete or not was hers to make, not Matteo's.

Realizing he was standing there awaiting her response to his earlier command, she shrugged.

He held out a blanket he'd brought back with him. "This will be your privacy screen. Now, take off your shirt for me, darlin'." When she didn't jump at his repeated command, he smiled, "Trust me, Dakota. I'm a professional."

"You're a medic, too?"

"No, but my brother Rafe insisted we all get basic EMT certification to make us more marketable when we went job hunting."

If only she could pretend she was being seen by one of the many medical personnel who'd checked her out after her fall from the bull, but this was Matteo Giardano. She'd had countless teenage fantasies of stripping for him but not when she was feeling old, beat-up, and vulnerable.

Matteo waited patiently for her to run all these thoughts through her head. Had he also been a military officer? He sure liked to spout orders.

All she'd come here for was some coffee and a cot to sleep on in his barn. When Dakota had parked outside, she'd noticed that the barn was larger and newer than the house. As always, Matt put his horses' needs in front of his own.

But Matteo was treating her exactly the way she'd expect him to. Just the way he'd taken care of her after she'd fallen off her bike in senior year. He'd insisted she ride in his truck to school and back every day afterward. He'd also made it his mission to drive her to the rest of their 4-H events that school year.

Had that been why she'd thought of Matteo when she'd been hurting and needing someone to take care of her?

Okay, I've already shown him some of my weaknesses.

With his medical knowledge, though, he wasn't going to be happy to find out she'd downplayed her injury. He'd asked her to rate her pain. Admittedly, it was more like an eight going on thirty, not a five/six. "Fine. Let's get this over with."

He grinned triumphantly. "I'll hold the blanket up so you can use both hands."

He did as promised. Most likely, he couldn't see anything below her neck, but she felt his intense gaze on her face. "It's getting warm in here."

Only the heat wasn't coming from the oven or the furnace but instead from Matteo's body.

She fumbled with the buttons on her shirt. Even her fingers and wrists ached from trying to keep her face out of the dirt after she'd been thrown off that bull. After a few minutes, she managed to unbutton the last one and opened the plackets. Quickly, she realized he wasn't going to be able to examine her like this, so she yanked the blanket out of his hands—unsuccessfully trying to stop her groan—and tossed it onto the back of her chair.

"Do what you have to do. I'll need help getting out of this shirt." What further indignities would she suffer as the result of this uncharacteristic show of weakness on her part?

He eased the sleeves down her arms and placed it on top of the blanket before turning toward her again. She waited, sitting half naked in Matteo's kitchen.

When he made no move to touch her, she glanced up at his face and saw horror as he stared at her chest and right side. The bruising had turned various shades of blue and purple yesterday and looked even worse than it felt. Or was he taking in all the scars from some of her past buck-offs.

Matteo didn't have to tell her in words; his facial expression told her that her body was a mess. But she'd earned every one of those marks and had nothing to be ashamed of. *Jeez.* If he thought this looked bad, he should have seen some of the injuries during her early days of bronc riding. Considering she rode almost every weekend during the regular season to stay at the height of her game, she'd had a good run—until Sunday.

She also liked to eat during the off months, which was one of the reasons she'd pursued this jackpot rodeo opportunity. Organizers at these events had no qualms about allowing a woman to ride bulls as long as they paid their entry fee.

She supposed she'd given them what they wanted, spill and all. Another year or so and she should be able to master bull riding, but she'd only have a few years left before retiring.

To what, she had no clue. Rodeo was all she'd ever done.

"If you call that a level five or six, I'd hate to think what a ten would look like. Sore muscles? Bullshit. How many ribs did you crack?"

Yeah, he had some medical knowledge all right. This injury would force her to take an unwanted break in order to heal properly before the new season began. She'd also miss bull-riding school. Time to come clean.

"One. X-rays didn't show any others, but there wasn't anything they could do for me at the hospital." *Other than tell me to take it easy for six fucking weeks.* The arena medics, who knew the rodeo athlete's mindset, were more realistic and simply begged her to stay out of the arena for a month.

His eyes widened. "And how long are you supposed to stay off broncs—and bulls?"

She tried to glance away, but the intensity of his gaze and his uncanny way of reading her thoughts kept her eyes locked with his.

"A few weeks."

"Only a few?"

"Okay, six by one estimate but only four by another."

He scowled at her. "How the hell did you think you could ride this weekend?"

She shrugged, then winced at the pain. "I didn't plan to ride broncs. Thought maybe I'd fall back on barrel racing."

"You can hardly breathe or walk. How are you going to sit a horse?"

She chose to evade the question. "I might not get the opportunity to ride, but I have some friends who offered to let me go on standby in case any of their barrel racers were injured."

"You're already hurt worse than they probably ever would be."

Dakota rolled her eyes because shrugging off his words would hurt too much. Maybe she hadn't thought this through, running on instinct and in survival mode. The only home she'd known since she was a little girl was the rodeo arena. She needed to get back to the arena as soon as possible.

"Any nausea or vomiting?" Matteo asked abruptly as he continued his examination.

"No." Although that might be because she hadn't felt like eating much since her spill; it hurt too much.

"Any fever or chills?"

"Nope."

"Take a deep breath for me."

Dakota did, trying to go deeper than she felt comfortable with to prove she was fine, but she winced in pain when she could stand it no longer.

"Show me where it hurt you just now."

She waved her hands to encompass the area from her hips to her shoulders. "I think every muscle in my body aches."

He didn't grin at her attempt at humor. "Coughing much?"

"No." *Hurts like a sonofabitch to cough.*

Then he asked her a few embarrassing questions about her recent bathroom habits and made her blush.

"Everything's been pretty normal."

"Good. Now I want you to point to where it hurts the most at the moment."

She pointed to her ribcage on the right side but refused to let him know how much pain she was in.

Don't be such a crybaby.

Tough it out.

Shake it off.

She shuddered at that gravelly voice from the past, the one that had resulted in her learning to shut down her feelings no matter what. Apparently not enough to be able to hide her discomfort right now, though. With a perceptive man like Matteo, she'd have to be mindful of showing further signs of weakness.

Matteo visually examined the bruising on her side as well as her trunk, back, and both arms. "I'll try to be gentle, but I need to make sure there's no swelling or damage to your internal organs."

"Do what you have to." *And get it over with, please.*

His hands were warmer than she'd expected as he tenderly palpated the area around her ribs—which hurt like hell—and her abdomen, which she barely felt. "No abdominal swelling. And you didn't wince when I touched you there, so I'm guessing that means you don't have any significant abdominal issues."

"Told you."

When his hands moved up to press the area below her breasts, goosebumps broke out on her arms, and her nipples became hard against the fabric of her bra. Heat rushed into her cheeks. She hoped he didn't notice her body's natural response to him—or that he wouldn't read it the wrong way.

"Sorry," he said. "It's getting chilly in here again. I'll try to hurry."

Craptastic! He totally noticed, even if he interpretted the reason all wrong.

The man had been completely professional during the exam, and here she was getting turned on by him. As if she was in any shape to do anything about it even if he had shown any interest in her sexually. When he pressed his fingers against one of her ribs, all embarrassment fled along with the breath whooshing out of her body. She couldn't hold back the moan of pain that escaped.

"Sorry." He sat back and met her gaze. "You've definitely cracked a rib, just like they said, and you might also have some bruising to other ribs along with your abdominal organs. But I don't see any swelling to indicate internal bleeding, which is good."

She nodded and took as deep of a breath as she could manage. "I just need some sleep. I'll be good as new tomorrow." Surely she couldn't feel much worse. Bone-weary, she leaned back in the chair and pulled the blanket tightly around her. "You wouldn't happen to have a bathtub, would you?"

He nodded. "I have a cast-iron clawfoot in the guest bathroom."

A soaking tub sounded like the most decadent, luxurious thing she could imagine. "That sounds perfect. Mind if I use it to soak a while?"

"Of course I don't. Consider this your home while you're here. I'll get you into the tub, then I'll go out to the barn and get my horses settled in for the night."

"For the night?"

"I want to do the bulk of my chores now so I can be in here with you."

"I don't want to keep you from your horses. Go!"

He placed a warm hand on her forearm and sparks almost flew from where they touched. "Your well-being comes first, Dakota. Promise you'll tell me if anything changes, or any new aches and pains come up. That includes during the night, even if you have to phone or text me at 3 a.m."

She cocked her head in confusion.

"I'll just be down the hall from you. If you're hurting too much to get me, use your phone."

Oh, that made sense. She couldn't think beyond the upcoming soak in the tub. "Okay, I will." She wouldn't report anything serious enough to have him hauling her to the emergency department, though.

"Before your bath, did the medics or ED doctors give you anything for the pain?"

"Yeah, but I don't do narcotics."

"You're not going to be driving for a while. They could help."

"I didn't fill it." She leaned forward and winced at the pain. "I do not do narcotics," she said, emphasizing each word.

He held out his hands as if to ward her off. "Fine then. What else did they suggest?"

"Ibuprofen, eight hundred milligrams at one time, no more than four times a day." *Not really working, though, because I pop 'em like candy during rodeo season.*

"Mine are two hundred milligrams. I'll give you four now. And some crackers to eat so the pills won't upset your stomach." He stood and opened the cabinet at the far end of the counter, pulling out a large bottle of pills. Maybe he took a lot of them too. He filled a glass with tap water, shook out four pills, and handed them to her before going to a pantry at the other end of the kitchen and pulling out a box of saltines. He opened a new sleeve and set them beside her. "I doubt those pills will really knock down the pain enough but hope they'll help you to be able to move around a little more easily."

She downed them with water, tossing her head back with a snap to help them down easier, which reminded her too late her neck muscles hurt too. "Thanks." She pulled out three crackers to chase them with.

"I can't believe you're able to function with such severe pain and bruising. You're one tough lady."

She had to be tough in her profession, or she wouldn't have made it this long on the rodeo circuit.

Dakota ate several more crackers, not realizing how hungry she was.

"Do you want to eat something before your bath?"

She shook her head, unaware that he was watching her every move. Soaking in the tub took precedence over eating.

"Let me help you out of those boots and jeans before you get up. You're in no shape to be pulling them off yourself."

While Dakota didn't like the idea of stripping completely down in front of him, he was right. She'd removed her boots the night she moved into the motel and hadn't put them back on until she'd gotten dressed this morning. The pain had been too excruciating to do so any sooner.

Did her socks have holes in them? She hoped not. And thank God she'd worn practical briefs today, nothing too revealing.

"Hold onto your chair or the table edge or something. I'll be as gentle as I can be." He lifted up her foot, cupping the heel as he tugged off the first boot. Although white-knuckling the seat of the chair with one hand and the edge of the table with the other, she refused to show him how much these minor movements hurt. Then he did the same with the right boot, but this time the pain from the jarring took her breath away. Her arm jerked forward reflexively, knocking over the glass on the table. Water spilled onto his denim shirt, soaking him as it plastered the fabric to his chest.

"I'm so sorry!" She set the glass upright and used a corner of the blanket to try and dry his shirt.

He waved away her concern and set the second boot on the floor. "No worries. I'll change into a dry one before I go back outside." He stood and quickly unbuttoned and removed the wet shirt, setting it over the back of a chair to dry.

Dakota's gaze zeroed in on his chest with its well-defined pecs and six-pack abs. *Whoa!* The man hadn't let his body go to pot, that's for sure. Her nipples responded to the view by bunching and tightening, and she pulled the blanket over her chest to hide her body's embarrassing response.

Chapter Five

"Thank you, Matteo." She wasn't sure if she meant that for helping her out of her boots or for the view he'd given her.

After he removed her socks—no holes as far as she could tell—she unfastened her jeans, and he helped her stand. She was in too much pain to shimmy the jeans down her legs, so she held onto the back of the chair and let him do it for her before sitting down again. Even that minimal amount of effort robbed her of breath.

He eased the Wranglers the rest of the way off in a matter-of-fact manner and draped them over another chair, seeming to ignore how close his face had come to her...panties.

Definitely no time for inhibition or embarrassment at this point. It wasn't as though he'd be thinking anything sexual about her in this condition, not that the thought hadn't crossed her mind while sitting practically naked with a shirtless Matteo in his kitchen.

Clearly, he hadn't been as affected by her beat-up body as she'd been with his magnificent one. He would put rodeo cowboys to shame in a competition for hottest bod.

Exhausted, she sat motionless.

"I'll bring your things in from the truck and leave them on the bed after I make it up."

"Just the small duffel bag, please." Dakota wouldn't be staying more than the night, because she hadn't given up on Albuquerque.

He helped her to her feet again. Once steady, though, she extricated herself from his hold. The intoxicating scent of his masculine soap or aftershave permeated the air around her. When a shiver coursed through her, he settled the blanket around her shoulders more securely. But that shiver had nothing to do with being cold. Matteo's hands on her upper arms and the nearness of his half-naked body left her wanting him to touch her again, only more intimately.

As if I'm in any shape for that kind of ride either.

"Thanks for everything, Matteo." She cleared her throat against the breathiness she heard there. "I hate barging in on people unexpectedly like this."

"Think nothing of it. I've got plenty of room."

"Well, I appreciate it." Being here with Matteo in his cozy house felt nice. Not that she wanted to get too comfortable, but what harm was there if she enjoyed a brief visit with all the creature comforts she normally went without? It wouldn't weaken her to accept a little hospitality from him.

"I'm just glad you're here with me and not out on the road somewhere." Before she could read anything into his words, he added, "I'd hate to think of you being all alone on Christmas Eve."

Suddenly, Dakota realized why he was bedding down his horses so early in the afternoon. She'd been so focused on her aches and pains that she'd totally ignored the probability that Matteo had holiday plans, especially given his close-knit family.

"Am I keeping you away from family parties or obligations? If so, I'll be fine here. I doubt I'll stay awake long after my bath."

"Let me pamper you a little bit. Consider it my Christmas present."

"But I don't have anything for you."

He chuckled. "Having you here is gift enough."

Was he lonely out here? He had his horses, but coming from a big family, she imagined he'd miss human contact on the days he wasn't on duty. His ranch was pretty isolated.

What about female friends? A man with Matteo's looks wouldn't stay single or lonely for long. And firefighters must have female groupies equivalent to the buckle bunnies who followed the rodeo cowboys.

Matteo pointed her in the direction of the guest room and indicated that she should go first. She walked at a snail's pace, each step draining her even more. Just that little bit of sitting had her muscles cramping up again.

Her expectations of what the room would look like disappeared the moment she entered the flowery room with a pastel-colored quilt on the bed and five pillows of varying shapes and sizes. The charming room had everything she'd need and so much more than she'd ever had—not that she planned to be here long enough to get used to it. Still, definitely not what she expected to find in a bachelor's home.

Maybe there *was* a woman in his life.

"What a beautiful, peaceful room."

"Okay, I know what you're thinking, but Mama decorated the room the way *she* liked. She used to come down to get away several times a year, but she hasn't stayed here in more than a year." He sounded a little sad about that.

Dakota remembered his parents as being supernice whenever she saw them at various 4-H events, and totally committed to their son's projects.

Shaking off thoughts of that earlier time, she turned slowly to face him, but her foot got tangled in the blanket, and she pitched forward. Her hands hit his hard chest as his strong arms grabbed for her to break her fall. When her hands wrapped around him, the blanket sailed to the floor as her forward momentum slammed her against his chest. She screamed in pain, but he held her tightly to stop the movement of her body.

The pain receded quickly, and she found herself bare skin against bare skin. A tingling coursed through her body, a response she never experienced before, not even during her brief but torrid romance with a bull rider in Phoenix. That had ended rather awkwardly when he hooked up with his ex-wife again.

Uncertain how to extricate herself from *this* awkward predicament without further embarrassment, she kept her gaze on his pecs. Not that the view helped curb her fantasies.

"I'm not usually so clumsy."

"You aren't usually walking around wrapped in a blanket, either."

"True." Obviously, he wasn't sexually aware of her. His voice sounded matter-of-fact about it all. Thank goodness, because nothing was going to happen tonight, and she'd be gone in the morning. "I guess I'd better get in that tub."

He pulled away but kept his hands on her biceps as if he wasn't sure she could stand on her own two feet anymore. "Bathroom's through that door." He nodded his head in the direction to her right. "There's another door to it from the hallway. Don't worry; I have my own so I won't be barging in on you. Now, I'll just start running the water and let you take it from there."

"Go take care of your horses. I can run my own bathwater."

"Well, I'll at least put the plug in, because it will be hard and painful for you to bend over."

She didn't want to think about bending over for Matteo.

"Thanks, then I want you to head straight to the barn. I'll be fine!"

He chuckled. "I think you're more concerned about my horses than about yourself." But he went into the bathroom and got the tub ready for her while she waited in the bedroom. "Okay, there's a clean robe behind the door. Help yourself to anything you find or need. Mama kept the place well-stocked from when she used to visit more regularly."

"Thanks, Matteo."

He nodded instead of responding. "I'll be back as quickly as I can. Promise me you'll let me know if you need anything in the meantime."

Did he expect to have her call him to help her get out of the tub? *Not a chance, fireman.*

"Keep your phone by the tub and call me if you need anything. Oh, I probably should program my number into your phone."

"That's okay. It's already in there." His grin read more into the admission than was necessary. "I needed the address for my GPS, so I put in the number too." She still didn't understand why she'd kept his contact info in the first place.

After he left, she glanced longingly at the bed. When was the last time she'd slept in a frilly bed like that one? Had she ever?

Don't get used to this, Alison. One night. That's all you're allowed in this fairy tale.

Her brain still sometimes reverted to calling herself by that name, but she'd been Dakota a lot more years than she'd used the name Alison. She'd chosen Dakota because it sounded fun, exciting, brave. And she'd left sad little Alison Parker behind in Aspen Corners long, long ago. For the first time, she wondered what might have happened if she'd stuck around. Would she and Matteo have dated? Had he experienced feelings for her other than as a high-school friend?

Shaking off her fantasies about the hunky firefighting cowboy she'd inflicted herself upon, Dakota walked stiffly into the bathroom, each step a painful reminder of Sunday's bull ride. She ran the bathwater and found the navy-blue terrycloth robe hanging on the back of the door just as Matteo had said. Was it his mama's or one he kept for other overnight female guests?

But wouldn't it be in *his* bedroom if here for one of his women to use?

Pulling herself out of her head once again, she saw that the tub had filled up more than halfway. Dakota turned off the water, gingerly removed her bra and panties, and stepped in, ignoring the pain as she hiked her leg over the side. Matteo might be right. Mounting a horse would be nearly impossible in her current condition.

After she had both feet in the tub, she eased herself into the hot water as quickly as she could. Leaning back in the tub, which happened to be perfectly shaped to her body, she sighed.

Heavenly.

Or maybe simply her first Christmas miracle in a long, long time.

Snippets of memories flitted across her mind's eye of a little red-headed girl discovering mountains of gifts on Christmas morning. Someone watched as she explored the treasures, but she couldn't tell who it was. Most definitely a woman, someone who'd always made her feel safe after….

Her eyes opened abruptly as the image of a car skidding on icy roads shattered her peaceful thoughts. She pushed the inexplicable memory out of her mind and closed her eyes again, resting her head against the tub. She wanted to focus on that vision of Christmas morning again, but it had flitted away.

Matt ducked into his bedroom after leaving Dakota to her bath and grabbed a dry chambray shirt before heading out to take care of the horses. He couldn't wipe the grin off his face. That she'd held on to his phone number and address all this time, even though she hadn't used them until now, made him think she definitely had intended to get in touch with him some day.

Sweet!

Her soft breasts pressing against his bare chest had sent sparks flying between the two of them. It had been torture tearing himself away, but he'd had to get out of there fast before she noticed his hard-on.

The woman's body was hotter than sin. And that hair! *Damn!*

Matt hurried through his barn chores so he could get back to Dakota as quickly as possible. He didn't feel too guilty about spending less time with his horses. After all, his original plan had been to leave for Breckenridge soon anyway.

Funny how finding Dakota practically on his doorstep had wiped away any need for sleep. But he'd better get his libido in check before he reentered the house. Her right torso was one massive bruise, and the last thing she'd be interested in was jumping into his bed—even crawling into it at this point would be a stretch.

How he could be lusting after a woman whose body had suffered so much trauma embarrassed him, but Alison had given him more than a few wet dreams in high school too. Not that he'd known what to do about an erection back then. He'd been a late bloomer when it came to sex.

But with all her talk about hitting the road and not giving herself time to heal, he didn't expect her to stick around long. While nothing would be happening between them while she was hurting the way she was, he had hopes for something down the road, even if he had to find her on the rodeo circuit next year. He sure hoped she wouldn't delete his number and needed to make sure he had hers before she left.

On his way back to the house, he stopped at her truck, opened the passenger door, and saw her saddle occupying the passenger seat. Behind the seat was just enough space to hold two duffel bags. After moving her saddle to the tack room, he returned to retrieve the smaller bag she'd asked for and carried it into the house.

There were no sounds coming from the guest room. He knocked, figuring he could deliver her bag and put fresh sheets on the bed while she soaked in the tub, then he'd get the heck out of there before she came out of the bathroom.

He knocked again a little louder but still no response. *Good.* He slowly opened the door. "Dakota? You decent?"

Silence. Not even the sound of water running or splashing to indicate she'd moved to cover herself. He pushed any thoughts of a naked Dakota out of his head and peeked into the bedroom. The bathroom door was closed. Quickly, he placed the duffel on the floor and called out, "I've got your bag. I'll just make up the bed right quick. Holler if you need anything." He figured if he told her what he was up to in here, she wouldn't freak out on him and think he was trying to sneak a peek or something.

Her silence confused him, but Matt stripped the quilt off the bed and changed the sheets before remaking the bed for her. What was Mama thinking with all these extra pillows? He tried to put them back the way Mama had, but it didn't look as nice.

When he finished, he glanced toward the bathroom. Still silence. Now he started to worry. What if she'd passed out and her head was submerged under the water? He couldn't very well leave her alone in there if she didn't respond.

Matt knocked sharply on the bathroom door. "Dakota? You okay? Awfully quiet in there."

When there was no response, he cautiously opened the door and peeked in. The back of her head leaned against the tub with her long ginger curls cascading toward the floor so they wouldn't get wet. She must have fallen asleep. How long should he leave her in the water? It would be getting cold soon in that cast-iron tub.

Unsure what to do, he simply stood there for a few minutes watching over her. At least he couldn't see her boobs, so she couldn't accuse him of anything lewd.

When she groaned and sat up with a start, he pulled the door shut as quietly as he could and knocked as if for the first time. "Need any help, Dakota? You've been in there a long time."

"No. Um, I'm fine. I'll be out in a few."

Her moans came through loud and clear, and he wished she'd ask him to help her out of the tub. While he didn't think seeing her naked would be good for his own chances of getting any sleep tonight, he stayed near the door, just in case she called out.

She didn't.

When the door opened after about five minutes, she gasped, apparently surprised to find him still there. She wore the robe Mama had left there, although it clung to her damp body in places that turned his thoughts to anything *but* his mother.

Assuming she hadn't heard what he'd told her about her bag or making up the bed, he repeated them. "Why don't you get dressed while I warm you up some supper."

"Don't go to any bother for me."

He heard her stomach growl at the mention of food, though. While he'd brought enough home, he'd wait for her to eat her fill before he took any. "I brought home some pot roast and veggies from a local café. I can vouch for how good it is, because I eat there all the time."

"You weren't expecting company. I don't want to eat your supper."

"There's way more than I can eat."

For some reason he couldn't name, Matt was happy to be able to keep Dakota here all to himself so he could take care of her as long as she'd let him.

Even though seeing her hurting so badly nearly killed him.

"I'll leave you alone so you can dress, but you're welcome to wear that robe, if it's easier." He left her alone in the guest room. In the kitchen, he transferred the food from the to-go sacks to microwavable bowls and started reheating everything.

While waiting, he pulled out his phone and realized he'd powered it down before his ride on Twinkle. When it came on, he saw there'd been two missed calls from Mama and numerous texts from Franco and Rafe. No doubt someone in his department had alerted Franco about the bad call; he'd worked at the Leadville station before moving to Denver.

Matt had better call Mama ASAP to explain why he couldn't be there tonight. He pulled out his phone.

"Matteo! We were just wondering when you'd be arriving."

"That's why I'm calling, Mama. Something came up. I hate to do this to you at the last minute, but I'm going to have to miss the Feast and midnight Mass this year."

Momentary silence on the other end was quickly followed by a barrage of rapid-fire questions. "What's wrong? Are you sick? Injured? Does this have to do with what happened at work last night?"

"Nothing's wrong, I just can't get away tonight." Mama would see right through a lie, so he didn't try to make up any excuses. But he wasn't ready to tell her that Alison Parker was at his house.

"How about tomorrow at Angelina's? We're preparing all your favorites—and I promise we won't bring any seafood or fish leftovers."

Matt's mouth watered at the thought of lasagna, ravioli, and all the side dishes and desserts they'd be making. It killed him to have to say no, but he couldn't commit to anything right now.

If Dakota left, he could still go to Angelina's early afternoon. There was always way more food than they could eat. But he might as well prepare Mama for the fact that he wouldn't be there. He never missed a Christmas family meal unless he was working.

But he intended to do everything he could to talk Dakota into sticking around a while. The thought of that stubborn woman heading off to Albuquerque and expecting to ride made his stomach more sour than eating Tony's latest seafood concoction. Last year it was squid of all things. His stomach turned just remembering having to take a bite of that creature to fulfill the annual traditional meal.

"I'm afraid I won't be there either, Mama. I'll let Angelina know, but I promise to come up after my next shift. New Year's Day at the latest."

"New Year's? But that's a week away!"

He needed to get off the phone before Dakota joined him. "Okay, New Year's Eve then."

"Tony and Rafe don't work that day," Mama said. She kept track of everyone's schedules in her head, especially around the holidays. "I'm not sure Franco will be able to make it, though."

About a year ago, his second oldest brother had taken a position with the Arson Investigation Unit in Denver. Unlike the rest of the family, Franco had always preferred city living. Matt missed working with him at the Leadville station, though.

"I hate having one of my children missing, but if you're sure everything's okay…"

"Everything's fine." Time to cut this conversation off before she heard Dakota in the background. "I hope you guys have a good one. I'll see you soon. Merry Christmas, Mama!"

After saying goodbye, Matt put the bowls into the microwave. He'd chosen beef and potatoes to make his noon meal the polar opposite of the Feast of the Seven Fishes that he'd expected to eat at Mama's tonight. If he'd gone, he probably would have gotten drunk on wine while trying to drown out the taste of all that fish.

Thankfully, the café had given him huge portions; they took good care of their first responders. Now they'd both be able to enjoy the meal. He checked the pantry and found some canned corn, which wouldn't take long to heat and would stretch the food further.

Matt was adding butter to the corn when Dakota entered the room. She'd decided to wear the robe, which clung to her breasts like a second skin.

"Smells delicious. You're sure I'm not depriving you of your supper?"

"Look at this feast! I couldn't possibly eat it all." He pointed to the bowls and pot on the stove. "Have a seat, and I'll serve you up a plate."

He put more meat on her plate than his, figuring she needed the protein to heal, then added the potatoes, carrots, and corn and placed it in front of her. She waited for him to sit down before digging in. Clearly, given the way she ate with gusto, her appetite hadn't suffered. Or maybe she hadn't eaten much in the past few days. With her injuries, she obviously couldn't take care of herself properly.

Matt hoped he could convince her to take a break from these post-season rodeo events and stick around a while, but he wouldn't say anything yet for fear of scaring her off. Surely she wouldn't leave as early as tomorrow, regardless. Hell, she couldn't even put on her jeans and boots without help.

They reminisced about old times in 4-H over supper, but when he asked her about her folks, she changed the subject.

"Do the rest of your siblings still live in Aspen Corners?"

"Just Rafe now. Tony got married last year and moved up near Eagle. Franco's in Denver, and Angelina and her husband built a place on the mountain between Aspen Corners and Breckenridge two years ago."

"You should go be with your family tomorrow."

No chance in hell would he be leaving her alone on Christmas.

"I pretty much told Mama earlier tonight that I probably wouldn't see her before New Year's, so we'll just have a quiet Christmas together."

"You're certain? I'm not even sure I'll—"

"I'm positive." He cut her off before she could talk about leaving. Maybe she'd forget about next weekend's rodeo.

Dakota resumed eating for a few minutes, but with half of the meal still on her plate, she set down her fork again. "I hate to leave so much food uneaten, but I can hardly keep my eyes open. Would you mind if I turned in early?"

It was barely four o'clock, but she'd been through some serious shit lately. "Of course not. Rest will do you a world of good."

"I hate keeping you from your family on Christmas Eve. I won't be very good company anyway." He opened his mouth to argue, but she held up her hand and continued. "Please go without me. You can bring me some of those cookies if I decide to stay tomorrow."

"I'm not going anywhere, Dakota. End of discussion. If you knew how much I detest seafood—the traditional menu for tonight—you'd see you're actually saving me from indigestion."

She smiled. "Okay, I'll try not to feel guilty."

"Please, don't."

"I can't eat another bite." Dakota stood with some difficulty. "Where should I scrape my plate?"

He jumped up to help her and took the dish from her hand. "You let me worry about that. I have some barn cats who will consider it their own special Christmas Eve dinner."

She smiled at him. "I love cats. I'd also love to meet your horses tomorrow."

Interesting. Maybe there was a fifty-fifty chance she'd be around come morning. He hoped she'd realize how absurd it would be to head to Albuquerque tomorrow.

"The cats are pretty wild, but the horses will love you to death."

Her eyes showed a mixture of excitement and exhaustion, mixed with a bit of pain. "I think I'm going to turn in now, Matteo. Thanks for everything."

"Don't mention it. I'm glad you're here."

Dakota turned toward the bedroom.

"Oh, I bumped up the heat in your bedroom," he added, "and pulled out some extra blankets and pillows if you need them." He couldn't imagine her needing any more pillows, though. "And put a clean glass next to the sink. Help yourself to anything you want or need in the fridge or wherever. *Mi casa es su casa.*" He knew he'd started to ramble but couldn't help himself. "If you can't find something, I'm in the room at the end of the hall. Call or text me, and I'll fix you up."

Dakota turned back to him and smiled again, her eyes too weary to radiate even a spark of light. "I may not act like it sometimes, Matteo, but I'm grateful to you for all you've done. I made the right choice in stopping here. I appreciate your hospitality."

He waved away her words, simply happy to have her here. Any

rancher in the area would have taken her in, although hearing her say how much she appreciated him was better than any Christmas present he could have wished for.

"Merry Christmas, Dakota, and goodnight."

Cheesy, Giardano. Who do you think you are—Babbo Natale*?*

But when her smile broadened, and he spotted a bit of sparkle in her eyes again, he didn't mind sounding like a dork. *Man, you haven't used that word since high school.* Maybe being around her again had him reverting to his teenage vocabulary.

"See you in the morning, Dakota." He almost called her Alison, but Dakota was growing on him. Somehow it fit her better.

Her smile faded instantly, though, and he wondered again if he had to worry about her disappearing as quickly as she'd reappeared, despite saying she wanted to meet his horses and cats.

"Night, Matteo. And Merry Christmas to you, too. Thanks again."

He watched her walk stiffly into the guest room and close the door.

Babbo Natale, if you'll grant me just one wish tonight, it would be to have Dakota here when I wake up in the morning.

Chapter Six

Dakota brushed her teeth, thankful to Matteo for leaving a clean glass by the sink so she wouldn't have to return to the kitchen. Every step drained her. She removed the robe before gingerly sinking naked into the bed. Putting on PJs would take more energy than she could muster.

She'd expected a soft mattress like the one in her camper but loved that this one was firm, just the way she liked them, and easier to get in and out of in her current condition. It didn't take long before the scent of lavender on the pillowcase soothed her weary, aching soul. Matt didn't look like the type to use fabric sprays so maybe he used scented dryer sheets. Or had his mother put sachets in the linen drawers? She seemed like the kind of woman who would add that touch.

A flash of memory flitted into her consciousness. Normally not one to indulge in perfumes or oils, Dakota had loved the scent of lavender for as long as she could remember. If it reminded her of something from her past, it must have been a good memory. But she was too tired to try and figure it out tonight.

The scraping of dishes made her feel guilty for not helping Matteo clean up, but she'd barely had the energy to do this much. So tired. Moments later, her mind drifted off to sleep.

Dakota jolted awake sometime during the night with faded images of a large woman who was soft in all the right places and gave the best hugs, but she couldn't for the life of her recall who she could be. A glimpse at the darkened window confirmed it wasn't morning yet. She tried to roll onto her right side to go back to sleep, but the pain in her ribs screamed at her to stay still and remain on her back.

Dakota didn't know what time it was yet. The room had no alarm clock, and she never wore a watch. A glance at the nightstand revealed she hadn't brought her phone into the bedroom. The silence in the house became deafening.

She hated keeping Matteo from his family this Christmas. If she were going to leave, now would be the perfect time, but this bed felt so amazing that she couldn't bring herself to vacate it yet. Maybe in a few hours, after she'd had a chance to sleep a little longer, she could reevaluate.

Still, thoughts of leaving Matteo and his ranch caused a pang in her chest that had nothing to do with her injuries. Dakota hadn't spent such a companionable evening with anyone in decades. She blinked away the uncharacteristic sting in her eyes.

Don't get too used to this place, cowgirl. It's only temporary.

The temptation to stay almost overwhelmed her; however, she refused to indulge in that fantasy. Even though her body needed a break from competing, she couldn't afford to sit one out. Her earnings had petered out toward the end of the regular season. She still had about eight hundred dollars on her debit card but needed to make it stretch until she could earn a living again.

Unfortunately, every time she moved, the excruciating pain reminded her how ridiculous barrel racing in Albuquerque would be. Matteo was right. She wouldn't be able to mount a horse, much less ride one at breakneck speed in a barrel race.

Maybe she could find a way to earn her keep for a few weeks. The only thing Matteo seemed to need was a cook, and that definitely wasn't her strong suit. She'd always chowed down on arena food or whatever she could afford from nearby cafés and restaurants. But how hard could it be to whip up something edible a couple of times a day? And it sounded like he was on duty two days at a time. On those days, she could fend for herself.

Dakota fell back to sleep, surprisingly at peace for the first time all year.

But the next time she awoke, doubts assailed her once more. She hadn't relied on anyone but herself since high school. She wouldn't mooch off Matteo's generosity. No, she needed to hit the road first thing in the morning. She might skip Albuquerque and go to West

Texas to try to find some barn or tack room work to tide her over until she could compete in another rodeo. Maybe in February, she'd be ready to go again.

This time when she closed her eyes, she didn't have that earlier sense of well-being. But this was the right thing to do.

Sometime before dawn, Matt woke to hear the engine of a truck turning over. His heart sank. Apparently, Dakota had made the decision to leave after all. While not surprised, he couldn't help but be disappointed that she hadn't waited to say goodbye.

Damned if he'd watch her leave. He tossed off the covers, willing himself to head toward the kitchen, not the window.

Stop worrying about her. She's self-reliant.

Apparently, she'd been on her own a long time. Matt needed to be needed. Clearly, Dakota wasn't one to ask for his or anyone else's help, although she had grudgingly accepted some assistance from him yesterday. He scratched his bedhead hair into some semblance of order as he walked down the hallway toward the kitchen to start the coffee maker.

After showering, shaving, and brushing his teeth, Matteo returned to the kitchen to pour a mug of coffee and make some instant oatmeal and toast for breakfast. More awake now, he glanced around but didn't find a note or anything to indicate Dakota had left. Hell, there was no sign that she'd even been here.

Time to take care of his horses, which would at least give him something to do for the next forty-five minutes or so. Maybe he'd go to Angelina's later this morning, but he wasn't sure yet. Heavy snow flurries fluttered around his head when he stepped off the porch, but he clearly made out Dakota's camper parked at the side of the lane. How the hell had she managed to unhitch the camper from her truck in the shape she was in? That had to have hurt like a mother. She must have wanted to get away pretty bad, but then wasn't the camper still being here proof that she planned to be back at some point? He just didn't know when. In that bucket of bolts she called a truck he doubted she'd get very far.

He met the horses' basic needs and lingered a bit to talk to them about his worries, not that they had any solutions. On the way back into the house, he glanced down the lane toward the county highway. Still no sign of her return. Matt sighed. How long should he wait around before going out to look for her? What if she had engine problems or, God forbid, had been in an accident? She had to be hurting from the exertion of unhitching the camper too.

Inside the house, he decided to check the bedroom. Sure enough, the duffel bag he'd brought in last night sat on top of the made bed. Her clothes and toiletries would be in there. She might leave the camper, but he doubted she'd leave that bag if it was so important to her last night.

Where did *you go, Dakota?*

Holding out hope she'd be back today, though, he texted Angelina to give his regrets. Should have done it last night, but he'd held out hope that he wouldn't be alone. He'd pretty much indicated to Mama that he wouldn't be there, so his sister probably already knew. Mama had a sixth sense about her kids, so he wouldn't call her until later. Right now, she'd definitely detect the worry in his voice.

Filling a travel mug with coffee, Matt decided to head to town to see if he could find Dakota. He glanced at his messages. Nothing. *Enough already.* He turned off the ringer so he wouldn't be distracted while driving, but he'd try to keep an eye on it for any calls or messages.

Ten minutes later, he left the ranch. He didn't lock the door in case Dakota returned before he came back. First, Matt would drive around Leadville, keeping an eye out for her or her truck.

He didn't have to look too hard. Her blue pickup sat parked on the left-hand side of the road about a mile before the city limits.

Dakota's Dodge. Did she break down? His heart rate ticked up a few notches. Was she okay? Had she passed out? Clearly, she'd been coming *from* Leadville, so had she been heading back to his ranch?

He quickly crossed the deserted two-lane road to the opposite shoulder and parked in front of her truck in case he needed to jumpstart her engine. When he checked inside, the cab was empty, except for a to-go bag from the café on the seat.

Damn. Where are you, Dakota?

Closer to town than his ranch, Matt glanced down the road toward Leadville but saw no sign of anyone walking on the shoulder. He'd definitely have noticed if she'd been walking between here and the ranch.

Had she been picked up by someone? Was she safe? Should he report her as missing?

Authorities wouldn't take his report seriously this soon, so he got back in his truck, pulled back into his lane, and sped into Leadville. He'd stop at the station first to see if any of the guys could help him search. If she'd come to town on foot, she would have had to pass the station. Maybe someone saw her.

Unless she's in the vehicle of some lunatic who's taken her out to some deserted place to do unspeakable things to her.

He'd barely walked inside the apparatus bay when he heard a woman's laugh, followed by a groan of pain, coming from the kitchen on the second level.

Dakota!

How had she managed to climb the stairs from the bay? Matteo reassured himself that at least she was safe. He shot up the stairs two at a time. When he opened the door, she sat at the breakfast bar with a mug of coffee cupped between her hands as if to warm them.

"You guys need to stop making me laugh. Hurts like hell."

Seeing Matt, she broke out in a smile. "You got my message."

"What message?" *Oh, hell.* When he pulled the phone out of his pocket, sure enough, there was a text from her, but it had only been sent about ten minutes ago.

***DAKOTA:* Truck broke down. At fire station to warm up. Roadside assistance hasn't called back yet.**

As he'd told himself earlier, the woman was self-reliant.

"The guys were telling me all about you rescuing that seventeen-year-old girl last week who got stuck in a baby swing at the playground, Matteo. I'd have paid money to see you in action."

He rolled his eyes at the embarrassing situation but wouldn't have minded half as much if he'd been rescuing Dakota from the tight fit. Before he could respond, the room erupted in a round of teasing about her calling him by his formal name. At work, he simply went by Matt.

He might as well have a cup of coffee too. He ignored the ribbing from the guys in the room but wasn't all that sad when the tones dropped and they went off on a call. He wished them a Merry Christmas and thanked God he wasn't on duty today. He wanted to be alone with Dakota.

Matt sat on the bar stool next to hers. "What happened to your truck?"

"No clue. Just sputtered out on me on my way back to your ranch."

What if that had happened up in the mountains or on some deserted stretch of highway?

"Hey, did you move my saddle last night?" she asked out of the blue.

"Huh? Oh, yeah. I figured you'd want it in the tack room in this weather."

"Perfect. I didn't think anyone would come into your driveway and steal it from my truck but wanted to be sure. It's worth more than that truck for sure."

Back to the matter at hand. "How'd you get here from where your truck broke down?"

"A Christmas angel stopped and drove me into town. When I mentioned that I knew you, he thought this would be a good place for me to wait."

I'm glad one of the good guys found her.

"Why'd you come to town in the first place?"

She gave him a lopsided grin and a half shrug. "I wanted to get us some breakfast, but it's probably frozen on my front seat now."

His eyes opened wider. "I wondered why you hadn't taken the camper." Matt felt like a little shit for thinking the worst of her. He glanced down, noticing her boots. "How'd you get into your boots?"

"It's much easier putting them on than taking them off."

Matt's gaze roamed slowly up her body as he thought about taking a few things off her body last night, then he remembered her condition.

"How'd you manage those stairs?"

"They nearly killed me! You guys need to put in an elevator."

"Usually, we're more concerned about getting down than coming back up."

She shrugged then took a sip of her coffee. "I managed."

"I can see that." At least none of the guys had offered to carry her up here. He couldn't believe he felt jealous of them, but he did. "What I'd like to know is how you managed to unhitch that camper by yourself in your condition."

"Oh, I'll be paying for that stunt tonight. It took me nearly an hour because I had to keep one hand pressed against my rib for counterpressure."

"Why didn't you come and get me?"

"You were sleeping. Besides, I wanted to surprise you with breakfast."

She'd been thinking about him? Matt sighed. Just when he was ready to bitch at this stubborn, infuriating woman, she went and melted his heart. "How long before the auto club shows up?"

"One of the guys—Paske, I think—told me to cancel the call. He's going to have his brother-in-law take care of my truck."

Matt had seen the lieutenant in here a few minutes ago. Surely the town's best mechanic wouldn't be working on Christmas Day, but maybe Paske had called in a favor.

Matt stood, wishing she'd called him instead of texting, but with his ringer off, he might not have noticed a call, either. He poured the rest of his coffee down the drain, rinsed his mug, and set it in the dishwasher. "Why don't I take you to the café for a hot breakfast? Then we can check on your truck."

Fifteen minutes later, they sat down in a booth at the café. She looked over the menu a moment. "That sampler looks amazing."

Dolly, who'd been waitressing here for more than thirty years, came to the table.

"Merry Christmas, Matt. Didn't expect to see you here today."

"Change of plans." He ordered the sampler for them both. Dakota asked for her eggs scrambled well done, just the way he liked his too.

"I noticed the guys at the station made fun of me calling you Matteo. Would you prefer Matt?"

He grinned. "I love the sound of my formal name coming from your lips. I mean, mouth."

She grinned, saying nothing about his correcting himself. "I'm glad. It's a beautiful name."

"Do you think that truck's worth saving?"

She laughed. "It was a piece of crap from the day I bought it off a roper/wrestler who'd won a new truck at a rodeo we competed at. It was right after I wrecked my other one, so I jumped at the offer."

"Were you hurt?"

"Nah, well, nowhere except in my wallet, even for that old thing."

He relaxed before she continued. He didn't want to think about her being injured in an accident.

"I had to replace it fast so I could make it to my next rodeo. Most likely, I'll have to sell this one for parts or scrap metal and look for something more reliable."

Smart girl.

She glanced away, nibbling on her plump lower lip. When she met his gaze again, his heart skipped a beat. *So beautiful.*

"If you don't mind me staying at your place a little longer, I'm a little strapped for cash."

Yes! Well, not about the financial part, but that she planned to stay a while. Matt reached across the table to squeeze the hand wrapped around her mug. "I told you last night, Dakota, you're welcome to stay as long as you'd like. I'm enjoying your company."

She raised an eyebrow, then grinned. "I was asleep by five o'clock last night. Sure doesn't take much to entertain you."

He gave her a noncommittal shrug and a grin. "Have to admit that, when I'm not working, things are pretty quiet out there. Just me, the horses, and the cats."

The first few months on the ranch had been the most difficult; he wasn't used to such intense silence. He wouldn't have traded his siblings for anything in the world but, growing up in a big family, peace and quiet had been hard to come by. Now, Matt valued his solitude. The ranch and his horses gave him a chance to unwind and rejuvenate after a rough shift, like that last one. His extended family and his firefighting family provided him with all the socializing he needed or wanted, then he just wanted to be alone.

But having Dakota here hadn't felt like an intrusion at all.

A wistful look crossed her face, and she smiled back. He wasn't sure what she was thinking, but she changed the subject. "The guys at the station seem nice."

He nodded. "We have some great crews. I've only worked at one other station—volunteering at Aspen Corners FD while in college—but I wouldn't trade Leadville's station for any other."

"How long have you been a firefighter?"

"Started as a volunteer in college after Papa was killed."

"Matteo, I'm so sorry! I didn't know!"

She squeezed his hand. He hadn't meant to be so blunt, but he'd forgotten that it had happened after she'd left Aspen Corners. He'd just assumed she'd known.

"Thanks. I miss him every single day."

"What happened, if you don't mind me asking?"

"He was killed in an avalanche trying to rescue a woman who'd fallen."

"How awful! That must have been devastating for all of you, but especially hard on your poor mother."

He nodded, probably too curtly, but he didn't really want to go into the aftermath. "He died doing a job he loved. It'll be eleven years this May." He paused a moment. "My two oldest brothers joined the ACFD soon after to honor Papa. Tony and I switched majors to fire service and volunteered at the home station until we graduated. Then we were hired on as career firefighters, Tony in Aspen Corners and me in Leadville."

"I can't think of a more fitting legacy for your papa."

Mama had told them later on that Papa probably had put himself in that dangerous position because he knew he had cancer and didn't want any of the other team members to risk their lives until they were ready to transport the woman to safety. But in Matt's mind, Papa would have beaten cancer if given the chance.

He sighed and shoved that thought down again. "Mama remarried last year and moved to Breckenridge. Her new husband is a battalion chief there."

"Another firefighter in the family."

Matt was still getting used to the fact that he had a stepfather, but nodded. "Rafe lives in our childhood home. He didn't want us to lose all those memories. We still come together there a couple times a year for gatherings."

An awkward silence ensued at the talk about the house in Aspen Corners. Matt wondered if she wanted to revisit the town where she'd once lived. She'd seemed happy enough there, although he had to admit he hadn't known her outside of 4-H and their truck rides to and from school. They'd only talked about horses when they were together, though, never anything personal. He'd never really met her parents. Whenever Matt picked her up for school, she'd been sitting outside waiting, no matter the weather conditions.

He couldn't figure out her story any better now than he could back then.

Dakota fiddled with her silverware, then asked, "What had you been studying in college before…that happened?" Thank goodness she hadn't probed any further on that subject.

"Animal science."

"To be a vet?"

He laughed. "No, I didn't have the grades for that. I just wanted to know more about running a ranch, since I hadn't grown up on one."

"I can see you going in that direction from what I remember about you in high school."

He nodded. "But I decided not to return to Colorado State the semester after… Anyway, I transferred to a nearby school where I studied fire science instead, so I could be around to help Mama and Angelina."

"I'm sure being closer to family was a comfort at a time like that."

He swallowed hard before he could speak again. "I'll be honest, it crushed me to change majors. But it seemed like what I needed to do at the time. Now I have my ranch and my horses and I love my job, so I'm satisfied. I wouldn't give up any of them for anything in the world."

Matt had never admitted to anyone how hard giving up on his ranching dream had been. Now he had no regrets and the best of both worlds.

Before Dakota could say anything more, Dolly brought them two huge platters filled with scrambled eggs, bacon, sausage, home fries, pancakes, *and* biscuits. After refilling their coffee mugs, Dolly left them alone again.

"I don't know if I can eat all this," Dakota said, her eyes taking it all in with a dubious look. But she didn't waste any time digging in. Neither did he, not wanting to continue this conversation anyway.

They spent the next ten minutes eating. He hadn't realized how hungry he was, and Dakota did her meal justice as well. Matt appreciated that her appetite had improved since last night.

When Dolly came back to check on them, he placed a to-go order for later. Looked like Dakota wouldn't be leaving his ranch anytime soon so he'd need to stock up, but he didn't want to go grocery shopping on Christmas Day. Neither of them were much on cooking, apparently. Too bad they were going to miss out on Angelina's and Mama's dishes today, but she didn't need to be sitting in a vehicle for any extended trips just yet.

Besides, he wanted Dakota all to himself for a while. Man, if his siblings found out he had a girl staying with him, half the family would be dropping by unexpectedly to check her out. He didn't want to subject Dakota—or himself—to that kind of scrutiny.

Dakota nearly cleaned her plate before sitting back with a groan. "I think my stomach is pressing against my cracked rib." She gently rubbed her right side, making him worry about how much she ought to be doing and how he'd keep her still while she recovered.

"Why don't we head back to the ranch? You need your rest."

"No, I'll be okay. I need to talk with the mechanic."

"Lieutenant Paske will notify me when his brother-in-law can look at the truck, but I doubt it will be today."

She paused a moment. "I keep forgetting it's a holiday. I hope they'll at least tow it today, but I need to pick up some things from inside the truck on our way back."

Matt waved for the check. "We can stop on the way. Then you probably need to go back to bed for a while."

"I couldn't sleep any more if I wanted to. But I *would* like to go back to the ranch and meet all your babies."

She reached for the check Dolly had just put down, but he beat her to it. "This one's on me," he said, knowing she didn't need to be spending any money unnecessarily. "You already bought us breakfast once, even if we didn't get to eat it yet."

"Well, thanks. I appreciate it. The other breakfast might only be fit for your cats."

"I'm not too sure about that, but they'd certainly appreciate it."

After laying a hefty tip on the table as Dolly's Christmas gift, he exited the booth and came around to Dakota's side to assist her, but she waved him off.

"I'm fine," she said, "even if I do waddle a bit after all that food."

She didn't look fine, wincing with each step. She'd be hurting tonight after all her running around today. "Take it slowly. We aren't in any hurry."

Dakota settled herself into the passenger seat of his truck. When she groaned while twisting to put on her seatbelt, Matt took the belt and extended it across her chest, which brought his face into close proximity to her breasts. He caught a whiff of her scent and watched as her chest rose and fell from the exertion of getting into his vehicle. Memories of her naked in his bathtub last night flooded him, even though he saw more of her breasts now than he had last night.

Being around Dakota for however long she stayed and not being able to touch her was going to be the toughest challenge in self-control he had ever faced.

But he didn't want her to be anywhere else.

He closed her door, adjusted his jeans as he rounded the hood, settled himself in the driver's seat, and started the engine. They made a quick stop to clean her belongings out of the truck and soon were on their way home.

"Sorry to be so much trouble."

"Cut it out. I love being able to help."

At the ranch, he gave Dakota a quick tour, trying not to jar her in the truck on the rutted dirt road, then headed toward the house. "I'll introduce you to Streaking Comet and Twinkle Littlestar after you rest up a bit."

"I don't need to rest yet. I want to meet them."

"I'm an EMT professional, remember? I say you need rest."

She paused as if to argue, then her shoulders sagged as if the fight had left her. "Fine." She must be exhausted to have given up so easily.

More determined than ever to get her inside where she could relax, he parked close to the house and helped her down from the cab. She insisted on going into the house under her own steam, but as he walked beside her carrying the to-go meal, he could tell from her gait and the tension in her face that she was hurting.

At the kitchen table, he removed her boots.

"I think I'll have another soak in that tub."

"Why don't you use the shower in my bedroom? There's a massage feature, or you can just let the main setting soothe those aching muscles."

Her features softened. "You don't mind? Because that sounds heavenly and much easier than getting in and out of a bathtub."

"I want you to make yourself at home while you're here."

His phone lit up, and he saw that the mechanic was headed out for Dakota's truck. When he told her, she bent down to pick up one of her boots and groaned.

"Where do you think you're going?"

"I need to meet him at my truck."

He took the boot out of her hand with little resistance. "I'll take care of it. You go get that shower."

The relief on her face made him certain this was the right decision. "Then let me get you some cash to pay for the tow."

"We'll take care of that later. I'll be back in thirty to forty minutes. Take all the time you need in the shower, then maybe lie down a while. It might be a good idea for you to take some more painkillers before your shower. They're on the counter in the kitchen."

"Thanks, Matteo. I feel like I'm always saying this, but I appreciate it."

He smiled, glad to see her choosing to take care of herself for once. "I'll be back as soon as I can."

He couldn't wait to get back to the house, although realistically he expected her to be sound asleep after that shower.

The mechanic showed up fifteen minutes later. While the man loaded Dakota's truck onto his flatbed truck, a Chevy Tahoe breezed past them. Matt thought for sure it was Rafe's, but what would he be doing down here on Christmas Day?

Crap! A quick glance at his phone showed several missed calls and texts from Mama and Rafe over the past two hours. Surely Mama hadn't sent Rafe down to check on him, but after his uncharacteristic cancellations last night and today—in addition to not answering their unseen calls and texts—he probably had them all thinking he was having a rough time following the bad call the other night.

Sad to say, he'd hardly had time to even think about that, what with Dakota showing up unexpectedly.

Matt gave the driver Dakota's information and tried to hurry him along, but he was in a chatty mood. It was a good ten minutes before he was on his way back to his ranch. He floored the accelerator and took the highway at about ninety miles an hour, hoping to get home before Dakota opened the door—and a whole can of worms.

Please don't let that be Rafe. Or worse yet, Mama.

Chapter Seven

As Dakota stepped out of Matteo's shower, her body tingling from a thirty-minute shower massage, she heard a knock at the front door. She'd hoped to be dressed before Matteo returned but wondered why he'd knock at his own door? Perhaps he had a Christmas visitor?

Dakota grabbed the robe he'd let her borrow last night and put it on. She winced as she twisted her arms and torso, then slowly made her way to the living room. A peek through the slim opening in the door's curtains didn't answer her question. Two tall men and a woman of average height stood on the porch. The darker-haired man and the woman with similar hair color looked toward the barn, but Dakota couldn't see their faces. The sandy-haired man focused on the woman more than anything else, but Dakota didn't recognize him.

Should she open the door or pretend no one was home? After all, whoever they were, they should be able to see that Matteo's truck was gone. Her heart thudded as she tried to figure out what to do. Matteo hadn't mentioned that he expected any visitors today.

As if the woman sensed Dakota's presence, she shifted her gaze to stare straight at her through the crack in the curtains.

Mrs. Giardano!

What was *she* doing here? Hadn't Matteo said his family was gathering at Angelina's for Christmas?

The darker-haired man turned to say something to Mrs. Giardano, then, as if becoming aware of something in her expression, he too stared at Dakota through the peephole. Definitely a much-older version of Rafe, the brother who had come to quite a few of the 4-H horse shows. She still didn't know who the other man was, but he wrapped an arm around Mrs. Giardano's back as if to protect her from something—or someone. Matteo said she'd remarried, so that must be her new husband.

But who did he think she needed protecting from? Dakota? Maybe he was just worried about his wife.

Taking a step back, Dakota looked down at the robe. She shouldn't answer the door dressed like this, but they'd already spotted her, and the thought of changing quickly and painlessly into anything else would be impossible. Undoubtedly, they had a spare key or knew where one was hidden and would be inside before Dakota could dress and return anyway.

In her current state, would they think something intimate was going on between her and Matteo?

Drawing a deep breath, she did the only thing she could. Dakota took the knob in hand and opened the door, smiling at the trio with a false sense of bravado.

"Merry Christmas!" Dakota said, zeroing in on Matteo's mama. "It's been a long time." She didn't know his mama's new name, so left it at that.

Neither she nor Rafe seemed to have a clue who she was, which wasn't surprising since she'd been away from Aspen Corners for a long time and had been a blonde back then. She hadn't been involved in anything but 4-H, so wouldn't have run across them other than at those competitions.

"Please, come in out of the cold." Dakota's skin, still wet from the shower, certainly felt the chill. Dakota stepped back and opened the door wider, clutching the robe across her upper chest with her other hand. "Matteo should be back any minute. He went to meet the mechanic towing my truck. It broke down outside Leadville this morning. He wanted me to hang out here and..."—*shower? Don't tell them that!*—"get warmed up."

Rambling now and not giving them the entire story about why she was here or when she'd arrived, she waited for them to come inside. She didn't particularly want them to know she'd spent the night, afraid they might jump to conclusions. It didn't matter about her, but she didn't want his mama to think he had a girl staying here.

Stop acting like you're in high school. He's a grown-ass man.

"Can I get you something to drink while you wait? There's a pot of coffee in the kitchen, although I probably should make a fresh one."

None of them said anything at first, then his mother asked, "I'm sorry, do we know each other?"

"Oh! Um, well, sorta. I was in 4-H with Matteo in high school." She held out her free hand to shake his mother's.

"Alison?" she asked before Dakota could give her a name. His mother's eyes opened wider. "Alison Parker!" How on earth had she recognized her, much less remembered her name? She'd tried so hard to be invisible in those days.

Matteo's mama bypassed her hand and wrapped her in a big hug. Dakota winced against the pain of the rib-crushing hug. Fortunately, she didn't hold her too long. When the woman released Dakota, she scrutinized her face a little too long for comfort. She couldn't possibly have seen Dakota's grimace of pain but might have felt her flinch. The men standing nearby probably noticed, though.

"I didn't recognize you with ginger hair," she said.

"That's not all that's changed, actually. I go by the name Dakota Mathison now."

"*The* Dakota Mathison?" the unknown man asked.

"Well, I'm not sure how many others there are, but if you mean the rodeo rider, then that's me."

He whistled between his teeth. "Imagine that! I've seen you ride." Dakota gave him a surprised look as he held out his hand. "Paul Janowski." He pulled Matteo's mama to his side with his other arm. "I married this beautiful woman last year."

"Oh!" Dakota shook his hand much more weakly than she normally would, but he was a big man, and she didn't want to jar her ribs or shoulders. "So nice to meet you." She realized her robe had opened a little at the neck and quickly closed the gaping neckline again.

"I see your love of horses carried over into a career," Rafe said, smiling as he extended his hand for her to shake as well.

An awkward silence ensued after the introductions had been made. "Would you all mind if I changed into something else? Just got out of the shower."

"Of course not," Matteo's mother said. She must be Mrs. Janowski now but hadn't really told her how to address her. "Paul, let's unload the vehicle. Rafe, go make a pot of coffee."

Sounded like they were planning to stay. Well, they'd probably come to see Matteo and wouldn't leave until he returned. But what if they were staying the night? Dakota wasn't sure where she'd sleep in that case. The barn or her camper, she supposed.

Please, Matteo, come home soon. She wasn't sure how she'd entertain his family much longer.

In the bedroom, she realized her large duffel bag was still in his truck. Rummaging through her small bag, she mostly had toiletries. Could she go to Matteo's room to find something to wear? First, she opened the dresser drawers in the bedroom. There were some clothes there, but knowing that they probably belonged to his mother, she felt she should ask permission first.

Before making a decision, she heard Mrs. Janowski let out an ecstatic, "Matteo! *Buon Natale!*"

He's back! Thank goodness!

Moments later, she answered a knock at the bedroom door and found Matteo standing there with her large duffel bag.

"You're a lifesaver! Thank you!" She reached for it, but he wouldn't release it to her.

"Let me set it down on the bed. I don't want you lifting anything this heavy."

Knowing that arguing with him would be futile, she stepped back to let him in. "Did you know your family was coming?"

Matteo chuffed. "Hardly, but it's my own fault. I missed their calls and texts, and they were worried because of…well, they just worry." He looked down at his boots making her wonder what they'd be worried about.

"I'm sure they wanted to see you for Christmas."

He nodded.

Guilt washed over her. "I hate that I've kept your family from being together today."

"Last night was the big celebration, so it's no biggie."

She felt even worse that he'd missed that because of her. Dakota nibbled her lower lip.

"Trust me. It's fine. Now, get dressed and join us. I'm sure Mama's brought a feast for us to enjoy."

"I couldn't eat another bite after that enormous breakfast." All she really wanted to do was go to bed. Her body ached all over, the beneficial effects of the shower long gone.

"Well, try to nibble a little. We don't want to hurt her feelings."

The thought of putting more food into her stomach made her cringe, but she nodded in agreement. "Just let her know we had breakfast not long ago and that we might want to hold off on eating again for a little while." She waved him toward the door. "Now, go! Have some coffee with them. I'll be out soon."

"Yes, ma'am."

As soon as he left the room, she slipped out of the robe, hung it behind the door, and tried to figure out how she was going to get back into those jeans. And what about a bra? Could she contort herself enough to get into one? She'd gone without earlier today.

Between her waning energy and the level of pain, she wanted to curl up in a ball and hide.

Ugh.

In the kitchen, Mama removed food from the bags they had carried in while Paul continued carrying in wrapped gifts. Christmas was a big deal to Mama.

"Coffee's ready," Rafe said.

"I'm sorry to pull you away from Angelina's today, Mama."

Mama gave him a stern look. "When she said you'd texted that you couldn't make it then you didn't answer our texts and calls, I had to check on you."

"We've had a hectic morning, and I didn't see the messages until a little while ago." She must have thought he'd intentionally avoided calling her.

"I heard about your bad run and the fatalities, *Bambino.*" She cupped his face on both sides. "After Tony's difficulties last year, we wanted to check on you sooner than later. How *are* you doing?"

Last year, the day after Angelina's wedding, Tony had been involved in a swift-water rescue gone bad that had resulted in the deaths of a toddler and her mother. A devastating time for Tony, who had never had a child die on his watch, and he'd had a rough time dealing with it afterward.

Sadly, the accident Matt's crew dealt with the other night hadn't been Matt's first and probably wouldn't be his last.

"I'm fine. Yeah, it was bad, but it's part of the job." Did Mama buy his nonchalant response? Probably not. She knew him better than that. "Having the horses here and then Dakota showing up yesterday took my mind off it, honestly."

While that made him feel a little guilty, because the Martin family wouldn't be able to put it out of their minds for a very long time, Matt was thankful he'd had the distractions.

Matt glanced toward the closed guest room door and wondered when Dakota would rejoin them. Was she having trouble getting dressed? Did she have anything besides jeans to wear? He knew how difficult it would be for her to get into her Wranglers given her injuries, especially considering how tight she wore them in the first place. Not that he was complaining. Somehow, though, she'd managed to get into them without him this morning.

Matt tried to decide how best to handle the situation of explaining her presence, not that they had anything to hide or be ashamed of. He just didn't want Mama to think this was anything more than what it was—one old school friend helping another one out.

While Mama placed the pan of lasagna in the oven to warm, Rafe opened a tin of cookies and made himself at home at the bar as if waiting for the show to begin. Matt had better explain before Dakota came back out—more for his mother than his big brother.

"Mama, about Dakota." Mama closed the oven and gave him a puzzled expression. "Alison." Hadn't she introduced herself to Mama as Dakota?

"Oh, that's right. It'll take some getting used to for me to call her that."

"Yeah, well, um, she got roughed up by a bull last week."

"A bull!?! *Dio Mio!* What was she doing with a bull? I just assumed she barrel raced."

Before he could respond, Paul interjected. "When I saw her last year, she rode broncs as well as any man I've ever seen. No bulls, though."

"Broncs aren't much safer than bulls," Rafe added.

"Well, bulls are a new event for her," Matt explained. He hoped a short-lived one too.

"You need to take good care of her, Matteo. She's fragile and hurting."

Matt pulled away and looked into Mama's eyes. "Yeah, Mama, she got banged up pretty bad." But something in her expression told him by *fragile* Mama meant something much deeper.

Before he could say anything more, the bedroom door opened, and all eyes turned to find Dakota standing there in a flirty, summery blue-green dress the color of Navajo jewelry. The dress had those thin straps that would make it so easy for him to slip them off her shoulders and place kisses there on her bare skin. Good thing the bruises hadn't extended to her shoulders, because he doubted she'd be wearing that dress if they had.

And wouldn't that be a damned shame?

The dress hugged her waist before flaring out over her hips. His gaze continued downward, taking in the intricate beading design that led to the wide band of lace on the hem at her knees. The peekaboo effect excited him even more than if he'd been able to see her thighs. But seeing her in her boots, he wondered what she'd look like without the dress, wearing nothing but the boots.

Despite the fact that her glorious mane of hair had been pulled to the nape of her neck in a clip or something, he'd never seen Dakota looking more beautiful. His mind went blank. This had to be the best Christmas present Matt had received in a long time.

"Everything smells wonderful, Mrs. Janowski." Apparently, introductions had been made before he arrived.

"Please," Mama waved away her words, "everyone calls me Mama."

"Mama it is." She flashed a shaky smile in Matt's direction. Were her eyes shining a little brighter? Before he could check on her, she turned back to Mama. "Everything smells wonderful, but I'm sure Matteo told you that I'll need to recover from the huge breakfast he treated me to before I can eat another bite."

Nope. I forgot that altogether.

Her hand went to her flat stomach, but his gaze rose to the bow far below the neckline. He zeroed in on her breasts encased in that tight bodice. He'd tried not to notice before, given her injuries, but…

Damn, she's hot!

Rafe was taking in her beauty too. A spike of jealousy hit Matt like nothing he'd experienced before, especially concerning one of his brothers. Matt wanted to grab his denim jacket—or maybe even a blanket—to keep her from getting cold. Okay, more so to keep Rafe's gaze off her.

Before he could offer anything, Dakota moved closer to the four of them, her stiff posture and slow gait signaling she still experienced a lot of pain from her injuries. But her wide smile told him she intended to ignore it.

When Mama insisted Matt open his gifts, Matt felt bad that he didn't have anything for Dakota to open, but he hadn't really expected to have anyone here on Christmas. Of course, Mama couldn't have known he'd have a guest, either.

Matt shrugged apologetically to Dakota who leaned closer and whispered, "Don't worry about me. Do it for your mama." He noted a slight catch in her throat and wondered what had caused it. "She went to a lot of trouble to bring them to you."

Remembering what he was supposed to be doing, Matt picked up the presents, setting them on the coffee table before he sat on the couch. "Mama, I have something for you in the truck. I'll bring it in momentarily." The store had wrapped the necklace and earrings for him, and he'd kept the box in the truck so he wouldn't forget to take it on Christmas Eve.

Everyone else grabbed a chair. He wished Dakota would come sit by him, but she also chose a kitchen chair, probably because it would be easier to get in and out of.

Don't be selfish, Matt.

The first gift he opened was a bottle of Prosecco and a note from Marc and Angelina saying they'd imported it from the Lombardy region of Italy. They'd agreed not to exchange gifts amongst the siblings. What the heck?

Damn. I need to get them something now too. Stick with the plan next time, Sis.

He asked Rafe to put it in the wine chiller Mama had given him last Christmas so he could share a Christmas toast with everyone today. It didn't get a lot of use with him because he preferred red wine over white.

The next gift came from Rafe and Tony. "I thought we agreed not to exchange gifts anymore," Matt objected.

"Just open it," his big brother urged. *Testy, testy!*

The flat package looked about the size of a calendar. When he opened it, he let out a laugh. That's exactly what it was. On the cover, he recognized quite a few members of the Aspen Corners Fire Department standing in front of their ladder truck, wearing their turnout pants with the suspenders either up or hanging down at their sides and not a shirt among them.

Matt laughed out loud as he met Rafe's gaze. "You guys did a beef-cake calendar?"

Rafe rolled his eyes. "It's a charity thing to help bring in more money for our water-rescue squad," he responded, more than a bit on the defensive.

Matt flipped through to find the pics of his two brothers—representing May and October in the calendar. "This is a great idea, but you two probably should have kept your shirts on."

"Keep going," Rafe said, slightly annoyed. "Marc's Mr. December."

He flipped a couple of more pages to find his newest brother shirtless in front of the ambulance. "No Fiona?" Matt joked, referring to the female paramedic who worked in the ACFD.

"She took the photos," Rafe said. "Said she knew what would appeal to women, our target audience."

"How's it selling?"

"Carmella's resort, Angelina's restaurant, and businesses throughout Aspen Corners sold more than fifteen hundred. Then Carmella put it on a few websites and as of last week, we've sold over twenty-three thousand copies."

"Seriously?" Matt whistled through his teeth. "That woman can sell anything."

"After expenses, we cleared so much we were able to put some in the general fund to replace that old ladder truck sooner than expected."

"That's awesome." Matt might need to mention this to the guys at his station.

"Can I see it?" He looked up to find Dakota standing next to the coffee table.

"Sure. Do you want to sit here or at the kitchen table?" He didn't expect her to sit on the couch with him, given her level of pain, but she surprised him and eased down beside him.

She leaned closer to whisper, "Do you think your station will do one of these sometime?"

Did he detect a note of wishful thinking in her voice? "Doubtful. The Aspen Corners Fire Department started up a new dive team, thanks to my brother Tony. When Carmella, the woman Tony was dating—and has since married—surprised him with a fundraiser at her resort in Aspen, the idea grew into a full-blown water rescue squad. If Leadville had a need or cause we wanted to get involved in, I suppose we could consider it."

The scent of strawberries drifted to him as he reached for the calendar. It was all he could do not to pull her a little closer.

She's your guest, not your date.

Unaware of where his mind had gone, Dakota kept her focus on the calendar as she slowly went page by page starting with January. Every now and then she'd smile, and he noticed her giving several of the guys the once-over from head to toe.

The September firefighter looked like he wasn't even wearing any clothes at all but simply held his helmet sideways against his junk to conceal it from the camera.

"Michael wore his briefs," Rafe explained before anyone asked, "not that you can tell." Matt looked closer but still didn't see a hint of anything but skin and muscle. Lots of muscle. He probably worked out for weeks to prepare for the shoot.

Matt wondered if she'd like to see *him* without his shirt and jeans while holding his helmet over his…

Dakota flipped to the next page and there was Tony. She gave him a slower than ever once-over from helmet to boots then back up again. Carmella had probably made him keep his pants on.

"Very nice," Dakota said before tearing her gaze away and looking sideways toward Matt. "He reminds me of you."

"That's because he's my little brother," Matt said.

Dakota's gaze returned to the page, and she stared at Tony a little longer than Matt thought necessary. She glanced up and over at Rafe and asked, "Can I buy a copy? To help the cause, of course." Her throaty laugh made his jeans get a little tighter.

Matt chimed in before his brother could respond. "Since I didn't give you anything for Christmas, you take this copy. My treat, if Rafe's okay with that." He glanced across the room and Rafe nodded. "I'll buy another one from you, Bro."

"Are you sure?" she asked.

"Absolutely," Matt said.

She smiled. "Thanks." He couldn't help but wonder where she'd hang a calendar since she spent so much time on the road. In her camper, he supposed.

"I'll look at this more closely later on." She stretched out to set it on the coffee table, groaning under her breath at the movement.

Matt hoped she'd be able to stretch out and relax again soon. She needed some time to heal.

Chapter Eight

Matt leaned forward and whispered, "You okay?"

"Yeah," she whispered back. "Sometimes I forget and move too fast or the wrong way."

Apparently, staring at half naked firefighters and EMT/Paramedics took her mind off her pain somewhat. He'd have to remember that, even though the effect was clearly only temporary.

"When's the last time you took any painkillers?" he whispered.

"I took four more ibuprofen before I went to town this morning."

He wished he had something stronger to offer her; ibuprofen wasn't cutting it with the severity of her injuries. The need to take care of and protect her slammed into him. "I hate seeing you in pain."

Mama must have overheard their conversation and retrieved some pillows from a rocker in the corner and brought them over to Dakota. "Let me put these behind you so you won't sink back too far into the sofa."

Seeing Mama looking after Dakota warmed his heart, but Dakota seemed to be thrown off by the gesture. Clearly, she wasn't used to being pampered, which was too bad, because once Mama found out someone needed her, she didn't ease up. Maybe Matt had inherited that trait from her; between the two of them, Dakota didn't stand a chance.

Luckily, after a few moments, Dakota smiled up at her before settling back into the cushions. "Thanks, Mrs—*Mama.* That's much better."

"Want me to open the Prosecco, *Matteo*?" Rafe asked, emphasizing his given name. Clearly, Rafe had picked up on Dakota calling him by his full name and was ribbing him a little. It didn't sound nearly as nice on his brother's lips as it did on Dakota's, though.

Matt glanced across the room at his brother, surprised to hear him teasing. That was usually Tony's forte, but he could take it no matter which brother dished it out. Matt refused to rise to the bait.

While Matt hated leaving her side, he needed to get her some more ibuprofen. He joined Rafe in the kitchen.

"Enjoying your role as nursemaid to your high-school sweetheart?" Rafe asked.

The brothers all teased each other about the women in their lives, although it had been a while since Matt had been the target, but it didn't sit well with him to have Rafe make those assumptions about Dakota.

"We aren't sweethearts. I'm just taking care of a friend who's been injured. When's the last time you rode a bull, much less fell off one? Show a little compassion."

Rafe raised both eyebrows at Matt's terse comeback, and the two remained silent a moment staring each other down. Then his brother smiled and shook his head, mumbling something under his breath about another one biting the dust.

Fine. If he wanted to think Matt and Dakota were an item, let him. It wasn't far from what Matt hoped for anyway. He just didn't see anything long-term happening with her, given Dakota's vagabond lifestyle.

Shaking out a few pills, he brought Dakota a glass of water and crackers to take them with. After she'd taken the pills and removed a few crackers, he took the glass and sleeve back to the table where Rafe poured the wine in several glasses.

"Would you like some Prosecco, Dakota?" Some wine might help her relax so the pain pills could kick in.

"Maybe a small glass. Thanks, Rafe."

Matt picked up two of the glasses Rafe had already poured and delivered them to Mama and Paul then returned to the kitchen.

Rafe slid Dakota's glass toward him along with the bottle, now more than half empty. "You can pour your own."

Seriously? But Matt chuckled at the running gag between the brothers, picking up the bottle to pour his own glass. Rafe wouldn't be drinking because he'd be driving the three of them home—*soon*, Matt hoped.

Dakota leaned back against the couch, the exhaustion clearly visible on her face. He hoped his family wouldn't stay much longer, because she needed some rest. She couldn't have had time for much of a nap, if she'd had any at all, after her shower.

Matt lifted his glass, meeting Dakota's gaze, and everyone followed. "To a holiday season filled with laughter, friends, and family."

A flicker of something in her eyes at the end of the toast caught him by surprise. Family must be a sore subject. Did she have any family left? He certainly hadn't heard her mention any last night or at the rodeo in October.

"You still have another present to open, Matteo," Mama said. Matt took a couple of swallows of his wine before he picked up the last box from the coffee table and returned to Dakota's side on the couch. The sooner he finished with gifts, the sooner they might be alone again.

How long did his family plan to stay? Now that they had seen Matt hadn't gone off the deep end after working the fatal crash the other night, hopefully they'd leave as soon as they finished the Christmas rituals. Though as host, he probably should offer them some of the food they'd brought down before sending them on their way.

He felt a pang of guilt over wanting to get rid of his family, especially Mama, after he'd just toasted them, but he wanted to spend as much time with Dakota as possible before she left. Every day she stayed would be like a gift for him, though.

"This one's from you, Mama." She smiled at his inane remark. Of course, she knew that.

Once the wrapping paper was tossed aside, he lifted the lid off the box and stared down at a framed picture of his dad in his SAR gear, probably right after a successful mission given his smile. It was the same photo that had been on Mama's mantel since before Papa was killed. The image left him speechless.

"I had copies made for each of your homes," Mama said.

Matt cleared his throat so that he'd be able to speak without embarrassing himself in front of everyone. "Thanks, Mama. It's always been one of my favorite photos of Papa." Matt stood and crossed over to where Mama sat in the rocker to give her a hug.

"Love you, Mama. Thanks."

"Love you too, *Bambino.*"

Luckily, she whispered the endearment and didn't embarrass him in front of Dakota. Matt hadn't always been the dutiful son—like last night—but he vowed to do better in the future. She'd always been there for him and his siblings, with and without Papa. "I'm sorry I didn't make it up to see you last night—or get to Angelina's today." He tried to keep his voice low so as not to have Dakota overhear him.

"You were where you needed to be. My mother's intuition told me something was up with you, although I didn't expect to find Alison—*Dakota*—here when we came down." She smiled in Dakota's direction across the room before focusing on him again, her voice still low. "I'm just glad you're okay. After hearing about the other night, I was worried. I always felt an odd pull toward her when you two were in 4-H together, as if she needed a mother figure in her life."

He turned toward Dakota to see her wipe away a tear and stand with Paul's help before Matt could reach her side. No way could she have overheard them, but something had upset her.

"Can I get you anything, Dakota?" Matt asked.

"No, thanks. I'm fine." Her voice sounded shaky. "I just need a minute, if you'll excuse me." Without waiting for his response, she slowly walked toward the bedroom, holding her side.

What had made Dakota cry?

Dakota splashed water on her face before staring at herself in the mirror. Red eyes spoke to how hard she'd been fighting back tears at the beautiful family scene she'd just witnessed. The love in the room made her heart ache for something she'd never been a part of.

Then a glimpse of a familiar, frilly room flitted across her mind's eye, but she couldn't remember where she'd seen it before and pushed it aside.

Taking a washcloth from the basket, she wet it and held it against her eyelids. She'd have to go back out there and face them but didn't want Matteo, especially, seeing that she'd been on the verge of crying. What was *wrong* with her?

When she removed the cloth, her eyes still looked a little puffy, so she fanned the air in front of her face as she continued to stare into the mirror. Drawing a deep breath, she straightened her dress and drew herself up, ignoring the pain. Matteo hadn't taken his eyes off of her when she first came out in this dress.

Thankfully, his mama, she supposed, had put a portable ironing board and iron in the closet. The pain of setting it up to iron the wrinkled mess had been worth it just to see how much Matt appreciated the dress on her. He probably hadn't expected her to have anything dressy in those duffel bags, which wasn't far from the truth.

But she'd bought this dress on a whim from a street vendor last summer during Cheyenne Frontier Days. She hadn't had an occasion to wear it—until today. While it was more of a summer dress, she'd wanted to look nice for his family for Christmas. At first, she'd been tempted to put on her denim jacket but since none of her bruises showed had decided against it. At least she hadn't needed to wrestle with a bra with this dress that had built-in cups.

His mama was one of those apple-pie mothers you read about but never thought actually existed. Dakota didn't remember her own mom, who had never been a part of her life as far as she could remember, so being cared for by Matteo's mama made her eyes sting again.

Don't start crying again!

Steeling herself against another bombardment of emotions, she plastered a smile on her face and left the safety of the bathroom. Again, the smell of lasagna hit her first, but she decided that eating would be less threatening than sitting around making small talk or watching all these displays of affection.

She noticed the beautiful blue glass jewelry Mama now wore. "Those are beautiful!"

Mama's hand went to the necklace, and she smiled affectionately at

Matteo. "My son knows my one vanity is handmade jewelry."

"Lieutenant Paske's wife makes them," he explained to Dakota. "When I saw the blue ones, I thought immediately of Mama."

Dakota wondered what color would make him think of her, then pushed that notion aside.

"Matteo, if you're hungry now, I would love to try Mama's lasagna."

He searched her face as if trying to find some crack in her armor, but Dakota remained strong and resolute. Apparently satisfied that she was okay, he said, "I always have room for Mama's cooking."

"Why don't I get everything ready for your dinner," Mama began, "and then we'll be on our way. I'm sure Angelina is holding dinner until we get back."

"We didn't take food away from your family's Christmas dinner, did we?" Dakota asked, mortified at the thought.

"Oh heavens, no! We made multiple pans of lasagna and ravioli. I know several of my sons aren't much on cooking, so Angelina and I like them to have leftovers. There's plenty here to last you two a couple of days."

Dakota wasn't sure which made her more nervous—being in the house with four other people, or being here alone with Matteo. But Mama didn't wait to put her plan into action, so it didn't really matter. Dakota wanted to help, but when she winced as she tried putting the bread in the oven, Matteo took it from her and suggested that she sit down and take it easy. Mama retrieved a platter of salami, pepperoni, and vegetables from the fridge.

"I don't know the last time I've seen a feast like this one!" Dakota said. "Do you always cook this much?"

Mama stopped what she was doing and stared at her as if she'd grown two heads. "It's Christmas! I always cook more than usual during the holidays."

"Every meal with Mama is a feast," Matteo chimed in. Dakota couldn't cook a lick. Clearly, though, she'd never have been able to live up to his mama's cooking.

Dakota's knowledge of holiday family traditions was nil. She hadn't had a Christmas or Thanksgiving dinner in…she couldn't remember how long.

"Your family is very lucky to have you, Mama." Calling her that didn't seem natural to her, but Dakota didn't want to disappoint the woman who had been so kind to her. However, Dakota couldn't wait for this woman to be on her way. She churned up too many long-buried emotions.

And yet when they gave their final farewells and the woman hugged Matteo, Dakota felt a pang of regret. Suddenly, she found herself being hugged as well. This time, Mama did so more gingerly; Dakota gave in to the warm feeling ever so briefly before pulling away.

"So good to see you again, Mama."

"Please take care of yourself, sweetie. And let Matteo spoil you a little while you're here."

"Oh, he already has."

Rafe and Paul didn't seem inclined to hug her but wished her a Merry Christmas before heading toward the door. For the first time since she'd found Matteo again, she wished she could stay wrapped up in his cozy little cocoon for a long time. A pipe dream, of course, but if he'd let her stay a while, she just might do her recuperating here. This place was a balm for her battered soul.

Matt wasn't sure what changed to make Dakota want to stay past the day when her truck—which she said now ran better than ever—had been fixed. But each day he woke up surprised to find her still here.

It was New Year's Eve now, and she hadn't left yet.

His cooking abilities couldn't be what kept her around. Dakota didn't seem to know her way around the kitchen any better than he did. On the day before his shift, he'd stocked up the fridge with things she could microwave while he was gone.

He'd planned on taking her up to Mama's for dinner tomorrow, but

Mama told him it was too soon for Dakota to sit in a truck that long. So yesterday, Mama had brought them enough food to last through the holiday weekend. "Stay home. Let her heal a bit longer before you make that drive to see us."

Matt wasn't too sure how long Dakota would be sticking around or if she'd be here for Mama's next family dinner, but he'd agreed.

Despite her injuries, Dakota spent a lot of time with him in the barn. She wasn't able to ride or do much more than feed and try to ingratiate herself with the cats. They weren't much on being touched, though. Of course, she'd tried to muck Comet's stall once, but when he'd caught her doing it, he had put a stop to it immediately.

There seemed to be no limit to the rubdowns his horses benefited from under Dakota's hands, though. Each night when Matt brought them into the barn, she'd grab the curry comb and brush and go to work on them as if her life depended on it. The look of peace that came over her face at those times warmed his heart.

Matt suddenly regretted that he hadn't really arranged anything special for them tonight other than picking up a bottle of champagne to toast in the New Year. He didn't want to spook her by getting close too quickly. There had been a couple of times where he had crossed that line, but tonight he could see in her eyes that she was on edge. Would she bolt if he pushed too far?

Last thing he wanted was for her to leave. Where would she go? Nobody expected her to be anywhere, as best he could tell. She never talked about family around him and hadn't mentioned anyone from the rodeo circuit since she'd shown up here. If she had someone else in her life, she'd have run to them first, right, instead of to him?

But why the hell wasn't there anyone who cared about her? Dakota was engaging and entertaining, easy to be with, and always willing to help out. Why didn't she have anyone who cared where she was or how she was doing? Something didn't seem right with this picture.

Maybe he'd find out more about her in the next couple of days—or weeks—if she stayed that long. Thankfully, she'd agreed to lay off the rodeo circuit until at least late February, maybe even early March. But she led a drifter's life if he'd ever seen one. Who knew when she'd decide it was time to move on?

"How'd you like that rubdown, girl?" Dakota pressed her face against Twinkle's cheek and patted the mare's neck, closing her eyes as she savored the moment. "You don't know how badly I want to ride you, girl."

Her words were spoken as if only for Twinkle's ears but gave Matt a glimpse into how difficult an injury was for someone like Dakota. She'd lived and breathed horses every day of her adult life, although in bronc riding, she wouldn't have her own horses to pamper and care for, much less for pleasure riding. Was that even something she'd enjoy? Was there some way to simulate the horseback riding experience for her without causing further pain or injury? His mind drew a blank. Well, other than the X-rated thoughts that popped up more and more often when he was around her.

An idea occurred to him. He'd give Luke Denton a call. The man worked with a lot of people with disabilities at his ranch and might be able to offer some advice.

As if suddenly aware of his presence, she turned her face toward him and smiled. "Your horses are about the sweetest ones I've ever met."

He chuffed. "That's because most of the ones you come across are trying to buck you into next year. But Comet and Twinkle are definitely on their best behavior. You're company and a novelty to them."

She spoke in Twinkle's direction. "I don't believe for a minute that you're behaving any differently with me, Twinkle, than you would if I wasn't here. You're a sweetheart." She kissed the horse on the nose, and it took everything in Matt not to feel jealous.

Jeez. You're such a goner.

"Hey, are you hungry, Dakota? I thought maybe we could have an early supper and then rent a video to ring in the New Year." He didn't want to make this out to be some kind of romantic New Year's Eve but did want it to be something more special than any other Wednesday night.

"Not super hungry, but a movie sounds good. Do you know what my favorite New Year's Eve one is?"

I didn't even know people had *favorite New Year's Eve movies.*

"Don't laugh," she added without waiting for him to respond.

Had he conveyed his thoughts to her? He'd have to be careful around her. "No judgment. I promise."

Dakota pushed straw around with her toe a moment before meeting his gaze again. "I don't think it's a guy flick at all. Never mind."

Now he was curious. "Dakota, what's the name of it?" He couldn't even be sure that the rental box in Leadville would have it, but now he needed to know.

She glanced down and rubbed the toe of her boot in the straw as her cheeks turned pink. *Adorable.* Not whatever title she'd mumbled, but Dakota herself. Still, he asked her to repeat the name, because now he wanted to know more than anything.

She met his gaze as if defying him to say a word about her choice. "*While You Were Sleeping.*"

Interesting.

Matt didn't picture Dakota as being into romantic movies, for some reason. Westerns maybe, but not sappy stuff like that one. "That's one of Mama's favorites too."

While the cheesy chick flicks did nothing for Matt, who had never been able to watch past the first part with that insufferably stereotypical Italian neighbor, watching it with Dakota might be eye-opening. Why did it top her list—at least as a New Year's Eve flick to watch? Matt wanted to know more about Dakota and what made her tick, and he had a feeling watching the movie tonight was going to reveal more about her.

"Mama left some of her favorite DVDs here to watch when she used to come to visit before she married Paul. I'll bet it's mixed in with my videos."

"If not, it's not that big a deal. I'm sure we can find something else."

No way would he miss this chance, even if he had to go buy a copy of it himself.

Both said goodnight to the horses and returned to the house. Anticipation for the upcoming evening together had his spirits running high. It would be all he could do not to cuddle with her on the couch, but she obviously didn't see him in a romantic way.

Too bad, because in just the short time they'd spent together, he sure as hell saw *her* that way.

Chapter Nine

At the front door, Dakota reached for the handle, but Matt beat her to it and opened it for her. "Why don't you heat the gnocchi while I look for the movie?"

"Sounds good." After being in the barn all day, she needed to pee, but first she removed her boots using the boot jack Matteo had placed just inside the door for her. It had been a great help to her on the days he was at the station. Such a considerate man.

A few minutes later, Dakota rummaged through the closet where she'd hung her clothes. She wanted something more comfortable to wear than jeans. Nothing too revealing or clingy. While she slept in comfy long johns—the men's sets, which were much warmer than the women's—no way would she parade herself around him in those. Fleece and flannel had never been her thing, though, because they made her too hot. She chose a soft cotton blouse and a flouncy skirt in a western print fabric. The elastic waistband didn't press too hard against her bruised body. She did put on some fuzzy socks, her one concession to comfy attire.

Pulling her hair into a low ponytail, stretching her arms to the point of pain, she wondered what on earth had possessed her to mention *While You Were Sleeping*. The movie's far-fetched premise was as unrealistic as they came. Still, Dakota always cried during the hospital wedding scene where the main character, Lucy, confessed why she'd gone on with the ruse for so long. She hated to show deep emotions in front of anyone, especially ugly crying in front of a man.

Maybe spending time with Matteo's mother, brother, and stepfather on Christmas had triggered some weird longing to be part of a loving Italian family.

Dakota identified with Lucy's longing for a family on many levels, but Dakota had better come up with a different reason for why she loved the movie. In reality, though, from that Christmas break her senior year when she'd borrowed the video from the library, she'd immediately pictured herself as Lucy, and Jack's family as Matteo's.

No way did she want Matteo to suspect how much she'd fantasized about being a part of his family back then. Dakota reminded herself of the advice Lucy's boss had given her in the movie:

"You're born into a family; you don't join them like the Marines."

Did Matteo realize how fortunate he was to have been born into the Giardano family? From what Dakota could tell, he appreciated his mama and siblings, even if he'd chosen to move away from them to live and work in Leadville. But it hadn't fazed him that they would drop everything on Christmas Day to rush down here to make sure he was okay. He acted as though it were normal.

When was the last time anyone had cared about Dakota that way?

Shake it off. No pity parties allowed.

She had lots of people on the rodeo circuit who'd have cared if they'd known. They just hadn't been at that event in Golden so probably didn't know about her injury.

Even if feelings did spark between her and Matteo, she wasn't the type of girl who settled down and had 2.5 children and a yard surrounded by a white picket fence. Not that the thought of having a short fling with him didn't appeal to her. Dakota's long-neglected hormones had left her hot and bothered on a number of occasions this past week.

As if her body would be able to do a damned thing about it, even if she wanted it to.

But why Matteo?

She'd been hanging around guys her entire adult life and none had affected her this way. Sure, there were hot cowboys at every rodeo, and she'd tumbled between the sheets (or in the hay) with a few when the need arose—or more likely after she'd had a few too many beers. She'd never had trouble leaving those guys behind, because her heart hadn't been involved.

With Matteo, it would be different.

She'd had the biggest crush on him back in high school, one she'd been too shy and awkward to act on. Not that he'd ever shown any interest in her as girlfriend material. Matteo had always had the more popular girls following him around school like buckle bunnies. She assumed he'd gone out with at least a few of them. Gangly Alison Parker had just been another 4-H'er who shared his love of horses.

Of course, she wouldn't have been able to date, even if he'd asked her out. She counted her lucky stars she'd been allowed to participate in 4-H, her only after-school activity. Except for a few rare weekend events, she'd always had to be home before dark.

Before letting the anger boil up inside her and spoil this evening for them both, Dakota pushed those memories away once again.

Within half an hour of coming in from the barn, they were seated at the table enjoying Mama's food. "This is delicious. I've never had gnocchi like this before."

"Mama knows gnocchi bolognese with spinach is one of my favorites. As a kid, it was the only way she could get me to eat spinach."

Dakota didn't remember having a favorite dish as a kid—or even a least favorite. Her meals usually came out of cans, and she could choose whatever canned soup or pasta she was in the mood for.

She lifted her bottle of Corona Extra to her lips and took a long draw. Despite his having a wine chiller, he seemed to prefer beer with his meals, rather than wine, which was fine by her.

After not feeling hungry earlier, she surprised herself by cleaning her plate. "I think I could live on meals like this."

"I've never taken Mama's cooking for granted. I'm just glad to see you're enjoying it—and that you're eating. Want some more?"

"I couldn't eat another bite, or this skirt won't be as loose as I'd like."

Matteo had been riding her since Christmas about eating enough to allow her body to heal. His persistence had galled her at first—definitely not the kind of riding she wanted from him—until she realized he probably just wanted her to get well enough to be on her way. Despite trying to give him lots of space this week, it wasn't her fault that he kept finding excuses to join in on whatever she was doing.

Out of the blue, it occurred to Dakota that maybe he *wanted* to spend time with someone—anyone—even her. Maybe he got lonely out here, although the horses took up a lot of his time outside of work. She'd certainly enjoyed their time together, though, so much so that she hadn't left when she could have once her truck had been repaired.

And her body *had* begun mending. Already she could move around more easily. Of course, choosing not to jostle herself around in the truck racing to the next event and trying to mount a horse way too soon had helped in the healing process too.

Just don't get too used to being here, Dakota.

As soon as she could, she'd need to figure out where her next rodeo would be. By both the hospital doctor's and the rodeo medic's estimation, she should be able to ride again by the end of January at the latest. There'd probably be some small rodeos around by then, but seeing the lack of safety measures at the last one in Golden, she might want to wait until the season officially started in March.

Until then, she had a safe place here to bide her time; the longer she let the rib heal the less likely she would reinjure it. Besides, being here with Matteo this past week had been—nice. And he seemed in no hurry to kick her out.

Matteo stood and picked up his plate. "Finished?" She realized they'd hardly spoken during the last part of supper. They'd eaten in companionable silence like an old married couple.

Whoa, Nellie! Don't start thinking like that!

Dakota nodded. "I can do the dishes."

He gave her a no-nonsense stare that melted something inside the pit of her stomach. She wasn't going to win the battle over the dishes tonight either, so she backed down and handed him her plate.

"While I clean up, why don't you rest a little in your room?"

His calling the room hers sounded funny. She hadn't had a room to call her own in such a long time.

"Thanks, but I'll be ready when you are." Standing, she breathed in and out slowly, waiting for the pain to subside before moving to the couch.

After finishing the dishes, Matteo popped a bowl of popcorn and pulled out two more beers, setting them on coasters on the coffee table. *Good.* Another beer might give her enough of a buzz to take the edge off the pain. As long as she didn't let it go to her head and lower her inhibitions enough to blurt out something she shouldn't reveal during the movie.

Matteo had found the movie earlier and put it in the DVD player while she took her spot at the end of the sofa. When he sat in the middle, a little closer than she'd expected, she found it even more difficult to relax. At least they weren't quite touching each other.

As the credits rolled, she turned to him. "Thanks for watching with me. I hope it doesn't put you to sleep." *But in reality, I hope it does.*

He gave her a half-smile. "I'm sure it will be great."

Wincing at the pain from bending over, she picked up her bottle and took a sip, hoping to nurse it through most of the movie. He groaned at the first scene with Joe Junior.

"Sorry," he said. "That guy always bugs me."

"Yeah, he's pretty annoying. Fortunately, he has a small part."

She took a long draw on her beer when they came to the scene where Lucy spent the night at Jack's family home for Christmas. Dakota's eyes stung, knowing exactly how Lucy felt now that she'd experienced a glimpse of what a real Christmas must be like with Matteo's family.

By the time the wedding scene was about to unfold, she placed her almost empty beer bottle on the table and stood. "Don't pause it for me, but I need to take a…break after the beer."

Unfortunately, he picked up the remote and hit pause. "It's getting close to midnight. I'll open up the champagne."

She wanted to decline a glass, but that wouldn't be in the spirit of the holiday.

"Just half a glass for me."

When she returned, the champagne bottle peeked out from the wine chiller and two flutes sat next to the uneaten popcorn. Before pressing play on the remote, he asked, "Have you ever been to Italy?"

The random question made more sense when she remembered that thread in the movie where Lucy had dreamed of traveling to Italy. "No. I've only left the country once to go to an event in Calgary."

"The Stampede?"

She laughed. "No, something much less prestigious." She wondered if saying she wanted to go to Italy would make him think that's why she loved the movie so much. But she had no interest in traveling beyond her rodeo circuit.

"How about you? I remember you going to Italy between junior and senior years. Don't you still have family there?"

"Extended family. Nonna passed away many years ago. Actually, she was my great-grandmother, but my mama lost her mother at a young age and her grandmother was more of a mother figure for her. Her papa would send her to spend summers with his mother, and eventually, she took us there every summer to do the same. I still have uncles and cousins in Marsala that I ought to visit again sometime. My sister and her husband went there on their honeymoon last year, and I've been meaning to take some vacation time and go back. Just haven't managed to do more than think about it yet."

Matteo's family stretched between two countries. How lucky could someone be?

Not ready to return to the movie yet—fearing the ugly cry she anticipated—she kept the chatter going. "Have you lived anywhere besides Aspen Corners and Leadville?"

"Went to college in Fort Collins for a while before transferring to Breckenridge. After that, I commuted from home. How about you?"

Dakota wasn't sure how to answer her own question. She chose to go with what she remembered. "I've been all over. Aspen Corners, of course, for a couple years. And after that, I ranched a while before joining the rodeo circuit. Since then, I've mostly lived near the arenas and rodeo grounds I've competed at."

No roots. A tumbling tumbleweed.

While she could handle crowds of strangers at the rodeos, having to engage one-on-one or with strangers had always freaked her out. She'd never felt safe in social situations as a child or teen and had always tried to become invisible.

No conversation seemed safe tonight. Before they went down any other trails leading to personal revelations, it was time to finish up this movie.

"I'm ready when you are," she said, pointing toward the television.

Matteo hit play, and Dakota steeled herself for what was to come.

Matt turned his attention to the TV again as Dakota sat silent and ramrod straight beside him. He tried to pay close enough attention so that he'd be able to discuss the movie later, because it seemed to mean something to her.

Once Sandra Bullock's character got away from her annoying neighbor and settled into Jack's parents' house, Matt warmed up a little more to the story line. While Christmas itself was never a big deal to him, Matt did enjoy the time spent with his family. He pitied the Lucy character for having to weave such a complicated web of deceit in order to feel the familial connection he'd always known. He hoped he'd never take his family for granted.

No doubt, all of Lucy's lies would come back to bite her in the ass, or it wouldn't be much of a movie. But Matt expected a happy ending eventually. Wasn't that a rule for chick flicks?

Once again, though, the scent of Dakota's hair began to distract and intoxicate him. Smelled like strawberries, something he'd never associated as an aphrodisiac before—until Dakota. No way would he be getting any sleep tonight, but sitting here beside her was just about the best way he could imagine ringing in the New Year.

Matt didn't know if she'd be around long once her injuries healed, but he had a strong feeling he'd be attending more regional rodeos in the coming year for opportunities to see her again.

A glance at his watch told him they had about five minutes before the start of the New Year. Matt leaned forward to pick up the champagne and popped open the bottle to pour them each a flute in preparation. At the stroke of midnight, he handed her a glass and lifted his own.

"To rekindled friendships continuing to grow in the New Year," he toasted.

She almost seemed disappointed by his words, but then smiled and clinked his glass. "To friendships." Each took a sip. Maybe if he hadn't limited himself to friendship, he'd have scored a kiss. But were they anything more than friends? He'd like them to be, when she was ready.

With half-filled glasses in hand, they returned their attention to the screen and watched as Lucy walked down the aisle in the hospital chapel to marry Peter. He must have missed something. Didn't she love Jack?

During Lucy's tearful explanation of why she'd lied to them all, he heard Dakota sniff and turned to see tears streaming down her cheek. She tried to surreptitiously wipe them away by pretending to scratch her cheek. Matt took her glass and set both of them on the coffee table before plucking a couple of tissues, cupping her chin to turn her toward him, and gently wiping away her tears.

She tried to laugh it off. "Sorry. That part always rips my heart out."

He half-listened to Lucy on the screen, wondering why the scene was so significant to Dakota, but the pull toward her became too strong to ignore. Her eyes sparkled with unshed tears. The urge to kiss her grew, and he leaned forward to see if she'd back away. When she didn't, he moved in a little closer…closer…and brushed his lips over her cheek, kissing away the tears. She still didn't pull away, so he turned her face toward him and did the same to the tears on her other cheek.

Matt wished he could absorb the emotional pain for her at the same time. He didn't like seeing her hurting, whether it be from a silly movie, a cracked rib, or anything else.

Dakota opened her mouth slightly and damned if she didn't kiss him. Her lips, tentative at first as if she wasn't sure about his reaction to her, grew bolder. When her lips brushed his, he opened his mouth in invitation and her breath mingled with his own. Despite the urge to let her know exactly how he felt about her, he didn't advance the kiss. He'd let her set the pace.

Dakota gently nibbled on his bottom lip, and his cock pressed against his zipper hard enough to make an imprint. She tugged lightly before closing her lips over his mouth and deepening the kiss with her tongue. All too soon, she pulled away, dashing his hopes. She paused a moment to search his eyes, and her rapid breaths fanned lightly over his face. He remained stock-still. Any moment, he expected her to retreat. He waited for what seemed an eternity for her to make her next move. *Jesus.* He hoped she wouldn't end this moment just yet.

Finally, she cupped his face—as if he were going anywhere—and pressed her lips more firmly against his. This time, he wouldn't sit here like a bump on a log. His hand went to the back of her head to tease the escaped tendrils of hair and the soft skin at the nape of her neck. She gasped, and her mouth opened slightly wider. He made a mental note that he seemed to have found one of Dakota's erogenous zones and continued to stroke her there while flicking his tongue playfully against her lips. She smelled clean, like sunshine on a summer day. When her lips parted a little more, his tongue slipped in and out, teasing hers. Her tongue joined the dance, and she hummed softly, expressing her enjoyment. He needed to adjust his position to keep his cock from being strangled but was afraid to move and break this spell.

He became lost in the kiss until Dakota stiffened and pulled away. Her cheeks had become nearly as red as her hair. Matt tried not to groan in frustration but sat back and stared into her eyes again before he said, "Happy New Year, darlin'."

Her tongue skimmed her lower lip as if to savor the taste of his kiss. He shifted his position because his desire for Dakota was nearly strangling him.

"Same to you, Matteo."

Matt refused to feel badly that the kiss had gone no further. This was way more than he'd ever hoped for in a first kiss with Dakota on

New Year's Eve or any other time. There could be no denying that this was not a chaste kiss she might have given a friend or even a casual date.

When she sat back against the sofa cushion and turned her attention to the screen again without another word, he picked up the remote. "Want me to rewind?"

"No!" She practically grabbed for the remote, groaning at the pain the movement caused. She turned toward him and added sheepishly, "Not on my account. I mean, I've seen this movie a thousand times. We can just continue where it is now—unless *you* want to go back."

He'd already lost his train of thought and didn't think he'd be able to concentrate on the movie anyway with this smokin' hot woman sitting beside him, so he pretended to watch the movie while her nearness and the memories of that potent kiss threatened to overtake his self-control.

He'd expected her to distance herself from him, but she surprised him by resting her head against his shoulder. When her head grew heavier, he wrapped his arm around her shoulders, and she nestled into the crook of his arm as if sitting here together like this were a common occurrence. He held the sleeping cowgirl next to him, content to sit here all night if that was what she needed from him.

Soon his own eyes started to droop a bit.

A jerking motion woke him suddenly, and he found a sleepy-eyed Dakota looking up at him. It was after two o'clock.

Dakota tried to move away but winced in pain.

"Easy does it." He sounded like he was talking to a skittish filly. "Take it slowly."

"Sorry, I must have fallen asleep."

"So did I," he admitted.

The movie had ended at some point, and the main menu of the DVD repeatedly played the theme music.

She used her hand against his thigh to push herself upright and groaned as she straightened up. "I'm so sorry! I can't believe I fell asleep on you!"

Her words brought new fantasies to mind. "You must have needed it; I didn't want to disturb you."

"Your arm must be numb."

He wasn't going to admit that and make her feel worse, so he grinned as he lowered his arm to his side to let the blood rush back in, creating a tingling sensation in his fingers.

"Did you make it through the entire movie?" she asked.

"Afraid not. Sorry."

She cocked her head. "Your impression of what you saw?"

He still wasn't sure he completely understood why the movie had upset Dakota enough to cry over but had to respond. "It's all about family—the one you're born into and the one you choose. As a firefighter, I have one of each type of family."

She smiled a little wistfully and nodded. Maybe he'd watch it again later and study that chapel scene more carefully in its entirety.

All he knew was that he'd remember this New Year's Eve forever for having Dakota kiss him, even if she did promptly fall asleep beside him afterward. Good thing he didn't have a fragile male ego.

"I guess I'll go to bed now." Her breathy voice washed over him. He wished she'd join him in his bed.

Don't press your luck.

"Thanks for making this New Year's Eve so special for me, Matteo."

"I can't think of anyone I'd rather have rung in the New Year with."

She leaned in and gave him a peck on the cheek, which only got his jets fired up again. "Sleep well."

Remembering his manners, he stood first and helped her to her feet then watched as she slowly ambled toward the bedroom. After sitting so long, she had to be stiff and sore. "Do you want something for the pain?"

She turned and forced a smile. "No, thanks. I'm fine." And then she walked into the room and quietly shut the door.

His skin felt seared where she'd pressed her lips against his cheek.

He wished they could have spent the night together in the living room even if all they did was hold each other. Dakota felt so right in his arms.

Matt gave himself a mental shake. Man, he sure was getting sappy about her, which probably wasn't a good idea. Dakota's free spirit would clash with his need for solid roots.

The New Year had more to offer him than he would ever have imagined a week ago. Matt had never turned away from a challenge, and he sure as hell wasn't backing down from this one.

Chapter Ten

Dakota's lips tingled from kissing Matteo's cheek a few minutes ago. But that sensation paled in comparison to their earlier kiss. How it had happened confounded her.

Oh yeah. The movie.

Matteo had kissed away her tears with such tenderness, it made her heart ache. She'd temporarily forgotten her rule about not getting sexually involved with him and went with her gut—kissing him.

Dakota appreciated that he hadn't probed her with questions about the source of her tears, though. He simply gave her space while also calming her. Crying in front of him might have embarrassed her at any other time. She prided herself on hiding her feelings and her weaknesses. But Matteo made her feel comfortable enough to express emotions she normally kept shut inside. Actually, she usually didn't even admit some of these emotions to herself.

The man did everything right when it came to bringing out her inner yearnings and making her long for something more. She needed to fight harder to keep this relationship from going in a physical direction, because she could never commit to anything more than superficial with him. Otherwise, she wouldn't be able to walk away when the time came to leave.

And she would have to leave eventually.

Matteo was a forever-after kind of guy, and she wasn't cut out for settling down. She'd never had stability growing up and wouldn't know how to act if she had to live in the same place for the rest of her life—or for the next year, for that matter.

Matteo would never leave this ranch or his job with the fire department to follow her around the circuit like some lovesick puppy. She wouldn't respect him if he did. The two of them were unsuitable to say the least, so then why had Dakota kissed him tonight? And kissed him again?

Because she'd been dreaming of having sex with Matteo before she even knew what sex was. While too sore right now to do anything more than lust after him, it wouldn't be fair to get that sexy cowboy/fireman in bed and then walk out on him. Would it?

Grabbing her long johns, she walked into the bathroom. After removing the ponytail and shaking out her hair, she stared at herself in the mirror hardly recognizing the woman looking back. The lines around her eyes had softened up during the week she'd spent here. That tough edge she wore like armor to keep others at a distance had slipped, if not fallen away completely. Was that due to not having to be "on" around people all the time—or did it have more to do with being in close proximity to a certain Italian American cowboy/fireman?

As she gingerly ran a brush through her hair, she resolved not to let him further erode the defense mechanisms she'd built up over a lifetime. They'd served her well up to now, and she'd need them again when she left this temporary haven.

But how was she going to keep herself safe from her own desires?

She hadn't come here to kindle anything with Matteo. She needed to focus all her energy on recharging her spirit, healing her body, and rebuilding her determination to make it as a bull rider during the upcoming rodeo season. With those two spills, her self-confidence had taken a brutal beating.

Dakota brought her fingers to her lips. Kissing Matteo had felt so good, so right. Unlike the cowboys on the circuit, Matteo would never be just another notch on her belt. She was able to forget those guys the minute she left their beds—and she'd *always* been the one who left first. Had she subconsciously compared all subsequent men over the years to the teenage fantasies she'd had of Matteo and found them all lacking?

She hadn't totally forgotten him since high school, just pushed those memories into the recesses of her mind. Of course, the innocent feelings she'd had for Matteo as a teen were nothing compared to her body's response to him tonight.

Undoubtedly, Matteo would be impossible to forget if we become intimate.

All the more reason *not* to jump in the sack with him, no matter how much he turned her on.

You'd better be careful, Dakota.

She sighed with regret and finished preparing for bed. Five minutes later, she eased herself onto the mattress, trying to ignore her stiff body and the pain in her ribs. She stared up at the ceiling, trying to quiet her mind.

What am I going to do about you, Matteo? How did you slip under my defenses so quickly?

Was it more about his family than him? His mama had treated her like one of her children. Even Rafe, although not as open toward her as the Janowskis, had been kind. What if she merely yearned to be part of the Giardano family, as Lucy did Jack's family in *While You Were Sleeping*?

Gaining a family was no reason to start a relationship with a man.

Oh, come on, Dakota. Be honest. Her attraction to Matteo had nothing to do with his extended family. He exuded hotness and had once been the boy of her dreams, the one she'd fantasized would rescue her from…

Dakota pushed those memories aside, even though they tried to persist. Regrettably, she found herself dragged back into those two years spent in Aspen Corners.

Alison and the man had moved there during her junior year. They'd moved every few years for as long as she could remember and for reasons she wasn't sure of. He didn't have a job outside the home, and whatever his business had been, it had probably been illegal.

He'd shown her no love, and she couldn't really say she had any positive feelings for him, either. She resented him for depriving her of…something she couldn't name.

The man insisted Alison call him Dad, but she'd never been comfortable doing so. She used that title only when she wanted to avoid his anger. He'd wanted to control her every thought and action, and she'd let him—up until she'd finally escaped from him. Dakota had no memory of abuse from the man but held no love for him, either.

At some point, the man, whose real name she'd banished from memory long ago, had noticed her relationship with Matteo. While it had been nothing more than friendship, he'd felt threatened by Matteo for some reason she couldn't understand.

On the night of her high-school graduation, when he'd packed up everything to move them to God-knew-where this time, Alison had become fed up. She'd almost gone to Matteo's home to ask for refuge but had instead gathered her few belongings and hitched a ride out of Aspen Corners to wherever.

Wherever turned out to be southern Utah. She'd found a job at a desolate ranch where she'd learned to rope cattle. She already knew how to barrel race. Eventually, those two skills and a nearby rodeo had led to her new career, and she hadn't looked back. Changing her name gave her some sense of hope that the man wouldn't find her and wreck her again the way he had when he'd kidnapped her as a child.

Kidnapped?

She wasn't sure where that thought came from. Had the man kidnapped her originally? Why couldn't she remember something that monumental?

He'd told her he'd taken her away from her drug-addicted mother, and that he could take better care of little Alison. She had no bad memories of her mother. The fleeting ones she did have seemed pleasant, but Dakota supposed that even a bad mother was still a mother.

A tear trickled from the corner of her eye before she realized she was crying. Thoughts of the two women from her childhood always left her raw. Usually, Dakota kept those thoughts at bay, but tonight her emotions were rawer because of the movie.

Why did I suggest we watch Sleeping*?*

Wiping the tears from her face, Dakota banished those memories to the far recesses of her mind yet again. Well, she tried to, anyway. But after an hour of lying in bed without being able to sleep, Dakota suddenly had an uncharacteristic urge to bake something, even though she had no clue how. Maybe she wanted to do something nice for

Matteo after all the meals he'd provided her with. With a shrug, she tossed back the covers.

Sometime in the middle of the night, a loud crashing sound woke Matt from a deep sleep. He automatically reached for the handgun in the nightstand drawer before remembering he wasn't alone in the house anymore. Still, he needed to make sure Dakota was okay. The commotion seemed to be coming from the kitchen.

He donned his jeans, tucking the handgun into the waistband at the middle of his back. Picking up his phone, he hurried down the hallway to find Dakota wearing a gray long john top, her bottom half hidden by the kitchen island. Though facing in his direction, she wasn't aware of him yet. While she appeared frustrated, she also had an unguarded look he didn't often see.

A metal mixing bowl stood in front of her, and her hand rested on a round cake pan. She frowned as if trying to solve a physics problem. Maybe he could help, as long as it didn't involve him doing any actual baking—or physics.

"Everything okay?"

She jumped, which sent the cake pan skittering to the floor, replicating the sound that had woken him up a few moments ago.

"Shit," she said. "Sorry. I wanted to surprise you, but…" She left the words hanging in the air as she stared down at the pan.

He crossed the room to retrieve the metal pan only to find another one a few feet away. He carried both to the sink and ran the hot water while inserting the stopper. "I'll wash these up for you. What are you making?"

"Apparently, a disaster. I don't know what got into me. I couldn't sleep, so I thought it might be nice to make a coffee cake for our New Year's breakfast, but my cell phone didn't have a signal, and the bag of flour didn't show any recipes on it. You don't seem to have any cookbooks around here." Her accusatory tone made him smile.

"I think the only ones I might have would have been left by Mama in your bedroom. She liked reading them for fun, I guess, during her visits. I don't think she took all of them with her."

Dakota had wanted to make them something for breakfast, though? He hadn't pictured her as the domestic type. "It sure was sweet of you to think about baking something for us." Or maybe she'd just grown tired of his scrambled eggs and to-go café fare.

"Your appreciation might be a bit premature. I also couldn't find the sugar but did see the cinnamon. Then I accidentally knocked that pan off the island and couldn't bend down to pick it back up." Her chin trembled. He needed to salvage the situation fast.

"I've been keeping the sugar in the freezer ever since it started attracting ants." He went to pull out the bag. "Here you go." He set it on the island. "But I'm not sure my flour is the right kind for coffee cake. I think Mama uses a special flour for those." He looked at the pans in the sink and went to the cabinet to pull out a rectangular glass pan. "She usually makes them in this type of pan, though."

"I told you I have no clue what I'm doing."

"Mama had no luck teaching any of us to bake, not even Angelina, although at some point my sister learned how to make the best cannoli I've ever eaten." He paused a moment, trying not to notice how hot she looked in the long john bottoms too. Who would have thought Duofolds would be sexy?

"Um, want me to see if Mama left any cookbooks behind?"

A smile of relief came over her. "That would be great. Thanks for helping me out."

"Sorry about the cell phone coverage out here. Some days are better than others." He pulled out his phone and unlocked it. "Feel free to google something using mine. Might work, if we have different carriers." He set it on the island in front of her.

Matt came back with a book on baking to find her already cracking eggs into the mixing bowl. Clearly, she'd found a recipe that suited the sparse list of ingredients she'd found, so he set the cookbook aside on the counter. "Can I help with anything?"

"No, I think I have it. Just don't get your hopes up. A domestic goddess I am not."

You're a goddess of all things.

With flour on her cheek and her hair pulled back from her face in a ponytail, she resembled an earth mother. Not something he'd have ever associated with Dakota before. *Sexy!*

"So, you couldn't sleep?" Surprisingly, he had managed to fall asleep fairly quickly, despite that kiss.

She gave a shrug and consulted his phone again. "I guess the nap on the couch ruined my chance of getting a good night's rest. But I probably should have found something else to occupy myself with in the middle of the night—like reading a cookbook." She flashed him a half-grin, quirking the side of her mouth up, and he couldn't help but smile back.

Damn but she had a sultry, heart-stopping grin.

"I just had a weird urge to bake something." She gave a flippant shrug.

"You really don't have to make anything for me, but I appreciate the effort." He joined her on the same side of the island, a little closer than earlier. "Before you get a hankering again, maybe we ought to lay in some supplies. You know I don't use this room for much more than making coffee and oatmeal and warming leftovers."

"So I gathered." She pointed to the bag on the island. "This flour expired a year ago."

"Sorry about that."

"Oh, no worries. I added extra cinnamon and some nutmeg to hide any staleness."

"I'm sure it will be wonderful." He picked up what was left of the bag of flour and tossed it out before she had any inclination to use it in anything else.

"It wasn't buggy, though, so I'm sure we'll live."

Her self-deprecating humor about the situation made him smile. "What can I do?" he asked again. He wasn't going to miss hanging out with her in here for anything.

"Preheat the oven to three-fifty, please."

After he took care of that, he watched her beat the batter—or was it dough?—by hand. Her breasts jiggled with the vigorous movements, and he decided it would be best if he stood on the other side of the island to hide his hard-on. He tried imagining her with nothing on but an apron, her breasts spilling out from the sides. He'd never fantasized about a woman in the kitchen before.

To fill the silence, he suggested, "If you can't sleep, maybe I can make us some cocoa or mulled wine before you try to fall asleep again. It's going on four o'clock, and I think we're going to need a little more sleep if we are going to get through the day."

"Did you have something special planned?"

He did but didn't want to spoil it yet. "Yes, but that'll be *my* New Year's surprise."

She waved her hand to take in the flour-dusted island and all the cooking items. "Some surprise this turned out to be, huh?"

Before she could grill him for details, he headed her off at the pass. "So, what do you say? Cocoa? Wine? Something stronger?"

"Cocoa sounds wonderful. We can sip it in the living room while the cake bakes. Maybe you can stoke up the fire again?"

His body's fire had been stoked for a while, but Matt nodded, happy to have something to do besides gawk at the sexy woman in his kitchen. He headed to the mudroom to bring in a few more logs. "Looks like there are still some embers from earlier." Soon he had the fire blazing and closed the doors of the insert.

Rather than sit on the couch where he might be tempted to start kissing her again, he pulled the rocking chair closer to the fire for her and arranged another chair for himself. They'd be sitting only a few feet apart, yet far enough away for him to behave himself. But he reminded himself she'd been the one to take their first kiss to the next level.

Back in the kitchen, he poured the milk in the saucepan and wondered how long her ribs would take to heal before they could get into a more physically intimate relationship, assuming she wanted one at some point. He wasn't going to be able to hide his feelings from her for much longer.

But first, he'd make damn sure *he* was ready for whatever type of relationship she wanted from him, which included a trip to the drugstore real soon.

"That's it," Matteo said early afternoon on New Year's Day. "Easy does it."

Dakota wasn't sure if he was talking to her or Comet as she climbed up the four steps to the mounting platform.

"I was thinking we'd need the para rider hoist I trained Comet on last year," Matteo remarked.

"It's essential for our paralyzed guests," Ryder Wilson explained, "but Luke made this block about six months ago due to the high demand for the hydraulic hoist. It works great for those with less severe injuries like yours, Dakota."

She'd met Luke Denton earlier. The Dentons and Wilsons were equal partners in running the Dreams Found Ranch near Fairchance. Apparently, Luke and Cassie had sold the ranch house to Ryder and Megan, who initially helped manage the place but now shared an equal partnership in the running of the equine therapy and mustang rescue operation.

While Dakota didn't know how the hoist Ryder and Matteo referred to worked, this platform seemed straightforward. The main thing she noticed was that the floor of the platform was much higher than a regular mounting block would be.

"I'm ready when you are, Matteo." Matt held Comet's reins and seemed nervous now that she was moments away from mounting a horse for the first time since her accident. This might push the boundaries laid down by the doc, but she knew it would make a huge difference in the speed of her recovery.

"Take ahold of the saddle horn to steady yourself."

Dakota did as he'd instructed and swung her right leg over Comet's back, settling herself into her saddle. Matteo had brought hers along knowing she'd be more comfortable in it.

Home. Dakota felt whole for the first time since that disastrous bull ride. Elated, she beamed at Matteo. "This is the best medicine I could ask for." Only she didn't have to ask. He'd instinctively known what she needed.

"And thank you, Comet, for being such a good boy," she cooed, patting his neck without bending too far forward. The gelding nickered as if he understood her words and the importance of standing still for her. She gave Matteo a nod as if ready to come out of the chute. "I'm ready."

"How's that rib?" Matteo asked as he handed her the reins. Despite this New Year's surprise's being his idea, furrows in Matteo's brows made her think he was second-guessing himself.

"I'm fine, Matteo." There'd only been a twinge of pain initially, but she didn't feel it seconds later. "Thank you *so* much for this." She could hardly get the words past the knot in her throat.

He smiled as relief flooded his face. "Glad it's working out."

"I can't believe I'm going to get to ride a horse this soon after my accident."

When Matteo had asked her if she'd be up for a ninety-minute drive, she'd chomped at the bit to go somewhere. Being sedentary wasn't her style. Soon after, he began loading up the horses. Was he taking them for the drive too? After they pulled out of his lane, he'd told her about where they were headed and what they'd be doing.

Until this moment, she hadn't been able to envision herself joining in on the horseback riding part of it, but clearly Matteo and Ryder had been in communication earlier. Everything had been ready for her when they arrived just before noon.

She turned to Ryder. "You have no idea what this is doing for my soul."

He grinned. "I have a pretty good idea. I hear that almost every day from someone."

"I'm usually on a horse nearly every day—for eight-second stints, anyway. Not exactly peaceful rides, but I've missed them something awful these past ten days. Thought I'd have to wait until late January before I could get in the saddle again."

She couldn't say she wanted to be on a bronc anytime soon, though. Unfortunately, there wasn't any money in riding sedate horses. And if she never rode another bull, it would be too soon.

Ryder nodded as if he understood. "Glad you could join us, Dakota."

"What a wonderful sanctuary you and Luke have here." Not only did they rescue abused and neglected mustangs, but the horses provided hope and joy for all the people she saw on the bustling ranch outside Fairchance.

They had an amazing operation here. Even on New Year's Day, several wheelchairs sat abandoned nearby at the fence surrounding the corral as three children took riding lessons from Megan, Ryder's wife. Parents and other children milled around chatting at the start of a row of bunkhouses in what once might have been a pasture. Several single-family cabins were situated on the other side of a dirt road. Another group of adults and children petted alpacas in a pen closer to the barn. So much activity!

"Ready to head into the corral?" Ryder asked. She glanced at the sedate pace the other riders used in the corral and wished she could ride faster, but first, she needed to see how her body took to the rhythm of a walking gait. She'd taken a heavy dose of ibuprofen on the way here after finding out she'd be riding, hoping to alleviate most discomfort.

I don't care how much it hurts. I'm riding this horse!

After leading Comet to the corral, Matteo turned her loose. She tried to stay out of Megan and her students' way as she became one with the horse. "You're such a good boy." She patted his neck, wincing as she leaned too far forward, compressing her ribs and muscles.

After several turns around the corral, she began to shift her focus beyond the fence. Luke, Ryder, and others saddled and bridled a group of about a dozen mustangs. Two adults in wheelchairs waited nearby and she got to see the hydraulic lift in action as the first one was hoisted into her horse's saddle. Her thighs had been placed into straps and a waist guard provided stability as she was lifted high above the horse. Ryder worked the remote that then eased her into the saddle.

Amazing.

Dakota had heard about para riders using hydraulic lifts to mount horses for dressage and other equestrian activities, but she only knew of one who had made it in rodeo circles—Amberley Snyder, who made it back into barrel racing after a catastrophic accident. What would have happened to Dakota's career if her fall from the bull had resulted in paralysis—or worse?

You're one lucky cowgirl.

Most riders going out on the trail didn't need the lift. Some had no apparent physical injury or disability. On the drive over, Matteo had explained Dreams Found Ranch offered equine therapy to anyone suffering with trauma or post-traumatic stress issues, whether they were combat warriors, first responders, or survivors of violent crime, abuse, or neglect.

Everyone here seemed to find peace and comfort around the animals.

Once the last of the riders were mounted, Luke got astride his palomino mustang Picasso. Luke had introduced her to Picasso and another of his mustangs, O'Keeffe, soon after she and Matteo arrived. She'd quickly learned Luke named all his horses after famous artists, probably because he and his wife, Cassie, were artists as well.

Ryder rode O'Keeffe over to where Matteo watched her like a hawk. Dakota slowed Comet to join them at the fence. "Luke and I will be out on the trail ride for the next ninety minutes or so." Earlier, she'd tried to encourage Matteo to go with them rather than babysit her, but he'd insisted on staying here.

"Everything going okay, Dakota?" Ryder asked.

"Perfectly," she answered.

"Hope you two can stay for our New Year's dinner. Cassie and Megan have prepared a feast."

"Wouldn't miss it for the world," Matteo answered.

Dakota hadn't met Cassie yet but looked forward to it; she'd never met anyone from Peru before. She felt embarrassed that she hadn't brought anything to contribute to the meal, but after serving Matteo the hardest coffee cake known to man, she wasn't sure they'd have appreciated her culinary efforts.

"See you soon." Ryder left, and they watched the group set out. The mountains beckoned to Dakota, too, but joining them would result in excruciating pain for her and might set her back a week or two in her recovery. Still, she envied the riders heading out with Luke and Ryder.

I'll bide my time—for now.

Chapter Eleven

Joy filled Dakota's heart as she watched the three blue merle Australian shepherd mix dogs cavort around the horses headed out on the trail ride, almost herding them at times. One of the dogs, Chance, was the mother of the other two. She and Suyana, whose name meant Hope in Cassie's native language, lived with Luke and Cassie up at the pass. Kachina, or Chee as Ryder called her, stayed here at the ranch with the Wilsons. Dakota had been told that two other pups from the same litter lived with friends in Denver, and the final one had found a home with Matteo's sister and her husband.

Dakota glanced at Matteo who had been looking at her, not the trail riders. "This is such an amazing place."

"Sure is. They've helped a lot of people find peace and healing."

Dakota hadn't realized it until now, but maybe she'd gravitated to horses all those years ago to find escape, harmony, and the sense of being loved that had been missing from her life.

Dakota smiled down at him from her perch on Comet. *Time to charm him into saying* yes.

"Why don't you mount up too, Matteo, and we can ride around the bunkhouses and maybe across that pasture a little bit." She pointed to the land next to the nearest house and barn.

He scowled, "You aren't overdoing it, are you?"

She pointed toward the line of riders on their way to the mountains. "Heading out with them would be overdoing it. I feel like I'm on the pony ride at the county fair. It's pretty flat around here, and we can stick to the places that have been graded for vehicles if that makes you happier."

Matteo scanned the area, assessing its suitability, she supposed. Dakota didn't normally let anyone dictate what she could or couldn't do, but Comet wasn't her horse, so she'd let Matteo come to his own conclusion. If all or most of the Dreams Found horses weren't in use right now she probably could have switched mounts, but better to play along and let him be in charge—today.

After what seemed like forever, he met her gaze again. "Promise me you'll let me know if you're in any pain and that we'll stick close to this area until we see how you handle it?"

Dakota couldn't wait until she didn't need a nursemaid, but today she appreciated him for giving her the chance to ride. Using her finger to make an X mark over her heart, she smiled again. "Promise. Now, saddle up. Comet and I are ready to go." But he needed to understand that she wasn't going to get off this horse until she was good and ready.

"All right, it's a deal." Matteo shook his head in surrender but didn't seem all that upset.

He opened the gate to let them out of the corral, relatching the gate before heading to the trailer to get Twinkle's saddle and bridle. While waiting, Dakota walked Comet around as she scouted out the path they might start out with, anxious to get going. She could sense Comet's excitement too. He seemed happy to be back where he'd been boarded until Matteo bought his own place. She didn't know the feeling of returning to a place she'd loved in the past.

As soon as Matteo joined them, Dakota used her knees to get Comet moving. "Follow me."

Dakota didn't look back as she rode away from the corral, but hearing the clomp of Twinkle's hooves behind her assured her he followed. She felt some twinges in her side and chest, but the pleasure outweighed any pain.

Rather than follow as she'd commanded, Matteo trotted up beside her, then slowed Twinkle's gait to match Comet's.

Dakota glanced sideways at him. "Have I told you how much I appreciate you for bringing me here today, Matteo?"

He shrugged with a grin. "Once or twice. It's good to see you smiling."

His words only broadened her smile. "You might have to pry me out of this saddle later." He seemed to size up the round shape of her butt in the saddle and the curve of her thigh against the horse's side. "Should be easier than you having to pry that teenager out of the baby swing."

Just as he had at the station, he cringed at the mention.

Man, I wish I could have seen him in action.

She couldn't help but notice the tight fit of his Wranglers and how rugged he looked in his sherpa coat and black Stetson. Emotions stirred inside her, ones she'd been trying to tamp down after last night, obviously without much success.

She'd have liked to follow behind him and enjoy the view of *his* ass during their gentle ride, but any time she lagged a little, he also slowed down, giving her concerned glances.

Too bad. Maybe next time.

When they came to the end of the row of bunkhouses, the gravel lane ended. Rather than circle around and head back to the barn, she urged Comet in the direction of the gate to the pasture.

"Would you mind opening the gate for us to continue our ride?"

Matteo "You doing okay? Any pain?"

She hadn't slowed up or in any way indicated any pain. She smiled, not certain how to convey to him she'd be fine. "Stop worrying about me, Matteo. I haven't felt this good since I got hurt. And Comet is about as gentle a mount as I'll ever have, so relax."

He searched her face a moment before grinning sheepishly. "It does my heart good to see you so joyful."

"I'm back in my element!" She pressed Comet's sides to pick up the pace of the walk again. Soon after, a motion out of the corner of her eye caught her attention. She glanced down to find Chance at Comet's heels, staring up at them as if making sure they didn't stray too far. "Are you worrying about me too, Chance?" The dog gave a quick yip in response. She must have doubled back, leaving the trail ride in the care of her babies.

Laughing, Dakota continued out at this laboriously slow pace. With the wide open pasture enticing her, Dakota wanted to let Comet trot or canter across the field, but she'd keep her promise not to overdo it.

Even at this near crawl, Dakota wouldn't trade this ride for anything in the world.

"I'm glad you didn't have to work at the station today. And not just because I wouldn't be here if you'd been working."

"It's always nice having a major holiday off, but this place has something going on every day of the year. We can come back again if you'd like, so don't try to do it all today. I just had a feeling getting you on the back of a horse again would outweigh the consequences."

"You know us rodeo types. We don't let a little pain keep us off our mounts."

His thoughtfulness touched her in a cold place deep inside.

She couldn't help but wonder what they might have been doing if they'd stayed at his house, though. Things certainly had heated up between them last night. Did she want to take their relationship into sexual territory or would it be safer to remain friends—without benefits? She'd had sex with cowboys who were friends before but had never been able to cross back into a friendship-only relationship after things cooled down.

Remaining friends with Matteo was more important to her than having a brief fling with him.

For this reason, it was probably best she not think about anything more than building on their friendship.

Great idea to get away from his ranch for the day, because Matteo wouldn't have been able to keep his hands—or lips—off her if they'd hung around his house or barn instead.

Still, thoughts of her riding *him* jarred him from his woolgathering. He attempted to shift to a more comfortable position in the saddle without success. This would be the most uncomfortable ride he'd taken in a long time.

They rode in the direction of the highway, nearly deserted due to the holiday. Matt understood the power of horses for helping a person when stressed or upset. How many times had he found solace with his horses? Seeing Dakota's smiles today showed him she understood that feeling as well.

Dakota took a deep breath. "Smells so good out here."

"I guess with most rodeos taking place in or near towns and cities, you don't get much of a chance to just spend time in a rural place like this."

"True enough. Not having my own ranch or horses doesn't help."

"Well, while you're staying with me, what's mine is yours."

She smiled at him. "I appreciate that. Can't wait until I can venture out a little more without all your restrictions, Matteo."

"Hey, I'm only following your doctor's orders. I doubt he'd be happy with you doing even this much so soon after your injury."

"The way I took his advice was not to ride at a *rodeo* event for six weeks. I don't think he meant for me to stay off horses altogether."

"I call bullshit."

Her grin told him she was aware of that already. "Can we not bring up bulls today?"

He nodded. "Just don't do anything to make me regret this."

"I made you a promise. I'm a woman of my word."

"Good, because that means a lot to me." His words sounded like he referred to more than this ride. Okay, maybe he did.

After they rode another thirty or so minutes around the perimeter of the fenced-in pasture, his phone buzzed, and he removed it from his pocket. "Ryder says they're heading back, if we want to get cleaned up for dinner."

The disappointment in her face made him feel bad about cutting off their ride, but she'd been on the horse well over an hour. She'd be hurting tonight and tomorrow, so they ought to head back before making it any worse. Hopefully the benefits would outweigh the pain.

They circled back to the barn and his trailer. He waved Megan over to help line up Comet at the mounting block they'd used earlier while he dismounted and climbed onto the platform. A groan escaped Dakota's mouth as she swung her leg over the back of Comet, and he steadied her with his arms. She met his gaze, and time stood still for a moment as if all the oxygen had been sucked out of the air.

I'm going to kiss her again if she doesn't kiss me first.

"I'll leave you two to take care of the horses," Megan called up to them, breaking the spell with a grin that told him she knew exactly what Matt had been thinking. "The trail riders just got back. Dinner's about ready. Meet us in the event barn over there." She pointed toward the new structure.

"I'll be right there, but why don't you go on in," he said to Dakota.

"I'll take care of Comet first." Lines had formed at the corners of her eyes, and he wondered if they'd overdone it, but she'd never admit it, even if they had.

After Matt helped Dakota down the stairs, they wiped down and currycombed both horses before Matt led the horses to the corral to join the others.

"They built this event barn last year," Matt said after rejoining Dakota and heading for the huge building. "They needed a place big enough for all their guests to join together for various activities—like eating. Sometimes they hold workshops in here when they have groups of people dealing with similar issues. They've also had music and dancing events in here."

Inside the building, two long farm tables, each about sixteen feet long, were nearly filled with ranch guests—both adults and children—which surprised Matt. He hadn't realized how many people were here. Some probably had been helping Cassie prepare the meal or might have just needed some down time from all the activities and had stayed in their cabins or bunkhouses.

The nearest table had guests in both wooden chairs and wheelchairs; the other table had two long, matching bench seats. No doubt Luke had made the tables and benches; his skill at creating beautiful furniture was renowned in the region. Matt had even heard he made some specialty kink furniture for clubs throughout the United States and even parts of Canada, but Matt had never been privy to seeing any of it.

Matt led them to the end of the second table where Megan and a woman Dakota hadn't met yet stood. The other woman stretched out her hand. "You must be Dakota. I'm Cassie, Luke's wife. Did you enjoy your ride?"

Dakota shook her hand. "Nice to meet you! And it was unbelievable! I thought it would be another month before I could ride again. This place is amazing!"

Cassie nodded. "Definitely a dream found for my Luke."

Matt watched the man himself as he walked up behind Cassie and wrapped his arms around her waist, kissing her on the side of her neck.

"You should be careful, sir," Cassie said with all seriousness. "My husband can be a jealous man."

"He has every reason to be jealous with a beautiful wife like you, Sweet Pea."

Cassie turned around and her smile radiated in Luke's direction as she encircled him with her arms.

Matt remembered back to the day nearly three years ago when Luke had come down the mountain with Cassie's Peruvian brother in tow after an avalanche near Iron Horse Pass had stranded Luke in Cassie's cabin for a couple of weeks. Matt later learned Luke and Cassie had headed to the JP to get hitched that very day, although he hadn't noticed much of a connection between them at first. She'd finally moved in with Luke following a woodland fire that summer that had destroyed her cabin. Obviously, love had won out, despite all life had thrown at them.

Matt turned to Dakota and caught a look of longing on her face as she watched the other couple share their reunion moment after having been apart only a few hours. Would she ever miss him that much? Or miss anyone, for that matter? Dakota didn't seem to get attached to people. Maybe she'd want to come back to visit his horses someday, although he hoped she'd want to visit him too.

Whenever she chose to leave. He planned to do his damnedest to have her stick around long enough to make sure she didn't forget him.

Dakota tore her gaze away from the Dentons, feeling as though she was intruding on their intimate moment. The love they showed for each other made her heart ache. She'd never seen anything so beautiful before.

She caught Matteo's gaze on her. If he'd been staring at her as she suspected, he didn't turn away to hide the fact. Dakota smiled when he took her hand and squeezed it measuredly.

"What would you like to drink?" Luke asked Dakota. "We have iced tea, coffee, cocoa, or soda."

"Thanks, but don't worry about us. We'll help ourselves," Matteo said. He turned to her, "Tea, pop, or something to warm you up?"

"Iced tea sounds good."

"Be right back." Matt and Luke went to the table laid out with beverages, leaving her with Ryder and the women.

Megan turned toward her husband. "Ryder, why don't you find a chair for Dakota? I think she'll be more comfortable at the end of the table, rather than on the bench seat."

"Sure thing, Red." Must be a nickname. Megan's hair was as ginger as Dakota's.

"I hate for you to go to any bother," Dakota demurred. "After all, I just mounted and rode a horse!"

Megan waved away her words. "All the more reason to let us take care of you today."

Making chitchat with non-rodeo people had never been her thing. "I'd love see your artwork sometime."

"I would love to show you around my studio sometime." Cassie had a quiet beauty about her and seemed reserved but friendly. "When the weather is better, you should come up to visit my studio on the mountain pass."

"Oh, I don't think I'll be around that long, but I appreciate the offer. Maybe our paths will cross again and I can catch an exhibit in a town where I'm doing a rodeo."

"I'm sure Matt can share upcoming exhibit information with you. I am so happy that you found your ride enjoyable. That will make Luke and Ryder happy. They love this place so much."

Cassie smiled somewhat wistfully. "I know he loved today's trail ride. We don't live here at the ranch any longer, so Luke enjoys any chance he gets to ride the back country." She glanced toward the stone fireplace at the far end of the barn where the three dogs lay curled up and sleeping from their workout. "And I know Chance and Suyana enjoyed their reunion with Chee today."

Dakota couldn't imagine giving up a place like this, although Luke didn't live all that far away and remained actively involved in its operation from what she could tell.

"Why don't you have a seat?" Megan suggested, pointing to the chair Ryder had placed at the end. "Matt can get a plate for you."

"No, that's fine," Dakota insisted. "I can serve myself. Really. I don't want to get used to being pampered." She wouldn't have anyone to do that for her when she returned to the circuit. "Besides, moving will help me heal faster." Even if it did hurt like the devil.

"Well, then, shall we?" Cassie extended her arm toward the buffet line where the other guests stood filling their plates. As she drew nearer, the dishes looked and smelled delicious, even though there were many Dakota didn't recognize. She'd always had a good appetite, as long as it wasn't her own cooking.

"You've prepared a feast! I'm so sorry I didn't know to bring anything." *But lucky for you that I didn't.*

"You're our guest!" Megan and Cassie insisted at the same time.

Cassie pointed to one dish that appeared to be a soup of some kind. "This is *caldo de gallina*, a traditional New Year's dish in my homeland."

"Wait until you try it," Megan added. "It's so good!"

Dakota didn't normally have much of a rapport with women, other than the few she competed against on the rodeo circuit. But these two were easy to talk to and didn't make her feel socially inept in any way.

With her plate piled high and a bowl of the Peruvian soup—no one would ever accuse her of being ladylike when it came to her appetite—she made her way back to the table. Matteo had placed her tea and his coffee near the last two plaid placemats at the end of the table.

"Can I get you anything before I sit down?" Matteo asked, having made it through the buffet in no time at all. Almost everyone had been through the line now.

"No. Thanks for the drink." She removed her outer jacket given how warm it was inside with all these people and placed it on the back of her chair before sitting down. Matteo slid onto the bench seat next to her, their arms brushing.

Luke stood next to where Matteo sat and tapped a knife against his glass. "This is the start of a New Year at Dreams Found Ranch. I want to thank all of you for joining us, whether it's for the day," he glanced down at her and Matteo, "or for the week." His gaze took in the two long tables of guests. "You're helping us kick off the year in a big way. We hope you find the same sense of peace and healing that we've discovered here."

He glanced down at Cassie with a smile then his gaze quickly moved to Ryder and Megan. Dakota wondered what the story was behind each couple and how they'd found their dreams. She'd certainly found both peace and healing at the ranch today.

"Thank you, Cassie, Megan, and all who helped prepare this meal for us. I know you've been working on it since yesterday, and we really appreciate you." The room erupted into applause for the cooks.

"Everyone please take a moment to give silent thanks however you choose." Luke bowed his head.

Dakota wasn't the praying kind but bowed her head and thanked Matteo for bringing her here and the Dentons and Wilsons for providing this place for all who needed it.

"Now, let's eat before this delicious food gets cold!" Luke took his seat between Matteo and Cassie.

Chatter began to erupt, and she took a taste of Cassie's soup. *Delicious!* A few more mouthfuls took the edge off her hunger. She leaned forward to meet the woman's gaze on the other side of Matteo. "Cassie, this is fabulous." No sense in asking for the recipe, though. Why ruin the memory of how good it tasted? "Tell me about where you're from."

Cassie's face lit up as she told Dakota about the town high in the Andes where she'd grown up. Luke chimed in about an upcoming trip they had planned to visit her family in February. "Peru's summer is our winter, so it's a nice time to get away. We go to Machu Picchu every year while down there. Next to our home on Iron Horse Pass, the Incan holy place has to be the most spiritual place I've ever been to."

Dakota sensed Cassie might be a spiritual person and was certain their cabin on the mountain exuded harmony and tranquility, much like the woman did.

Megan squeezed Ryder's hand and the two shared a silent communication then smiled at each other. Dakota wondered what they'd been thinking about but would never have asked. Turns out, she didn't have to.

"We found a place like that near Wilson Peak on our honeymoon almost three years back." The love in his eyes for his wife made Dakota's heart ache. "Sometimes it seems like we've always known each other, and other times I can't believe how recently we met." Ryder turned back to Dakota. "We try to go back there every chance we get, although it's harder to get away these days with the ranch doing so well."

Before even thinking about it, Dakota opened her mouth and offered, "I can't really cook or do all the other things you do here for your guests, but I know how to take care of horses. If you need someone to help out with the horses next month, I'm your gal. The rodeo circuit doesn't start back until late March, so the timing is great."

The Wilsons and Dentons seemed surprised by her offer. She almost added that she hadn't been serious when Ryder said, "That's generous of you to offer, Dakota. The horses would sure be in good hands with you."

"She's been great with my horses," Matteo added.

Luke quickly jumped on her offer. "We have some volunteers coming for one of the weeks we'll be gone, but maybe you could take the other. Matt, you're welcome to join in when you aren't on shift or working with the forest service."

Dakota turned toward him. "You work with the forest service too?"

He shrugged. "Once a month, I take my four days off to help with wildland fire maintenance year-round—mostly thinning the canopy and undergrowth and joining local engine crews serving as holding forces on prescribed burns so they don't get out of control. It all helps toward preventing the next big wildland fire, we hope. But my February stint with forestry service will be early in the month. I should be home before you leave, Luke, not that a wildfire is out of the question."

Matteo never ceased to amaze her with his commitment to the fire service and his community. The thought of being useful to anyone made her feel good inside, but she'd never really gone out and pursued opportunities to help in her adult life. Her sole focus for so long had been on chasing buckles.

Being so readily accepted by Matteo's friends gave her a sense of belonging and being needed that she hadn't felt in a long time, if ever.

"Just say when," she finally responded to Ryder. "I'm not going anywhere for a while."

Dakota met Matteo's gaze and smiled, hoping that sticking around was okay with him. She couldn't read his expression—a mix of happiness but was there also a tinge of regret?

Then he grinned. "I'm sure Comet and Twinkle will enjoy having another chance to visit their friends up here too." He turned toward Ryder. "I'll join you on my days off. It'll be like old times."

Having Matteo here too would be nice. She didn't know how much more time they'd have together. Dakota wasn't going to be able to stick around once professional rodeo events started popping up in late March.

I need to guard my heart, though, or I'm going to be in for a world of hurt when I do leave.

Chapter Twelve

Three weeks later

Matt exited the ladder truck following the two-alarm fire on the outskirts of town. It had been a brutal call. Frozen hoses only complicated matters. The house was a total loss, but at least they'd managed to rescue everyone in the family, including their pets, without injury. Matt had searched as hard as he could to salvage some things for the family from the ruins, but he'd found pitifully few items—a partially burned wedding album and a singed silverware chest. Matt couldn't imagine what it would be like to lose everything he owned in a fire, but possessions could be replaced. If he lost a loved one or his horses, he'd be devastated.

They couldn't clean their turnout gear until closer to shift change in the morning, because they didn't have any backup gear, but did assess the extent of the damage. Matt brushed and inspected his gear before heading up the back stairs to shower off the smoke and soot from his body.

After their showers, several of the crew members made their way down the hallway to the kitchen. "Hey, Dakota!" Ackerman nudged Matt, who looked up to find Dakota standing in the kitchen next to the table.

"What brings you here?" Matt asked. Before she could answer he noticed how the other guys gawked at her like lovesick puppies. Matt walked over to give her a peck on the cheek, partly as a territorial signal for his brothers to back off. Dakota didn't seem taken aback. In fact, she gave him a hug and peck on the cheek back.

"I heard about the fire when I came to town to grocery shop and thought you might appreciate some ice cream," she said facing him before turning to the other guys. "Matt told me how much it soothes your dry throats after a fire."

Wow. She remembered me saying that?

Matt didn't even recall telling her.

Dakota went to the freezer and pulled out a two-gallon tub of Neapolitan, his favorite because he could have a little of each flavor.

"This was really sweet of you, Dakota." Ackerman pulled some bowls from the cupboard. The other guys expressed their thanks too.

"This is a special treat." Matt brought the ice cream scoop to the table to serve it up. "Thanks for going to the trouble."

"What trouble?" she asked. "I just picked it up at the grocery."

"Hey," Matt said, "you thought about us, and that makes it special."

"We really appreciate this," Paske added. "Makes me glad I came in on my day off to go on this run."

That peck on the cheek a few minutes ago was the first time they'd shown any affection for each other away from the privacy of the ranch, although it was on par with the types of touches and kisses they'd been exchanging over the past few weeks. The woman had left him as horny as hell, but Dakota had been sending him mixed signals as to whether she wanted more than friendship. Okay, and Matt had also been afraid to take it to a more intimate level because of her injury.

Inflicting pain isn't my thing.

He wanted to give her more time to heal, showing her how he felt about her in nonsexual ways, but wished they had more time together to cultivate something. He'd taken her to his doctor but she'd only extended the time Dakota needed to heal to early February.

One thing in his favor, Dakota hadn't talked about missing the circuit as much lately as she had when she first showed up. She refused to take it easy at the ranch, though. The woman drove herself harder than anyone he knew and seemed to have a need to push the physical boundaries for whatever task she set her mind to.

Had spending time at Dreams Found Ranch on New Year's Day and helping around Matt's ranch given her a new perspective on what she could do after her days of riding the rodeo circuit ended? Not that she sounded like she was ready to hang up her rodeo hat anytime soon.

But at least he didn't hear her pining to ride another bull.

Matt watched as the crew, seated around the table eating their ice cream, bantered back and forth with Dakota. She'd developed an easy rapport with them; hell, she fit right in wherever she was. She seemed to like coming here when he was on duty, because she'd found an excuse to stop by for some reason at least one day of every shift this month.

He'd like to think she missed him and got lonely at the ranch without him. Of course, she was used to hanging out with cowboys on the circuit. His brothers at the station treated her like one of the guys—well, almost. Good thing they did, because if one of them made a move on her, he'd hate to have to break a nose or something.

Not that Matt had staked any claims on her himself other than the occasional touch or peck on the cheek. Now that she was almost fully mended, maybe he ought to think about wooing her more vigorously.

If I'm going to have any chance of keeping her here, I need to get to work on that—soon.

Dakota laughed out loud at Lieutenant Paske's story about his oldest son's misadventures in high school. She'd first met the man when her truck had broken down but hadn't expected him to be on Matteo's shift today. In fact, there were twice as many men in the station as on a normal shift. The fire must have been bad enough that they'd called in backup to help.

She didn't want to ask if there'd been any fatalities or serious injuries, but their mood seemed to be more tired than distraught. She hoped there was nothing more than a loss of property.

Dakota liked hearing Paske talk about his family, envying him for having that bond with his wife and kids. He hardly talked about anything else, unlike the others at the station, half of whom were unmarried or divorced. They mostly talked about hunting, sports, and fire-service training around her.

Dakota glanced over to find Matteo staring at her intently. He'd surprised her with that public show of affection earlier. Was he staking his claim around the single guys? She did a mental shake of her head. Lately, his touches and occasional pecks on the cheek had left her longing for more, but they never went anywhere. Had his mama taught him to behave like a gentleman *all* the time?

Too bad. Being so close to him all the time and not having him put the moves on her drove her to distraction.

Of course, that didn't seem to keep her away from him.

You can't even get through his two-day shifts without finding a reason to stop by the station.

What was keeping him at a distance? Was he afraid she'd break like a china doll if they had sex? Damn that bull and the doctor anyway, but she was almost as good as new and wished she'd never admitted to Matteo how long she'd been told to stay off horses. Apparently, he took it to include Italian stallions too.

Maybe Dakota should take this stallion by the reins and show him what she was made of. He brought out more sexual desire in her than she'd ever experienced. For her, sex had always been a physical release—and she needed that release now more than ever to relieve the pressure that had been building up between them since New Year's Eve.

But no matter how much she liked Matteo, he didn't seem like the kind of guy who took sex as casually as had the men from her past. Dakota didn't want to be tied down either, though. She just wanted to have a little fun.

Although settling down had taken on new meaning after meeting the Dentons and Wilsons. She'd been in touch with them since New Year's and would be heading to their ranch in a few weeks to help while Luke and Cassie visited family in Peru. She couldn't wait. She hoped she'd have something to offer the people who came to the ranch in search of peace and healing, but more than likely she'd be the one who benefited most.

Matteo had said he'd bring up his horses and stay with her on his days off that week.

She missed Matteo when he was at work, especially in the evenings when they shared a meal then watched a movie, played cards, or did whatever activity they could come up with—well, short of having sex together.

Confound it, her feelings for Matteo grew stronger each day. She didn't know if a relationship between them was in the cards but wanted to see if their chemistry would self-combust if they took it to the next level.

Maybe after his shift ended tomorrow morning—or this weekend at the latest—she'd get him into bed with her and see where this went. If it was a bust, she wouldn't be around all that much longer.

Now, all she needed to do was decide how to make the moment look spontaneous rather than orchestrated.

On Saturday morning, Matt couldn't wait any longer to start working on his skijoring practice course. Keeping Dakota away from the hard work of setting it up would be a challenge, though. He'd come home from the station yesterday morning to find her carrying heavy water buckets to Comet's and Twinkle's stalls.

When he'd asked what happened to Jason, Dakota told him he'd called to say he wasn't feeling well. She'd assured him she could handle the job herself, but why she hadn't waited the two hours for him to get home and help, he wasn't sure. The horses still had water from when Jason had been there the evening before.

If left to her own devices, Dakota would continue to try and prove she could do as much as either he or Jason did around here, despite her injuries.

Okay, the doctor said she'd be able to resume all activities in a week or so. His bigger concern, if he wanted to be selfish about it, was her leaving his ranch for good. Her week at Dreams Found Ranch bought him some time and the circuit wouldn't really get going until mid to late

March. Then what?

Maybe he should try to make her feel needed by giving her more to do around here.

Jason's truck pulled up outside the barn and the teen came in looking good as new. "Feeling better?" Matt and Dakota asked him at the same time.

"Yeah. Mom said it was just a twenty-four-hour thing."

They took care of the horses, giving Dakota the job of dispensing feed. With Leadville's annual skijoring competition only six weeks away, he and Jason needed to set up the training course this weekend, a task that involved a lot of lifting to create the jumps and gates that would be close to what they could expect at the festival.

How would they manage that without Dakota offering to help? He could assign her the job of driving the Bobcat to move the piles of snow from the field to the practice course. Even that involved twisting that might not feel so good for her. But at least she wouldn't be lifting anything heavy.

The next worry that popped into his head as he mucked Twinkle's stall was how to keep her from competing this year. Matt hadn't missed the local event in years and wouldn't dream of doing so this year. But no way did he want Dakota on the course as a rider or a skier. People with much more skijoring experience had died or suffered serious injuries competing, and he didn't want anything to happen to her.

Not on my watch, assuming she's still here then.

"Hey, Mr. G.," Jason began as he pushed the wheelbarrow down the aisle toward the barn door. "When are you going to start training for the festival?"

"The skijoring festival?" Dakota asked.

Well, so much for keeping it under wraps a while longer. Of course, he'd told her about it when they'd run into each other at that Amarillo rodeo last fall, and no doubt she'd heard some buzz about it in town.

Her eyes lit up. "Sounds like a lot of fun." *Damn.*

If he tried to tell her it was too dangerous for her, it would be like tossing down a gauntlet she no doubt would pick up. So he'd downplay his own interest. "It helps break up the monotony of winter at least."

"Mr. G. has won in the Open division for professional skijorers the last two years," Jason said. "Wait until you see him and Twinkle out on that course."

Shut up, kid. You're not helping here.

"So, what does training involve?"

Matt sighed. There'd be no hiding it from her anyway, especially if she spent any time around the other firefighters. "We set up a mock course out in the pasture," he pointed to the barn wall beyond which was the field they'd use. "I train both Twinkle and Comet to race and alternate between them, although Twinkle's been the fastest so far."

Dakota glanced in Comet's direction. "Maybe I can work with Comet this year."

No, you can't. "You have no business riding a horse racing across the field at breakneck speed."

She narrowed her eyes and set her lips as if waving the gauntlet back in his face. "I'll be good as new next week. Your own doctor said so."

Maybe I need a new doctor.

"Skijoring is taxing on anyone's body," he tried to reason, "much less someone with a rib injury. You ever even skied before?"

"I'd rather be on the horse, but I'm game for learning to ski too."

"It's not an easy sport to learn. Maybe you should wait until next year." Would this event bring her back to the ranch during future off-seasons, because he'd love to teach her skijoring when she was in better shape physically. Besides, he was going to miss her when she left.

"I'm a quick learner. Don't count me out for this year's competition. Now, what do we do to get this training course set up?" she asked, as if everything had been settled.

Resigned that he'd been outmaneuvered and thinking this might show her she still had a ways to go in mending her broken rib, he had no choice but to let her help this weekend. But no way did he intend to let her ride one of his horses on the course, doctor or no doctor.

The three of them spent the next five hours working on the course.

He and Jason had it down to a science by now. He'd put enough punch in the snow to keep the horses safe and enough jumps for the skier to make it a challenge. He was ready to saddle Twinkle for a run-through when he caught Dakota wincing as she stepped down from the Bobcat.

Damn it all. He'd been so focused on getting the course laid out, he'd pushed her too hard. They hadn't even stopped for lunch or a coffee break.

Time for damage control. "Jason, Dakota, thanks for your help. I'll test it out tomorrow, but I'm beat." *It was only a small white lie, Mama.*

Jason gave him a surprised look but didn't say anything. "What time do you want me?"

"Let's plan on ten."

"I'll be here a little early to help in the barn." Before the boy headed back to his truck, he turned to Dakota. "You sure drive a mean Bobcat, Dakota. See you tomorrow."

When all she could muster was a smile and a nod, Matt knew she had to be in a world of pain or just plain worn-out. Time to get her into the house. He'd leave the Bobcat here for any touch-ups he'd need to do in the morning.

They walked slowly toward the house. "I'll dig up some supper for us." The snow crunched under their boots as they made it slowly back to the house. "How're you doing?"

"Fine."

Like hell. But he didn't argue.

"It'll be at least forty-five minutes before supper's ready. Why don't you take a long, hot soak in the tub? Might loosen up those sore muscles."

She opened her mouth as though to argue, then nodded. "Sounds like heaven. I won't be too long."

Inside the house, she shucked her boots with some difficulty at the bootjack inside the door but didn't ask him to help. Then she walked stiffly into her bedroom and closed the door behind her.

Matteo sighed and went into the kitchen, pulling out a frozen meal, opening it, and preheating the oven. Not wanting to wait for the beeper, he placed their Salisbury steak family-sized container on a baking sheet on the center rack.

Before he could head to the pantry for side items, the door opened again. Dakota stood there, her shirt open to the waist but still mostly dressed, and sheepishly asked, "Would you help me take my jeans off?" That was as close to an admission that she'd overdone it today as he'd ever hear.

"Absolutely." *Don't sound so eager, Matt.*

He followed her into the bedroom where she unbuttoned and unzipped her jeans and slid them with excruciating slowness over her hips before she sat on the edge of the bed.

Matt couldn't help but notice her lacy pink bra and panties. He hadn't expected something so feminine.

Why not? She's a woman, even if she is a tough one.

She extended her legs outward. "I really appreciate this."

"No problem." He bent over—in part to hide his growing erection, but also so she wouldn't have to raise her legs in the air and put pressure on her sore and injured muscles.

He tugged the Wranglers off in one smooth movement, forcing his gaze past her crotch and to her face. "I've been told I give a mean massage, Dakota. If you'd like, I could give you one to relieve any tight muscles."

She stared at him a long while, making him wonder what was taking her so long to accept his offer, then smiled. "I might take you up on that after supper. Then I can return the favor. I know you're beat too."

Busted!

He'd told her earlier how tired he was, but as much as he'd love to have her hands on his back, shoulders, and other parts of his anatomy, he didn't have the willpower to resist where that might lead. No reciprocal massage for him. At least she hadn't rejected his offer for one, though.

Hurrying into the bathroom, he closed the room door behind him to put some distance between them and started running the water for her, trying not to think about her undressing in a few moments. He'd held back from making any moves on her since their kiss on New Year's, but that didn't mean he couldn't fantasize about the things he'd like to do with her.

Back in the kitchen, he rinsed off two baking potatoes and oiled them up to be ready for placing in the microwave. His mind went to rubbing oil into Dakota's skin a little later. He tried to quell his X-rated thoughts, but his mind had a will of its own.

I need to get some massage oil the next time I'm in town.

What might the massage lead to? Kissing her again? Not a brotherly peck on the cheek but a full-blown, curl-her-toes kiss?

Matt trailed his lips to the hollow in her shoulder and gently drew her skin into his mouth.

He wasn't juvenile enough to leave a hickey but would put enough pressure there to make her think he might.

His hand skimmed down to brush over an erect nipple, then he pinched it between his thumb and forefinger just enough to make her gasp.

His erection strained against the zipper of his jeans.

His lips lowered to take the erect nipple into his mouth, and he sucked harder than he had on her shoulder. This time she moaned deep in her throat, and he wanted nothing more than to bury himself inside her.

A groan from her room broke into his explicit fantasies. His mind flashed back to what her torso had looked like the night she'd arrived here. He hadn't seen it since, but the bruising should have mostly faded by now. He walked toward the bedroom and rapped lightly on the door.

"Need any help?"

Silence for a long moment. He was almost ready to go inside and make sure she was all right when he heard a faint, "No thanks. I'll be right out."

He could kick himself for letting his focus on building the skijoring course make him forget about her health and well-being. She might not be up for a full-body massage, because lying on her chest and stomach might still be painful, but he could offer a shoulder rub before supper. Maybe a leg massage after.

Matt had returned his focus to the meal when the door opened. Dakota stood there dressed in nothing but a long T-shirt that came to midthigh. Her shapely legs made him want to start that leg massage first, but then his gaze drifted upward. Her skin must still be a little wet, because the shirt clung to her nipples like a second skin—nipples that were as erect as they had been in his fantasy a few minutes ago.

"What can I do to help?" she asked, apparently oblivious to the effect she had on him.

He remembered what he'd been doing and turned away to open the oven door and check on their dinner, not that he could see anything with the lid on it. "Nothing. Everything's under control."

Except for my cock.

Wanting to hide the evidence, he picked up a dish towel and pretended to dry his non-wet hands. Maybe he should hand the towel to her instead. Wanting to place himself behind her before she noticed his state of arousal, he gestured toward one of the kitchen chairs. "Have a seat. Offer's still open for that massage if you're interested."

Without hesitation, she separated her hair in the back and let half of it cascade over each breast, thankfully hiding her nipples from his gaze. She took her seat. "I'm all yours, Matteo. You can start here, if you'd like."

I wish. But at this point, he'd take what he could get. Being able to touch any part of her would satisfy his needs for now. *Hope so, at least.* He opened the cupboard and pulled out the bottle of extra-virgin olive oil.

"Sorry I don't have scented massage oils, but Mama says EVOO is good for all kinds of things."

"Whatever you have is fine. I'm more interested in the magic your hands will work on me."

Oh, Sweet Lady, if you only knew the magic I'd like to work on your body.

"Should I remove my shirt?"

His step faltered at her innocent question. "Might make it a little easier." *For my hands maybe.*

Without any sense of modesty or hesitation, Dakota stood and, moving a little stiffly from the workout today, removed her shirt. She still wore her panties, but they were pretty skimpy and left nothing to his unbridled imagination. At least he couldn't see her naked breasts, because she now held the shirt up against them.

Matt stared at her pale skin and the faded freckles dotting her shoulders. Fighting back the urge to bend down and kiss the back of her neck, he removed the cap on the bottle and set it on the table then poured a small amount of oil into the palm of his hand. He coated both palms and rubbed them together to warm the oil before applying slight pressure to her shoulders. She gasped.

"Sorry. Is it cold?"

"No, not at all. I just…wasn't ready."

Neither was he, apparently, because he temporarily forgot how to give a shoulder rub. Slowly, his muscle memory kicked in, and he gently kneaded the backs of her shoulders with his thumbs, feeling the knots lying beneath the surface. "You weren't kidding when you said your muscles were tight."

"I've missed getting regular massages from the trainers at the arenas." Dakota knew what a good massage should feel like.

I need to up my game.

As he worked the tension from her muscles, she emitted soft moans that turned him on even more. Whose idea was it for him to give her a massage before supper?

I wonder if she'd think it strange if I took a shower—a very cold one—before supper?

Chapter Thirteen

Feeling Matteo's hands working over the knots in her shoulder muscles sometimes elicited a groan of pain but more often than not made her moan with something closer to passion. She'd wanted to have sex with him tonight in the worst way but hadn't expected to light up like a firecracker the moment he touched her. Actually, even before that, when she came out of the bedroom and his smoldering eyes from across the room had made her wet—not from her bath, either.

"You have some mean skills," she told him.

He chuckled. "Thanks. Don't tell anyone, but I learned most of what I know from Franco. We used to do shoulder and neck massages on each other after a rough shift. With all the crap we carry, we were usually hurting when we got home."

Dakota didn't know much about Franco, who had been at college when she hung out with Matteo in high school and wasn't as interested in horses as Rafe had been. At the moment, though, his brothers were the furthest thing from her mind.

"Let me know anytime you need a massage," she offered.

"Thanks. I'll do that."

As Matteo's hands worked up the side of her neck, her head lolled in the opposite direction to give him better access. Already, she could feel the stress she'd stored in her muscles over the past month being released from her body.

"Mmm." Her moans became more blatantly sexual, but he seemed to be all business. Was he remotely interested in having sex with her? While she'd planned to make her move tonight, that was before she'd strained every muscle in her body moving mounds of snow with the Bobcat.

Why hadn't she stopped before reaching the breaking point?

Because you're too stubborn and proud for your own good.

She closed her eyes, unable to think about anything but the motions of his fingers and no longer caring about what sounds she made. No sense hiding the fact that he turned her on, even while simply kneading her sore muscles.

Matteo remained quiet as he worked. After a moment, though, something caught her attention and made her stomach growl.

"What smells so wonderful?"

"Damn! I forgot all about our supper!"

Matteo quickly wiped his hands on a towel and ran to the stove. He opened the door, grabbed some oven mitts, and pulled the pan out of the oven. It hadn't smelled burned, so she wondered why he'd gotten so flustered.

Maybe he's more affected than he's letting on.

He turned toward her and shrugged with a grin. "I'll finish your massage after we eat. You must be starving."

He always seemed aware of her needs; she hadn't eaten since breakfast. Of course, he might have heard her stomach rumbling too.

"Are you sure I can't help with something?"

"Nope. Sit right there."

He put two large baking potatoes into the microwave then pulled out plates and silverware to set the table. Dakota felt useless, but at least her shoulders weren't as stiff.

She still hoped for another kind of release tonight, one that would benefit both her and Matteo. For now, though, she donned her long T-shirt again.

About ten minutes later, he sat down to eat with her. While discussing plans for finishing up the course tomorrow, he shared more details about how the festival worked. While she had every intention of being a participant, she wanted to find ways to help too. Having spent so much time at the fire station these past few weeks, she'd begun to feel like a part of Matteo's community. It might be the first time she'd felt anything close to that before. Surprisingly, it didn't unsettle her as much as it once might have.

After they finished supper, Dakota insisted on helping with the cleanup, and for some reason he let her.

"I'll be back in a few." Matteo went into his bedroom.

He was gone longer than he'd need to be for a bathroom break, making her wonder what was taking him so long. Was that the shower running? Ten minutes later, he returned as she placed the last plate in the drainer.

"Want to watch a movie tonight?" she asked.

"Sounds great. Wine or beer?" He moved toward the fridge.

"I think wine might be fun." *And romantic.* After drying her hands, she went to the entertainment center to look for a movie. *Eight Seconds* and *Cowboy Up* caught her eye. She smiled. Tonight, she wanted sexy, so she'd wait to pull those out later on when it was time to get psyched up to start back on the circuit.

"How does *The Horse Whisperer* sound?" she asked over her shoulder.

"Good choice! I'll pop the corn."

Not a supersexy movie, but it did have Robert Redford and horses—and the love story kind of snuck up on you.

"How are you feeling?" Matteo asked, sitting down on the couch next to her as the movie intro started. He placed the bowl of popcorn on the coffee table.

"Great." *Horny as all get-out, though.*

"Want me to finish that massage?"

Hell yeah.

"My legs muscles are still a little tight. But I don't want you to miss the movie."

"It starts out slow. I've seen it a few times before."

Matteo stood again and moved the popcorn bowl next to her. "In case you get the munchies while I work my magic." He winked at her, and her girly bits leaped for joy.

The movie forgotten by both of them now, he pushed the coffee table away from the couch and knelt just beyond her knees. She spread her legs a little wider. His gaze went to the space where her panties grew wet, not that he could see that far under her shirt. Refocusing his attention, he took her left leg and began working the muscles in her calf.

Dakota hadn't realized how tight those muscles were until he kneaded them. She leaned back against the cushions and closed her eyes. Perhaps that would encourage Matteo to take a few more peeks at her crotch. She didn't want to be the only one getting excited tonight.

When he released her leg and gently placed her foot on the floor, she was afraid he'd finished, but he only maneuvered himself around to start on the other calf. She smiled.

"You do have magic hands, Matteo."

"Glad you like them." If she hadn't already become enamored of the man, this would have done it.

Ignoring the niggling voice inside that warned her not to let him get too close and wreck a good friendship, she stretched out her left leg, spreading herself open for him a little more. His hands paused momentarily before he resumed working on her right calf.

She imagined his gaze bearing down on her thighs and scooted farther down on the couch, letting the hem of her shirt ride up to give him a clearer look. Could he see how wet she'd become for him?

"If you wouldn't mind, my thighs are a little sore too."

She didn't open her eyes, but disappointment flooded her when his hands remained on her calf.

Come on, Matteo. Help a girl out here!

Matt could barely move without squeezing his hard-on in a vise. Dakota probably wasn't aware that scooting down like that had made her T-shirt ride up to the tops of her creamy thighs.

Damn!

He had a clear shot of the black lace on her pink panties—and now she wanted him to massage her thighs? There wouldn't be enough cold water in the well for him. Actually, he might need a hand job, truth be told, because his half-assed attempt at a cold shower after supper hadn't helped a bit. Too bad it would have to be his own hand. It was too soon for her to be having sex, even if she wanted to. He didn't want to hurt her but wasn't sure he could take it nice and easy their first time together.

"Would it be easier if you sat next to me with my leg across your lap?"

Her innocent question sent his fantasies soaring to a whole new level. "Maybe." He choked the word out past the lump in his throat then met her gaze. She smiled like an angel. How could she not know the effect she had on him?

Matt stood and moved the still-full bowl of popcorn back to the table and braced himself for what might be the hardest thing he'd ever done with Dakota—touching her but stopping significantly short of how far he'd like to go.

Sitting next to her on the couch, the effect of the strawberry scent of her hair shot straight to his groin. How the hell was he supposed to hide his erection now?

"I really appreciate this, Matteo. My entire body is tense."

So is mine, Sweet Lady. So is mine.

He started massaging closer to her left knee when she stretched out the length of the couch and let her right leg slide off until her foot reached the floor.

Be a gentleman. Don't look.

Screw that!

With the hem of her shirt pulled tight, having slid even farther up her thighs, he saw that a few ginger hairs had strayed from the confines of her panties.

So ginger *was* her natural color.

When he reached a knot in her adductor muscle, she moaned deep in her throat.

Jesus, just take me now.

Good thing she couldn't see his crotch because his cock throbbed mercilessly against his zipper, begging to be turned loose. He tried to massage out the knot on the inside of her thigh, because he couldn't do anything about the one in his pants, but he wasn't going to make it much longer.

Matt took a deep breath and let it out slowly but froze when she opened her legs wider to give him better access and her knee pressed against his raging hard-on.

She froze. He froze. Then a provocative smile spread across her face.

Why, you little witch. She'd known exactly what she was doing to him all along.

Time to up the ante here. Satisfied that he'd taken care of her adductor sufficiently, his hands moved up her thigh. This time, he ignored any of her other muscles and lightly traced the leg opening of her panties, his fingers brushing her stray curly hairs.

When she tilted her hips in further invitation, he let his fingers slip inside to find her hot and wet for him. He took another breath and blew it out.

Reality washed over him. "You're still hurting from the bull ride, so we don't have to do anything too athletic tonight if you aren't up to it."

I don't have to be a caveman when I make love to her, right?

Dakota opened her eyelids and met his gaze. "I'm feeling much less pain after your massages tonight. I need a different kind of release more than anything else right now, however I can get it."

"You and me both, Sweet Lady."

His fingertip rubbed against her swollen clit, but this wasn't how he wanted them to make love the first time. He pulled away, tugged her panties back in place, and set her other leg on the floor as he stood up.

"Let's finish this in my bedroom."

"I thought you'd never ask." She held out her hand, and he helped her into a seated position first before lifting her onto her feet.

Continuing the fantasy he'd had in the kitchen earlier, he picked her up and carried her down the hallway. At the entrance to his room, he pivoted so she could reach the light switch.

"Turn the knob to the left." The dimmer switch lowered the intense lighting to just the right amount. "That's perfect."

He lowered her feet to the ground and pulled her against his full length, no longer trying to hide his arousal from her. His hands swept down her back as he pulled up on her T-shirt while she unbuttoned his denim shirt. He interrupted her efforts long enough to pull the tee over her head and tossed it on a chair before staring down at her bare breasts.

"Jesus, you're beautiful, Dakota."

"No fair. I get to see you too."

Matt quickly shucked his shirt, and the rest of his clothes soon came off until the only thing left between them were her skimpy panties.

Matt walked to the king-sized bed and placed two pillows midway down the mattress. Her fingertips skimmed over his right shoulder blade. His tattoo. He didn't want to think about Papa in this moment but turned to face her.

"All my brothers decided we'd have the Maltese Cross tattooed somewhere on our bodies as a memorial, along with Papa's name and years of birth and death."

"What a beautiful tribute. I know how much you loved your papa."

He nodded. "While he didn't actually serve as a firefighter, he lost his life in service with the search and rescue squad attached to our local fire department, so we thought the firefighter's cross was the perfect symbol for him."

"I'm sure it would mean a lot to him."

Matteo smiled. "I chose to have mine placed on my back, because Papa always had mine."

While he loved his Papa, he didn't intend to derail this moment with Dakota going down that dark road. Reclaiming the moment, Matt leaned closer and cupped her chin to lift her face toward his.

"Where were we?"

"I think you were about to have your way with me."

"Oh yeah." He leaned down and kissed her. When the kiss ended, he helped to ease her onto her back with her hair spilling around her head on the pillows and her feet dangling over the edge of the mattress.

"Are you in any pain?"

"Matteo! Please!"

Her bruising had faded a lot since that first night she'd arrived. Still, he planned to go easy and avoid putting any weight or pressure on her ribs.

Matt skimmed her panties down her legs and stared a long moment at her glorious ginger mound. He couldn't wait to have his first taste of her.

Mine. At long last.

Dakota waited for him to do something more than stare. Was he having second thoughts? Remnants of her high-school insecurities around Matteo came back. She'd never felt that Alison Parker who'd lived a life filled with lies was ever good enough for Matteo Giardano. But was Dakota Mathison, the woman she'd created but who wasn't real either, any better suited for him?

Just when her level of self-consciousness nearly exploded into her calling this off tonight, he climbed onto the bed, straddled her hips, and leaned over her, keeping his weight on his hands and knees. His erect cock pressed against her abdomen. She needed him inside her more than her next breath at the moment.

"What did I ever do to deserve having such a gorgeous woman in my bed, Sweet Lady?"

So he *did* want her in that way! As always, that endearment made her feel feminine and cherished, but that he thought she was gorgeous blew her away.

"If you knew how many times I fantasized about being in your bed in high school, Matteo—" She stopped, realizing too late what she'd admitted.

But he only smiled. "You wanted to do the naughty with me too?"

Too?

"I'll admit," he continued, "there were some rough nights senior year when I wanted to do nothing more than take you into the hay loft—if I'd had one—and make you mine right then and there."

A thrill ran down the length of her body at hearing those words. She interlaced her fingers behind his neck and pulled him closer. "Then what are you waiting for, cowboy fireman?" She'd meshed two of her hottest fantasies into one but had to admit the firefighter one was unique to her daydreams of Matteo.

His lips brushed hers, gently at first then he pressed his tongue between them and tangled with her own in a passionate kiss that robbed her of breath. He retreated after a moment and sucked her lower lip into his mouth before releasing it, leaving her lip feeling fuller and hypersensitive.

As much as she loved the attention he was giving her mouth, she wanted to feel him drive his cock inside her and ride her for all he was worth. Not that he was likely to. At some point, he'd remember her injuries, healed or not, and would call a halt. In the meantime, she wouldn't do anything to remind him of them.

She released his neck and moved her hands to cup his pecs, repeatedly scraping the nails of her thumbs against the peaks of his nipples, making them harder. That must have given him ideas because soon he scooted down her body as his mouth blazed a trail to one of her nipples, and he suckled gently at first until his teeth nipped the peak harder.

"Oh God, yes!" She arched her back, feeling the pain in her chest muscles but hoping he hadn't noticed her wincing.

Her girly bits screamed for him to keep moving down her body, but he didn't seem to be in any hurry. The thorough attention he paid to both her nipples only fired her up for what she hoped was still to come.

When he pulled away to crawl off the mattress, she felt the loss intensely. "Scoot to the edge here." They weren't done! *Thank God!* She complied without being told twice and slid onto the pillow he held in place to elevate her hips. The bundle of nerves at the junction of her thighs throbbed in anticipation.

When he didn't touch or kiss her immediately, she met his gaze and saw that he was simply standing between her legs and staring at her. Confused at first, she soon began wringing her hands, afraid he might not find her body to his liking.

Then he grinned, leaned over to separate her hands, and held them on either side of her head. His face was inches above hers now, and his intense stare made her even wetter.

"I had some pretty vivid fantasies in high school about you, including this one, thanks to two older brothers and their magazines."

He'd fantasized about me too? Really?

Releasing her hands, Matteo knelt at the foot of the bed and positioned his head between her thighs then placed one of her legs over each of his shoulders before bending closer to the core of her sex. Again, he stopped to stare, but she didn't become self-conscious this time. Slowly, he spread her lower lips open with his thumbs and blew gently on her sex. Oddly enough, that only made her wetter.

His mouth laid a row of nibbles and kisses up the inside of her left thigh before he inhaled the scent of her deeply and started down the other one. Once again, he lifted his head and stared, only this time she didn't become self-conscious. He truly seemed to be enjoying her body, making her feel adored.

No other man had treated her with such care and reverence. Normally, sex had been an animalistic release—fast and furious, then forgotten about just as quickly.

Not so with Matteo. She'd remember his slow lovemaking for the rest of her life and hold him up as the measure against every man who followed.

But tonight she didn't want to think about any man other than Matteo.

When he flicked his tongue over her clit at last, her hips bucked off the mattress, making her wince. She squeezed her eyes shut and breathed slowly in and out until the pain subsided. Clearly, she was using muscles she hadn't been acquainted with since being injured and hadn't been aware they were so stiff and sore.

Fortunately, he didn't seem to notice her flash of pain. Instead, Matteo drew her tiny bundle of nerves into his mouth and gently sucked until she nearly wept with the sensations sweeping through her. Her vaginal muscles clenched in anticipation of feeling him deep inside her, but she didn't want to rush him. Not one little bit!

She wanted to see this through to its climactic ending and if he thought she was in pain, that would be the end of it. Besides, the pleasure far outweighed any pain.

Time to cowgirl up and give in to all the sensations.

Chapter Fourteen

Matt had never seen anything more beautiful than Dakota's sex. His boyhood fantasies of Alison had been dull compared to the reality of Dakota.

He thrust his middle finger inside her. So wet. So ready. But he had no intention of taking her fast. He'd waited too long for this moment and wanted to savor every bit of it.

When his tongue played with her clit again, her sudden intake of breath told him she might not last long. Maybe he'd better give her some satisfaction before continuing at a slower pace. He withdrew his finger then plunged two inside her.

"Oh, Matteo! Please!"

He grinned as he flicked his tongue against her clit until she mewled like a kitten.

Come for me, Sweet Lady.

"I can't hold back. Please, I need you inside me! Now!"

Oh, no, sweetheart. He'd be calling the shots here, and he wasn't ready for tonight's experience to end. A woman as passionate as Dakota would be able to come multiple times within a relatively short period of time.

While his tongue worked its magic, he increased the speed of his fingers, filling her, pulling out, and repeating. She grabbed onto the back of his head to hold him there—as if he planned on going anywhere anytime soon. When he sensed she was at the tipping point, he pulled her nubbin into his mouth again and sucked—harder than he had minutes ago.

"Yes! Oh, God! I'm going to come!"

Bet your sweet ass you are.

Her hips bucked, and she moaned then screamed. While the sounds conveyed her enjoyment, he wondered if some of her moans might be from pain. He'd temporarily forgotten about her injury but didn't plan to stop now until she told him to or she went over the edge.

The slight restraint of pressing his hands against her hips to hold her onto the mattress pulled some invisible trigger within her. She exploded, giving him a wilder ride than any bronc she'd ever ridden. Dakota's scream could probably be heard five miles down the road. What a beautiful sound. The woman held nothing back.

Certain that his tongue might be causing her discomfort now, he slowed its movements as she took panting breaths and came back to earth. When her body relaxed fully against the mattress, she seemed spent—for the time being at least.

He pulled his fingers out of her and stared at her. Eyes closed, her lower lip tucked between her teeth, she had to be the sexiest woman he'd ever seen.

"Open your eyes."

She did so, and he slowly licked her juices off his fingers, savoring every drop. She surprised him by the look of wonder on her face, before he stood and stretched out beside her on the bed. Lying on his side, he propped his head on his palm.

Before he could remark on it, she reached out to stroke his cheek before working her way down his chest and abdomen and finally surrounding his cock with her hand. "Now it's your turn, cowboy fireman."

He wasn't about to argue with her, up to a point, but she needed time to recover before they took this relationship to the next step.

"Have your way with me." Matt rolled onto his back. Her hand slipped off his cock, and Dakota didn't miss a beat as she gingerly scooted off the mattress. She picked up the pillow that had been under her hips earlier, as well as another, and placed them on the floor between his legs before kneeling on them. She trailed kisses from his knee to his thigh, up one side and down the other, much as he had done earlier.

His cock bobbed, waiting impatiently for her hand or her hot mouth to take him. He closed his eyes, giving in to the sensations. At long last, she flicked her tongue against the underside of his cock, and his hips bucked uncontrollably.

I'm so glad it won't be a hand job. He could do that himself.

"That feels incredible."

She took him inside her warm, wet mouth. The woman knew exactly how much pressure to use and where to touch him with her teeth and tongue to bring him to the edge quickly. He wouldn't last long if she continued so, to slow her movements, he placed his hand on the top of her head. She tilted her head up to meet his gaze with his cock still firmly in her mouth.

Jesus, take me now!

Matt nearly came in her mouth just looking at her, but he needed to find something out before they went any further. If he'd been thinking with the right head earlier, he'd have done this sooner. Slowly extricating his cock from her mouth, he helped her to lie beside him again. He propped himself on his elbow, brushing the hair back from her face and tucking it behind her ear.

"Dakota, I want to be inside you in the worst way, but I need to ask if you had any pain earlier."

She shrugged, which was tantamount to admitting *yes. Damn.* Just what he thought. Knowing that he'd hurt her in any way killed his mood instantly.

She must have read the reaction on his face. "What you were doing with your mouth and fingers felt so good, Matteo, that I hardly noticed. Not until later, anyway." So, she *had* felt pain.

When she reached for his cock, he stayed her hand. "I never want to hurt you. Let's make a few adjustments to make this as comfortable as possible for you."

She opened her eyes wider. *Why had that surprised her?* Wouldn't any guy want to put her comfort first? He'd never do anything to cause her pain.

"I'm fine. Really. I'm almost healed already. I just aggravated things on the Bobcat today."

The woman didn't respect her body's limitations. Maybe he needed to just call it a night. "Listen, I'm good with just holding you tonight. We'll give it more time for your rib to heal, per doctor's orders."

She narrowed her eyes. "If you think I'm going to wait a week or longer before giving you the orgasm you deserve after what you gave me earlier, then I'll pack up right now and go."

She'd leave over this? Just when he thought he might have to rethink his plan, a grin broke out on her face. Clearly, she wasn't serious about leaving. Not this time, anyway.

"Don't get so feisty, Sweet Lady. I'll definitely take a raincheck. Why don't we get some sleep first?"

He didn't know if she'd get up and leave or stay, until she smiled slightly and lay down on the pillow. Now he wished he'd let her finish him off before he got all noble. But as long as she stuck around, there'd be other opportunities.

Dakota lay spooned in Matteo's embrace for more than an hour, unable to sleep or relax. He, on the other hand, had fallen asleep almost immediately. Okay, he'd worked hard today and said he rarely slept much at the station, but she'd worked hard too and still wanted him to make love to her. Sure, he'd gotten her off, but how could he just fall asleep and not let her reciprocate?

I want to have sex with him, damn it!

Maybe he wasn't as into her as she'd been into him. His words and actions belied that notion, but Matteo was a gentleman and wouldn't be rude to her. If he truly did find her sexy, then how could he just go off to dreamland and leave her horny like this?

What was she going to do with this infuriating man? One minute he ran hot, the next, cold. She tried to console herself that he'd shut down out of worry about hurting her, not because he'd lost interest. She had been hurting but didn't want to leave him with that raging hard-on.

Of course, that problem had resolved itself all too quickly. While she longed to have him buried deep inside her, he was going to make her wait.

Determined to let him sleep a few hours before initiating anything more, she gingerly turned onto her other side, facing toward him. She'd thought she could sleep on her injured side, but maybe that's why she hadn't fallen asleep yet.

A sense of longing for something just out of reach permeated her thoughts as she did the relaxed breathing exercise that usually knocked her out on restless nights. Not longing for another orgasm, but what?

Matteo slept so peacefully. He must be used to falling asleep fast, never knowing when they'd get a call at the station. She might have to ask him what his technique was. Of course, he'd told her before that he didn't sleep well on duty and this was his first night in his own bed since his shift ended Friday morning, so maybe he was simply exhausted.

Dakota's eyelids finally grew heavy. Warm arms wrapped around her, pulling her against the soft hairs on his chest.

"Don't you worry, Pumpkin. I'll keep you safe here with me."

The woman's voice comforted the little girl. She did feel safe, for the first time in a long while.

Then the bad man came and yanked her away from her grandmother's arms. "Nana! Want stay with you!"

"You're my kid. You'll go where I tell you."

"Noooo! Nana! Stop him!"

The arms holding her became hard and ruthless. She fought to extricate herself from his grasp, but beating against his chest was like pounding a brick wall with her tiny hands.

"Wake up, Dakota. You're safe. You're with me. It's Matt."

Dakota's eyes bolted open. Cold sweat on her forehead chilled her to the bone. She pulled up on the blanket as if wresting it away from the bad man, only to realize she was in bed with Matteo, not locked into an all-too-real nightmare. It took her a few seconds to push those lingering images out of her head.

Matteo stroked her cheek. "You were having a bad dream."

She tried to recapture the feeling of being with the woman who must have been her grandmother, but the negative energy from the end of the nightmare clung to her instead.

"Sometimes helps to talk about it."

Safe. Home. Matteo.

He made her feel things she hadn't felt since she was a little girl.

Regardless, she shook her head vehemently. What could she say? She wasn't supposed to talk about the secret.

She didn't even know what secret that was.

"I can't remember anything." *Much.* "Mostly a sense of being safe and wanted." *Until I was ripped away.*

He stroked her hair, continuing to calm her fears as he might a spooked horse.

"I don't normally dream," she said. "At least, I don't remember them, if I do. I wonder what brought it on."

"You were screaming for your nonna—actually, you called her Nana."

"I don't have a nana." *Did I, once upon a time?* Or was this just a nonsense dream that had no basis in reality?

"Nobody said dreams had to make sense."

Something about the man in the nightmare made Dakota uncomfortable with being touched at the moment, so she rolled onto her back, her insides feeling raw from the movement, and stared up at the ceiling.

"Maybe you can go back to sleep. It's still hours until morning."

She nodded. "Sorry I woke you."

"Don't worry about me. I'll be able to fall asleep again in no time. One of the perks of being a firefighter."

She turned her head toward his face. "I was meaning to ask you how you do that."

He shrugged. "They're always telling us to get more sleep at the station, but I don't do as well there. When I need sleep, though, I do a combination of relaxation techniques and imagery of places that relax me."

"What places do you imagine?"

"Mostly my place now. The mountains. A glacial lake."

"Nice."

"I can teach you the steps, if you'd like."

Dakota wasn't sure she was ready to go back to sleep. "How sleepy are you?"

"Not very," he answered.

A slow smile spread across Dakota's face. Time for a diversion. She slid her hand sideways until she touched his bare chest. His skin was hot to the touch, which is probably why he slept shirtless. When he didn't stop her, she rolled onto her side again to face him and began exploring his pecs, pinching his nipples one at a time, and then sliding down over his six-pack abs to his erection, which was as hard as it had been earlier.

"Okay, totally not sleepy now," he said as his hand cupped her breast and pinched her nipple. "What did you have in mind?"

"On your knees, fireman, hands holding onto the headboard."

"I'm intrigued."

After he'd positioned himself per her instructions, she slowly maneuvered herself onto her back with her head on the pillows near the headboard. "Now, straddle my face."

Dakota intended to finish what she should have last night. She grabbed his cock, making sure the position was right to take him fully. She wanted to blow him away, not just give him a blow job.

"Stop the second you feel any pain."

Sure. Not. She looked up at him and smiled. "I'm tough. Riding saddle broncs means pain is my middle name." She'd leave the bull out of it at this point, uncertain whether she'd ever want to experience that much pain again.

"Dakota…" he warned her.

Before he pulled away, she insisted, "I'm fine! And now I'm going to make sure *you're* feeling no pain for a while."

Her mouth wrapped around the tip of his cock, skipping the foreplay because who knew how long he'd let her do this without calling another halt to their lovemaking? After kissing, licking, and nibbling him, she took his cock deeper until the tip hit the back of her throat then pulled slowly away letting her teeth gently scrape the sides as she partially retreated. Matteo's hissing sound made it clear he enjoyed that and she had him where she wanted him.

She couldn't wait to take him down her throat, but first she continued to tease him with her teeth while flicking her tongue against the underside of the plum-shaped head.

"I've always had a fantasy about a redhead going down on me, but damn, this blows that lame fantasy all to hell."

She smiled around his cock as she took him in and out of her mouth rapidly, each time taking him a little farther until mentally ready to ease him into the opening of her throat.

"Jesus!"

You ain't seen nothin' yet, fireman.

Her fingers played with the hair on his balls in part to hold him in her throat for several seconds until her gag reflex subsided. His cock throbbed, and she took another half inch of him as she pulled at his short hairs adding to the intensity of his sensations. She retreated until his shaft had barely left her throat, then took him in again.

"Incredible."

She couldn't give him verbal responses but cupping his balls, she gripped them more forcefully and began raising and lowering her head to take him in and out of her throat more rapidly.

"Can I come down your throat? If not, I'm not sure I'm going to last much longer."

Dakota nodded but wasn't sure that conveyed her message, so she pumped his cock in and out of her throat faster, hopefully making it clear she wanted him to come whenever he was ready.

She didn't have long to wait.

"Jesus, *God*!" He gripped the headboard so hard she thought he might bend the wrought iron. Soon his seed blasted down her throat in a dozen pulsating explosions.

She closed her eyes and held his still-throbbing cock inside her throat, swallowing around it to provide him with continued sensation.

"Thank you. I've never... Damn, that was hot, Alison!" The rest of his body stiffened. "I mean, Dakota. Sorry. My brain shut down for a minute."

Was he thinking about making love to her as a teenager? The thought made her smile as he pulled out of her throat. She regretted that he wasn't buried deep inside her right now, but that would happen sooner rather than later.

But if I wait for him to think my body is ready, it'll never happen.

Once again, she'd be willing to take her stallion by the reins.

As he eased his cock out of her mouth, she smiled up at him. The sheer ecstasy on his face made her heart soar. She'd done that for him. And apparently no other woman had deep-throated him before, which made this moment even more special.

He kissed her forehead before retreating off the bed. "Be right back."

Matteo went to the bathroom to clean up, she supposed, because he brought back a warm washcloth. He gently wiped the cum off her face. His consideration for her always warmed her heart. After he tossed the cloth on the floor, he moved into Dakota's arms and curled against her side. She lifted her head and rested it on his chest, closing her eyes.

"That…was…unbelievable." His heart pounding in her ear almost drowned out his words. Dakota smiled but didn't need his validation. His physical and verbal responses told her all she needed to know.

They lay there for a while, his breathing steadying as he held her tightly against him, stroking her hair.

Dakota had never felt more content than in this moment. How would she ever be able to ride away from this man?

Chapter Fifteen

Dakota's nerves were shot. Even though she'd been with Mama, Paul, and Rafe on Christmas Day, this would be her first meeting of the extended family and she'd been on edge for days about this Sunday dinner.

"Stop worrying." Matteo reached across the truck's seat to squeeze her hand. "You've already won over Mama, Rafe, and Paul. They love you, and everyone else will too."

"But you said Paul and Rafe were on duty today, which means I only know you and Mama." She sighed. "I'm just not good in social settings."

"Says who?"

"Okay, specifically, family gatherings freak me out a little. I don't know why, they just do." When was the last time she'd been in one—well, other than this past Christmas?

"I assure you that you aren't going to have any problems with my family. Mama raised us all to be welcoming, charming, and polite." He grinned at her, but instead of coming across as angelic, he made her wet for him.

"You've certainly nailed charming." For the past week or so, he'd definitely turned on the charms—up to a point. As expected, though, he hadn't taken her for the ride she'd been wanting. Still, she wished they could go back to his ranch and make love right this very moment.

Don't think about having sex on the way to his Mama's!

Matteo pulled into the parking lot of Mama and Paul's condo, and Dakota took a slow, deep breath. Now she worried if she'd be able to tell the difference between them genuinely liking her or merely being polite because that was how their mama had raised them.

Grrr! It was so much easier when I didn't have a need to be accepted by other people.

"Relax, or you'll start making *me* nervous," Matteo teased as he stroked her cheek. At least she thought he was kidding. He didn't appear nervous at all as he took her hand and they walked up the sidewalk to the entrance. He did manage to infuse some much-needed warmth into her. She thought he'd let go of her hand when they reached the door, but he continued to hold it. Matt opened the door, and it surprised her that it was unlocked.

The aroma of Italian cooking hit her immediately, and her stomach growled. Next, she heard the conversations—seemingly several at once—both male and female voices.

"We're here," Matteo called out as he guided her toward the back of the condo. She hardly had time to take in the decor, although she noted the colors were warm and inviting. Just before he brought her around the corner to where the voices and laughter came from, he leaned in and kissed her cold cheek.

Her face warmed immediately as she thought about where those lips had been on her body over the past week.

He smiled at her. "There, that's better. You have a little color in your cheeks now."

Don't be thinking about having sex with the man when you're about to meet his family!

Unfortunately, sex had yet to happen even a week after that incredible night in his bed. He still worried about hurting her, even though her rib was completely healed other than an occasional twinge of pain when she twisted or bent the wrong way.

They went into the kitchen and one of the brothers she hadn't met yet came forward. "Hi, Dakota. I'm Franco."

She shook the hand he extended. "Nice to meet you, Franco. Matteo has told me a lot about you."

He gave his brother the side eye before smiling again as he spoke to Dakota. "Don't believe half of it. Can I pour you a drink? Water? Wine? Something stronger?"

"I'll get her something," Matteo said. "I know I'll have to pour my own anyway."

"Damn right you will, Bro. Why don't I take your coat then, Dakota?" Once again, his demeanor lightened up when he addressed her. Was this that welcoming charm their mother had instilled in them? Apparently, it didn't extend to one another.

"White or red?" Matteo asked as he helped her out of her coat before handing it to Franco who carried it into another room.

"Red, please."

Matteo's gaze swept the length of her before he smiled in appreciation as he poured her a glass, then one for himself. She wore the same dress she had on Christmas Day, so it couldn't be the novelty of seeing what she wore.

Wiping her hands on her apron, Mama crossed the room and approached them. "Dakota, you are looking well! Look at those rosy cheeks! Welcome to my home at last!"

Rather than extend a hand, Mama wrapped her in a hug. Intense feelings washed over Dakota at the contact, but she had no time to deal with these unfamiliar, raw emotions and let them dissipate.

"Nice to see you again too, Mama. Thanks for inviting me."

"I'm so happy you're able to travel again now. We missed you both at New Year's dinner."

"Thank you so much for leaving us such incredible food, though." Dakota pointed to her now-healed side. "All healed now, though, thanks to your son." Dakota smiled, unable to see Matteo's expression at the moment.

Mama glanced over Dakota's shoulder. "Good to hear, Bambino. Now, give your mama a hug."

While the two embraced, Dakota glanced around the kitchen and saw two couples she didn't recognize; they appeared to be waiting for her to finish with Mama. All four started toward her, and Dakota held her breath. She remembered both men from the charity calendar photos.

"Nice to meet you," said the one she thought was Matteo's brother. "I'm Tony, and this is Carmella, my wife."

"A pleasure," Dakota said as she shook both their hands. "Mr.

October, right?"

He grinned. "Guilty as charged."

"Paul said you ride in the rodeo," Tony mentioned. Apparently, she'd come up in the conversation.

"I do, and I hope to be back on the road competing again when events start up again in March."

"Sounds like an exciting life," Carmella commented.

She used to think so, but there was something to be said for the quiet, stable lives these people led. "It has its moments," Dakota said, not really wanting to dive into her feelings about chasing more championship buckles. "Matteo says you run your family's resort."

"I do. It has its moments too," she said with a laugh. "This season is our busiest with all the skiers, but my brother and I have made a pact not to work every weekend anymore, so now we take turns. I try to schedule it so that I can join Tony at these monthly dinners, because Mama's food is better than anything I can make."

In that moment, she bonded with Carmella over their inability to cook. "I'm sure you do better than I do, Carmella. I don't usually have access to a kitchen on the circuit." *As if having a kitchen at Matteo's has improved your cooking any.*

"I'd love to give you some lessons," said the dark-haired woman who had Matteo's chocolate-colored eyes. "I'm Matt's little sister, Angelina." She held out her arms and wrapped Dakota in a hug much as her mother had done. When Angelina pulled away, she continued. "I own a little restaurant here in town. Matt could use some lessons too," she gave him a sideways glance, "if you both want to come in some morning or afternoon before things get busy."

"Haven't you given up on me by now, Sis?" Matt asked.

"I'll admit, I have more confidence in Dakota's abilities than yours, but at least the two of you will be able to work together to prepare whatever meal I teach you."

Matteo glanced at Dakota as if waiting to see what her interest level was. While she didn't see any point in learning to cook, she did love to eat Italian food—assuming that's the type of food Angelina's restaurant served. "I'm game, if you are."

"Done!" Angelina said without waiting for Matteo's response. "Before you leave today, let's pick a day that works for us all."

"May I barge in for another lesson myself?" Carmella asked.

"Absolutely. Tony, do you want to join us? It gets trickier juggling the calendars from both stations as well as the resort, but I'm sure we can find a weekday that works for us all. Mondays are my slow days."

"Skijoring season's coming up," Matteo began, "and I need to train on my days off," Matteo said. "Why don't we aim for after the festival?"

Angelina seemed a little disappointed and looked toward Dakota. "How early in March will you be heading back to the rodeo circuit?"

She'd let Matteo know she'd be leaving in March, but she hadn't gotten around to checking to see when events would start up in earnest. "Probably the end of the month." She glanced at Matteo. "I want to check out this skijoring festival I keep hearing about first." Matteo narrowed his eyes.

"You planning to compete? Because you'd be a lot more entertaining than my brother." Tony pointed toward Matteo.

"She doesn't know how to ski," Matteo responded before she had a chance to answer. After seeing how much skiing was involved and how much Matteo loved the sport, she'd already considered learning sometime, but that would probably have to happen during the rodeo break next winter.

"Come to Aspen for a few days," Carmella offered "and I'll give you lessons."

Matteo glared at his sister-in-law, making Dakota consider competing this year more seriously. Besides, skijoring would give her a chance to warm up before returning to the rodeo circuit.

Dakota turned to Carmella. "I'd love that! Thanks so much! I'm not worried about the horseback riding part of it, of course, but I honestly have no idea what to do on a pair of skis."

Matteo ran his fingers through his hair, and Dakota hid her smile from him when he met her gaze again. "Skijoring is a dangerous sport,

Dakota. It can take years to become proficient enough to win."

She smiled at him. *Who's worrying now?* "I didn't say I need to win or compete at the professional level. I just miss competing. Period. I'm sure I'd be placed in one of the novice or amateur divisions, so you don't have to worry about me beating you, Matteo."

He stared at her as if that was the furthest thing from his mind, but Dakota focused on Carmella again. "You can teach me enough in a few days?"

"Well, if you haven't had *any* experience, we might need to do several days one week, then have you come back the next week to take it to the next level."

Clearly, Carmella didn't realize how quickly she picked up sports. But with only a month before the festival—and her promise to spend a week of that at Dreams Found Ranch—she'd better get going.

"Can we start this week?" Dakota asked.

"Absolutely! I don't do a lot of personal lessons anymore, but I'd love to get out of the office and join you on the slopes."

"I can help on my days off," the other man said as he extended his hand. "I'm Marc, by the way. Angelina's husband and Carmella's brother." She shook his hand, remembering him as Mr. December in her calendar. She hadn't realized the families had been united in marriage twice.

"It's a two-and-a-half-hour drive to Aspen this time of year with Independence Pass closed," Matteo pointed out. *Damn.* She hadn't thought about the amount of time she'd have to spend on the road driving back and forth.

"No worries. You can stay with Tony and me in Wolcott," Carmella offered, "unless you'd prefer staying at the resort. I'm sure there will be rooms available during midweek. You'll be my guest, of course."

That these people would open up their home and treat her like family touched Dakota in ways she wasn't ready to analyze. But she wouldn't feel comfortable staying with two people she barely knew and didn't feel right taking advantage of Carmella by lodging at her resort for free at such a busy time, either.

On the other hand, there was no way she could afford to pay for rooms and lessons. Everyone was being so helpful and encouraging—well, everyone except Matteo. Maybe she needed to just accept their offers to help.

"You won't be putting anybody out," Carmella assured her, as if thinking that was her biggest concern.

She *really* wanted to compete in that festival. Maybe in part to show off to Matteo a bit, although she didn't understand that, given he'd already seen her compete at the Amarillo rodeo. Besides, he was a pro at skijoring. No way would they be competing in the same divisions.

Maybe that bull ride had opened her eyes a little. Her remaining years were numbered in rodeoing. She needed to find new activities to provide that adrenaline rush and allow her to keep riding horses after her rodeo days came to an end.

Dakota made up her mind. "I'll be sure to come midweek so I won't put anyone out." She didn't look in Matteo's direction but had a feeling his eyes were shooting daggers at her.

Is the woman insane?

Dakota still hadn't healed fully from her bull ride, and now she planned to take skiing lessons where she could possibly fall and reinjure that rib—or break something else?

She obviously wasn't going to listen to reason, so he decided it would be better to discuss this away from his oh-so-helpful family who seemed hell-bent on undermining his efforts to keep her safe.

Before he could say anything, Mama came to the rescue. "You can discuss your plans for skiing and cooking lessons over dinner. Boys, help me carry all this food into the dining room."

"Would you mind holding this for me?" Matt asked, extending his wine glass to Dakota. He hadn't made eye contact with her since she'd made her declaration that she'd be taking ski lessons from Carmella and possibly Marc. She didn't seem to share his concerns or fears.

It's not like you have any claim on what she does with her body.

Mama's sons, including Marc now, lined up at the island, as they'd done at her meals many times before. Matt picked up a hot dish with the potholders sitting nearby while others carried a dish, tray, or basket.

"Follow me," he said to Dakota.

He needed to let go of this need to protect her. Dakota was an independent woman who'd made her own decisions for more than a decade without any help from him. He'd stated his concerns, and they hadn't swayed her any. The woman definitely liked to push the boundaries of personal safety, and he needed to accept the fact that she'd ultimately do whatever the hell she wanted to, safety be damned.

After placing the dish on the buffet, he took his glass from her and guided her by the elbow to her seat.

"I've been looking forward to this ever since Matteo told me we'd be coming for dinner, Mama. You've outdone yourself again."

Dakota's words took Matt by surprise, given how nervous she'd been earlier about coming here. Of course, who wouldn't be looking forward to Mama's food? Dakota had been more reluctant about meeting the rest of the family. But they'd welcomed her in as if she were one of their own as they'd done with Carmella last year. And Marc, too—at least by the time the ceremony took place. Mama had accepted him long before, but he and his brothers had been the holdouts.

A round of praise for Mama went up. Matt appreciated the way everyone had welcomed Dakota in, though the two of them weren't really a couple or anything. He couldn't even stay angry with Carmella or Marc for their offers to help Dakota compete in the festival.

Maybe she won't be any good at skiing.

Although given her athletic abilities, he knew there was slim hope of that.

Franco sat down next to Matt and the two caught up on what was happening at the Leadville station with the firefighters his brother had once worked with.

"How are things on the arson side of the fire service?" Matt asked.

"Dark." But he didn't elaborate. Matt wondered what cases he'd been working on. Every time he heard about an arson around Denver, he wondered if his brother would be on the detail. Most of the arson cases in Lake County had to do with insurance fraud, but he suspected things got uglier in the city.

"You always did seem more interested in the analysis and aftermath of a fire, though. Probably because you'd thought about becoming a police officer at one point."

"True. But I'm glad I went in this direction now that all's said and done."

Papa wouldn't have had a problem with Franco continuing to pursue law enforcement as a career, but when Rafe had changed his major to fire service, Franco followed suit. He'd always tried to emulate their oldest brother, even more so than Tony or Matt had done.

"So, Dakota," Franco began, leaning forward to see her on the other side of Matt, "you'll have to keep me posted on when you are competing in the Denver area. I'd love to come out to see you ride."

Since when is Franco interested in the rodeo? Since never.

What the hell was going on with his family today?

"Thanks, Franco. I haven't looked at the schedule of events yet, but I'll let you know."

Matt really didn't want to think about that right now.

Chapter Sixteen

Dakota had waited long enough. Tonight would be their night. They'd spent the day running the skijoring course. He'd even let her pull him while riding Twinkle for the first time. If she could ride a horse, she certainly could ride her Italian stallion next.

She'd been thinking about making love with Matteo for weeks, and in a few days they'd be at Dreams Found Ranch. The man's lascivious gazes conveyed that he felt the same way, but he hadn't made a move on her. She hadn't felt any pain in a long time and assured him truthfully that today had been pain free.

One thing she'd come away with today was the decision to compete in the skijoring festival. She'd spent the last two days at the resort in Aspen taking ski lessons. She clearly had a lot to learn to become an expert like Matteo, but she felt confident she could compete well enough in the Sport division intended for amateur skiers, because she'd taken to the slopes like she'd been born to them. Of course, her riding skills couldn't be beat and weren't a concern according to one of the festival organizers she'd spoken with.

Tonight, though, her only goal was to set the mood for sport of another kind when Matteo came in from the barn. She'd bought some candles on her way back from Aspen and placed them in the middle of the coffee table. She wore the dress he'd loved her in on Christmas Day as well as at his mama's condo earlier this month. Without an extensive wardrobe to choose from, he'd be seeing a lot of her one and only dress when she wasn't wearing jeans.

The music of Cody Johnson—a rodeo singer she'd heard perform at RodeoHouston—played on the boom box in the corner. Dakota wanted dance tonight, much more so than her initial idea of cuddling on the couch and watching a movie. Dancing would be sexier and further show him that her body had healed. Then they could two-step down the hall and into the bedroom.

She wanted tonight to be romantic—slow at first with lots of touching, then more urgent when the passion burst between them. No holding back. She'd waited long enough.

Dakota moved the kitchen table and chairs aside and pushed the coffee table up against the couch to open up more room for dancing. She glanced at the time. Where was Matteo? He seemed to be taking longer than usual.

She'd almost put on her coat to join him in the barn when the door swung open. Matteo stood there with an armful of fresh-split firewood. Perhaps he wanted a romantic evening too, although he seemed to enjoy sitting by the fire most nights.

As he hung his coat on the hook, his gaze roamed slowly down her body and back up again before he broke out in a huge grin. "What have we here?"

She swept her arm wide to have him take in the change in decor. "Dakota's Roadhouse. All the beer and dancing a cowboy could ask for."

His eyes smoldered. "Let me build us a fire, then I'm all in." With his arms full of wood, he used the bootjack to remove his boots before crossing the room and dumping the wood into the bin. When he would have bent down to open the fireplace doors, she tugged at his arm and spun him around. She loved how the lacy band at the hem swished as she moved—and she planned to move tonight.

"We're going to make our own heat tonight, fireman."

She couldn't decide which fantasy suited him best—cowboy or fireman—so she'd use them both. The strains of "Lucky" pulsed from the stereo. Perfect beat. He sashayed her around the room, avoiding the table legs and chairs as best they could.

"You've got some moves, Matteo." She hadn't expected him to be such a good dancer.

"You're not doing so bad yourself."

"My rib's healed. I'm ready to move!" She executed some twists and turns to demonstrate that fact.

"Looks like. Anytime you want to show up in nothing but an apron, just be sure I'm around to watch you cook."

Puzzled at first, she laughed out loud when she realized he was referencing the lyrics of the song on the stereo. Dakota stored that tidbit away for a future seduction scene. But for tonight, she had other plans.

"Proud," the next song on the album, slowed the pace. Dakota snuggled into his embrace, wrapping her arms around him tighter and pressing her breasts against his chest. She brought her head to rest on his shoulder, and they swayed silently to the music as she drank in the scent of hay and sweat from the time he'd spent in the barn.

Nothing sexier than a cowboy fireman.

Matteo's hand stroked her back as she ran her hand up and down before settling on his butt where she drew him in closer. Wait till he discovered she wasn't wearing any panties. His erect cock pressed hard against her lower abdomen. She smiled and squeezed his butt through his Wranglers.

"Why don't we move this into the bedroom? I feel the need to ride a certain cowboy tonight."

He pulled away to search her eyes, then smiled as he slid his hand between them and cupped her breast. "Thought you'd never ask, cowgirl." He pinched her nipple, making it even harder, and bent to kiss her. His tongue entered her mouth; she offered no resistance.

Long, slow, deep. Just the way we'll be making love tonight.

They separated, breathing hard, and started for the bedroom. Matteo stripped off his shirt, leaving it behind on the hallway floor.

"You just sit right here in the front row, cowboy." Dakota guided him to the edge of the bed, then took several steps back before beginning to gyrate to the music coming from the other room. Clasping the sides of her dress, she swished its skirt in the air, alternating back and forth and giving him brief glimpses of her thighs. He sat mesmerized, grinning.

His bare chest and hard nipples made her want to sink her teeth into them, but she didn't want to rush things. She'd waited a long time for this and knew she'd explode like a firecracker the minute he touched her intimately.

Slowly, she lifted the dress over her head and tossed it on a nearby chair. She now wore nothing but her boots and his gaze took her in as he slowly went from her boots to her breasts then back again to her boots. His erection strained against his jeans. Maybe he just had a thing for naked ladies—his eyes were glued now to the ginger curls at the apex of her thighs, but she had a feeling the boots added to his interest as well.

If his hot stare were a torch, she'd be on fire now. Hell, she *was* on fire, just a different kind.

He crooked his finger to beckon her closer, and she swaggered to the beat of the music, stopping a few feet away. He pointed to his Wranglers. "I might need some help with these first. Not sure I can get them off without hurting certain parts of my anatomy." Her gaze went straight to his crotch, and she gave him a seductive smile.

"On your feet, cowboy."

Matteo stood, and she unhooked his belt buckle and then undid the button. He lifted her chin and kissed her as she carefully slid the zipper down and then helped rid him of his Wranglers and the boxer briefs that were molded to his body. Their lips remained locked despite their contortions, and she couldn't prevent a giggle from erupting. When he pinched both her nipples, though, she gasped and broke contact. Apparently, he wanted her to take this more seriously. *Fine.* She wrapped her hand around his cock and gave him a squeeze. She couldn't wait to have him buried inside her. *Soon!*

Matteo removed her hand. "We aren't in any hurry, Sweet Lady." He motioned with his hands for her to turn around. "I want to have a good long look at this sexy woman in my bedroom wearing nothing but boots—and her ginger hair." *Above and below.*

Her hips swayed seductively as she eased slightly away from him, then turned around and bent over at the waist to give him an even better view. Before she could stand upright again, he began rubbing his cock down the crack of her ass.

Whoa! How sexy would it be for him to take me in this position?

But he didn't enter her. Instead, he let the precum on the head of his cock coat her cleft, which would make his entry easier when the time came.

"I'm so hot for you, woman."

She stood up and turned around, nudging him backward toward the bed. "You can see how hot—and wet—I am. Now I'm ready to ride you like you've never been ridden before, cowboy."

The backs of Matteo's knees hit the edge of the mattress, and he sat abruptly, pulling Dakota with him as he lay back on the bed. She didn't seem any the worse for wear from all her dancing—or riding Twinkle earlier—so maybe her rib really had healed.

God, I hope so. I'm not going to be able to stop unless she tells me to.

He didn't want to hurt her but couldn't wait to pound himself into her hot, wet pussy.

"Open that drawer," he said, pointing the nightstand.

She did so and grinned back at him. "Someone sure is prepared."

He shrugged, unapologetically. "Or hopeful. I've been looking forward to this night for a while now."

She seemed to peruse the selection and chose a contoured one before rolling the condom onto his erection. He'd have to remember those were her preference.

He wanted to roll her onto her back, but instead, she knelt on the bed, a knee on either side of his hips, and straddled him. He reached up to cup her firm, full breasts, pinching her nipples, deciding to let her make the first move. She didn't disappoint and wasted no time lowering herself over him, guiding his cock just inside her.

So tight. Jesus, take me now.

On second thought, don't! Give me just a little longer in paradise.

It took all he had to keep his hips still, letting her set the pace. Slowly, advancing and retreating as she continued to gyrate her hips, she slid him inside her inch by inch, coating the rubber with her juices, until his full length was inside her. She grinned down at him. "I've been waiting for this for a long time."

"You and me both."

She took a deep breath then leaned forward, placing her hands on either side of his head. He lifted up to take one of her nipples into his mouth as she slid almost completely off his cock, then moved back onto his shaft, making her nipple plop out of his mouth. He'd have his work cut out for him to maintain the connection between them. When she pulled away from his cock the next time, he grabbed onto her nipple again but this time pumped his hips into her to keep them joined at both points.

Matt pistoned in and out of her while nibbling and sometimes biting her hard nipple on the breast cupped in his hand. He slid his hand between their bodies as best he could, searching for her clit, but she pushed his hand aside.

"I'm going to come the minute you touch me," she warned, "but I'm not ready yet."

Sounded like she was more than ready, but he remembered his vow to let her set the pace, so he moved his hand up to cup her other breast and continued to feast.

All too soon, she lifted her body away from his mouth, and he stared up at her. Too bad they hadn't thought to put her hat on, because he could picture her in that as well as the boots she still wore. Might not be original as fantasies went, though there was a good reason that certain ones were popular. But the reality of *this* cowgirl would blow all those mediocre fantasies of the past out of the water.

Using her knees to lift herself up, she pulled almost off his cock, then plunged down again. Soon she had set a rhythm of riding him that nearly brought him to the brink too. He didn't want this to end any more than she did but didn't have the willpower to slow down her ride. Seeing that she wasn't wincing in pain, he decided to give her a bit of a bronc ride and began lifting and lowering his hips, pounding into her luscious body.

Faster. Then, slower.

Shit, he didn't know what he wanted anymore.

Yeah, he did. He wanted Dakota.

When she closed her eyes, she appeared to be close to the brink. He again placed his hand near her short ginger curls and searched for her clit, then touched the hard button, wet from her juices, and she cried out.

"Matteo! I want you to come inside me. Now!"

"Only if you come with me. Ride me, darlin'!"

She nodded, unable to say the word, apparently. He increased the strokes of his finger and his hips as she got into the rhythm with him and rode him for all she was worth, raising her right hand high above her head as if she were actually riding a bronc.

"I'm coming!" she shouted.

He could feel her body squeezing his cock and helped her over the edge as he exploded inside her. "Jesus, woman!" She dropped down onto his chest, and he held her tight as he pumped the last few times. Both of them were breathing hard for several minutes, unable to speak.

Dakota lifted her head and smiled. "Best ride I've had in…forever."

He grinned. "Definitely not the longest, though. I'll do better next time."

"You just holler, and I'll hop on."

Rolling onto his side, he laid her on her back, brushing the hair back from her face. "God, I love your hair."

"So you've said."

"Don't ever cut it."

"Not even trim?"

"Well, maybe an inch or two, but no more."

"You're getting awfully bossy."

True. He had no hold on her, and now that her body had healed, she could leave at any moment. "How's that rib?"

"Still attached, despite you trying to buck me off."

He shook his head. "I mean, did you have any pain?"

"Matteo, I'm fine! I healed up long ago! And the next time I ride

Comet, there will be zero restrictions. I figure riding him would only be half as strenuous as what we just did." She smiled.

He thought a minute, then grinned back. "Probably. But don't go riding far from the house without being armed."

"Why?"

"Mountain lions. And bears will be coming out of their dens in another month or two."

She nodded, but didn't tell him she'd be gone long before that. He knew she carried, because she'd mentioned shooting anyone who came into her camper uninvited. He relaxed a little at the thought of her being out there alone, knowing she probably could protect herself.

She splayed her hand open on his chest, over his heart. "Your heart's still beating as wildly as mine."

"That was an incredible workout. Why don't we take a shower together?"

"I have a better idea. Why don't you dispose of that condom and put on a new one and we can go at it again?"

Matt liked how she thought. "Be right back."

Minutes later, he was back and reaching for a foil packet in the drawer. He handed it to her. "I'll let you do the honors."

She smiled as she knelt beside him and slowly opened the packet with her teeth then removed the condom. His cock stirred at the seductive way she looked at him as she covered him. Once it had been rolled in place, her fingers danced down to his cock, and she folded her hand around him. He was at full staff now.

"Glad you aren't ready to put the hose away, fireman, because I have a fire that needs putting out."

He smiled and rolled on top of her, cupping her face and lowering his mouth to hers. His tongue traced her lower lip until she opened for him. God, he couldn't get enough of her.

But you'd better get your fill—before she leaves.

Matt tried not to let that thought put a damper on their lovemaking tonight.

Hours later, he woke with a start from a troubling dream. Dakota looked down at him, worry in her eyes. "Everything okay? I think you were having a nightmare."

He couldn't remember anything tangible—just that he'd seen her ginger hair…

Oh God!

Matt sat up on the edge of the bed with his back turned toward her. Dakota had been in the burning wreckage out on Highway 24. The dream had started out being about the Martin family, but somehow he'd placed her in the burning vehicle that had morphed into her pickup truck.

She came up behind him and stroked his back. "It's over now, Matteo, but I'm here if you'd like to talk about it."

Not a chance.

"It was a jumbled-up mess. Doubt I could put it into words." *Even if I wanted to.*

Her gentle touch soothed him somewhat but only made the thought of anything like that happening to her hurt worse. Wanting to erase those fleeting glimpses from his mind, he lay back down and pulled her on top of him.

Dakota smiled seconds before he pulled her by the hair until her lips met his, losing himself in her. She hadn't been in that wreck. He'd been sleep-deprived from his shift, which probably accounted for the nightmare slipping into his unconscious mind. He just needed to replace those thoughts with something more…

Alive.

"You're shaking."

Pull your shit together, man.

"I'll grab another blanket."

"Let me." Dakota got out of bed and strutted to the cedar chest at the bottom of the bed where she'd tossed her dress earlier. Watching her naked body erased any remnants of his nightmare.

He grinned as she returned to the bed and shook the blanket out over the comforter. "Since we're both awake," she suggested, "maybe we ought to find something to occupy ourselves."

Hell, yeah.

As she crawled under the covers and returned to his side, he pulled her into his arms, kissing her soundly. She stretched out over the length of him and smiled. *Good.* She'd forgotten about his bad dream. And soon so did Matt.

After making love, she fell asleep in his arms. Fearing those terrifying images would return, sleep eluded him for the longest time. But he must have succumbed at some point because he woke again when Dakota jumped up from the bed.

"Matteo! We need to take care of the horses!"

He groggily glanced toward the windows, then his watch. "It's only an hour later than normal. They'll be fine."

"But your alarm clock…"

"It's off. I use my watch."

"Why is it still dark in here?"

"Room-darkening shades and curtains. They help me sleep in the middle of the day when I need to catch up after a rough shift." And for him, *all* shifts were rough when it came to getting adequate sleep. Not that last night had been any better in his own bed.

He sat up and rubbed the grittiness from his eyes. At least with Dakota he'd had some fun to compensate for the lack of z's. Way better than sleep.

As they went about their chores, though, he couldn't shake the feeling of impending disaster. In no time, she'd be off on her own and he wouldn't be able to protect her. He doubted warning her about some nebulous threat, mostly of his own conjuring, would carry any weight with her. She'd just do whatever she wanted, anyway.

Matt pushed away the persistent images from his dream. His mind must have merged his worrying about her with a flashback from that horrific accident. The two weren't related.

Dakota would be fine. Well, until the next time she decided to ride a bull.

Chapter Seventeen

They arrived at Dreams Found Ranch three days later. Matteo would be going back on duty in the morning—Valentine's Day—but he'd insisted on driving the truck and trailer up with the horses this morning. She sighed. He still worried about her doing so much. She hoped Ryder wouldn't treat her with kid gloves like Matteo did.

Now that she was able to do strenuous riding again—and before Matteo returned to his ranch this evening—they'd decided to enjoy a trail ride with the Wilsons. Well, Ryder and his sister, Marcia, in this case. She'd been visiting from Santa Fe for a few days but planned to head back home tomorrow now that Dakota had arrived. Megan had stayed back at the corral to give riding lessons to the little ones. She was so good with them. Dakota wondered if she and Ryder would be having a family of their own someday. The love she saw between them made her heart ache, wondering whether she'd ever experience that herself.

She glanced over at Matteo. While she had strong feelings for him, she wasn't sure she was capable of loving any man. But he sure opened up the door to some great possibilities, with or without love.

Only the four of them had set out on this trail ride, rather than the dozen or so who had ridden out on New Year's Day. Ahead, Dakota spotted a large aspen grove, its greenish-white tree bark recognizable in the distance although the trees were bare of leaves at this time of year.

Ryder reined in and checked on them as they passed him by. "Dakota, you look like you're in heaven."

"I am! Comet's being quite gentle today, but you should see him running the skijoring course."

"Oh, I usually get down to the festival to help out with the horses. Comet and Twinkle are both very competitive."

Dakota and Matteo had worked both his horses hard the past few days, preparing them for the festival, which was only a little more than two weeks away. She'd fallen in love with this sport already, even though she still needed to work on her skiing skills.

Dakota bent over to pat the horse's neck after Ryder returned to where his sister rode. "Comet, you're such a good boy. Thank you for letting me ride you today." The horse whinnied and bobbed his head in response as if he understood Dakota's words—and he probably did. The two had formed a tight bond over the past few weeks. She'd also taken care of Twinkle, of course, but the mare had a stronger attachment to Matteo.

A sharp wind blew down the side of the mountain and across the field, making her appreciate Matteo's suggestion that she dress in several layers today.

As they entered the aspen grove, she heard running water. Soon they came upon a mostly frozen brook that still had a trickle of water dancing over the icy rocks. The horses took turns drinking their fill, while the riders remained mounted, chatting with each other.

"It's so peaceful out here," Marcia said. "This is one of my favorite places on the ranch."

Dakota nodded. "I can see why."

"Because of how much I love this spot," Matteo began, "I made sure to find a place with a stream when looking for my own ranch. Water makes such a peaceful, calming sound."

She wondered if that was something he used to help him regroup after a bad shift at the station. "I can't wait to explore more of your property, Matteo." So far, they'd only had time for skijoring training, not pleasure rides.

Matteo used the horses and his ranch to find solace when the horrors he witnessed at work bore down on him. Knowing that gave Dakota comfort. She wished she'd been able to do more than distract him the other night after his nightmare. Maybe Carmella or Angelina could offer some suggestions.

After another ten minutes' rest, they returned to the trail, skirting the brook as they rode up the mountainside. Earlier, Ryder had pointed out Iron Horse Pass where Luke and Cassie lived. The two had flown to Peru yesterday, so she'd missed seeing them again.

She hadn't taken care of horses since her teens, but it was something she found herself enjoying even more over these past weeks than she had back then. Working alongside Matteo had been a lot of fun too. The two of them had so much in common and worked well together. She wouldn't have traded her time at either ranch for anything.

Just don't get too used to it, Dakota. You're only visiting at both places.

The times when Matt had fallen back to let Dakota ride single file through tight spots on the trail had been torture for him. Her hair cascaded down her back, swaying back and forth as Comet slowly climbed or meandered along the path. How many times had he fantasized about grabbing Dakota by a fistful of hair while she sat astride the gelding, pulling her head back, and planting a deep kiss firmly on her sweet lips?

Okay, let's be real. That fantasy was PG-rated compared to the galloping-horse position he'd been daydreaming about all day. Matt would be mounted on Twinkle as Dakota faced him and lowered herself onto his cock before Twinkle entered a canter or gallop.

Damn!

Matt adjusted himself in his saddle, hoping no one noticed his raging hard-on, but staring at Dakota's ass encased in tight jeans, perfectly molded by the well-worn saddle, had pushed any tamer fantasies out of the way.

Having to work all weekend without a visit at the station from Dakota would be torture, but at least he knew she'd be in good hands here. And she wouldn't be driving her own vehicle, so if his nightmare had been prophetic, then he didn't have to worry—this time, anyway.

Comet stopped abruptly. Thankfully, Twinkle had been paying attention and did the same. He glanced up at Dakota's face to see she'd caught him staring at her ass.

Smooth move, Matt.

Dakota grinned, not seeming to be upset with him. She raised her index finger to the lips he'd been fantasizing about kissing a moment ago, then pointed with her other hand to a spot where a mule deer doe chomped on a mountain shrub of some kind. The animals were a dime a dozen up here, so his attention rapidly returned to Dakota, a much more interesting sight to him.

But watching Dakota stare intently and in awe at the doe piqued his curiosity. She didn't seem to go on trail rides or get out in nature often, even though there must be plenty of days when she wasn't competing. Maybe she needed a horse of her own.

But she'd been rodeoing for more than a decade and didn't seem interested in having her own horse. The sport treated no one with any kindness, not that she had any plans for retiring from the arena yet. Eventually, though, she'd have to leave the brutal, demanding circuit and settle down someplace where she could enjoy a safer, more peaceful life.

Or would she miss the cheering crowds and adrenaline rush that came with riding whatever beast she wanted to conquer at the moment? That rush had gotten old for Matt long ago but apparently not for her. Of course, he'd just replaced it with the blood-pumping action of the fire service and skijoring.

When Dakota turned toward him again after watching the deer, a radiant smile spread across her face, her cheeks rosy from the brisk breeze.

So incredibly beautiful.

He grinned back at her, pointing toward Ryder and Marcia. "I guess we'd better catch up." But he could have stared at her all day if given the chance.

The four rode in companionable silence another hour or so before heading back to the house and barn. He'd be heading back home soon after they had supper so that he could get some sleep before shift change in the morning. Missing sleep during his days off always made for some long-ass workdays, especially when they had a lot of calls.

But Matt made a commitment to himself to take Dakota on trail rides at his place next month, if she stayed around long enough after the festival.

Nine Days Later

Dakota hated that her time at Dreams Found Ranch had come to an end. She'd been allowed to do much more here than Matteo let her do at his place. She hardly felt the effects of her broken rib anymore, and when she returned to his place, she intended to demand that he ease up on the restrictions he'd imposed.

Regardless, when he was on duty, she could start riding around his property more to see the places he hadn't shown her yet.

"Kahlo, girl, how are you doing today?" She murmured softly as she approached the skittish mare slowly from the front so as not to spook her.

Working with the horses, especially the newest adoptees like Kahlo who still showed some signs of their abuse and neglect, made her want to rescue her own horse. But what business did she have owning a horse with her vagabond life? Sure, she could haul a trailer around from rodeo to rodeo, but that was no life for the horse. It would need roots and a place to heal away from crowds. Besides, a trailer that would also have a place for her to sleep would be far beyond her means. She wasn't ready to get rid of her camper yet. It had been the only home she'd known after so many years of sleeping in motels and occasionally in the rodeo grounds stables when helping out some friends with their horses.

But that Shasta, as much as she loved it, was nothing compared to a place like this or even Matteo's ranch. These were real homes. She'd found healing of her own at both ranches.

The horse's ears pointed forward, signaling that she was okay with Dakota coming closer. Pulling a carrot from her jacket pocket, she held it out and the horse gnawed it down to a nub in no time.

"Hey, Sweet Lady."

She looked up to see Matteo standing several yards away. A smile broke out on her face at the sight of Matteo. "Welcome back!"

He kept his distance, aware of Kahlo's dislike of men or sudden movements. Dakota stroked the horse's neck. "Matteo's a good one, girl. You okay with him getting a little closer?"

Kahlo seemed to size him up but didn't make any indication she wanted him near her.

"How's she been?

"We've been getting closer to each other. But she's still cautious, even with me."

He didn't come closer than ten feet. The distance killed her. She'd missed him these past few days. He'd headed for Dreams Found immediately after shift change Monday morning and stayed to help Ryder with some fencing work until the night before his next shift. With their horses staying there too, they'd practically moved in to help while the Dentons were in Peru.

When Dakota had first arrived on Friday, Megan had assigned her to a small cabin slightly removed from the bunkhouses and other occupied cabins where their guests stayed. She and Matteo had missed each other so much during last weekend's shift that they'd enjoyed hot sex every night, hoping nobody could hear them. Not that keeping her screams down was always achieved.

Had Megan anticipated that, even though she'd only seen them together before she and Matteo had become lovers?

"Did you and Ryder finish repairing the fences?" she asked him. Matteo looked beat. He never slept well at the station.

"Sure did." He pulled a carrot out of his pocket, having learned how much Kahlo liked them. He extended it to Dakota. "Do you want to feed this to her?"

"I just gave her one. Why don't you?" she asked.

"Because I don't want to get kicked or bitten."

She laughed with him but beckoned him closer with her hand. "Ryder said she needs to get used to both men and women before she'll be fully rehabilitated." The thought of the horse being rejected and sent away to some other sanctuary physically hurt Dakota's heart, not that she'd heard of Dreams Found ever doing that with any of their rescues—horse or human. They stayed at the ranch until they were ready to return to the world outside this sanctuary.

"Hey, girl," he said softly, holding out the carrot as he slowly came closer. Kahlo squealed, tossing her head away from him in a blatant rejection.

"Matteo's okay, Kahlo," she said, patting the horse's neck to calm her. "You can trust him. I do." As he drew nearer, she wrapped her free arm around him, pulling him closer to show the mare she deemed him safe. She continued to stroke the horse's neck, whispering calming words to her as Matteo slowly raised the carrot for the horse to see.

Kahlo alternately eyed the treat in his hand then Matteo, not wanting to chance the close contact but badly desiring the carrot. "Here, girl," he coaxed softly. "I've brought your favorite treat."

That Matteo had noticed what the horse liked endeared him to Dakota even more. His gentle ways. and the many kindnesses he showed to injured horses and wounded people like Kahlo and Dakota, made the thought of leaving his place next month almost too painful to imagine.

Dakota watched as Kahlo's ears pointed forward then upward, back and forth, as she tried to figure out how to get that carrot without contact with this man she didn't know well.

"That's my girl," Matteo said. "Take a nibble."

Kahlo took a bite then retreated backward to chew, continuing to stare at the rest of the outstretched carrot. Apparently seeing that he meant her no harm, she came forward and took a bigger bite, not backing away to chew it this time. Matteo's quiet approach would win Kahlo over, just as they had Dakota. Finally, Kahlo took the rest of the carrot into her mouth.

"You sure have a way with the ladies."

Matteo kissed Dakota on the cheek. "Only certain ones seem thrilled with my charms. She's just tolerating me."

She turned toward him to kiss him, and the two paid no attention to the horse for a few moments.

"So, this is where you two lovebirds are," Ryder said as he climbed over the corral fence. "Megan said supper will be ready in about fifteen minutes, if you're hungry for something more than each other."

Dakota couldn't help but blush, even though they hadn't tried to hide anything from the other couple. Still, she felt like she was back in high school and had been caught doing something she shouldn't.

Not that I'd ever have done anything like this back then.

"You two sure have a way with Kahlo. She won't let me near her yet. I'm sure her new owner will do just fine with her. She needs more than we can give her right now."

Dakota's heart jumped into her throat as tears stung her eyes. She hated the thought of never seeing Kahlo again after growing so attached to her this week. Dakota turned toward the mare and blinked away the tears before either man saw her show of weakness.

"Glad you decided to buy her, Matt."

Dakota turned to Matteo, and a tear splashed onto her cheek. "You bought Kahlo?"

He nodded, smiling. "And Van Gogh," he said pointing across the corral, "for Jason's early graduation present. He's going to need his own horse when he goes away to college."

Dakota fought the urge to launch herself into his arms, because she didn't want to spook Kahlo. Not having to say goodbye to this special horse would make her remaining weeks with Matteo much more wonderful.

She turned to the mare. "Did you hear that, Kahlo? You're coming home with us!"

Home with us.

Matt loved the sound of those words. When Ryder told him earlier today that they had three more horses coming in unexpectedly next week, Matt had asked if he'd consider selling Kahlo, knowing how much Dakota needed the horse. Even though Kahlo wasn't one of the horses they'd intended to adopt out, Ryder had seen the connection between Dakota and Kahlo as well.

Matt had made arrangements to purchase a horse for Jason months ago without knowing which horse would be available. The boy had worked so hard at Matt's place that he wanted to repay him with his own horse. Matt sure would miss having Jason helping out when he went away to college in the fall but had known the day had to come eventually. If he hadn't wanted to go to college, Matt might have tried to find a way to hire him on but didn't really have enough work for him to do full-time.

"We wouldn't let Kahlo go to just anyone," Ryder had said, "but you've rescued two mustangs from bad situations already, so I know you'll be able to see to her needs. And Dakota's great with her. We sure haven't been able to get that close to Kahlo yet."

Matt had built his barn big enough for six horses. Only three would be permanent residents, although he'd keep a spot open for Jason to board his horse anytime he came home from college. He'd cleared it with Jason's dad already, and when Darren and Annette found out Matt was giving him a horse, they decided to buy Jason a small horse trailer.

Who knows? Maybe Kahlo would be the bargaining chip he needed to lure Dakota away from the rodeo circuit. He didn't like using ulterior motives—and he had planned on getting a few more horses eventually—but nothing wrong with putting out two hotspots with one pass of the line.

Kahlo scampered off to the far end of the corral when she decided she'd had enough human contact for a while. In an instant, Dakota launched herself at Matt, who caught her just as she started raining a dozen kisses all over his face.

"Thank you, thank you, thank you! I hated the thought of not seeing her again."

Matt chuckled as he twirled her around in a circle.

"Gee, I hope you're going to miss the rest of us here that much,"

Ryder said.

"Oh, I am!" she said to Ryder as Matt lowered her boots to the ground. "But I wasn't as worried about you guys as I was about Kahlo."

"She sure did bond with you this week," Ryder said.

"When can we take her home?" she asked, her gaze going from one man to the other.

"We can take Twinkle and Comet home today and come back for Kahlo and Van Gogh tomorrow." He needed to get a four-horse trailer if he wanted to transport all his horses at once—that would leave room for another someday. But he'd better not bite off more than he could chew right now.

Ryder offered to bring the other two, but he'd be needed here with Luke not due back from Peru for a couple of days. They were already short-staffed, although he said they'd anticipated this and hadn't overbooked guests this week.

"Tonight, we can prepare stalls for the new additions," Matt said, turning toward her, "but don't tell Jason I'm giving him Van Gogh yet.

She zipped her lips with a twist of her fingers making him want to kiss her more thoroughly. "Van Gogh will be wonderful with him!" She smiled over at the gelding, unaware of Matt's thoughts. "He's going to be over the moon when you tell him."

Matt nodded. Never one to keep a secret, though, he couldn't wait to tell him.

Ryder climbed back over the fence. "We'd better get in to supper before Megan feeds the meat to the dogs and the veggies to the alpacas." Ryder grinned, clearly not serious. "I'm sure they'll get their share anyway. She spoils them rotten."

Dakota had gotten familiar with Cassie and Luke's alpacas too. So personable. She wondered if she'd get a chance to visit them at their mountain before she left the area next month.

Chapter Eighteen

The next afternoon at Matt's ranch, Dakota looked around the barn to make sure everything was in place before they unloaded Kahlo and Van Gogh into their stalls. The new feed and water containers had been filled to welcome them. Fresh straw had been strewn on the floor for bedding.

They'd chosen the two stalls at the end of the aisle farthest from Comet and Twinkle to allow the horses to communicate with each other without being too close together or getting territorial. At Dreams Found, the two pairs of horses had been separated, but she hoped they'd all get along—especially Kahlo, who'd be staying here a lot longer.

"All set?" Matteo asked.

"I think so."

They decided it best to get Kahlo and Van Gogh settled before bringing the other horses in from the corral. They could acclimate together for the first few hours.

"Let's bring Kahlo in first. She'll be the most skittish."

Dakota took the lead with Kahlo, of course. The mare hadn't been won over by Matteo's charms yet, but it would only be a matter of time. Besides, in some weird way, Dakota felt as if she was part owner of the horse, given all the time she'd spent with her at Dreams Found.

Whatever happened—or didn't—between her and Matteo, she hoped she'd be able to visit the horse from time to time during her breaks from the rodeo circuit—and the other horses too. Matteo probably wouldn't mind, unless he got serious about another woman and it became awkward for Dakota to be around.

Easing the mare backwards out of the trailer, Dakota helped calm her with pats to the neck and gentle words until the mare relaxed enough to be led into the barn. Her ears gave away her curiosity—and her caution—as the horse looked around at her new surroundings both outside and in.

"Here you go, girl," Dakota crooned as the horse's nostrils flared, taking in the smells of her new environment. "Welcome to your new home. You're going to like it here. I know I do."

She realized too late that her words made it sound like this was her home too, but Matteo was outside with Jason's horse and wouldn't have overheard her. Dakota pointed out where her food and water were, as if the horse needed to be told. Inside the stall, Dakota unclipped the lead from the halter, and Kahlo made a beeline to the large water bucket first.

Dakota looked around to make sure everything was safe and in order before assuring Kahlo she'd be right back, closing and locking the stall door behind her. As she left the barn, the sound of Jason's old truck drew her gaze down the lane, and the excitement of the surprise in store for the boy made her feel like a kid on Christmas morning.

A glimpse of presents under a six-foot tree at the house of the woman she'd dreamed about recently flashed across her mind's eye. She didn't have many memories of happy Christmases, but this one left her with a feeling of warmth and joy.

"Hey, Mr. G! What's up? Wow, a new horse?" His elation was palpable, even though he couldn't know what Matteo had planned.

"Two actually," Matteo said. "Dakota already got Kahlo settled. Why don't you take Van Gogh in? I'll show you his stall." She wondered when Matteo would tell him the news. Matteo handed the young man the lead, but Jason didn't move before turning toward the horse.

"Hey, handsome boy." Jason greeted the horse with a couple pats on the neck. "Welcome to your new home! You're going to like it here."

Matteo and Dakota exchanged a secretive smile.

"Come on, boy. Let me show you your new digs."

As Jason led the horse away from the trailer, Matteo took Dakota's hand and walked ahead of the teen and his horse, making her feel as much a part of the surprise as Matteo.

Inside the barn, Dakota hurried ahead to Kahlo's stall to comfort her as the strange male approached. "It's okay, Kahlo. He's a friend too." Kahlo chose to move to the far corner of the stall, as far away from Jason as possible.

Jason glanced toward Kahlo's stall. "I can see I'm going to be spending more time out here now with four horses to help take care of."

She'd appreciate the help when Matteo was on duty, but she and Matteo could probably manage the four horses the other days. However, Dakota reminded herself that she was the interloper here. Besides, once he found out Van Gogh was his horse, Jason would be around a lot to bond with the gelding.

Turning toward the stall across from Kahlo's, streamers in Jason's school colors wound around the bars, Dakota waited to see if Matteo would do the reveal today.

Jason did a double take between the two stalls, then gave Matteo a puzzled look.

"We're counting on you to help, because Van Gogh is your early graduation present. So you'll need to take especially good care of him."

Van Gogh gave the boy a nudge with his nose as if to punctuate the announcement. "What? He's mine?!"

The teen's face lit up and Dakota felt her eyes sting with unshed tears. Jason wrapped his arms around the horse's neck and buried his face as if trying to hide a few tears of his own.

"Ryder tells me he's fast," Matt said. "You've only got two weeks to train him, but maybe he'll be ready to race at the festival."

Jason pulled away from the horse to meet Matteo's gaze. "If I can find someone to ride him, it would be great to ski with my own horse."

"I'd be happy to ride him for you, Jason," Dakota offered. From what she understood, she could ride unlimited times that weekend.

Jason gave her a hug, taking her off guard. "Thanks so much! Can you hold him for a minute?"

She took the lead rope from Jason before he rushed over to give

Matteo an even bigger hug. Matteo clapped him on the back, and she saw him blink away a few tears. He had such a big heart, and suddenly she remembered how much it meant to Matteo when a ranch had gifted him with Dipper, the horse he'd worked with throughout high school. Perhaps Matteo didn't want Jason to have to wait so long to learn that the horse would be his, or he just couldn't put off a surprise.

"Thanks so much, Mr. G. I won't let either of you or Van Gogh down." The boy looked back at his horse. "I'll take the best care of him I can."

"If I didn't have confidence that you'd do exactly that, I wouldn't have given him to you. You've shown me how responsible you are since you've been working for me, Jason."

The smile left the boy's face. "I'm going to hate leaving him when I go to college, but I'll try to come home from Fort Collins every weekend to help out with him."

Jason missed the grin Matteo gave Dakota, but neither would spoil his parents' surprise about the new horse trailer he'd be receiving.

Matteo took some time to explain Van Gogh's history and some of his known triggers before Dakota explained the situation with Kahlo and that, for the foreseeable future, she'd be the only one caring for the mare. But with her time limited, she'd have to make sure Kahlo would be okay around the guys too.

"Why don't you get Van Gogh settled in? I need to clean out the trailer."

"Let me help." Dakota went to the faucet and filled two buckets to carry outside.

"You stretch out the hose, Dakota. I'll get those buckets." She rolled her eyes but didn't argue. One of these days, she intended to show him that she could lift as much as he could. Well, almost as much. With his firefighter skills, he probably could carry more weight than she could even before her injury. Still, she didn't like being thought of as weaker than any man.

Despite her frustration over that, she enjoyed working together with Matteo doing chores around the place. While there wasn't a lot of work that had to be done, she always looked for something to occupy her hands and mind during his days on duty.

She wanted to find something more to occupy her time, but with Kahlo here and her being able to do more riding without a lot of help, she might start exploring Matteo's place, with or without him.

Dakota glanced down at the menu in the Greek restaurant Matteo's sister-in-law had brought her to for a late lunch.

Carmella had put her through some grueling paces on the slopes today—cramming two days of lessons into one after Dakota texted her last night asking if she could head home a day early. Dakota told herself she wanted to be at the ranch to begin training for the Ski Joring Festival, but if she were honest, she missed Matteo so badly she couldn't stand it.

Cowgirl, you've got it bad. What are you going to do when you leave for good?

Hell, if Matteo kept trying to wrap her in cotton to keep her from getting hurt, she might be ready to leave sooner. But she had no intention of cutting out before competing at the festival. She missed being in the rodeo arena.

Of course, if Matteo wouldn't train with her, then she'd work with Jason. They were already working on her riding and his skiing, but could reverse roles on Thursday and Friday while Matteo was on duty. Matteo might be stubborn, but she could be stubborn too.

"I can't wait to see you run the course at the festival, Dakota."

"You've taught me so much in such a short time. I just hope I can manage to stay upright." She laughed.

"You're going to do great. I'm curious, though. What does Matt think about you competing? He didn't seem too thrilled when the subject came up at dinner earlier this month."

"I think he knows me well enough not to try and stop me, if that's what you mean. I've been doing rodeo for a long time and am no stranger to a few spills." Dakota laughed and rolled her eyes.

Carmella shook her head with a grin. "The Giardano brothers are very protective of their women."

Dakota started to correct her assumption that she was Matteo's woman, but Carmella continued, "I'm not sure there's much more I can show you here, so it's good that you're working with the horses on perfecting your skills for the competition."

Both turned their attention back to their menus. "I can give you some food recommendations, if you'd like," Carmella offered. "Tony and I come here all the time. In fact, he proposed to me at that table right over there." She pointed to a secluded spot near the fireplace.

"How wonderful!" The two had been married less than a year and a half but still acted like newlyweds together. "I'm sure I can use any suggestions you have. I eat mostly a steak-and-potatoes diet on the rodeo circuit."

The two ordered, Dakota appreciating Carmella's help with her menu selections. Because she planned to head back to Matteo's as soon as they finished, she drank water instead of wine or beer.

"Sorry Tony couldn't join us." Worry lines instantly creased Carmella's forehead, and she took a sip of wine before continuing, making Dakota wonder if something was wrong. She'd never pry, though.

"Tony's had a couple of rough nights," the woman volunteered. "I don't know what triggered him, but he isn't sleeping well."

Tony too? Dakota had been wondering how to broach the subject of helping Matteo, so Carmella's revelation provided the perfect segue.

"I'm so sorry to hear that, Carmella. Matteo has been having some nightmares lately too."

Carmella's eyes opened wider. At first, Dakota wondered if it was the admission that Dakota and Tony's brother were sleeping together, but her next words indicated that wasn't the case.

"I didn't know Matt was having a hard time, but I'm sure Tony hasn't said anything to his brothers about his recent nightmares, either. They try to keep things like this away from each other—and sometimes from the women in the family too, I suppose."

"Tony's opening up more about the aftereffects of a traumatic call he went on when we first started dating. I keep trying to get him to be more forthcoming about the stresses of the job rather than keep things bottled up. I finally gave him an ultimatum about being honest with me about what happens each shift, although I give him some time to decompress when he gets home. But if we hadn't come to this agreement, I might not hear about the bad calls at all. I work so far away from Aspen Corners. Marc's been good about giving me a heads-up after a particularly bad call, though, because they work the same shift."

The life of a first responder's spouse must be difficult. "I can't really get anything out of Matteo, only that he's sorry he woke me."

Carmella rolled her eyes. "Typical Giardano firefighter. I have a feeling most in the fire and emergency services are that way. They want to be macho and show us they can handle everything, but some of what they face on the job is too horrific to even imagine. I'm sure every first responder keeps a lot of the details to themselves, but the Aspen Corners Fire Department is good about getting everyone together for an after-incident review on particularly difficult calls."

Dakota wondered if the Leadville firefighters, police, and paramedics did the same. Matteo hadn't really shared anything about that with her. She heard about some incidents while hanging around town or at the station, but even that major fire last month had been swept under the rug with a couple gallons of ice cream.

"Have you noticed any behavioral changes in Matt lately? Excessive drinking or anything?"

Dakota shook her head. "Not around me anyway. He may get a little quiet, but I think he uses the horses to let go of the stress."

"That's good. For Tony, it's scuba diving."

A silence fell between them as Dakota tried to think back for any signs of trouble she might not have been aware of. "I don't know how they do it." Dakota couldn't imagine having a career where she had to deal with death and destruction on a daily basis. "I feel so helpless when he wakes up in the middle of a nightmare, though."

Carmella reached across the table and patted the top of Dakota's hand. "It'll get easier for him to open up the more time you spend together."

How much longer do we have, though? And who could Matteo turn to after she left? More than likely, he'd wake up alone with no one there to provide any comfort.

That thought left Dakota feeling empty.

"Any advice on what to do when he wakes up from one of these nightmares—or when I wake him up from one?"

"I know the natural inclination is to wake them up, but it's best not to. We have no idea where their mind is at that point. We should protect ourselves and not risk any wild swings at our faces or somewhere equally vulnerable while they're rehashing a rescue. Tony's first question when he wakes from a nightmare is whether he hurt me. I'm sure Matt would be equally concerned about hurting you. He seems to care a lot about you."

Dakota had feelings for Matteo too and didn't try to hide that from Carmella. "I never thought about him doing anything to me." Matteo wouldn't lash out at her—not intentionally, anyway.

"He can't control what's happening at that point. I usually try to talk firmly and calmly to ease Tony out of his trance. I say his name repeatedly, which helps too."

"How did you know how to handle the nightmares? Do they give spouses advice or recommendations at the department?"

Carmella hitched the corner of her mouth. "They might, but we weren't even dating when he had the first one. I learned those tips after Marc returned from Iraq with a combat injury. The counselors told us that touching a combat vet in the middle of a PTSD episode isn't a good idea, either, but Tony hasn't ever struck out at me."

"Your brother served in Iraq?"

Carmella nodded. "He was a Navy corpsman serving with a Marine unit and was discharged after a serious lung injury. Ryder Wilson was one of his Marines."

Dakota hadn't been aware that Ryder was a Marine.

"Thankfully, Marc's fully recovered from the physical wounds, and

I think he's doing better with the psychological aftereffects too. At least I hope so. Angelina hasn't mentioned anything in a long time."

So many selfless people in Matteo's family. They made a real difference in the world. What had she ever done to help anyone else?

Dakota wondered if she could handle being a firefighter, though. She'd never really thought about anything other than pursuing her rodeo career. Sure, she had to deal with the occasional injury but nothing on the scale of what military members and first responders faced on the job.

"Any other advice for me?"

"Once he comes out of it and is back in the present, just hold him. Stroke his back. Do whatever to help him reacclimate. If you can get him to tell you anything about the dream or the bad call that precipitated it, brownie points."

"I'll do my best."

But she hated to think about him facing those times alone.

Matt rolled over, pulling Dakota on top of him without having her break contact with his cock. It was so good to have her home tonight.

When she winced, he stopped. She hadn't shown any sign of pain from her rib injury in weeks.

"Did I hurt you?"

She shook her head, then smiled. "Just a little sore."

"From your skiing lesson today?"

Dakota nodded. "Carmella put me through my paces, but I'm glad I'm done with lessons. Now I'm ready to put them into practice sessions for the festival." She grinned, waiting for him to react.

Even though he'd known she hadn't given up on the idea, hearing the reminder, with the event only a little more than a week away, made his stomach sour.

The mood gone, he eased her off him without saying anything. She stretched out beside him, and he got up to dispose of the condom and clean up before returning to the bed and pulling her into his arms.

He'd been giving it a lot of thought, and if anyone was going to teach her to do skijoring, it would be Matt. "We can start training after morning chores tomorrow."

Dakota sat up and stared down at him, a wide smile on her face. "You'll train me?"

"I want you to know how to do it safely, so yeah. I'll do it."

She bent down to kiss him. "Thank you so much! I've missed the adrenaline rush so much." Again, she seemed to flinch at the movement.

"Did you hurt yourself today?"

"Nah. Just overdid it. It's been a while since I've done anything so strenuous." She gave him a sultry stare.

Matt grinned. "Show me where it hurts."

Dakota smiled and moved his hand to the inside of her thigh. "It's a little tight here." Matt's cock came back to life instantly, and she noticed before he could adjust the sheets. "You know what they say. If you don't use it, you lose it." Without skipping a beat, she pulled another condom from the drawer and rolled it onto his cock before mounting him again.

"Let's ride, cowboy."

Despite how slowly Matteo and Twinkle pulled her through the course, the exhilaration of doing the jumps, catching as much air as possible, then landing on her skis and gliding to the next jump had Dakota's blood racing too.

Now she wanted more speed. How she'd talked him into training with her, Dakota didn't know, but she needed to set him straight.

"Would you go that slowly with another competitor, Matteo?"

"What?" Matteo said as he dismounted. "Twinkle went all out."

"For a novice skijorer maybe." She removed her helmet, certain that she wasn't going to get anywhere with him and would have to wait and train with Jason while Matteo was at work. "Let me saddle up Comet, and I'll show you how I want to be pulled through the course next time."

Twenty minutes later, they were lined up at the beginning of the course. "Ready?" She sat astride Comet, the rope tied firmly over the saddle horn.

Matteo held onto the other end of the rope. "Whenever you are."

Dakota leaned over and whispered in Comet's ear, "Let's show him what we're made of, boy." Digging her heels into Comet's sides, they took off and were soon at a breakneck speed. As they neared the first jump, Matteo lined himself up and took the ramp, catching lots of air as he flew off the other end. *Beautiful.* Would she ever be that good?

Turning her attention back to the job at hand, she guided Comet around the next jump, setting Matteo up perfectly. *God, I love this!* The only thing better would be to watch this man in action, but she didn't want him getting injured. She needed to keep her focus on the ride this time.

Without slowing down, they worked their way through the course in what was record time for her. She wasn't sure how fast Matteo normally breezed through it, though.

She pulled up on the reins and watched the snow and ice fly as Matteo brought his skis to a stop.

"Damn, Dakota! That was a great run!"

She smiled, happy to hear those words. "Maybe we ought to team up for one of the runs at the festival."

He paused a moment, leading her to think he'd nix the idea outright, but he didn't. "Sounds good to me. I don't usually have anyone willing to ride that fast and hard. We could take first place with a run like that."

Being on the same team as Matteo gave her a thrill. While she wasn't good enough on skis to be pulled that fast, she could definitely ride a horse that hard.

"Let's do it! Take me through the course again with you riding Van Gogh. He's not as fast as Twinkle or Comet yet, but they're spent from the first two runs, and you'll want to help get him ready if he's going to compete this year."

Matteo didn't hold back the way he had on her last run, so perhaps she'd gotten through to him. She'd be feeling it later, but the thrill outweighed the pain.

She and Matteo made a great team. Maybe they could get in some more great runs on his course in the weeks after the festival, unless the snow and ice melted.

What about the circuit? It'll be here before you know it.

She'd think about that later. Now that she was feeling better from her injury, the thought of signing up for bull-riding school again had begun to interest her. Maybe she could see if there was one offered somewhere close to Leadville. If not, the one in Colorado Springs wasn't that far away.

The need to know if she could master the sport outweighed any fear of getting back onto the back of a bull. Not that she'd say anything to Matteo until she'd been accepted. One less thing for him to worry about.

Chapter Nineteen

The first day of racing in the Leadville Ski Joring Festival weekend dawned clear but cold, which did Matt's heart good. He'd been waiting for this for a whole year. If the temps stayed low like this, it should make for some fast runs on the track. At least no blizzards had been predicted.

As soon as his shift had ended yesterday, he'd headed to the ranch and crashed for a few hours to make up for lost sleep. He could fuel up on coffee all weekend and sleep most of the day Monday before going back to work Tuesday.

He hadn't found a four-horse trailer he could afford yet, so they'd made a return trip to load up Van Gogh. Dakota said she'd prefer to bed down with the horses at the fairground stables for the two nights rather than haul her camper to town, which was fine with him. Although he was damned curious about what was inside that Shasta. He had yet to be invited in.

Matt had offered to let Mama and Paul stay in his house so they wouldn't have to drive back and forth to Breckenridge. As an added bonus, Paul offered to help take care of Kahlo, who wouldn't be able to join them this weekend.

On Thursday, Dakota and Jason had both practiced skiing on the course at the ranch, similar to the amateur one they would encounter in the Sport division at the festival. While Matt hadn't been there to watch, Dakota told him they were ready.

Even though she was new to skijoring, Matt trusted his own riding abilities, and she'd drawn a rider for her other ski run with many years of experience at the Leadville event. However, Matt couldn't help but worry. Unfortunately, nothing much they could do now but make the runs down the track and let the chips fall where they may.

God, please keep everyone safe this weekend—especially Dakota.

Matt also asked Papa to watch over the competitors and the horses, as he did every year.

He loved how she'd gotten involved in the festival this year, volunteering to take care of the horses and to be available as a rider to anyone in either division who needed one. She sure had taken to life in Leadville, but did that mean she'd want to stick around?

Don't go there, Matt. She's not planning on settling down here—or anywhere else, apparently.

Early Saturday morning, they left the fairgrounds to transport Comet and Twinkle to the Harrison Street area for the day's activities. Jason had wanted to ride Van Gogh into the downtown area so they wouldn't need to make two trailer runs.

On the short drive over, Dakota remarked, "I hated leaving Kahlo out of the fun, but I know she's not ready to be around noisy crowds like these yet. Maybe next year."

Next year?

Before getting his hopes up, Matt cautioned himself that Dakota hadn't said *she'd* still be around then, only that she thought Kahlo would be up to skijoring in a year.

"Jason's so excited about skiing with his own horse this year," she said. The kid had competed as a rider last year but had trained the horse hard the past few weeks to prepare Van Gogh for his first runs at the festival.

Mama and some of his family would be arriving soon to watch them compete. For some reason, Dakota hadn't wanted his family to know when she'd be on the track, but Mama had insisted on not missing any of their runs. Was Dakota worried about performing well in front of Mama? If so, it could mean she had a lot of respect for his mother's opinion, which warmed his heart.

When Mama asked Matt recently where their relationship might be headed, he hadn't been able to answer. She had to know Dakota was special to him and that they had an intimate relationship, but that wasn't anything he intended to discuss with his mama.

But where were they headed?

I don't know myself.

Dakota took a deep breath as her adrenaline ramped up and she prepared to take off on her first ski run Saturday. Each day, she could ski twice—once with her match team and once with her random draw rider. Earlier, she'd ridden Van Gogh for Jason in their match run. Now she couldn't wait to ski down the course, wondering how it would compare with the one they'd made at the ranch.

All she needed to do to finish in the money would be to have the fastest rides and fastest ski runs down Harrison Street—without penalties.

Piece of cake!

With Matteo as her rider on Comet, she had a good chance of doing that. She knew the speed this horse was capable of, so Matteo had better not hold back on her. Luckily, her second ski run should be good too, because she'd drawn the legendary rider Jeff on his horse Rocket. If she executed fast, clean runs both times, she'd have it in the bag.

Her gaze locked with Matteo's as she waited to start. Once she'd been handed the rope, they'd have four minutes to cross the starting line and onto the track. Not that she'd need that much time.

I am ready!

And between her rides and ski runs in the Sport division and her rides later today in the Open Division for Bruce, a legendary skier, as well as for Matt, she had a chance to score big in both divisions as either skier or rider, depending on the division.

Call me competitive.

The rope had been tied around Comet's saddle horn. An official led Matteo and the horse onto the track before handing her the other end of the rope to hold onto. Gripping it in her left hand and the baton for grabbing rings in her right, Dakota gave Matteo a nod. He surveyed the track briefly and took off. When the slack in the rope grew taut, she jerked onto the track, her arm feeling like it was being pulled out of its socket.

She shifted her focus to the first ring lying just ahead of her first jump. They went from zero to thirty miles an hour, and she easily slipped the baton through to grab the first ring. Any misses of rings or gates would result in penalties, throwing her out of any contention for prize money. Knowing where the rings were located after scouting out the track earlier as Jason's rider gave her an advantage here. Dakota tucked her arms and legs in to reduce the drag, just as Carmella had taught her, before being slung up the four-foot ramp for the first jump and sailing through the air. Nothing was going to slow her down on this run.

Dakota nailed the landing and skied to the opposite side of the track to go through her first gate before veering sharply back to the right for the second jump, nabbing two rings this time. Five rings had been placed on the track. So far, so good. And Matteo pulled her onto this ramp even faster than he had the first. Knowing he had confidence in her abilities made her adrenaline pump even harder. She wanted that overall championship buckle to add to her collection tomorrow.

Exhilarated, she shouted, "Faster!" While he hadn't slacked off as far as she could tell, she didn't want to take any chances losing this great time in the end. She wanted these competitors to know who they were dealing with.

Just wait till next year. I'll be running and *riding in the Open division then.*

Dakota sailed past the second gate, clipping it slightly but not knocking it over, and grabbed her last ring before crossing the track again and getting into her tuck for the last jump. As she started up the ramp, though, her right ski suddenly slid off the edge. She wound up taking the ramp on one ski, her equilibrium off-kilter. She'd need to get it together and nail the landing because if she didn't cross the finish line on both skis, there would be penalties. She pulled her legs in tighter to help control the landing and managed to pull it off somewhat gracefully, considering that slipup.

Matteo glanced backward, apparently aware that something had gone wrong, but didn't slow down. "Keep going! I'm fine!" God love him, but he and Comet didn't let up. He must have trusted her to recover.

Thanks, my cowboy fireman!

Dakota tucked her body tight again for the final gate then crossed over the finish line. She thought she'd made excellent time, despite that little blip with the ski.

Matteo guided Comet to a careful stop on the packed snow, leaped out of his saddle, and sprinted up to her. Still holding onto the horse's reins, he grabbed her upper arms and sized her up and down as if looking for injuries. "You okay? You had me worried."

"Of course, I'm fine! Skijoring is just as big a thrill as nailing a solid eight seconds on a bronc! Just lost my footing for a minute on that last jump, but thanks for not slowing down."

"By the time I looked back, you seemed to have things under control, so I kept booking it."

"Fourteen point ninety-nine seconds for Dakota Mathison with Matt Giordano riding Comet."

Hot damn!

"We did great!" Dakota screamed before throwing her arms around his neck. He lifted her off the ground and kissed her in celebration. When Matteo set her back down again, his lips pressed hard against hers in a deeper kiss that curled her toes in her ski boots. After a few moments, Comet whinnied, and they pulled away to lavish some praise on him too.

"Can't wait to review the video," Dakota said a few minutes later, already wondering how to shave off a little more time tomorrow morning, "but I think I executed a very good assault on the track so far for my first day."

"Sweet Lady, any legendary here would love to post that time. But we'll try and figure out what happened at that one spot and make sure it doesn't happen again."

"Sounds good."

"Dakota, what an incredible run!" She turned to find Matteo's mama approaching them. Mama wrapped her in an embrace Dakota hadn't expected, but she couldn't get over how reassuring it felt to have the woman's approval and encouragement.

"Thanks, Mama! I'm pretty happy with it."

"You might have found a new sport to love," Paul pointed out. "I heard one of the organizers saying he didn't remember ever seeing a rider who also skied on the same day in the same division. Bodacious, I think was how he described it!"

That she'd done something memorable and noteworthy without even realizing it thrilled Dakota even more. "I guess that's why they looked so incredulous when I registered last night. All those changes from cowboy boots to ski boots and back again has been a challenge, but it's been worth it. I love the challenge of combining the two disciplines of skiing and riding—not to mention the speed." Dakota glanced at Matteo whose smile warmed her to the core. "Best of all, skijoring events occur in January to March when I don't have anything else on my schedule. Hopefully, Matteo will let me train at his place next year. He sets up an awesome practice track on the ranch."

"You're always welcome at my ranch, Sweet Lady. You know that."

Well, as long as you're unattached at least.

She wasn't sure any future girlfriends would be as welcoming as he was, especially after the steamy times they'd had together. She'd definitely be considered an old flame to them at this point. They'd burned up the sheets—and whatever else they'd made love on—the past few weeks.

Man, will I ever miss him when it comes time for me to move on.

"I've got to get out of these ski boots and back into my cowboy ones." In about twenty minutes, she'd be riding Van Gogh for Dan, a longtime local skier in the event.

Maybe all the lucky draws were a sign that she was destined to become a legendary herself in the sport of skijoring someday.

Later that afternoon, Matt had needed to cut short his volunteer time with the EMS station in order to prepare for his two ski runs in the Open division. He'd promised the EMS supervisor that he'd volunteer for two hours tomorrow after he finished riding for Dakota in their match in the Sport division.

He'd missed Dakota's ski run with Jeff but heard he gave her an awesome 15.01 second ride. She was sitting in first place for skiing in the Sport division for today. He had no doubt she was destined to win multiple top prizes this weekend—in both divisions. Unbelievable talent!

In his first ski run half an hour ago, his rider and horse, both new to the Leadville event, had pulled Matt through the track at a breakneck speed despite the jumps being a lot higher than in the Sport division. Matt executed a flawless and competition-stealing run through the professional course landing him in first place for now.

There were just two teams separating him from his next run with Dakota. There weren't as many running in the Open division, so his chances of holding onto that lead were good. Dakota came up to him leading Twinkle.

"She's so excited to race again. I hope you're ready for a fast run, Matteo."

"You know it. Comet and Twinkle love the sport, and Van Gogh sure has taken to it too."

Matt gave Dakota a quick kiss before patting Twinkle's neck. "You two go just as fast as you can," he told them. "I'll keep up."

Their names were called, and she got into the saddle and rode to the starting area. After they had gotten the rope situated and taken their places, the announcer gave them the go-ahead and with Matteo's nod, Dakota spurred Twinkle who streaked onto the track. Given how hard the rope yanked his arm, Matt could tell this would be a great run.

He navigated the three alternating jumps and gates grabbing every single ring, until she catapulted him across the finish line for his new personal best time—14.95 seconds.

Damn, his cowgirl could ride!

Dakota ran up to him after dismounting, pulling Twinkle with her. "That was awesome! We flew down the track!"

"Sure did. You and Twinkle were great!"

"And you anticipated every move and jump so well! We make a great team!"

"You said it!"

After a quick kiss, Dakota headed off to cool Twinkle down but said she'd rejoin him soon.

Tony clapped him on the back. "Not bad for an old man."

"Watch the old man jokes, little brother." Rafe glared at Tony before turning to Matt and smiling, lowering his voice so only the two of them could hear. "Your cowgirl sure did give your sorry ass a ride for the money today."

Matt heard the innuendo in Rafe's remark but ignored both his brothers' teasing. His heart raced from the exhilaration of competing with Dakota again.

"Great run, Matteo," Mama said as she gave him a hug and a peck on the cheek. "I'm so proud of you."

"Impressive run, Matt." Paul extended his hand to congratulate him. "Looked like a hell of an adrenaline rush. I might have to look into competing next year."

Mama swatted him on the chest. "You don't need to take up any more dangerous activities, Paul."

"Glad you guys could make it, Sis and Marc," Matt told them.

Angelina approached with Marc's hand in hers, and she gave Matt a big hug. "You two make such a great team!"

"Thanks!" He agreed with his sister's assessment, in more ways than one, but left it at that.

He hoped Dakota would come back for next year's festival because the two of them could become legends in this event in no time with rides and runs like they'd put in today. Of course, he didn't want her to leave in the first place, but seeing her competitive spirit coming out today, it would only be a matter of time before she felt the pull to return to the rodeo world. But at least the Leadville Ski Joring Festival wouldn't conflict with that schedule, and they might even compete in some other skijoring regional events during her downtimes.

On Sunday, Matt and Comet gave Dakota another great time in the Sport division. Coupled with her earlier run with Jeff, which earned her another incredible time, she might have aced top prize for skier in the Sport division. Good thing he hadn't missed watching them this time. After he dismounted, his family—just Mama, Paul, and Rafe today due to work schedules—soon joined in to congratulate them.

"I'm afraid I need to head back over to the EMS station to finish volunteering before my Open division runs later on," Matt apologized.

"Need any more volunteers?" Rafe asked. "My uniform's in the truck."

"We've been accident-free so far, but I'm sure another EMT wouldn't hurt in case we get into a serious situation." The sun was a little warmer today and the track seemed to be getting a little mushy, never a good sign.

Matt turned to Dakota. "I won't get off duty before your ride for Jason, but if things are quiet, I might be able to sneak away, especially with Rafe there now." He needed to volunteer for some other event next time. He was running ragged this year but hadn't usually competed in the Sport division before, either. To his Mama and Paul, he added, "You won't want to miss Dakota riding for Jason's ski run. It should be another great run."

"Can't wait." Mama smiled at first Dakota then Matt. "We'll be here all day."

The group chatted a few more minutes, then Matt gave Mama a kiss on the cheek.

"Why don't I cool Comet down while you go get ready?" Dakota offered.

"That'd be great." He gave her a kiss, wishing all their kisses didn't have to be cut so short today but watched as she set off with the gelding. They might meet up at the trailer before he left for the EMS station, but Rafe would be around, and he didn't want to invite any more teasing.

As he and his brother walked away, Matt suggested that Rafe bring his uniform to the trailer area and change into his uniform there. He let him know the cross streets where they'd parked.

After he'd changed into his uniform, he went outside to wait for Rafe in case he didn't know which trailer was his, but Dakota approached him first.

"You burned up the track again today, Sweet Lady."

"With the help of you and others! Being part of a team is fun and adds more of a challenge." Her phone buzzed, and she glanced down at it furrowing her brows. "I've gotta run."

"What's up?"

"Jason's having a case of nerves, I guess. Worried about the track getting too sloppy. I'll saddle Van Gogh and head over a little early to calm him down." Before she left, Dakota gave him the once-over. "Have I ever told you how sexy you are in that uniform?"

He grinned. "Maybe once or twice, although I thought you preferred me *out* of uniform."

She laughed. "Naked would my preference, now that you mention it. Don't injure anything important on your runs this afternoon. I have plans for you later on tonight."

"You do know that Mama and Paul are staying with us at the ranch tonight, right? I didn't want them driving back at night."

She grinned. "I doubt they'll follow us out to the barn when we bed down the horses for the night. And your mom asked for total control of the kitchen tonight and tomorrow, which I heartily granted."

"I like how you think. We'll get some time alone *and* some of Mama's great meals."

She slapped him on the butt as they parted, and he paused to watch her as she walked away.

My woman is fine, coming and going.

At least he hoped to make her his woman someday.

"Stop staring at her ass and show a little class, Brother." Rafe said.

"I wasn't staring at her—just get in there and get your uniform on. I'm late. I'll meet you there."

Rafe showed up ten minutes after him at the EMS station, and Matteo introduced him to the crew members he hadn't already met at a regional training exercise.

Other than a spectator's minor medical issue, everything remained calm during the first half hour of his shift, but Matt was antsy to see Jason and Dakota's run. Rafe agreed to cover for him for ten or fifteen minutes but would text him if he was needed back at the EMS station.

When he arrived at the track, the team just ahead of Jason was finishing up. He chose a vantage point near the end of the track. Ironically, he would be near the jump that Dakota had almost wiped out on. Matt studied the last jump in the Sport run from the sidelines but didn't see anything amiss. Jason hadn't seemed to have any trouble yesterday, but the track did look a little slushier with a little less punch. That didn't bode well for his own times later on, either.

The announcer called out the names of Jason and Dakota and seconds later the sound of Van Gogh's hooves pounding down Harrison Street followed. He watched the determination on Dakota's face as she gave it her all for Jason. Matt normally didn't worry about her as rider. She knew horses.

He shifted his gaze to Jason, seeing equal determination on his face as he flew through the track. His form looked great and he was familiar with Van Gogh and Dakota both.

As rider and horse whipped past Matt, Jason lined up with the last jump. He started up the ramp perfectly, then the unthinkable happened as he lost traction with his right ski and hurtled off the snow mound, landing hard on the ground. Dakota pulled up on the reins as the rope went slack after Jason lost his grip, aware of the problem but too late to prevent Jason's hard fall. Like all the skiers, he wore a helmet, but Matt worried about broken bones, internal bleeding, or a traumatic brain injury due to the jarring impact as he hit the ground.

Heart in his throat, Matt ran onto the course just as he heard the announcer on the loudspeaker calling for EMS. When he reached the teen's crumpled body, he checked Jason's breathing and whether he had a pulse. Relieved to discover both were present, he looked for any bleeding, but detected no major external bleeds. He continued his initial assessment, albeit without medical instruments. He should have brought something along, but it had been so quiet, he hadn't expected anything like this to happen.

Jason's pupils were equal and responsive to the LED flashlight on Matt's phone. Concerned about a neck or spine injury, Matt held Jason's head still and made sure his airway remained open. How much longer before the paramedic came and took over?

"Jason, it's Matt. You're going to be okay." A spectator brought him a blanket, and Matt instructed them to cover Jason to keep him from going into shock; the snow-covered ground had to be frigid. "Just take it easy, Jason. Help is on the way."

"How is he?" Dakota hunkered down on one knee beside him, her other leg trembling uncontrollably.

"He'll be fine. The ambulance crew is on the way." Matt didn't want to say anything Jason might overhear, but his being unconscious this long didn't look good in his opinion.

Damn it. Why Jason?

Chapter Twenty

"I knew something was wrong when the rope went slack but by the time I could rein in Van Gogh and slow him down, it was too late."

Matt wished he could take Dakota into his arms right now and hold her now to reassure her that she hadn't done anything wrong, but he couldn't let go of Jason's head.

"You did everything anyone could do in that situation."

Jason's parents came running up, Annette screaming his name in near hysterics. "Open your eyes, Jason! It's Mom. Please, open your eyes for me!"

Matt glanced up at Darren, an engineer at the firehouse, and silently pleaded with the boy's dad to get his wife away so that she wouldn't freak out their son.

"Come on, Annette," Darren said, wrapping his arm around her and forcefully pulling her away just as the EMS crew arrived on the scene. "We need to let them do their jobs."

Matt shared his initial assessment with the paramedic, and she checked Jason's vitals.

"Anything I can do?" Rafe asked.

"Yeah, take Dakota over there while they finish their examination." He pointed to the place where Matt had recently stood. He glanced over to see Paul walking Van Gogh around in a circle to start cooling him down after his race had ended so abruptly.

Dakota would probably regain her composure soon enough and take charge of the horse again, but at the moment, she was nearly as upset as Jason's mom. He'd have thought she'd dealt with lots of rodeo accidents in her career, but perhaps she cared more about Jason than she did those rodeo cowboys.

Refocusing his attention on Jason, he continued to hold his head still as the EMT applied the neck brace. The paramedic reported that Jason's blood pressure had dropped to a dangerously low level, indicating shock might be setting in. Seconds later, an ambulance pulled up, and Matt helped load Jason into the back.

A blast from the air horn forced the crowd to part so they could transport him to the trauma center. Matt looked on until Rafe and Dakota rejoined him.

"Head to the hospital." Rafe said.

"I still have an hour left on my shift."

"The supervisor said he can spare you." His brother squeezed his shoulder supportively. "Go! I'll cover the rest of your shift."

"Thanks." No doubt Rafe knew Matt wouldn't be of much use to them given his current state of mind. While he hated to shirk his duties, he needed to find out how extensive Jason's injuries were.

"I'll get my truck and drive us to the hospital," Paul said.

"Thanks. I'll find someone to take care of the horses in case we don't get back for a while," Matt said.

"Already took care of that," Paul assured him.

"Van Gogh!" Dakota searched frantically for the horse as if remembering him for the first time.

"It's okay," Paul reassured her, patting her on the back. "I took him back to the trailer after the accident, and the cowboy volunteers are going to make sure your trailer and horses make it back to the fairgrounds tonight."

"I appreciate you taking care of that, Paul." Matt had nothing else to worry about now except for Jason. He didn't even care about missing his own runs this afternoon.

"I can't believe I deserted Van Gogh like that," Dakota said, wringing her hands. "My main thought was with Jason, and I just handed the reins to someone in a festival jacket."

"You did the right thing." Matt rubbed her arm through her coat before turning to Paul to find out where they'd parked. "We'll meet you at your vehicle after we grab some things from our horse trailer."

"Why don't we just pick you both up near your trailer then?" Paul suggested. "Save some time."

Matt nodded and took Dakota's hand, wondering where her gloves were. Her hands were as cold as ice. Of course, she might be experiencing the shock of the accident herself. On the way to the horse trailer, he tried to stop her from beating herself up.

"You didn't do anything wrong, Dakota. Jason just didn't recover from the slip of the ski. But your reaction time was as fast as it could be." She remained silent and he continued, "Don't be too hard on yourself."

"Working on a team is a lot harder than just being responsible for myself." Her words were almost inaudible, but he heard them.

Matt squeezed her hand. "But being on a team can make you twice as strong too. I don't know that I could have handled it any better."

He dealt with injuries and accidents every day on the job, but when it hit close to home, he couldn't handle it emotionally. Detachment would be hard to find with Jason's injury.

This was going to be a long night.

Dakota couldn't stop shaking or get warm. They'd been waiting in the emergency department for what seemed like hours but probably hadn't been that long. Matteo took her hand, which felt so cold inside his warmer one, then brought Dakota to her feet.

"He'll be okay," Matteo assured her, but she didn't believe him.

What if I killed him?

All to get a faster time.

Matteo gave her a hug that helped warm her somewhat, and she felt the loss of his heat when he pulled away and sat down on the two-person bench nearby. But he immediately pulled her onto his lap and wrapped his arms around her.

"These things happen sometimes. You nearly wiped out on the same jump." His words provided little comfort.

"But everything had been going perfectly with the run. I don't know how—"

"Shh." He pressed her head against his shoulder and stroked her hair. Surrendering, she let him envelop her in his warmth and security as he continued to try to ease her mind.

"It's not your fault, Sweet Lady. You have no control over how the skier takes the jumps other than going slower. How would you have felt if I rode slower on your ski runs?"

"I'd have been pissed."

"Well, Jason's competitive too. Nobody blames you, Sweet Lady."

Irrational or not, Dakota still blamed herself but wouldn't say anything more to Matteo. She glanced across the room to the doors leading to the examination rooms. Jason's parents hadn't come out yet to say how Jason was doing. How much longer would it take?

Several guys from the fire station had arrived too, none in uniform but she recognized them all the same. She loved the sense of family within the firefighting community. They pulled together in good times and, like today, in bad. She'd never had anyone waiting for her when she'd been bucked off and taken to the ED. Jason wasn't even a member of the fire station, but he was the son of a firefighter and therefore family.

Time passed at a snail's pace, something she remembered from her own times waiting to be evaluated in the ED. Mama sat next to Paul and continued to pray her rosary. Dakota never gave religion a second thought but offered up healing vibes to the universe, in case they would help.

She must have dozed after a while, comfortable in Matteo's arms but awoke when she felt his body stiffen. Jason's dad came through the double doors. Dakota sat up and waited for an update.

"Wow! What's everyone doing here?"

"We just wanted to be here for you guys," Lieutenant Paske said, "and check on Jason's condition."

Darren smiled. "Jason's going to be okay."

Everyone in the waiting room cheered but soon muffled the noise to a sedate level. Dakota noticed that even some people who appeared to be awaiting news about other patients joined in.

Community.

Some of the tension left Dakota's body.

"Thank you, God," Matteo muttered.

"For real." Dakota slid off Matteo's lap, somewhat embarrassed now at her show of weakness and neediness, but she'd needed to be held by Matteo until she'd been assured Jason hadn't died.

"He's got a mild concussion but no brain bleeds. He also has a broken arm," Darren continued, "but he's going to be okay, which is all that matters. They're keeping him overnight but looks like he's out of the woods."

Matteo took her by the hand as they moved closer to Jason's dad who continued speaking, not just to them but to everyone else who'd shown up. "You guys don't have to hang around tonight, but..." his voice cracked, "...we appreciate your support and your being here for us."

Before leaving the ED, several firefighters wished them well and told Darren to call on them for anything they needed in the days and weeks to come.

Dakota wasn't sure what to say, feeling responsible for the accident, but when they approached Jason's dad, Darren asked if he could give her a hug. Taken aback, she nodded. A bear of a man, he wrapped his arms around her then whispered, "Don't worry. He's going to be fine."

Tears stung her eyes that he'd actually be reassuring her as they pulled apart. She cleared the tightness from her throat and met his gaze. "Let me know if there's anything I can do for you or Annette. And tell Jason we'll take good care of Van Gogh until he can get back out to the ranch."

Darren nodded. "That'll make him feel a lot better. He's already asking if his horse is okay."

Matteo gave his friend a bear hug. "Anything you guys need, just let me know."

"I appreciate that, brother. The other engineers have offered to swap shifts with me—I could probably milk this for a getaway to the beach for a week or so." The men exchanged a laugh, several slapping him on the back, before he said he needed to get back to his wife and son. Jason's dad hit the buzzer to be allowed into the back.

Dakota turned around to find Paul and Mama standing and waiting for them. They walked outside together. "We'll take you out to where you're parked," Paul said. "Need any help with the horses?"

"I think we've got it," Matteo answered, then thought again. "Actually, Paul, if you could hang out with Van Gogh while we run Comet and Twinkle home first, that would be great. And thanks for taking care of him after the accident. I really need to get myself a bigger trailer."

"I know a guy who has a decent four-horse trailer for sale. If you want to check it out, let me know," Paul offered.

"That would be great, Paul." The man was only about ten or twelve years older than Rafe, but he came across to Dakota as a fatherly figure to Mama's kids, even if they didn't see him that way. But then they had memories of their papa that would make it hard to see anyone else in that role.

Paul turned toward his wife. "Angela, why don't you go on back to the ranch and relax?"

She took his hand and looked up at her husband as the four walked toward the truck. "I'll stay with you and Van Gogh."

The two shared a smile. "Sounds good to me."

After settling into the back seat next to Mama and behind Matteo, Dakota took a long, slow breath. Mama reached across the seat to squeeze her hand. "Everything's going to be okay. Kids are resilient. Trust me. With four boys, this I know."

Dakota nodded. Jason would be fine it seemed, but Dakota had some decisions to make. Not the least of which would be postponing her return to the rodeo circuit. She felt partially to blame for this predicament, regardless of whether she could have prevented anything. Matteo would need help with the horses, especially on the days he worked. She might offer to help Darren and Annette too, while Jason was laid up. Was her cooking ability strong enough to take over a dinner or two when they got home?

Don't go overboard. Just pick up something for them from the café.

Oddly enough, though, the thought of staying longer at Matteo's ranch, rather than kicking off the rodeo season, didn't upset her as much as it would have last December when all she'd wanted to do was get back to the rodeo.

Dakota wasn't sure what that meant and didn't intend to analyze it right now.

Lying in bed later that night with Dakota curled against his side and her head resting on his chest, Matt stared up at the ceiling—not that he could actually see anything in the dark room. He would never have wished for anything bad to happen to Jason, but while getting the horses bedded down in the barn tonight, Dakota had offered to stick around until April.

A reprieve, but for all the wrong reasons.

While he wanted her to stay for him, rather than out of a sense of obligation, it would buy him more time to win her over. At some point, he would have to find another high-school kid to help out when Jason left for college in August.

He'd rather have Dakota stick around but didn't intend to bring that up with her. That she planned to stay a while longer to help out worked for him. He'd take whatever he could get.

"You okay, Sweet Lady?"

She nodded before returning her head to rest on his pecs. He brushed her hair in long strokes, the strawberry scent wafting to his nose. He loved having her here like this. It would have been a rough night to be alone.

Seeing Jason's crumpled body on the course—not knowing whether he was dead or alive until he'd performed his initial assessment—had taken a few years off his life. Still, Matt hadn't been able to do much to help him in those first few minutes. Maybe he should think about going back to school for more medical training.

"What are you thinking about?" she asked.

"That I'm grateful the ambulance arrived so quickly."

"They were amazing. But you helped to stabilize him immediately. I'm glad you came over to watch us."

He shrugged. "Without any gear, there wasn't much I could do. Scared the hell out of me. Even though I'm supposed to handle an emergency like that with professionalism, it's different when it's someone you know and love."

"I can't imagine, but seeing you take charge like that—well, it was pretty damned awesome." Dakota placed a kiss on his chest and rolled onto her side. "We'd better get some sleep."

"Good night." After a moment, she asked, "Matteo?"

"Yeah, babe?"

"Do you have any idea how loud this bed squeaks?" She rolled onto her back again, and he noticed the squeak for the first time. "How am I going to face your mama over the breakfast table after that?"

Having Mama and Paul just down the hall suddenly seemed a little awkward.

"I'm afraid to move and have her hear the bed creaking and think we're having sex in here."

He chuckled. "But we aren't." Plans for a quickie in the barn hadn't materialized given their tattered nerves after they'd returned from loading up the trailer after they'd left the hospital.

They'd just happened to make it back in time for the awards, though. They'd both taken first place for their Saturday runs—she in the Sport division and he in the Open. Dakota had also won for Sunday's ski runs, giving her the overall best. He hadn't been eligible for overall after having to forfeit his rides after Jason's accident but was thrilled for Dakota. He'd almost thought she'd wear her shiny new buckle to bed with her, but it lay beside her prize Ski Joring Festival jacket on the dresser instead.

"How do you know they aren't doing the deed themselves right now?"

She raised up on her elbow to meet his gaze, wincing when she heard the bed squeak again. "Do not make my mind go there, Matteo!"

"Hey, believe me, I don't want to picture Mama and Paul having sex either." He gave an exaggerated shudder. "But come on. After such a long, stressful day, my guess is that they're sound asleep by now."

She thought it over a while and lay back down but didn't turn away this time.

"Besides, Mama's had five kids and two husbands. I'm sure she knows what men and women do in bed."

"Even when it's her son with someone he isn't married to? She seems kinda religious to me."

The thought of being married to this woman sounded like the perfect solution to that problem, but you can't put strings on a tumbleweed. He had no idea how long she planned to stick around after Jason healed up. Dakota was nowhere near ready for settling down.

"Mama's a realist. She knows she didn't raise any Italian monks. Even Angelina lived with Marc before they tied the knot."

"Well, it's still going to feel a little awkward. I'm not used to having parental figures in my life that I have to please or appease."

She never said anything about her own mother. He wondered if she even remembered her.

"Consider my mama your mama. She thinks the world of you already."

She brought herself up on an elbow again and met his gaze. "You think so?" She wasn't going to get any sleep at this rate.

"I know so. She was as proud of you after your runs as she was of me after mine."

"That means a lot to me." He couldn't see her face clearly but noticed her voice had grown thick with emotion.

"I'm pretty proud of you too, Sweet Lady."

She bent down to give him a quick kiss before pulling the covers over her and snuggling closer to him.

"Good night, Matteo."

"Night, sweetheart."

Her breathing evened out soon after, and he wondered if she'd even heard him. At least one of them could sleep now. He wasn't sure he'd be able to for a while. This day had felt more like a week. But they sure had ended it on a great note.

Dakota and Matteo came in from the barn to the smell of bacon and eggs. Her stomach growled in appreciation. His mama made even simple food smell and taste out of this world.

"Get out of those wet things and cleaned up for breakfast," Mama ordered. "It will be ready in five minutes."

Maybe Matteo was right, and Mama thought of her as one of her kids now. Dakota smiled as she removed her outerwear and boots before the two of them went to his bedroom and stripped out of their muddy jeans. Matteo also removed his shirt, giving her a view that took her breath away. To distract herself, she ran a brush through her hair. "I can get used to having your mama cooking for us. Just saying."

"You'll be cooking like a pro in no time. Your first lesson at Angelina's is coming up, isn't it?"

"*Our* first lesson, remember?"

He gave her a lopsided grin. "I was hoping to be the official taste tester instead."

She waggled her finger at him. "Not a chance, fireman. How did you not learn how to cook at the fire station, you working 48-hour shifts and all?"

He shrugged. "I hear Rafe isn't much better in Aspen Corners, and Tony used to stop by to help out with the cooking on our big brother's shifts."

"Well, you're going to have a heart attack if you keep eating those to-go meals. They'll make you fat."

His mouth opened wide with indignation. He pressed his hand over his shirtless waist. "Not an ounce of fat on this body."

She laughed, appreciating the view. "I didn't say it's there now, but what about ten years from now when you have a beer belly?"

"Are you saying I need to give up beer too, woman?"

She grinned. "Not around me, because I sure don't intend to."

It occurred to her that they sounded like they'd been married for years when they hadn't even been together more than a couple months. The thought of being married to Matteo left her with a warm spot in her heart.

In their clean clothes, they returned to the kitchen hand in hand and soon were seated at the table across from the older couple.

After the platter of bacon and toast, as well as a bowl of scrambled eggs, had been passed around the table once, Mama asked, "Guess what Paul and I did right after the New Year?"

Dakota didn't know how to answer, but Matteo stopped chewing his bacon and swallowed. "What's that?"

"We did DNA testing!" Mama smiled, waiting for their reactions. Dakota didn't say anything as it didn't really affect her.

Matt swallowed, a puzzled look on his face. "I thought you already knew where you're from—Sicily."

She shrugged. "True. I'm three-quarters southern European—no surprise there—and the rest of my DNA is from other areas of eastern and northern Europe. No, nothing unusual came up for me, but Paul's results were much more interesting." She turned toward her husband and waited for him to continue the story.

Paul nodded, setting down his fork. "I'm about half Eastern European and half Native American."

"That's cool!" Matteo said. "I've always wanted to have Native American blood."

"Well, I pretty much knew that part already—from my mother's side—but that's not the fascinating part." He glanced at Mama who smiled encouragingly before Paul turned toward Matteo and Dakota alternately. "The big surprise was finding a half brother in the system—one I didn't know anything about before now."

"Holy—" as if remembering his mama sat at the table, Matteo altered whatever he'd started to say "—crap! Have you met him yet?"

He shook his head. "He lives in Canada. I'm guessing my dad and his mom hooked up while Dad worked some pipeline jobs up there. He's older than me and was born before Dad married my mom."

Dakota didn't really hear much more of the conversation as her mind latched onto the idea of doing a DNA test of her own. Could anyone from her past be looking for her in some database? What if it was someone she didn't really want to be reunited with? The only person Dakota really wanted to find would be the grandmother she'd been having dreams about.

"Did he reach out to you first?" Dakota asked, curious how this worked.

"Actually, I initiated contact," Paul explained. "The very day the results came in, I saw the close connection and sent him a message asking for details of his parentage and birth. Surprisingly, he came back pretty fast confirming that we shared the same dad."

If she took the test, would she be able to control where her information went? Without knowing the name of the woman she called *Nana*, could she inadvertently reach out to someone connected to the asshole who had taken her away?

Dakota shuddered, and Matteo squeezed her hand until she made eye contact. "You okay?"

She nodded. "Just a chill." A total lie, but she wasn't ready to say more about this now.

"Want me to light the fireplace?"

"No. I'm fine." She needed to move the focus away from her. "Paul, tell us more about this half brother of yours. Are you planning to keep in touch with him?"

Matteo searched her face a moment until she almost became too uncomfortable before he turned back toward Paul, who was telling them how he hoped to take Mama on a trip to Alberta sometime to meet this newfound brother.

Dakota didn't remember much else from breakfast. The wheels continued to spin in her head about the possibility of opening up a Pandora's box, which could happen if she put her DNA out there. Was she ready for the fallout of such an action?

No clue. But I want to know who I am. And if Nana is looking for me.

Chapter Twenty-One

As he cuddled with Dakota on the couch Monday night watching some movie he couldn't remember the name of, Matt could tell something was bothering her. Dakota had been aloof all day after Mama and Paul had left. He'd tried to coax her out of her silence, but she'd insisted everything was fine and had remained tight-lipped.

Was she already regretting her offer to stick around while Jason's arm healed? If she didn't want to stay, he might as well cut the rope now.

"You know, anytime you need to be somewhere else while Jason's recovering, I can find someone to help with the horses on my shift days."

Dakota sat up and turned to meet his gaze, her eyes growing wide. "Are you tired of me being here already?"

What? "Hell, no! Nothing like that. You just seem to be a million miles away tonight. I thought maybe you had regrets."

She glanced back at the television a moment before returning her focus to him. "Sorry about that. I've just…had something on my mind."

"Anything you want to talk about?"

She nibbled her lower lip between her teeth and took a while before answering. "Not sure I'm ready yet."

This didn't sound good. "Well, I'm here whenever you are."

She nodded. "I appreciate that." She settled against his shoulder again, and they returned to watching the movie, although it was a lost cause for him at this point. He hoped it would be over soon.

Matteo idly stroked her hair, trying to relieve some of the tension she seemed to be under. He wished she'd tell him what was bothering her, but Dakota was a private person. She'd let him know what was going on eventually—he hoped.

Then again, maybe he needed to push her a bit. The minute the movie ended, he said, "I'm worried about you, Sweet Lady. If nothing else, I'm a good listener. Maybe I can help."

She scooted away and searched his eyes a moment. "Sorry, Matteo. I'm…" He waited, but then she said, "I think I'll turn in early."

Matt tried to hide his disappointment. That she didn't trust him enough to confide in him hurt his pride. Nevertheless, he couldn't force her to open up to him. He sighed.

Give her time.

"I have to get up early for work. Might as well join you." He stood and helped her up from the couch then walked with her to their bedroom. Dakota immediately picked up her toiletries bag and phone and walked toward the bathroom.

"Holler if you need me to wash your back." he said only half-jokingly.

She turned toward him, but there was no spark of interest. "Not tonight. I'm beat. But thanks." Her smile didn't reach her eyes.

What the hell was wrong? Had he unknowingly said or done something to upset her? While he waited for her to return, he thought back over the time they'd spent together after Mama and Paul left but couldn't remember saying anything insensitive that might have upset her.

Was she still upset about Jason's accident? The woman had proven to be as strong as he, even stronger in some ways. She didn't freak out worrying about him every time he went to work, so he'd decided to cut her some slack too.

Not that he'd ever totally stop worrying about her.

Matt lay in bed the longest time waiting for Dakota to come back out, although it probably was only about fifteen minutes. He didn't hear her run the shower, but she'd probably taken one before the movie like he had, now that he thought about it. Maybe she was in there scrolling through phone or email messages, not that her phone ever seemed to ping. Was she looking up rodeo events to register for? After all, it was only a matter of time before her reason for sticking around here would end, and she'd return to the rodeo.

When the bathroom door opened, she came out dressed in the long T-shirt she'd worn her first night at his place. She'd said she wasn't interested in having sex tonight, but he wished she'd worn those long johns instead. He'd had so many fantasies of her in that nightshirt, including some they'd already acted out.

Get your mind on her and not her body.

Matt just wanted to lighten her mood or take away whatever she was worrying about. He pulled the comforter back and patted the mattress; Dakota crawled into the bed and curled up beside him, face to face. At least she wasn't physically distancing herself. *Nice.* Maybe she wasn't mad at him then, just…preoccupied about something.

"What are your plans for tomorrow?" he asked, hoping to get her to talk about something, anything.

Dakota stiffened, making him even more curious about what was going on. "Taking care of the horses. Might take Kahlo for a ride after neglecting her for three days. I can let the others hang out in the corral. Maybe go into town a while."

Nothing new about any of that. "Great. Why don't you stop by the station if you go into Leadville?" He loved it when she found a reason to stop by, which she did at least once during most of his shifts.

"I'll try." After another long pause, she said, "Matteo, I envy you knowing who your people are. Having such a strong, loving family."

Is that's what had been on her mind all day?

"Mama and Papa made family a priority. I suppose that's one of the reasons they kept us connected to our relatives here and back in Italy. Growing up, I used to spend summers in Sicily with my Nonna."

She stiffened, but before he could ask her why, she revealed something he hadn't expected. "I've been having dreams about my Nana." Not wanting to interrupt, he waited for her to tell him more. "But I have no memory of her except for what's been in my dreams. I don't even know what's real or what her name was, other than Nana." She paused a moment, and Matt kissed her forehead.

At this point, she hadn't told him anything about her dreams—or nightmares—but having no memory of someone as important as her grandmother had to be difficult.

"That has to be frustrating." He couldn't imagine a life without having had Nonna in it, however briefly, but he'd been a teenager before he'd known what Nonna's given name was. She'd always just been Nonna to him and his siblings.

Both their grandmothers had passed before Rafe had been born, but all the kids had formed a special bond with Mama's grandmother.

"She called me *Pumpkin* in the dream, so I don't know my actual name, either."

That confused him. "Isn't it Alison?"

She hesitated several moments, then shook her head. "I don't think so. I remember him giving me that name before we moved to Aspen Corners, but there were others before that—I remember Becca and Samantha earlier in my life. But if he kept changing my name, I doubt any of them was my birth name."

Matteo pulled away to search her eyes. What on earth was she talking about? "Who's *he*?"

She didn't meet his gaze. "The man who I believe took me from my grandmother."

"Took you?"

She nodded. "I think I was kidnapped when I was around five or six." What the hell had she gone through? "One of my nightmares showed that scene to me. I thought it was nonsense, but it seemed so real that I'm starting to believe it happened."

"You're sure your mind didn't conjure something up? I've certainly had some insane dreams lately that aren't based in reality." He remembered how vivid the one where she'd been injured in a car accident had been. Thank God *that* had been a total figment of his imagination—caused by the stress he'd felt at the idea of losing her, perhaps.

She weighed his words a moment. "Could be, but my gut says it's real. Growing up, I always felt like something was off with that guy. We moved around a lot."

"Pipeline jobs, right?"

She bit the inside of her lower lip. Would she tell him the truth this time? Did she trust him enough yet to reveal her secrets? Or did she even know what the truth was? Had she been lied to as a kid?

"I don't think so, actually. Honestly, whatever he did I think it was illegal. Maybe he dealt in drugs." She shuddered, and he pulled her closer and stroked her cheek. "All I know is that he gave us new names and dyed my hair a new color—well, any color but red—at every place we resettled."

"I thought you said you dyed your own hair in high school."

She shook her head. "No. But I remember having black, blonde, and brown hair, anything but my natural color. I suppose it would have been too recognizable if anyone from my past searched for me." She sighed. "Maybe no one ever did."

Her voice cracked, and he pulled her head down onto his chest, stroking her head and hair. "I doubt that's true, but it's such a big country, and he didn't keep you in any one place long enough for anyone to find you. Besides, Amber Alerts didn't become a thing until you were already an adult."

"Yeah, I don't know how anyone would have recognized me anyway." She was quiet a moment as he continued to stroke her hair. "I don't even know why he wanted me so badly, because he hardly had anything to do with my life other than trying to control me as much as he could."

His chest grew damp from her tears, breaking his heart. "Matteo, I don't even know who I am." The anguish in her voice broke his heart.

"Shh." He couldn't imagine not knowing who he was or where he came from. "That has to be scary and unsettling, but pieces are coming back to you. Maybe you'll remember the whole truth at some point."

"I don't see how. I've blocked most of it out for so many years. These dreams only started after I came here."

That admission meant a lot to him. "I've heard that sometimes you have to feel safe before you can unblock past traumatic memories." Did that mean she felt safe here with him?

I hope so.

Now, how could he try and fix this?

Still, he couldn't get over the magnitude of what she was telling him. "So who do you think kidnapped you?" Perhaps the authorities would have a missing person's report on her, but without knowing which state or name to search under, there wasn't much he could do. She might even have been pronounced dead by now.

"That's partly what's going on with me tonight. I've been thinking about doing that DNA testing thing."

"Like Mama and Paul did?"

She nodded. "I don't know of any other way to connect to people I can't remember the names of, although…"

He waited, but when she didn't say more, he asked, "What are you worried most about?"

More silence. Just when he figured she wouldn't be answering she said, "Finding him."

"The man who took you away from your grandmother?"

She nodded.

"What makes you think he's related to you?"

"In one of my dreams, Nana mentioned a court granting her custody of me. And he argued with her that I was his kid." She shuddered and curled up closer to Matt. "I'm afraid of him, Matteo."

Matt's heart raced. Had this guy sexually molested or abused her in any way? The man had a weird vibe about him, but if Matt had been aware the man had been harming Alison in any way, he'd have kicked down that door and taken her to a safer place—probably in his own home. Mama and Papa would have taken her in without question.

"Not physical abuse. Just wanting to manage my every move."

"I remember he didn't like you hanging out with me beyond the time needed for our 4-H activities."

She lifted her head and met his gaze. "I think you scared him." She grinned ever so briefly. "He thought you'd take me away from him once I turned eighteen. So he planned to pack us up the night we graduated and move somewhere else. I'd had enough by then and would turn eighteen that October, so I decided it was time to live my own life. I hiked to Frisco and found someone traveling west on I-70 who dropped me off in Utah."

He stared at her as if she'd grown another head. "You hitchhiked all the way to Utah?"

She grinned. "Calm down. I took a handgun and bullets from his arms collection, so I would have been able to protect myself if anyone tried anything. And I was lucky to find one person who could take me that far away."

He sighed. "Woman, do you know how freaked out I was that you accepted a ride to Leadville when your truck broke down Christmas Day? Luckily, you were offered a ride from someone decent, but who knows who could have stopped to pick you up that morning and what might have happened to you?"

"Relax, Matteo. I mean it. Nothing happened either time." He wondered how many other times she'd put herself in danger over the years. She rested her head in the crook of his shoulder again with her hand on his chest over his wildly beating heart.

"In Utah, I worked on a ranch and eventually put my skills at barrel race and cattle roping to use in a local rodeo. Turned out to be the beginnings of my career in rodeo."

"I'm glad it all worked out well for you." *And that you survived.*

"Me too." She remained silent a while, and he wondered if she'd fallen asleep. Then she continued. "I've had to look over my shoulder every day since I ran away. Had to make up yet another new name. At least I got to stop dying my hair. I'd honestly forgotten that I'd ever been a redhead."

"Well, you know how I feel about your red hair."

She nodded, then spoke in a near whisper. "Matteo, I never knew when he'd find me and take me away again."

"That's a lousy way to live, but he can't do that ever again."

"Sure can't. I haven't been watching over my shoulder since I came here. Not that he couldn't show up, but I've decided not to give him that much power over my life anymore."

Was this guy the reason she carried a handgun with her all the time? Not that she shouldn't be prepared to protect herself from any other asshole who might come after her too.

He kissed her on the forehead. "Proud of you." He'd better make sure he had a handgun with him at all times when they were together, in case there ever was a threat against her.

She lifted her head again and beamed at him, despite her tear-clumped eyelashes. "I have a confession to make."

He cocked his head and waited.

"Earlier, in the bathroom, I ordered one of the DNA test kits."

So that's what had taken her so long in there.

"I hope you find what you're looking for, but is there any way someone could track you down through that?"

"I don't see how. It seems very private. Everything's done by email." She paused then added, "and I made up a new username that hides my current identity. Even opened a new email account, just in case."

"Good thinking. With the notoriety Dakota Mathison has out West here, you can't be too careful. Don't want some nut job showing up at one of your events."

"You and me both."

Matt wondered if he'd be able to spot the guy if he turned up in Leadville. It had been a long time, and he could have changed his appearance in addition to aging.

In some ways, Matt wanted to meet up with him just to give him his due for what he'd done to Alison—no, *Dakota*. She'd been Dakota longer than Alison and all those other fake names combined. Clearly, that's who she identified as now.

He preferred Dakota too. The name fit her personality more. He couldn't imagine calling her anything else.

Dakota sat at the kitchen table staring down at the kit that had arrived today, only a week after ordering. She wished she hadn't told Matteo she'd sent away for one, in case she chickened out and threw it away unused. She didn't want him to think her a coward, but this truly was the riskiest thing she'd ever done since running away from that man.

Would she find a distant cousin or someone else who could lead her to other living relatives, namely the woman she called Nana in her dreams? Or would she be inviting that jerk back into her life? He'd claimed she belonged to him—did he mean biologically or by some other relationship?

Matteo came in the door, brushing lingering snowflakes off his coat. Earlier, she'd asked if he could take care of the horses without her, thinking she'd deal with the DNA kit in his absence, but here she sat with the package yet to be opened.

"I'll be glad when the weather warms up." Matteo removed his hat and boots. When he glanced at the table, his face lit up. "Hey, is that the DNA kit?"

She nodded, not as enthusiastic as he was about it. "Now I'm afraid to do it."

There. I just admitted to him that I'm afraid of something.

"Why? This could be the answer to finding your family." He shrugged out of his coat and hung it on a peg near the door.

"But what if I don't find the people I want to have in my life?"

"Then you ignore the rest and move on. Hell, you don't have to respond to anyone if you don't want to. And if you do have to resort to letter writing at some point, just set up another PO box in Aspen or Breck or somewhere they can't trace you to. We can check it when we visit my family."

She hadn't thought of that. "I guess I could." She stared at the package again. What excuse did she have now?

None. Just put on your big girl panties and do it.

She picked up the box and opened it, reading over the instructions while Matteo went to the spare bathroom to wash up.

"Sounds simple enough," she told him when he returned.

I can spit. No problem.

But she didn't intend to do it in front of Matteo. "I'll be back in a few."

She carried the kit into his bedroom, did the deed, closed the vial, and put it into the postage-paid envelope. She'd give it to Matteo to mail in town Monday when he went to work. No need to make a special trip. She wasn't in any hurry after all these years.

"All done," she announced when she returned to the room.

"Why don't we take it to the post office now and then grab some supper in town?"

So much for stalling two more days.

Maybe he noticed she hadn't put anything on to eat, although she'd told him she'd do so while he was in the barn. Her focus had totally been on that kit.

"I'm in the mood for a filet at Quincys." Matteo wasn't referring to a fish fillet, either. The man loved his steaks, but luckily, so did she.

"Sounds good." As distracted as she was, she'd probably burn the kitchen down if she tried to make anything for them tonight.

Twenty minutes later, they were in his truck heading toward Leadville. The envelope with the spit vial inside lay on her lap ready to be dropped off.

Please don't let this be a disastrous decision.

She wasn't a praying person, but maybe the universe would hear her and come to her assistance.

When Matteo pulled up to the mail chute, she stared at the package one last time before handing it to him to toss inside. And then it was done. No turning back now.

"You're awfully quiet," Matteo said ten minutes later after they'd been seated inside the old-fashioned tavern.

"Still concerned about what that test might stir up, I guess."

"Think positively. You might find your nana after all these years."

She nodded. That would be the perfect outcome. Matteo was right, of course. She had control over whether she chose to reach out to or respond to anyone. What was another fake identity in her life at this point?

Matteo squeezed her hand from across the table. “Stop worrying. Everything will turn out as it’s meant to be.”

She gave him a weak smile. “I love your optimism.”

“Mama always says most of what you worry about doesn’t even happen. So no point worrying about stuff you can’t control.”

“She’s a smart woman.”

Matteo nodded. “That she is.”

Besides, Dakota never used to be a worrier, so why start now? She picked up the menu to see what sounded good and pushed away any more thoughts about that stupid DNA kit.

A week went by, and a constant feeling of unease settled into the pit of Dakota’s stomach, as if she were waiting for the next shoe to drop. The instructions on the DNA kit said it could be six to eight weeks before she’d receive her emailed link to the results, so why was she expecting to hear from them so soon? While she couldn’t name where her insecurity sprang from, she wished it would go away.

Everything with Matteo had been going well, and even though the current rodeo season had begun, she didn’t mind sticking around a while longer at Matteo’s ranch while Jason’s arm healed.

She’d had a blast at the skijoring festival earlier this month, and she and Matteo had even played around on his home course a couple times since then. If she were honest with herself, she didn’t really miss being on the circuit yet. The work of riding broncs took a brutal toll on her body, and the pay got lower all the time for her in the unsanctioned saddle bronc events that permitted women to compete. Maybe the male egos were too fragile to be beaten by a woman.

She gave a mental shrug, not concerned about them in the least.

There was good money in riding bulls—for the guys on the pro circuit, at least. While she might not get rich doing the rogue events, she did need to decide where she wanted to go when she left here. Maybe it was time to take the bull by the horns, so to speak, and conquer that unmet challenge. She'd never let herself be bested by the broncs, so why do so with those one-ton ornery creatures?

Dakota whipped out her phone and looked up the class schedule for nearby bull-riding schools. One within a ninety-minute drive offered a four-day session next month. *Perfect.* Jason should be as good as new by then, so on the days Matteo worked, she wouldn't have to worry about taking care of the horses.

She checked the registration fee and should be able to cover it. She filled out the online interest form telling them of her qualifications. Hopefully, they'd accept her.

As an added bonus, this would give her something to occupy her thoughts while waiting on the DNA test results.

Yeah, she totally needed some distractions. Maybe if Matteo had been home, she'd have mentioned her plans, but knowing him, he'd just try and talk her out of it.

I definitely need to get back in the game if I want any chance of returning to rodeo life.

What else do I know?

Chapter Twenty-Two

Three Weeks Later

Matt had spent three of his days off this week in Glenwood Springs working his April commitment to the U.S. Forest Service but was glad to finally be on his way home.

God, I miss Dakota.

When the forest ranger in charge said they'd accomplished everything they'd set out to do, Matt hit the road. Normally, he'd have hung out to have a few beers with the other men and women who'd been part of the mission, but not this time. He didn't have to be back on shift until the day after tomorrow, which meant he'd be able to spend a whole day with Dakota.

Matt became a lovesick puppy every time they were apart. But she'd stuck around to help while Jason was healing. Another week or so and Jason would be as good as new. With rodeos popping up everywhere now, Matt expected Dakota to be heading off to compete any day. He could already tell she was getting restless.

Matt pushed away his worries about her leaving. He'd enjoy the time they had together. But it sucked that he had to leave *her* to keep his monthly commitment to the forest service when all he wanted to do was spend every moment they had left together.

Man, you have it bad.

And he had a job to do. He'd never shirk his responsibilities to the fire service, whether here at home or wherever he was sent.

After parking his truck, he heard Dakota talking to someone on the other side of the barn. When he walked over to the corral, he saw her audience was Kahlo.

"Anyway," she continued, "you be good for Matteo and Jason while I'm gone." *Gone? Already?* "They'd never hurt you."

"You're leaving?"

Dakota turned around and gave him a bright smile over the fence. "Welcome back, Matteo! How'd it go?"

"Same old." He didn't want to talk about that. "When are you leaving?"

Her smile faded momentarily before she cocked her head in confusion. "Tomorrow, but I won't be gone long. I signed up for some lessons in Colorado Springs that last until Friday."

What kind of class had she signed up for? At least it was only four days, and he'd be on duty at the firehouse for two of them.

"I've been trying to get Kahlo used to the idea of me not being here, so I let Jason feed her today. He's able to do almost everything again, and she tolerated him well enough." Dakota turned to the horse and patted her neck. "Didn't you, girl?"

He figured she'd tell him what this was all about when she wanted him to know. *Her life. Her business.* Sounded like she'd be returning to the ranch afterward at least.

"I'm going to unpack and shower." He needed some time to get his head on straight and not come across as a jerk every time she brought up the inevitable talk about leaving. If he pushed too hard for her to stay, it might only make her want to leave sooner.

"I'll check on supper." She climbed over the fence, and Kahlo ran off to join the other horses in the pasture.

They headed toward the house hand in hand. Inside the kitchen, he smelled something wonderful that reminded him of Nonna.

"Smells delicious."

"Thank your sister. I've been going up there for weekly lessons—and a little shopping. She said this dish was something your grandmother taught her and one of your favorites that didn't involve beef."

He nodded. "I thought of Nonna the moment I walked into the house. Took me right back to my summers in Sicily."

She smiled. "It didn't hurt that this is one of the easiest dishes Angelina's demonstrated so far. I think she realized she needed to simplify things a little for me."

He pulled her into his arms at long last. "Sweet Lady, there's nothing wrong with your cooking. And it sure beats my own." He placed a kiss on her lips but cut it off too soon. He really needed to clean up before doing anything more. Matt turned toward the hallway to the bedroom. "I'll be back soon."

When they sat down to eat, chatting was kept to a minimum while they enjoyed the meal, and he waited for her to tell him more about her upcoming class. When she didn't, he decided to focus more on their dinner. "This pork tenderloin is delicious."

"Thanks. I was afraid mine wouldn't be as good as Angelina's."

He was going to miss Dakota's cooking when she left too. "It's possibly even better than hers." She beamed at his words, and he took a few more bites. Pretty darn close to Nonna's too.

"Angelina's a great chef."

"You keep cooking like this, and you'll give her a run for her money." He realized it sounded like he wanted her to come back just to cook for him. "Of course, when you get back, feel free to get things cooking anytime—in the kitchen, the bedroom, the barn—anywhere you want." He grinned as he waggled his eyebrows, hoping she'd be in the mood to make love tonight. If they were going to be apart most of the week, he needed to hear her screaming in ecstasy at least once to tide him over.

"It's good to know you're going to miss me." She smiled. "I always miss you when you're gone."

He liked the sound of that. "You're welcome here as long as you want to stay." They continued to eat and Matt shared a little about what he'd been doing in Glenwood Springs, then she caught him up on what she and Jason had accomplished with the horses while he was gone.

"I can't wait for the school to begin. I'm determined to show those bulls what I'm made of."

Matt lowered his fork. What had she just said? "Bulls?"

Her eyes lit with excitement. "Yeah, I can't believe it, either, but I was accepted at a bull-riding school—one of the best!" Her enthusiasm dampened only slightly as she added, "Okay, they had a recent cancellation. But when I'm done there, they'll be happy they offered the spot to me."

"Have you forgotten what happened last December?"

She shrugged with a smile, seemingly oblivious to his concern. "Nope. Haven't forgotten, but the memory of the pain faded long ago. Now I just have to learn how not to let a bull get the best of me again. I'll also know what my chances are for riding in competition after this opportunity."

Matt couldn't help coming off as overprotective, which he knew would only piss her off, but damn it, someone needed to look out for her health and safety. She could break her neck this time! How could he make her see the dangers?

"What's the track record for injuries at this school?"

Dakota cocked her head and narrowed her eyes. "Their track record is excellent for the least number of injuries. I researched them already, and they take all the necessary safety precautions for their students."

Says who?

"What's the name of this school?"

"That is important, why? I've made my decision to take this class, and I won't allow you to try and prevent me from furthering my career."

Dakota reached across the table and placed her hand over his. "Look, I know you worry about me and want to be protective, but this is no different than you walking into a burning building."

Seriously? "I wear protective gear and have years of training under my belt."

"Exactly, and I'll be wearing a helmet, vest, face mask, and mouth guard—all the latest gear bull riders use to stay safe."

Would that be enough? Those vests wouldn't keep a bull from kicking her and giving her a thoracic injury.

"The main reason I'm going to this school is to get the training I'll need. You had to start somewhere, and I'm sure there was a time you didn't have all that experience and fire training, either."

What she was choosing to do had no comparison to his career. "I don't take unnecessary risks in my job. I also trust my incident commander and officers not to send me into unsafe conditions where I might be injured. Who's going to be watching out for your best interests?"

She pulled her hand back and glared at him. "I am. I've been looking out for myself for fourteen years, maybe even longer, and I know how to assess the situation better now than I did in December. Getting on a bull at a jackpot rodeo where nobody gave a shit what happened to me was an unnecessary risk. Maybe I did it just for the thrill of it after letting my impatience get the better of me. In retrospect, I should have waited for the bull-riding school I was supposed to go to in January."

Dakota drew a deep breath before continuing. "But I'm not going to be walking into an unsafe situation again. This is why I need to do this training to become better at assessing the situations."

"Why bulls?" Not that broncs were that much safer, but what could he do?

"Why not? Look, I'm afraid for you every time you leave this ranch to report for duty, Matteo. But have I ever tried to stop you from doing what you love because I'm worried about you?"

She worried about *him*?

Dakota continued before he could ask why. "But I try to take it in stride every time you go to work or out to do forestry maintenance. I expect you to do the same for me when I go to this school and when I go back onto the rodeo circuit."

This was the first time in a long while that Dakota had talked about returning, and she left no question that she'd be going back. Apparently, nothing he could say would stop her. He had no claim on her and no right to tell her what to do. He had obligations and wouldn't be able to follow her around the circuit, either, trying to keep her safe.

Not that she'd want him to. Maybe if he put a ring on her finger—

Whoa! Don't put the buggy in front of the horse, cowboy.

Needing time to figure out what he should say at this point, he stood without another word and took his empty plate to the sink, rinsing it off and placing it in the dishwasher. How could he make her see that there was no comparison between bull riding and fighting fires? She clearly wasn't going to listen to reason anyway.

Maybe the school would use washed-up bulls that wouldn't be killers. Matt took a deep breath, trying to steady his erratic heartbeat, and turned to face her. "I'll be off duty the last day of the class. Mind if I come and watch?" If nothing else, he could administer first aid until the paramedics arrived if she got bucked off.

Dakota grinned as she brought her own dishes over. "I'd love to have you watch me after I've had a couple of days to learn how to ride those beasts."

I just hope you don't get hurt before I can get there.

"Go on, you old cuss. Just try and buck me off before I get my eight seconds out of your old hide."

Silverback snorted and dipped his head down before jerking it toward her face. Dakota yanked her head back, avoiding contact. Even though she wore a protective mask to guard her lower face, she didn't want to wind up with a concussion before she got out of the chute.

Apparently, this bull didn't care for her smack talk. *Well, tough.*

Matteo had texted her that he was in the stands, and she intended to show him what she was made of. She'd already learned a lot in the past few days. Silverback might be older than the bull she got bucked off of in December, but he still had a lot of the devil in him.

Dakota assumed the instructors gave you nastier bulls as your skills improved, based on the milder temperaments of the previous bulls she'd ridden this week once she'd graduated from the mechanical bull. She'd managed eight seconds yesterday but didn't feel that bull was enough of a challenge. He probably needed to be put out to pasture.

This time, she'd cover on a respectable bull.

At her nod, the gateman pulled the rope, and the gate swung open to her left. The beast tore out of the chute ornerier than any other bull she'd ridden at the school. *Yes!* Silverback spun, bucked, and contorted his body as he tried to toss her off, but she held tight to the bull rope. Her instructor must have thought she could handle a rougher ride—and she intended to prove to him and Matteo that she could.

All she could hear were Silverback's snorts and the pounding of the sonofabitch's hooves as he spun until she became dizzy. But she kept her left hand high above her helmeted head to make sure she didn't accidentally touch the bull at any point. So far, she'd even managed to remain close to upright. This needed to be a perfect ride with maximum points.

Time stood still even though it could only have been a matter of seconds. How long had she been on this beast?

Hold on. Hold on! Hold on, damn it!!

The bullfighters came into her line of vision. She must be getting close to covering if they were here to distract the bull at the buzzer. Or did she look so precarious on the bull's back that they were readying themselves to pull her out of harm's way if she was thrown? The bullfighters saved many a rider from stomping hooves and piercing horns.

Nah, I still have a solid grip on the bull rope.

Until Silverback spun in the opposite direction, and she lost that grip. She flew off the back of the bull, landing hard on the ground. She hadn't heard the buzzer but wasn't sure if that was because of the ringing in her ears. One of the bullfighters quickly grabbed her arm and half-dragged her back to the chute to make a hasty exit.

"Did I cover?"

"Damn close, darlin'," one said. "Seven point six."

Damn it! Not close enough!

"That was a fine ride, Dakota," Caleb, her instructor, said, with a slap on her back.

"Eight seconds is a fine ride. Not a second shorter." To make matters worse, the classmate she'd been trying to beat today *had* covered earlier.

Dakota turned to glare at Silverback who seemed to be taking his victory lap for bucking her off. "You haven't beat me, you sonofabitch. And you won't keep me from trying again."

"There's a jackpot rodeo coming up in Grand Junction next weekend." Caleb smiled at her, waiting for her reaction. "You almost covered on Silverback, and he'll be there too. You might draw him or any number of other good bulls."

"Dakota, are you okay?" She turned at the sound of Matteo's voice. He did not look happy, so he must have overheard her instructor. Of course, he'd just watched her go flying off a bull, too.

Before he could warn her against it, she turned to Caleb, "Sign me up."

"Will do."

Refusing to face Matteo, she began removing her protective gear.

"Another jackpot? I thought you'd sworn off those after the one in December."

Fire in her eyes, she turned on him. "I was this close." She pinched her thumb and pointer finger together at his eye level. "I'll cover next time. I can feel it. Besides, if my instructors will be there, then I know it'll be safer than the one in Golden."

Matteo didn't say another word about that, but she doubted he'd had his last say about her riding next weekend. Too bad. Victory was so close she could taste it.

Matt stewed all the way back to the ranch as he followed Dakota's truck home. He'd thought the school would satisfy her obsession with bull riding and show her they were nothing to mess around with—but no. The damned fool woman had signed up for another jackpot rodeo.

This one just might get her killed.

She pulled up next to the barn and Matt parked closer to the house. Without a word, she went into the barn, probably to turn the horses out for some exercise. He walked into the house, not ready to face her for fear he'd blow his stack, which wouldn't help anything. Dakota couldn't be strong-armed. She'd do whatever the hell she wanted.

But he'd already gone the route of trying to talk some sense into her, and that hadn't worked.

Then he got an idea. He went over to the bookcase and pulled out a movie. If this didn't open her eyes, nothing would.

By the time she entered the house, he had the movie cued up, baked potatoes in the microwave, and a frozen dinner in the oven.

"Thanks for starting supper."

"No problem. Wanted to welcome you home. Horses okay?"

"Yeah." She smiled as she removed her boots. "Anxious to go out and play, just like kids."

Her words sent his mind off on a tangent of whether Dakota ever wanted to have kids. She'd probably be an unconventional mom, but no doubt one who would be a lot of fun for any kid.

If she survived long enough for motherhood.

He'd been careful to use protection whenever they'd had sex. She'd told him that her periods were sporadic and she probably wouldn't get pregnant, but neither of them was ready for anything as serious as parenting right now. Hell, he wasn't sure if this relationship would survive Dakota's reckless behavior.

"I thought we might watch a movie after supper."

"Sounds great! I'll go clean up and join you. Why don't you get out the salad fixings, and we can whip up one together."

Matt nodded and had pulled out everything that would go into their salads by the time she returned. Damn it all, he couldn't help himself. He pulled her into his arms and held her tight. "So glad you're home."

And in one piece.

She laughed but hugged him back. "I was only gone four days."

"Felt like a lifetime." He pulled away but kept his arms wrapped around her as he met her gaze. He bent down to kiss her, and she opened her mouth so that he could deepen the kiss. He'd probably not be getting any tonight after the object lesson he planned on giving her, so he might as well take what he could now.

After a few moments, she pulled away. "We'd better get to slicing and dicing or these salads aren't going to get made."

They each took several vegetables and began prepping. She didn't like peppers, so he left those out of her salad. And she knew not to put raw mushrooms anywhere near his. He enjoyed prepping meals with her. One more thing to miss when she went back to the rodeo circuit.

Supper went by with Dakota giving him a blow-by-blow of her week at the bull-riding school. She laughed about the many buck-offs she'd endured as if they were a mere nuisance. Matt simmered, biding his time. He intended to get through to her tonight, one way or another. He had to report to the firehouse tomorrow, so he wouldn't have much more time.

After supper, the dishes were cleared and loaded into the dishwasher. "Want some popcorn?" Matt asked.

"God, no! I'm stuffed."

He took her hand and led her across the room. They sat down on the couch and he picked up the remote. The movie came on, and he waited for her reaction.

"*Eight Seconds*! One of my favorite rodeo movies."

Favorite? How could anyone want to watch it more than once after the actor playing Lane Frost, the renowned real-life bull rider, was killed in a buck-off?

Maybe all she remembered was the bull riding. He decided to let the film play out. Matt wanted to see what her response would be to the fatal ride. When the inevitable came, he heard a sniffle from her. Good. She wasn't totally unemotional about the senseless loss of life in the dangerous sport.

He took her hand and squeezed it. "I see that image every time I think of you riding a bull, Dakota."

She brushed away the tears from her cheeks before turning to him. "It's tragic, but it was a fluke. Not that many cowboys have been killed like Lane was."

Seriously?

A surge of energy propelled him from the couch, and he turned to face her. "One is too many for a frivolous sport."

"Frivolous?"

"Nobody needs to ride a bull. There's no reason for it other than as entertainment. Even if you didn't get killed, you could wind up paralyzed or otherwise seriously injured."

Dakota's breathing became shallow as she stood and squared off with him. "Is that what this was about? You thought you could scare me off of my dream of bull riding from watching this movie?"

He didn't admit it but didn't have to. She clenched and unclenched her hand, and he was glad there was some space between them or she might have decked him.

"Seriously, Matteo! How would you feel if I pulled out *Backdraft*"—she pointed toward the shelf of movies—"to show you that firefighters sometimes die doing their jobs?"

"*Backdraft* isn't about firefighters dying, it's about the brotherhood and how we band together."

"But some firefighters died in the movie! I watched it once when you were at work, and it scared me shitless."

"Why would you watch something if it scared you?"

"Because I wanted to know more about what you face every day."

"I've never been involved in a backdraft in my life. We know a lot more about how fire behaves now than they did then, so our officers would order us out before anything like that would happen."

He didn't mention that for some departments situational awareness was lacking, and the signs were missed, but he trusted his own officers.

She took a deep breath as if praying for patience or divine guidance or something.

"Okay. I wouldn't have tried to scare you with *Backdraft* any more than you should have tried that on me with *Eight Seconds*. We watch movies about our professions because we love what we do."

"I save lives in my job. Yours is pure entertainment. Any loss of life is completely unnecessary. It's nothing but a deadly sport!"

"Athletes die playing football too. Do you consider that a deadly sport?"

Was she going to twist everything around? "We aren't talking about football here."

"Okay, what was the closest call you've had as a firefighter?"

He didn't have to think about that, because he'd only had one mayday call and it hadn't even been two years ago. "We were fighting a structure fire, two-story residence, and the roof collapsed on me."

The look of horror on her face told him to spare her the details about how long he was unconscious, because there had never been any long-term effects from it. Besides, it wasn't important to what they were arguing about anyway. "The homeowners had made some renovations and weakened the structure."

"How badly were you hurt?"

He shrugged. "Spent the night in the hospital, but I was back at work on my next shift."

"I'm glad it wasn't anything more serious. But you can see that sometimes despite all our training, we can get hurt. It's a part of life unless we live in a bubble." She brought herself up to her full height again, the challenge back in her voice. "What I can't live with is some man hovering over and trying to protect me to the point that I can't breathe. That's not living."

"I don't want to see you killed, Dakota!"

"Nobody asked you to watch!"

From all she'd said earlier, that couldn't be closer to the truth. He was losing her, and there wasn't a damned thing he could do about it. He just hoped she'd survive her reckless decisions.

Chapter Twenty-Three

Dakota turned away and drew in a deep breath, but her lungs felt constricted and her body shook uncontrollably. She needed to dial it back a little.

"Look, Matteo, I'm not hurting anyone doing what I do. If you choose to see it that way and to be unreasonable about it, that's not on me."

But she refused to stay with a man who thought he had the right to control her life. "Bottom line is, I'm going to that rodeo, and afterward I'll be returning to the circuit the first opportunity I have." Obviously, she couldn't return here, not if that's what he thought of her and her career.

Once she thought she could face him again and formulate words without hurting him the way he'd hurt her, she turned around.

Clearly, he had no confidence in her abilities to master bull riding. Be that as it may, she didn't need his approval or vote of confidence. As long as she felt she could do it, she would.

No man will ever tell me what I can or cannot do. Never again.

"Matteo, the rodeo isn't frivolous for me any more than what you do is for you. If you can't accept what I do for a living, that's your problem, not mine."

His continued silence started to piss her off too. But not as much as knowing that he saw no value to her wanting to provide entertainment for others, not to mention enjoying the adrenaline rushes she so loved so much. What had happened to him over the years?

"When did you turn against rodeo? You used to perform yourself."

"Yeah, when I was in high school and college. That was a long time ago. I grew up."

"So now you're saying I'm behaving like a child?"

"That's not what I said." He raked his fingers through his hair.

"Yes, you did. You also said my livelihood is nothing but some frivolous sport." She drew in and expelled a breath through her mouth as she tried to keep from losing her shit.

Suddenly, Dakota was unable to stand still. She turned toward the bedroom, but the need to fight his attacks against her very identity won over, and she returned to within a few feet of where he stood, on the fringe of his personal space.

"I don't answer to you or any man, Matteo Giardano! I am a grown-ass woman and *I*," she jabbed her finger at her chest over her breaking heart, "decide what I do and when I do it. *You*," she jabbed the same finger into his rock-hard chest for emphasis, "have no say over me or the decisions I make in my life."

"Let's sit back down, Dakota, and work this out."

The desire to give him a chance to dig himself out of the hole he'd dug warred with her desire to leave here for good.

"Believe me," he continued, "I'm not trying to tell you what to do."

"Like hell. What else would you call what you just did?"

He ran his fingers through his hair. *Good.* He was finally as frustrated with this bullshit as she was. Seeing him upset made her feel good in some way.

She took a step back. Silent. Waiting.

"Dakota, I'm just trying to get you to be realistic about the inherent dangers in pursing bull riding as a career path."

The man couldn't help himself. *What an ass!*

"You make it sound like I'm a novice, rather than someone who's been polishing her rodeo skills since high school. I'm not still some seventeen-year-old with stars in her eyes. I know what I'm doing and what the risks are." She held up her hand to keep him from interrupting. "Obviously, you don't respect what I do or what my dreams are. You're just like *him*! We are done with this discussion."

Without another word, she turned around and headed for the bedroom. In a matter of minutes, she'd piled all of her belongings into her duffel bags. There wasn't much more than when she'd shown up here in December, although she had bought a few new dresses and skirts recently that she'd never had the chance to put on—or take off—for Matteo.

But I'm fine with that.

He'd shown his true self tonight, trying to control her life. She couldn't wait to get out of here. A brief flash of worry over the horses came over her. She'd miss them more than Matteo, that's for sure. She pulled her phone out of her pocket and asked Jason if he'd be able to come and let them out Tuesday and Wednesday while Matteo was at work next week. He quickly responded that he could.

Dakota went into the bathroom and gathered up her toiletries then surveyed both rooms before carrying her bags back toward the living area.

"Where are you going?"

"Grand Junction. I have a rodeo coming up." She refused to look at him as she headed for the door. "I texted Jason. He'll take care of the horses while you're at work." She hadn't asked the young man if he'd be available beyond this week's shift but was certain he would be. He'd missed being out here while he was recuperating.

"Dakota, I don't want you driving off mad."

Anger bubbled up inside her again. She spun around. "Well, that's too damned bad, Matteo, because you can't stop me."

He held his hands out to his sides in a helpless gesture. "I'm not going to try, but why don't you at least wait until morning?"

"Why? So you can continue your campaign to undermine my choices? To get me to concede my power and independence to you? Not happening! Being under the same roof with an overprotective, paternalistic misogynist is more than I can stand right now."

"What do you mean? I'm only trying to protect you, Dakota. Trying to get you to see reason."

"Oh, so now I can't understand the consequences of my decisions or actions? Explain to me how what I'm doing is unreasonable—in your opinion—but that your equally dangerous decisions aren't."

"Stop twisting around everything I say."

"Then stop talking and think about what you've been saying to me tonight." She waved him off. "You can mull it over without me. I'm going to say goodbye to the horses and then hook up my camper and be out of your way."

She wanted to add *for good*, even though it sounded a bit childish, but deep down she knew it was over with Matteo. She couldn't be with someone who couldn't accept her for who she was or respect her choices.

She hoped she'd be able to set up her camper on the rodeo grounds even though the event was still a week away, but if not, she'd find a nearby campground until she could move.

Walking around the barn, she whistled for the horses. Kahlo came running first and Dakota swallowed against a lump forming in her throat. The horse had become used to Jason and Matteo over the recent weeks. She'd be all right without Dakota.

But will I be all right without her?

She climbed over the fence and greeted the mare with open arms, wrapping them around the horse's neck. "I'm going to miss you, girl. You be good now, you hear? Nobody here will hurt you."

Dakota couldn't say the same about what Matteo's words had done to her, though. She didn't know how long it would take to bounce back. She'd thought they shared something special, but apparently that was true only as long as she kowtowed to his expectations.

That's not who I am and if he doesn't want me for myself, he doesn't get me at all.

On the second day of Matt's next shift, the engineer backed the truck into the bay after the third false alarm at the high school this week. Matt figured some students must be trying to get out of taking a test or something. His lieutenant had met with the principal today to set up a time to talk to the student body assembly about the dangers of and penalties for pulling alarms when there wasn't a fire or other emergency.

After removing his turnout gear, Matt stored it for the next run. No smoke or soot, so at least they didn't have to scrub everything down.

Matt walked outside for some fresh air rather than join the guys upstairs right away. The late April weather had started growing warmer, and the sun shone brightly today, even though the chance of snow was strong this weekend. They'd still have significant snowfalls for at least another month, maybe longer.

Would Dakota's bull-riding plans this weekend be derailed if it snowed?

I hope so.

Nothing he'd said had changed her mind about going, that's for sure. The woman had a mind of her own, and he might as well accept that she wouldn't walk to the beat of any man's drum.

The thought of not seeing her when he came home after his shift and not being able to wake up with her these past three mornings soured his stomach. She'd become such a part of the ranch that he couldn't remember back to a time when she hadn't been there.

I miss her.

His phone buzzed and he looked down to see a text had come in from Mama.

***MAMA:* I'm stopping by tomorrow morning.**

As much as he loved his mama, he wasn't in any mood for a visit. The woman had an uncanny way of sensing when her kids were hurting. Of course, maybe it was blowing off her Sunday dinner the other day. He hadn't felt up to being around family—and seeing how Mama, Tony, and Angelina all had found the loves of their lives when Matt had just lost his.

And he had no doubt that it was over. Dakota hadn't left anything behind.

Knowing Dakota, she'd probably miss the horses more than him. He didn't understand how she could misconstrue everything he'd said to her. He only had her health and safety in mind. He didn't want to control her life, but he didn't want to see her killed or maimed, either.

But she'd been looking to pick a fight, and Lord knew he gave her all the ammo she'd needed.

Let it go.

Matt had rehashed last Friday night's fight over these past five days until his brain grew numb. As far as he was concerned, he'd said nothing as awful as she'd made his words out to be.

The following morning, after a fairly quiet night, Matt made his way back to the ranch. Mama's vehicle was parked next to the house. No doubt she was inside making him breakfast.

He had no appetite, not even for Mama's cooking.

Might as well face the music. If she probed too much, he could always say he needed to check on the horses, but Jason had already turned them out and probably mucked their stalls before school this morning. Not much he really needed to do.

Matt opened the door to the smell of bacon. *Damn.* Maybe he could eat after all. It would be the first time in days.

"Bambino! You're just in time!" Mama turned the griddle on and met him near the door where he'd just removed his shoes. She wrapped her arms around him.

Her not mentioning Dakota made him wonder if somehow Mama had heard that she was gone, even though Matt hadn't told anyone in the family or at the station yet. He kept hoping she'd come to her senses and return.

"Get cleaned up. I'm making pancakes. Then we can talk."

Matt immediately knew she was aware that something was up.

"Sounds good." *Well, the pancakes part did.* "I'll be right back." In the bedroom, he stripped out of his clothes and jumped into the shower even though he'd taken one at the station after his shift. Anything to postpone the expected confrontation with Mama. Matt had no doubt Mama would have words with him if she heard he'd run Dakota off.

And no doubt that's how Mama would see it. She thought the world of Dakota and worried about her as much as Matt did.

When he returned to the kitchen, she pulled a cookie sheet out of the oven with three stacks of pancakes on it. She'd already poured him a mug of coffee, and the maple syrup and butter sat beside his plate. She let him get through his first stack while she ate half of hers before she brought up Dakota.

"Have you heard from her?"

Matt slowed his chewing to buy himself more time before answering, then swallowed.

"It's over, Mama. She's gone." He forced the words out of his constricted throat.

"Nothing is final until we die."

Poor choice of words. Dakota might very well die this weekend, if not on Silverback then on some other damned bull.

"Why don't you tell me what happened?"

He recounted the fight, leaving nothing out. No point sugarcoating it. Mama would see through any half-truths or lies.

"I can see how she might be upset."

What about him? Didn't he have a right to be upset too? Whose side was she on?

"I couldn't just sit by while she went off to get herself killed."

"And what are you doing now?"

He realized that's exactly what the result had been. She was gone and he was sitting by waiting to hear that she was dead or severely injured—not that he would have been notified one way or another. He'd planned to look on the Facebook page of this rodeo outfit for the news.

"Bambino, the hardest thing I ever did was let your papa go and do all the dangerous things he felt driven to do."

"That was different. Papa was saving lives. She's just riding bulls for the sport of it."

Mama smiled wistfully. "Before you kids came along, Papa did ice climbing, hiked fourteeners in the middle of winter, and one year even bungee jumped from a hot-air balloon."

What the…? Why had he never heard about this? "Papa was a thrill-seeker?"

"Of the worst kind." She shook her head but smiled anyway.

He'd never seen that side of Papa. The man had put family and the people of Aspen Corners ahead of any wild, selfish pursuits.

"What changed or got him to settle down?"

"I got pregnant with Rafe and told Papa I didn't intend to go through life as a widowed single mother, so he needed to settle down and behave responsibly so that his children would have him around for decades." Mama shook her head. "Of course, then he replaced his wild adventures with the adrenaline rush of being a part of search and rescue." She shook her head. "He knew I couldn't very well deny him doing something to give back to the community in such a meaningful way."

"But that's not what Dakota's doing. She's doing it just for the sport and challenge of it."

"She's young."

"She's thirty-two. In rodeo years, that's ancient."

Mama smiled. "Don't tell me that that's old." Then she grew serious again. "Matteo, Dakota has never known what it's like to be part of a family or community. Rodeo *is* her family. She goes around the circuit with a lot of the same people. They know her. It's probably the first bond she's ever known. They accepted her and gave her what was missing in her life."

Mama's words hit him like a ton of bricks. Why hadn't he been able to look at the rodeo like that before this?

But he'd treated her like family too. "*I* accepted her—not just over the past few months, but back in high school too."

She nodded. "But she didn't choose to run to you or our family back in Aspen Corners. I don't know what she was running from. I sense that she wanted her independence from everyone back then. Perhaps she was trying to find herself."

Matt didn't want to reveal things Dakota had shared in confidence about her past and the lack of an identity but everything started making more sense. "She left for good reasons, even if she didn't choose the safest way to get away."

Mama patted his hand with a smile. "Always so protective. You and your brothers are just like your papa. But remember that she did choose to come to *you* last December when she was hurting and needed help. I think you planted a seed all those years ago that came to fruition."

He grinned. "I think I planted an acorn, rather than a willow tree." His smile faded. "And now I've run her off, just like *he* did." Perhaps even for the same reasons—trying to exert control over her life.

Mama cocked her head, but Matt had probably said more than he should have already. When he didn't respond to her curiosity, she continued. "Bottom line, Matteo, is that you can't tell Dakota to give up the only family and community she's ever known until she finds something to replace it with."

"Do you think she'll ever be open to considering me family?"

"It's entirely possible that one day she'll choose to settle down with someone. I would love for that to be you, but I don't think she's ready for any strong ties yet. She needs to see how important a stable, solid family and community can be before she gives up the only one she now knows."

He prayed she'd live long enough to discover that all he wanted was what was best for her. And to love her.

Maybe if I'd told her that…

"There's another thing you need to be careful about."

Matt waited, knowing whatever it was would be profound and true. Mama had an uncanny way of sizing people up.

"I know my sons are traditional Italian men and feel they need to protect those in their lives they deem to be weaker."

"I never meant to make her feel weaker. God, she's one of the strongest women I know. Like you."

Mama smiled indulgently. "I appreciate the flattery, but I know of no woman who could stand up to Dakota's physical strength. But have you told her that's how you view her?"

Matt thought back over their months together and couldn't specifically recall a time that he had. "Not that I remember."

"Which means, no. Dakota has a need to prove something—not just to herself but to the men of the world who want to keep her and other women down."

"I'm not sexist, Mama."

She shrugged. "Not intentionally, but you are. I think you expect women to be like me—to stay home and take care of their families. That was *my* choice, but I don't know that Dakota will ever be fulfilled by that definition of womanhood. She needs to show the world that she can do anything a man can do—and often do it better than they can."

"Like riding broncs and bulls."

Mama nodded. "Exactly. Perhaps someday she'll replace that ambition with something else, but I wouldn't expect it to be anything sedate and safe. It's not in her nature."

"You're probably right."

"In many ways, that's exactly what I decided to do when your father chose to pursue the building-trades career he did and then later on joining the search and rescue team."

"How'd you do it?"

"I had a strong faith, so I prayed a lot."

Had Mama paused to get him to think about going back to church or otherwise becoming more spiritual? Matt didn't know if his faith would get any stronger than it was now.

"And I made sure that he didn't do anything reckless unless there was absolutely no other choice."

"She's taking as many safety measures as she can to keep from being injured." *Or killed.*

"Then chances are she won't be hurt while pursuing her dreams." She leaned forward. "But none of us is promised tomorrow, Matteo. You'll have to decide how much of your well-being you're willing to risk if you choose to pursue a long-term relationship with Dakota, especially before you decide on something as solemn and permanent as marriage."

"I don't think either of us is ready to take that step."

"I would agree. Wait until you can resolve your conflicts and learn to accept each other as you are. She's always going to be a thrill-seeker—just like you. Do you think I don't worry about all the men in my life being hurt on the job? And what about you with your skijoring hobby?"

Mama always supported him in whatever he did, even showing up to cheer him on during the skijoring festival, just as she did for his brothers. Maybe if he could be supportive rather than letting fear cloud his judgment…

"I like Dakota a lot," Mama said, "and I think she'd be good for you. You will always want to protect her, but you can't change who she is at her core. You need to find some middle ground you can both live with." Mama stood and Matt did the same. She wrapped her arms around him. "Don't let her go, Bambino, without exploring every possible way that you can work this out."

Matt nodded. "She's the most important woman in my life after you, Mama. I don't want to lose her."

"Then do what you need to do to win her back."

Chapter Twenty-Four

Dakota hadn't been able to move the camper onto the grounds until Thursday night. Friday morning, she'd strolled around talking with some of the other cowboys and cowgirls who planned to compete this weekend, hoping to see some familiar faces.

To be honest, the only face she'd hoped to find was Matteo's, but of course he hadn't shown up and wouldn't after the words they'd had last week.

At last, she found someone she recognized. "Jackie!" The woman turned to face her, a puzzled look on her face. "It's me, Dakota Mathison."

Even that didn't seem to click with her, then she suddenly smiled. "Dakota! Long time, no see!"

"Yeah, had a run-in with a bull in December and have been off the circuit since then."

The woman had been one of Dakota's stiffest competitors in bronc riding. "I guess I haven't seen you since last fall."

She didn't seem to have missed her, either. "I'm planning to give bull riding another try tomorrow."

Jackie's eyes opened wider. "Really? Impressive."

"Well, let's wait and see how it goes before making that determination. I did go to bull-riding school, though, so hopefully I've learned some things since my buck-off right before Christmas."

An awkward silence fell between them. They hadn't really been friends before, so she didn't know what they had in common. There really wasn't anything else to talk about.

"I'd better get back to the gang," Jackie said. "Good to see you again, Dakota."

Jackie didn't invite her to join whoever the gang was, so she found herself meandering around the grounds alone again, scoping out the chutes and envisioning herself on a bull tomorrow, ready to barrel into the ring on a hyped-up one-ton beast for her eight-second adrenaline rush.

No, it was more than that. She had something to prove.

To whom?

Matteo was the only person who would care whether she covered or got bucked off. She would have loved having him in the stands tomorrow while she competed to hear what he thought about—

Whoa, Nellie! I compete for me, *no one else! I need to prove to* myself *that I can do this.*

Not to mention try to bring the sport into modern times. She'd been trying to show the rodeo world that women could compete with the guys and do just as well. Knowing how slow change came to the rodeo, she probably wouldn't still be competing when women were allowed to go up against the boys in the roughstock events at sanctioned rodeos.

In the early 1900s, they'd competed together until some unfortunate woman died riding a bronc, and suddenly riding bucking broncs and bulls was deemed too dangerous for the so-called weaker sex. The sport continued after the deaths of numerous cowboys, though. Double standards everywhere.

Dakota wasn't the only woman riding broncs and now bulls at these unsanctioned events and exhibitions. She was out to prove that women were just as capable as men. One of these days, maybe the sexist men in charge would open their eyes, and equality would return to the sport.

Not feeling hungry, she decided to skip supper and return to her camper early. She wondered what Matteo was having tonight. She hoped he hadn't forgotten to eat altogether. Their times together cooking and eating were some of her favorites, as dull as that might seem to the old Dakota.

Whoa, Nellie!

Who said there was a new Dakota? She hadn't changed, not really. She still loved to perform and challenge herself to be better than any man at whatever she set her sights on.

And she would—tomorrow.

She needed a good night's rest to be ready to show the bull she'd drawn what she was made of. It hadn't been Silverback, unfortunately, but Caleb assured her she'd gotten an equally worthy one. Half the score would be for the bull, and she wanted one that would challenge her to get the highest score possible.

Lying in bed that night, though, unable to sleep, her thoughts inevitably turned to Matteo. As much as she hated to admit it, she missed him—even his stubborn, overprotective ways.

She turned onto her side and punched her pillow. No, she didn't miss him enough to invite him back into her life if he thought he'd be telling her what to do—and not do.

Still, he had his uses. He made her feel special and could make her laugh even on a bad day. Not that she'd had that many bad days since she'd shown up at his ranch.

Once again, she shifted position, but sleep wouldn't claim her. She hadn't been active enough today to wear herself out. Instead, her mind kept returning to Matteo and all the sweet, sexy things he'd done for, with, and to her.

Okay, he wasn't overbearing all the time. Often, he could be a lot of fun to be with.

Then there were the horses. She missed them almost as much as she did Matteo and wondered how Kahlo was adjusting to not having her around at all. Guilt washed over her as Dakota experienced what it must have been like for the horse feeling as if Dakota had deserted her.

Heck, she even missed the guys at the firehouse, Dolly at the café, Jason, and all the people she'd come to know in Leadville this year.

When had she ever gotten herself so attached to people and horses before?

Never.

Too bad she'd severed those ties already. She had no experience with having to think about anyone but herself. Still, perhaps there was a new Dakota after all.

Now what did she plan to do differently in her life to pursue that? The thought of venturing onto a new path scared the shit out of her—much more so than riding a bull.

The next afternoon, her moment of reckoning arrived. As she prepared her bull rope for the ride, she listened to the small but enthusiastic crowds cheering on the riders ahead of her. At least the snow had held off. Sunny but cold, not that she'd notice.

Dakota rubbed her leather glove down the bull rope several times to produce friction and heat up the rosin. When it was tacky enough, she loosely secured the rope around the bull with Caleb's help.

She'd be riding next. She didn't know much about the bull she was about to mount, but these would be the longest eight seconds of his life. Dakota took a deep breath and spread her left leg over the back of the bull before seating herself on its back.

Once on top of the bull, she settled in and handed the tail of the bull rope to the man on the top of the chute. Dakota rubbed the rope again to heat up the rosin once more and wedged her gloved right hand inside the rope's handle. As the guy tightened the rope, she positioned the handle just where she wanted it.

Using her left hand, she pulled the rope across the palm of her leather glove. The bull started to protest by trying to buck her off, but she wrapped the rope under her wrist and brought it halfway across her palm before looping the free end between her fingers.

Almost ready. Dakota laid the remaining rope on the bull's back in front of her and slid toward the bull's neck until the back of her hand was practically against the crotch of her Wranglers.

Let's go!

Giving her nod, the gate swung open, and the bull took off. He immediately began bucking and twisting in an effort to throw her off. She kept her focus on the bull, but barely cleared the chute before he slammed her against the gate, banging her leg from knee to hip.

Sonofabitch!

Everything had happened so fast, she hadn't had time to get her rhythm going, but the pain caused her to release the handle. Trying to extricate herself from harm, she latched onto the fence and Caleb pulled her out of the ring to safety.

"You okay?" Caleb asked.

"Hell, no." She turned toward the score board, praying she'd get an option for a reride.

"I'm sure they'll give you one," he said, knowing what she wanted. "I doubt it'll be today, though. They've already given three rerides and had two others granted the option, but they don't have any more bulls in reserve."

When the *RR* appeared next to her name on the board, she breathed a sigh of relief. "That's okay. I'll head over to find out who I'm riding so I can check out some video tonight, if I can find any. I want to be better prepared for my next ride."

I intend to cover tomorrow.

If it kills me.

Poor choice of words, Dakota.

She limped alongside the chutes toward the judges' stand, hoping she could find out which bull she'd be riding tomorrow. She was the last bull rider of the day, so they'd probably draw for rerides soon.

Most of the cowboys and cowgirls would be headed to nearby bars, but she didn't want her faculties dulled by alcohol before she got on the back on another bull.

Instead, she'd return to her camper to nurse her wounds, watch videos, and prepare for her ride. At least she'd have another chance to prove herself tomorrow.

"Are you okay, Dakota?"

Her heart soared as the familiar voice rose above the cacophony of noise from the stands, then she remembered how they'd parted company. She turned around quickly to find Matteo standing there, worry in his eyes.

Obviously, he'd seen that disaster of a ride. Why had he come here?

To tell her *I told you so* or to try and talk her out of riding again? Too bad on both counts.

"That cuss didn't give me a chance to show him what I can do."

"You hit that fence pretty hard. Want me to check you out?"

"I'm fine."

"Well, you gave it your best. At least it's over now."

Dakota cocked her head. "Over for today maybe. I have a reride tomorrow."

Was that a flash of fire in his eyes? If so, he quickly tamped it back down. "Where are you hurt?"

"Right smack in the middle of my pride."

"Dakota, you were limping a minute ago."

She waved away his concern. "Nothing to worry about. I'll walk it out. Headed back to my camper."

Alone, thank you very much.

"Have you eaten today?"

She nodded. "Steak and eggs."

"Sounds like breakfast. Can I take you to supper?"

Would there be strings attached? "Not if you're going to try and talk me out of my reride tomorrow."

Matteo shook his head with a half grin. "We'll stay away from that subject, unless you want to bring it up." He grew serious again. "But I've been doing a lot of thinking since you left. We need to talk."

Lord knew she didn't intend to talk about it, either. Matteo had never lied to her before, so she took him at his word. "I suppose I could eat." Her appetite had suddenly returned, even though a few minutes ago she'd planned to skip supper altogether.

But he'd piqued her curiosity about what he wanted to talk with her about, if not about their argument over her riding bulls. "What did you have in mind?"

"I made us a reservation for seven."

She cocked her head. "A reservation?" Had he been that sure she'd accept?

His grin broadened. She'd missed his smiles. "Call me an optimist."

Don't let your guard down, cowgirl.

"Sounds nice."

What did she have to lose? He'd already trampled over her heart. But maybe there was still some hope left.

Matt watched Dakota as she talked to the judges, a little worried about which bull she'd draw for tomorrow. But he needed to just accept the fact that she was going to ride and pray nothing bad happened. Watching her being bucked off today and crashing against the chute had been painful enough, but he wouldn't be able to turn away for a second during her ride tomorrow. *No way.*

He couldn't wait to talk with her and hoped she still wanted to have a relationship with him. They needed to work some things out between them before he'd know for sure.

Tonight's dinner would be an attempt to make up for giving her such a hard time about riding bulls. He wanted to leave a better impression with her in case she ever wanted to return to him and his ranch. One thing was certain, keeping her from doing the things she loved wouldn't make their relationship stronger.

His gaze lowered to the turquoise and black chaps framing her ass in those tight-fitting Wranglers. He couldn't help but appreciate the view. When she turned toward him, he quickly readjusted his focus to her face, and she flashed him a big smile, clearly aware of what he'd been staring at. But then she went back to her conversation. After about ten minutes, she rejoined him.

"Checking out my ass earlier, cowboy fireman?" He'd missed her teasing him like that.

Hearing the old Dakota coming through made him smile too. God, he'd missed her. "Maybe."

"Chaps make everyone's ass look great. Not to mention a man's crotch." Her gaze went to his groin. "You ought to consider getting a pair yourself."

"Already have them. Just don't have any reason to wear them much anymore."

She met his gaze. "Too bad." Her banter made him wonder if perhaps he had a chance at reconciling with her. Then she switched gears completely. Her smile was even bigger than the one she'd flashed at him a few minutes ago. "I drew Silverback!"

For a brief moment, he closed his eyes, breaking contact with her, while trying to figure out how to respond. That bull had thrown her too, but she'd almost covered on him at the school. Maybe this time would be the charm, since she knew how the animal responded.

He took a deep breath and plastered a smile onto his face. When he opened his eyes again, he said, "You've got this, Sweet Lady." He hoped he sounded encouraging, even if he lacked enthusiasm.

She smiled. "Bet your ass I do, cowboy fireman. I know this bull. I can still feel him twisting and turning under me. So I won't have to study him as hard. I'm going to succeed this time." She took his hand. "Matteo, I know how you feel about me riding bulls. I just wanted you to know it means a lot to me that you'd come here to watch me despite how you feel."

Apparently, he'd passed the test. "I really do want you to succeed, Sweet Lady. Now, why don't we head to dinner?"

She released his hand and glanced down at herself. "I'm a little dusty from my ride. I need to change. How dressy is this place?"

He gave her the once over and shook his head. "You look great to me." She hadn't really hit the ground and her chaps had taken the brunt of it, so he saw no dirt on her jeans or shirt.

"No way. It's not often I get to eat at a place that requires reservations. Besides, I went shopping with Angelina the last time I was in Breckenridge. I'd love to dress up a little."

"You're fine just the way you are, but we have time if you want to change into something else."

"Come on. I'll show you the way to my camper."

He couldn't get over how she'd acted since he'd shown up. He'd expected the cold shoulder—or worse—considering how they'd parted company a week ago. But he gladly took her hand as she led him toward the camper. She went inside to change while he waited outside.

Matt's only thoughts at the moment were about having an intimate dinner with Dakota and seeing where they could go from here. When he decided to come to Grand Junction to watch her ride, he'd made plans to take her out afterward—whether to celebrate or commiserate, he didn't care. He'd found a local place that served the steaks they both loved in a building that had once housed a horse-drawn fire department a century ago.

When she came outside, she took his breath away. She wore a medium-gray cable-knit sweater and black Wranglers. The sweater's pattern formed a V over the curve of her breasts and hugged them like a second skin.

Matt whistled. "I didn't think it possible, but you look even more beautiful."

She smiled. "Thank you. I thought this would be warm enough that I could leave my coat behind."

He started to suggest she bring one along, in case they had a break-down, but Matt would make sure she stayed warm in that eventuality.

"Let's head over to the parking lot and take my truck."

They remained quiet on the drive to the restaurant. He ran the speech he had practiced all the way up here over in his mind once more.

I've got to make things right with her.

He planned to redeem himself before this night was done, he hoped. At least they'd be in a public place. If she got pissed at something he said, she probably wouldn't make a scene.

At the restaurant, seated in one of the smaller rooms, he scanned the area with its red brick walls. If he hadn't read their website and the history of the place, he wouldn't have known the place had once been a fire station. But if these walls could talk, he imagined they'd have some stories to tell.

Now he needed to put out the smoldering fire he'd started last week.

They picked up their menus and his eye went to the extensive list of wines and cocktails, but when the server asked what she'd like to drink, Dakota asked for water.

"Same for me, please."

"You can have wine if you'd like," she assured him. "I just don't want to dull my senses before tomorrow's reride."

He didn't want her to do anything to put her in jeopardy, either. "No, water's fine."

She turned her attention to the menu. "My gosh, this place is a little pricey."

"Don't worry about that. I wanted to treat you for going above and beyond around the ranch. I also thought we'd be celebrating your eight-second ride, but I guess we'll have to do that tomorrow."

Her eyes opened wider, then she smiled. "Thanks for the vote of confidence. I'm good with celebrating early, but you already paid me for working at the ranch."

"Not as much as you deserved." Since March, he'd tried to pay her something from his own paychecks so that a total lack of income wouldn't be the reason she returned to the rodeo circuit. But it sounded like rodeoing was where her heart lay, so he needed to accept the fact that she wouldn't be sticking around.

Matt wanted to have a deeper relationship with Dakota under whatever terms she set. He hoped they could become more than lovers at some point, because he wanted to keep her in his life. Even if that meant he had to watch her put her life and health at risk pursuing the dangerous thrills she seemed to need to prove herself or for whatever reason she did it.

"So what are your plans after this rodeo?" he asked after they'd placed their orders.

"Not sure. I feel like I'm at a crossroads but not sure which way to go. All depends on tomorrow, I guess."

"What drives you to do what you do?"

She shrugged. "Like you, I love a good adrenaline rush."

"I think there's more to it than that."

She searched his eyes before glancing down. "Maybe." She remained pensive for the longest time before adding, "I've always felt a need to prove something."

"To who?"

"I don't know." Her brows furrowed as she thought about the question a bit. "I think bull riding is just the next thing I have to prove to myself." He thought there might be more she was going to say, but she remained quiet.

"Well, I hope you know you have nothing to prove to me. And if you think you do, bull riding would definitely not be the way to do it."

Her eyes narrowed.

Shit. That didn't come out right.

"But I can understand having something you want to conquer," he added. "My challenges all just tend to be fire-service related."

And then there's you, Sweet Lady.

She seemed to stand down. Crisis averted. Hell, they hadn't even been served their salads yet. *Don't blow this.*

"I know it's not as noble as fighting fires and saving lives, but I need to do this. For me."

"I was out of line when I put down what you do as not being as important as what I do. Lots of athletes put their safety on the line for the sports they love." She opened her mouth to say something, but he raised his hand to halt her words. He wanted to finish while he had her attention.

"Mama told me something about Papa recently that opened my eyes to what the rodeo means to you." He told her about Papa's daredevil bungee jumping escapade.

Her eyes opened wide. "From a hot-air balloon? That's insane!"

At least he hadn't given her a new sport to aspire to. "I thought so too. But the thing is, it made me realize that we're all wired differently. Some of us have a thrill-seeking gene and need to pursue death-defying acts to feel more alive, I guess."

"But I'd never take crazy risks like that."

"I know you wouldn't. Which is why I wanted to apologize for going off the deep end about the bull riding. I know it's dangerous, but

I also know you are taking all the precautions you can to avoid injuries."

He took her hand and held it on the tabletop between them. "I've also taken the time to put myself in your place thinking about my own risks and dangers. It's a lot easier being the person doing these activities than it is to be sitting at home worrying about someone we care about, that's for sure."

She nodded. "How does your Mama do it? First her husband's search and rescue work and now her four sons, second husband, and son-in-law all going into harm's way? She must have nerves of steel."

He grinned. "Mama's faith is what keeps her going."

Dakota hitched the corner of her mouth. "I've never been much of a religious person."

"Me neither."

"Not that I didn't try and bargain with God, or whoever's in charge, when Jason was injured."

"Yeah, I know what you mean. I rarely go on a call without sending a prayer out to the universe to protect me and my brothers. Sometimes I call on Papa too." He leaned a little closer. "And you can bet your sweet little ass I'll be praying like crazy tomorrow when you get onto Silverback again."

The server brought their salads, but before she took a bite, Dakota said, "Flying off that bull today freaked me out a little. Okay, mostly pissed me off, but that sense of helplessness and lack of control isn't something I want to experience again."

Maybe she'd figure this out and opt out of the ride. He waited to see if she had second thoughts, but then she continued. "I plan to apply even more resin to the bull rope and fight like hell tomorrow to remain mounted for my full eight seconds."

"Well, I have faith in you. You've got this, Sweet Lady. You know that bull from your ride at the school."

She nodded. "As long as he doesn't pull out any new moves."

"What happens when you succeed?"

"I guess I'll have bragging rights. And the satisfaction of knowing I did it."

"I don't see you as the braggart type. Who is it you intend to brag about it to?"

"Good question." She thought a moment, then shrugged. "I suppose word could get out on the circuit that Dakota Mathison is back in a big way, and they'll remember me again."

Her words seemed incongruous with what Mama had said about the rodeo being her family, but perhaps the folks here in Grand Junction weren't the ones she'd been close to in the past.

But would they only accept her if she was successful? Didn't sound like much of a family to him.

"What if you don't cover tomorrow and there's no buzz?"

She glanced away, seemingly uncomfortable, before narrowing her gaze on him again. "Still doubting my ability to do it, Matteo?"

Shit. Her defenses were up again. He'd asked a simple question. There was no guarantee of success, after all. Cowboys got bucked off three out of four attempts sometimes in bull riding.

Before he could figure out how to get them back on a smoother footing, she continued. "I thought you came here to be supportive and to talk things over. What was all that talk about us being thrill-seekers and that you understood why I do what I do? Was it all just bullshit, Matteo?" She leaned closer. "Because, cowboy fireman, you just stepped in it big time."

"No, Dakota, that isn't it. I want a relationship with you. I want to see us have some sort of future together. I just worry to what extent you would go to achieve this goal of covering on a bull."

"I plan to do whatever it takes in order to achieve my goals. If I need more training, I'll seek that out, just like you'd do for something you wanted to achieve in your career." She glanced away and took a deep breath before addressing him again. "Where's the issue here? Are you still stuck on my being a woman trying to do this, and you can't allow someone you see as weak and helpless going after what she wants?"

He raked his fingers through his hair, momentarily taken aback. They'd suddenly gone off the rails again. How was he going to get them back on track?

Chapter Twenty-Five

"No, that's not it at all. You're the strongest woman I know next to Mama." How could he get her to see he only wanted what was best for her and to keep her safe? "Look, I want you in my life, Dakota, and I'm working on being okay with you doing these things I'd run from."

He glanced down at the table, trying to find the right words before he went on. "It's hard for me, but I'm trying. I meant everything I said about Papa. And I take risks too, but they're calculated risks. I know what to do to protect myself, because I have people who care about me and my well-being, and I don't want to hurt them."

Dakota's eyes opened wider and it took her a few moments to continue. "You really mean that, don't you? You're truly concerned about what happens to me, not trying to get me to change or conform so you can control me?"

"Of course. My greatest concern is your welfare."

"You aren't just trying to control me?"

What the—? "No! I care about you, Dakota. More than anything."

She remained quiet for a long time, studying his face as if for an ulterior motive or perhaps processing his words. "You do, don't you?" she whispered, as if it were some monumental revelation.

Hadn't he been showing her that from the day she arrived last December? Matt took her hand. "Sweet Lady, more than you'll ever know. I'm so proud of you and your accomplishments. I want to watch you grow and succeed at everything you set out to conquer."

When she went silent again, he stroked the side of her hand with his thumb. "I don't want to control you, Dakota—as if I could." He allowed himself to smile for the first time in a long while, hoping to lighten the mood. Still nothing. He felt a need to fill the silence.

"Dakota, I worry about you being injured again, so I'll have to work on not letting my fears take over again. But I want to see where our relationship goes. I want us to grow together. I plan on supporting and cheering for you tomorrow when you ride Silverback. I can't say I won't be scared for you, but I promise to rein it in. Believe me, I want you to cover on that bull like you've never covered before—and I have faith that you can do it. But I'll still care about you no matter what you do or don't do in life." He wished they weren't in this restaurant and that he could take her in his arms and kiss her right now.

"I appreciate that, Matteo. Nobody ever cared enough to be in my corner before."

"I'm one hundred percent there for you, Sweet Lady. And I'll be cheering louder for you than anyone else whenever I can be at one of your events. All I know at this moment, though, is that the thought of watching you ride out of my life again for good definitely isn't something I can stand."

The smile faded from her face. "But I'm not the type of woman who can settle down in one place for long. That day will come eventually, and I don't want to hurt you, Matteo."

"Why don't you let me worry about how to handle that day?" *If it comes.* He hadn't given up on winning her over yet and showing her what life with him could be like.

"I'll admit, this is the longest I've stayed in one place since I was a teenager. Before last week, anytime I thought about returning to the rodeo circuit this year, I weighed it against saying goodbye to you—and your horses—and I kept coming up with reasons not to leave."

"You've certainly secured your place in the hearts of each of the horses, including Jason's Van Gogh."

He had to wonder if he was on equal footing with his horses or whether he might edge them out slightly in her affections, but he wouldn't ask. His ego might not be able to handle her response. On the other hand, the fact that his horses meant so much to her made him feel even more strongly that she was the right woman for him.

"How's Kahlo doing? I love them all, but she holds a special place in my heart. She was so afraid of everything when she came."

"She missed you, but she's tolerating Jason and me as far as taking care of her needs. We haven't been able to ride her, of course."

Squeezing her hand, he leaned closer across the table. "Dakota, you mean more to me than any woman I've ever known besides Mama." She opened her eyes wider as if this was news to her. He needed to remedy that.

"I know I have no strings on you, Sweet Lady, and would never want you to feel tied down by me and my ranch. I just want you to know that you always have a place to come to when you need a break from the rodeo circuit, even if it's just for a night or two."

While it would kill him to watch her leave and not come back—the way he thought she had last week—she wasn't one to be roped and tied down. He didn't want to crush her free spirit.

She didn't say anything, but he thought her eyes grew a little bright with unshed tears. Before she started to cry, he needed to lighten the mood. "And I'm not just saying that because we have incredible sex together, although exploring your body is at the top of my list of favorite pastimes."

That made her laugh and broke the tension.

"I love making love with you, Matteo." She smiled almost shyly as if embarrassed to admit it for some reason.

Her declaration surprised and pleased him, although it sounded like a *but* was on the way.

"I also love being at your ranch. And spending time with your horses. And hanging out with you and the guys at the firehouse. Until you, there's been no one in my life who mattered." She glanced down.

He placed his index finger over her lips. "Let's leave it at that for now. We're still exploring this relationship. If you're willing to put up with me and my traditional Italian male ways, then we can figure out what works for us."

A slow smile spread across her face as she met his gaze again. "Well, I guess if you promise not to box me into your archaic ideas of what a woman can and cannot do…"

"Sweet Lady, you've proven to me that you're capable of doing anything you set your mind to, including showing a two-thousand-pound bull who's the boss tomorrow."

She beamed at him. *God, I love that smile.*

"Well, since you put it that way, I'd love to return to your place. I missed it—and you—so much this past week." She grew serious almost immediately and nibbled on her lower lip. Maybe he hadn't managed to avoid that *but* after all.

"I came to another realization after I left—I missed Leadville. Not just the firehouse, but also the folks at the café."

He let out the breath he'd been holding. "Sounds like Leadville has gotten under your skin too."

She was quiet a long time. "I've never been a part of a place like that. The rodeo community is so…transient." She glanced away again before whispering, "I don't think anyone even missed me when I didn't show up for the beginning of the season in March."

So his earlier instinct had been right. The people she'd thought were her "family" hadn't been there for her or cared enough to check in on her when events had started up again.

He took her hand in both of his. "Dakota, I'm sorry to hear that. I know how much the rodeo community means to you."

She tried to shrug it off and pull her hand away, but he didn't let go of their connection. He wanted her to know he was here for her. Again, he went for some levity. "Maybe you were a threat to some of the shakier male egos."

Dakota rolled her eyes and grinned. Then she became serious again and cleared her throat. "Rodeo's a competitive sport, but we try to be there for each other. I think a bigger culprit was my venturing away from the professionally sanctioned rodeos a few years ago. That might have been when things started falling apart. Maintaining a sense of family is hard to come by when everyone's running scattershot to so many smaller rodeos all over the West."

She took a deep breath. "The money was a lot better for us renegade women but, until yesterday, I don't think I realized just how much things had changed for me as far as community goes."

When she became lost in her thoughts, he waited a few moments before asking, "What happened yesterday?"

She stared down at their joined hands and didn't make eye contact as she answered. "I ran into a woman bronc rider I'd competed against for the past few years. Struck up a conversation and"—she met his gaze, and he felt the pain she was feeling as if punched right in his chest—"she hardly remembered me. Hadn't even wondered where I was when I didn't show up for the first competitions a month ago."

"Last night, I lay awake trying to figure out why that was." She took another deep breath and let it out slowly, meeting his gaze finally. "I have to blame myself for a lot of it. I really hadn't reached out to anyone last December. Nobody other than those at the Golden rodeo would have even known about my buck-off and injury." She swallowed hard. "I realized that, as much as I thought of these people as being my people—my family, inside and outside the arena—I'd never invested myself in their lives and they hadn't done so in mine, either."

He stroked the knuckles of her hand, feeling the hurt in her words. Then he leaned closer. "Well, Sweet Lady, I'm glad you reached out to me last December. I assure you that you were missed by me this past week. And by Mama."

Dakota's eyes opened wider. "She knows I left?"

He nodded. "When I didn't show up for her monthly dinner last Sunday, her radar went into overdrive."

"She cares so much about you, Matteo. I hope you and your siblings know how fortunate you are to have a mother like her."

The loss of Dakota's mother and grandmother broke his heart for her.

"Was she upset that I ran off without telling her goodbye?"

He chuckled. "A little, but not at you. I think she knows her sons don't always make the right moves when dealing with women, which is probably the reason only one of her four sons are married. Still not sure how Tony managed it, but I'd say it had more to do with Carmella setting him straight on a few things."

His throat suddenly dry, he released her hand and took a sip of water. "The rest of my family didn't know you were gone, but if they had, they'd probably have kicked my butt all the way to Utah for letting you go. Then there are the guys at the station. I think they missed you *almost* as much as I did."

A tear spilled onto each of her cheeks. "They did?"

He nodded with a grin, hoping to lighten the mood and cheer her up. "And not just because you didn't bring us ice cream this week, either."

She smiled, which did his spirits a world of good too. "I promise to bring you guys some ice cream Monday after you start your next shift."

Matteo sensed that they'd managed to jump over a big hurdle in this fragile relationship. She'd confided things to him she hadn't before, probably because they hadn't been clear yet to her before this weekend.

Time to see where he really stood with her.

"So you'll come back home with me tomorrow?" His heart beat wildly as he waited for her answer.

She gave a slight nod. "If you'll have me. Sorry I ran off in such a huff. I'm not very good at dealing with confrontation or anyone trying to—"

"—control you." He nodded. "I got it. Will try not to do that again. Mama helped set me straight on some things. You had every right to be pissed at me."

"I can't wait to see her again. And I promise not to run off the next time you tick me off."

"You make it sound like it's a given that I will."

She gave him a *no-duh* look.

"Okay, okay. I'm sure I will at some point."

She smiled. "But I'll try to give you the benefit of the doubt, even if you push my buttons. And we will talk things over, like we're doing tonight." She sighed. "Having a serious relationship—or strong connections to anyone—is new territory for me, though. I have a lot to learn about how to handle conflict and emotional stuff, Matteo."

He brushed his thumb over the knuckles on her hand. "You're my first serious romantic relationship, Sweet Lady. We'll figure this out together."

Next time he screwed up with her, he hoped to straighten things out without bringing Mama in to sort things out for him. Already, he understood Dakota a lot better.

They spent the rest of the meal talking about the horses and his plans to help Dreams Found Ranch by taking in some of their older rescue horses so they could focus on the new ones arriving this week. The Wilsons and Dentons had more horses than they could handle but with so many mustangs needing a safe place to heal and recover from all forms of trauma, they had a hard time turning any away.

The excitement in Dakota's voice as she talked about working with more horses told him this might help her find a new purpose in life, along with continuing her own healing. He wanted nothing more for her than to build a bright future with him.

After dinner, Matteo drove them back to the rodeo grounds, and they made their way to her camper. She pulled out the key and put it into the lock but didn't open the side door right away.

Dakota turned toward him. "I've never had anyone in here before, but you're welcome to stay with me tonight if you'd like." One thing was certain, they'd be cozy inside. But she needed to feel connected to him physically. Something major had shifted in their relationship today, and she, for one, wanted to explore whatever that was.

"Thanks. I'd love to."

She swung open the door, and they removed their boots before she indicated that he could enter first, but he insisted she do so. Always the gentleman. Sometimes she wanted that.

Not tonight.

She wanted him buried deep inside her as quickly as possible.

Inside, she placed her boots in the corner, leaving room for his, and they both hung their coats on hooks. Before she turned around, he pressed his erection against her backside and pulled her by the waist against him, making her instantly wet and ready to ride. Clearly, he needed this too.

He flipped her around and pressed her onto the mattress, lying atop her. "I think we'll both be more comfortable in the horizontal position." His lips nibbled against hers and she opened for him as he deepened the kiss, but then he pulled away. "Do me a favor?" he asked after kissing her into a frenzy.

"Anything." Her voice came out breathy with a hint of huskiness. She began opening his blue plaid shirt, figuring whatever it was would involve them both being naked. His shirt had snaps rather than buttons so she wasted no time, ripping it as she pulled. He might have to buy a new one, but who cared.

"Wear your chaps for me tonight. Nothing else."

A slow grin spread across her face. "I left them on the backseat of the truck."

"I'll be right back. Strip down while I'm gone."

"Yes, sir!"

She might not like him ordering her around career-wise but had no problem taking orders in the bedroom—or camper, as it were. She was out of her sweater before he exited the door, then remembered that the truck was locked and grabbed the key fob to unlock it before he'd need to come back and ask her to do so.

She'd shimmied out of her Wranglers and removed her socks by the time he came back inside carrying the chaps. "Let me just get out of these panties."

"Glad I got back in time for that. Stand up first." He sat down on the mattress.

Standing would be no small feat in the cramped space, but she did as he instructed. His gaze zeroed in on her peach-colored underwear. As he watched, she hooked her thumbs inside the silky fabric and undulated her hips while shimmying them down her legs. She remained laser-focused on his face, and the momentary appreciation she glimpsed in his eyes made her even hotter.

As she pitched the wet panties in his direction, he caught them in one hand and tossed her the chaps with his other. He brought her panties to his nose and sniffed her scent. "God, you smell good. Leather and spice—a heady combination." The crotch of his jeans bulged; she couldn't wait to get him out of them.

Making eye contact, she wrapped the band of the chaps around her waist and buckled it into place before reaching for the zipper.

He stayed her hand. "I'll do that. Spread your legs."

His hands reached between her thighs to pull the flaps through, the backs of his hands brushing against her short hairs, leaving her tingling.

He zipped each leg, then stared a moment at her curls framed between the chaps, breathing in her scent. If he didn't throw her on the bed and enter her soon, she'd die. But he didn't seem to be in such a hurry any longer.

He glanced up at her. "Turn around."

She did so, bending over to give him a full view of her ass cheeks framed by the turquoise leather.

"Sweet Jesus. Better than I imagined." He cupped the curve of her ass with each hand, letting her panties fall to the floor. Then he stood and pulled her upright, her butt rubbing against his erection.

Did he plan to enter her from behind too, rather than let her ride him? She was game for whatever, as long as it happened soon. Thoughts of them entangled on that mattress in whatever position he asked for made her even wetter. She waited for him to express his wants.

"We'll fit together perfectly." Matteo planted a quick kiss on her ass cheek. "Bend over and hold on tight."

Oh God! Her knees nearly buckled at the command, but she managed to bend again at the waist and keep her legs straight.

His hand wasted no time finding her sex. "So wet for me. I've missed you, Sweet Lady."

"I've missed you too." She hoped her voice conveyed how badly she needed him inside her—now!

"Glad you parked away from the other campers." He trailed more kisses down her back. She felt like a teenager in the backseat of a car.

"Why's that?" Her mind barely worked any longer. When was he going to enter her?

"Because we're going to be rocking this camper and you're going to be screaming, and I'd prefer not to have anyone banging down the door to check on you."

"Oh!" Three fingers plunged inside her, taking her by surprise. He wasn't going to take this slow after all.

Thank God!

Chapter Twenty-Six

"I have a better idea," Matteo said. Dakota missed his fingers when he pulled them out of her, but hoped his plan was to remedy that soon with his cock. "Turn around. Help me get out of these clothes."

Dakota ran her fingers through the springy hair on his pecs and bent to take a nibble at his nip. Hard. Just like his cock pressing against her sex. Her hips ground against his erection.

She took a step back, locked gazes with him, and removed his belt, tossing it aside.

"Lie back. I'll be gentle." When he did, she unbuttoned and unzipped his fly. After pulling and tugging the Wranglers off his hips, she wasted no time freeing his erection from his boxer briefs. But when she would have lowered her mouth to him, he pushed her away.

"I want the jeans off before we go any farther."

She complied in a matter of seconds. "Better?"

He grinned. "It's a start. Let's try this." He scooted to the edge of the mattress then turned around to move the pillows sideways to the center of the bed. Matteo stretched out, resting his head on the pillow. His penis rose proud and hard. She knew what she wanted to do but had decided to let him call the shots tonight. He beckoned her forward with his finger, still glistening from being inside her moments ago.

"I want you inside me, cowboy fireman. *Now.*"

"Turn around and spread your legs for me, cowgirl."

Her clit throbbed, but she did as he ordered. Apparently, tonight was all about his seeing her ass in these chaps.

His hands on either of her butt cheeks, he squeezed, slapping one then the other. *Hot!* Then he pulled her onto the mattress.

Feeling off-balance, she tried to turn around first, but he kept a firm grip on her hips. He scooted a little further onto the bed, allowing her to get her knees on either side of his hips.

Reverse cowgirl? Dakota's heart skipped a beat, then she smiled, happy to oblige.

"Lower yourself onto my cock slowly, cowgirl. I don't want to hurt you, and this might be a little tricky at first."

She shook her head and did as he told her to do, positioning herself above him before slowly easing herself onto his thick cock. She had to lean back toward him a little before being able to fully seat herself on him.

"So wet."

"You made me wet. Now, what are you going to do about it?"

"Cowgirl, question is how hard do you want to ride *this* bull?"

Dakota giggled and raised her left hand high over her head. He grabbed onto her hips and lifted her up and down as they increased their pace. "Giddy up, cowgirl. Only I'm going to give you a helluva lot more than eight seconds."

She'd never felt so full. Her thighs squeezed his hips, and Matteo grabbed her hips and bucked up into her heat. Each time his cock pressed against her G-spot, she lost control and let herself be consumed by the sensations rolling through her body. She leaned forward a little, and he groaned. She wasn't sure if she'd hurt him or if it felt good, but he didn't tell her to stop, so using her legs and hips to lift and fall, she was able to increase the pace even more.

"Sweet Jesus. I'm not going to last long, Dakota."

"Don't hold back! We can slow it down next time!"

With that, they both increased their thrusts and lunges. His hand slapped her ass until she screamed for more.

Her mewling cries increased as he sped up the tempo again.

I'm so close.

"I need you to come for me, Sweet Lady. Now!"

"I am!" Even without any added stimulation, the spasms roiled through her body until she lost her mind. Tears streamed down her cheeks.

"God, yes!" Matteo cried. "Don't stop!"

As if I could.

Her heart raced as they neared the peak, then he exploded inside her, thrusting several more times to milk his orgasm for all it was worth. Dakota continued to ride him long after her own orgasm had begun to fade. She'd never felt more connected with him as she did in this moment.

His hands grabbed her hips again and slowed her down.

"So damned hot. Remind me to rent a mechanical bull sometime. Not in public." He fought to catch his breath. "In the barn…Just us."

She stretched out her cramped legs and collapsed backward on top of him, not wanting to break the connection with him yet. She gasped to fill her lungs too.

Suddenly, he pulled out and rolled her onto her back. She stared up at him and saw a look of horror on his face. "We have a problem."

What? The fact that I can't fathom what you're talking about? She couldn't even formulate the one-word question to ask him what was wrong.

He stroked her face. "I've never been careless with a woman. I'm sorry. I got so caught up in the moment…"

He hadn't put on a condom! Not that she'd thought of one, either. Surely with her absence of periods most of the time, they had nothing to worry about. Still, it only took one slipup.

She brushed her fingers through his hair. "I'm sure it will be fine. I probably only have three or four periods a year. What are the chances?"

He rolled onto his back, looking up at the ceiling as he raked his fingers through his hair. "God, I can't believe I did that."

"I'm serious. Don't worry about it."

Although an unwanted pregnancy would certainly put a damper on her rodeo plans, she didn't truly think anything would come of it. How could she get him to put that behind them?

"Can we just bask in the glow a little while? That was incredible."

He didn't smile, still hung up on the fact that she'd ridden him bareback.

"Matteo, we both had a responsibility to think of it, and neither of us did. I am not going to beat myself up about it, and neither should you. I assure you, it's nothing, but I can take a pregnancy test in a few weeks if you're worried. And if it's an STD you're worried about, I'm clean. How about you?"

"Same. I'm more worried about you getting pregnant. I want you to know I'm not trying to do that to get you to stop riding broncs—or bulls."

That thought hadn't even occurred to her. Was he being truthful? After all, he had been very careful up until…no way. He would probably worry even more about her becoming pregnant and the risks involved with that.

"I know you wouldn't do that. Let's clean up and forget about it." The deed was done, after all. And, again, what were the chances?

She turned onto her side and reached for paper towels and wipes. Having a sink in here would have been nice right about now, but they'd have to work with what they had. They could go over to the showers later if they wanted to do a better job. Which they did.

Hours later, Dakota lay awake long after Matteo had dozed off, curling herself up against his side with her head against his shoulder. Not the best position to sleep in, but she couldn't get drowsy anyway.

What a day—and night.

She couldn't believe they'd only been together four months. In some ways, it felt as though she'd known him her entire life—not just the year and a half in high school and the time she'd been at the ranch since December.

He made her feel comfortable in ways she'd never been with another man. Dakota could get used to having someone looking out for her, even if he sometimes got overprotective and bossy. Tonight, he'd been bossy in all the right ways.

She'd always heard that Italian men liked to rule the roost in their homes, although she hadn't noticed Matteo's brother Tony bossing Carmella around. Maybe they'd come to a truce, just as Dakota and Matteo had tonight. Then again, his mama might have tried to raise more progressive Italian sons, rather than traditional ones.

Matteo possessed the right mix of both traits in Dakota's opinion.

He just needed to balance them and not let one take over.

Clearly, something she'd said or done over dinner had gotten through to him; it was as if he'd flipped a light switch on the bull-riding issue. At least, she hoped that was behind them. She didn't want to fight anymore—although the make-up sex was better than ever. Even if they did lose their minds temporarily.

What would she do on the off chance she got pregnant? She shrugged away the thought. What was the likelihood? When had her last period even been? She really didn't keep track of them. A gyno had wanted her to take the pill to regulate them, but it had become a hassle and not something she needed to worry all that much about, since she hadn't been sexually active in a while.

No doubt, Matteo would go all traditional and insist that she marry him. But she wasn't ready for that step, either. However, the thought of being part of his big Italian family left a warm spot in her heart. So much love and support for each other, no doubt a reflection of how his mama and papa had raised them. Even if the Giardano brothers did rib each other a lot, they did so with love.

What would it have been like if she'd had siblings? Maybe she did and just didn't remember them, but no brothers or sisters had popped up in any of the memories that had begun breaking through from her subconscious.

Still no word about her DNA results. Surely she'd hear something this week. It had been six weeks since she'd sent the kit back.

Her heart beat a little faster as she thought about the results, but all she could do was wait and see—and follow her instincts on whether to reach out to any matches.

She breathed slowly and deeply, trying to regulate her erratic heart-beat.

Don't worry until you have something to worry about.

She closed her eyes, willing herself to sleep. Funny that she was more worried about those DNA results than anything to do with unprotected sex with Matteo.

But she needed her sleep. Tomorrow afternoon, she had a date with an old nemesis, one she intended to conquer this time.

"Silverback, we meet again."

Dakota wouldn't let this ornery bull deprive her of a completed ride this time.

"Today's my day. You won't cheat me the second time around."

The bull snorted in derision, but she climbed onto the wall of the chute and then took her place on the beast's back. She wedged her gloved hand into the handle of the tacky bull rope until confident she could maintain a solid grip for the full ride.

As he'd done at the school, the sorry cuss tossed his head back as if to bash her face in, but she was ready for the move and avoided contact. Wearing full protective gear, she refused to let this bull get the best of her.

At her nod, the gate swung open and Silverback tore out of the chute, bucking and twisting toward the left. She spurred him on, keeping her toes pointed out and her eyes on the back of Silverback's head as she tried to rack up maximum points for this ride. The jarring and crushing of her ribs and internal organs with each buck made her feel each of her thirty-two years, but she held tight with her right hand and kept her left one high in the air.

Silverback instinctively switched things up and twisted to the right, trying to throw her off, but she wouldn't let go. Suddenly, she heard the buzzer as the bullfighters circled around her. Letting go of her bull rope, Dakota was thrown to the dirt at the feet of one of the bullfighters. She scrambled to her feet and was quickly ushered to the side of the arena, where she climbed over the rails before turning back and making eye contact with the beast.

Thank you for that ride, Silverback, but today was my turn.

"You were fantastic!" She glanced up and saw Matteo standing below her outside of the railing, a huge smile on his face.

"Thanks!" She turned toward the scoreboard and squinted. "What's my score?" She removed her protective face mask.

"They haven't announced it yet, but you covered!" Matteo's enthusiasm made her feel ten feet tall.

Dakota climbed down from the rails and launched herself at him. "I did it!" Unexpectedly, he wrapped his arms around her and spun her around—as if she wasn't already on cloud nine.

Matteo grinned down at her. "I'm so proud of you, Dakota. You set out to conquer that bull, and you did it." Matteo's praise meant so much to her, especially given how much he'd dreaded her doing this in the first place.

Caleb approached and clapped her on the back. Matteo stepped back to give them room. "You covered, Dakota! That was one helluva ride. Nobody's managed eight seconds on Silverback for the two years I've owned him."

Hearing that made her spirits soar even higher. Then a cheer went up in the crowd, and she heard the announcer give her score. "Eighty-six point five for Dakota Mathison on Silverback."

Yes!

Both rider and bull had to have done well to earn a rating like that. So not only had she covered, but she'd won first place. That meant a buckle and some cash. She already had plans for that money but wasn't ready to share those with Matteo yet.

"Here, drink this." Matteo held out a sweating water bottle.

"Thanks!" She chugged down the cold water without coming up for air then tossed the bottle in a nearby recycling bin. "I really needed that." She'd forgotten how dusty the arena could be.

"Dakota," her instructor said, "you should come to Boulder next weekend. We'll be there for another jackpot rodeo. I think you've found your calling with the bulls."

She glanced at Matteo, but his face remained expressionless. *My choice.* Dakota turned to her instructor. "I appreciate the vote of confidence, Caleb." Was she really about to say this? She took a deep breath. "But I've already proven myself—to me." Not to mention to Matteo. "I have no desire to launch a bull-riding career at my age."

"You sure?" Matteo asked, seemingly incredulous.

She smiled at him, grateful that he wasn't trying to smother her with all his worries about what could happen to her if she did. "One hundred percent." She turned to Caleb. "I don't know where I'm going from here, but I'm ready to retire the bull rope. I've seen too many life-altering accidents, and I'm not going out on a stretcher." She didn't mention the deaths caused by bulls and thankfully hadn't witnessed any herself other than in the movies. Matteo wrapped an arm around her. "Thanks for everything you did for me, Caleb. I'll be sure to recommend your school to anyone interested in your bull- or bronc-riding classes."

"How'd you like to teach saddle bronc riding for us this summer? We have a lot of ladies asking us to add a class specifically for the gals."

Was she interested in teaching? Of course, there were a lot of guys she'd like to teach a thing or two, but maybe she could help the next generation of women take on that fight now that she was hanging up her spurs.

"Not sure what my plans are at the moment, but give me a shout when things are closer to ready, and I'll see. Thanks for asking!"

She said goodbye to Caleb and, when they were alone again, she glanced up at Matteo. "Thank you for letting me make my own decision without trying to persuade me one way or another."

"I sure didn't expect to hear you say you were done even before the adrenaline stopped rushing through you. But I'd be lying if I said I wasn't thrilled with your decision to walk away while on top."

"I don't know if I'm on top after covering just once, but I think that's all I needed." She pinched his side playfully as they walked toward the truck to pack up and go home. "I might have taken him up on Boulder if you'd tried to talk me out of doing it, though."

"Seriously?"

She smiled, assuring him she certainly was.

"Then I'll make sure I keep my opinions to myself from now on, unless they're asked for."

"Smart thinking, cowboy fireman." She patted him on the ass. "I can't wait to ride you tonight. Now it's your turn to wear the chaps."

"I'm in no hurry to get back, with Jason in charge of things tonight, so if you can forego seeing me in chaps a while longer, that camper is still set up. Let's take a little detour after they award you your prizes."

"I'm down with that." Half an hour later, he led her in the direction of the campground. While she couldn't wait to get back to the ranch and his horses, she needed to expend a little excess energy. No better way than making love with this man she'd almost begun to fall in love with.

There, she'd admitted it.

To myself, at least.

Chapter Twenty-Seven

Back at the ranch after Grand Junction, Dakota already found herself becoming restless on the second day of Matteo's shift. Being in the arena had reignited her love of the rodeo. While she hadn't walked away from bronc riding, she had hoped that riding the bulls would have satisfied her longer than this.

Was she ready to hang up her spurs? Covering on Silverback had fulfilled something inside her. But now she'd accomplished all she'd be allowed to do as a woman in the rodeo world. Maybe someday the regulations wouldn't be so limiting and she could compete again, but that would have to happen soon. She'd be thirty-three in October and her daredevil years were coming to an end.

Thinking that teaching other women would keep pressure on the officials with the professional rodeo associations to open up the sport more, Dakota called Caleb and agreed to teach at least one class of women saddle-bronc riders. He told her the school would be starting in early August. Would that give her the satisfaction she needed? *Maybe.* If not, what on earth would she do to make a living if she didn't return to the rodeo? All she knew was rodeoing and a bit of ranch life.

But it's not like Matteo's invited you to move in.

Not that he seemed to want her to leave, either. Regardless, she couldn't sponge off him forever, even though she tried to do her part around here to earn her keep.

She supposed she could return to the professional circuit doing barrel racing again. Maybe Matteo would let her train Kahlo for that. The inherent risks weren't as great as with bronc riding, but then neither were the thrills, so it didn't appeal to her now any more than it had in the past.

When would Luke and Ryder be sending them more rescue horses?

What "us"? Don't you mean, Matteo?

But more horses would give her greater responsibilities and occupy more of her time. The four-horse trailer they'd bought from Paul's friend had been picked up two weeks ago. When Darren told him he and his wife were still looking for a two-horse trailer for Jason, Matteo had quoted him a good price so they could give it to him for graduation. But in the meantime, they could use both trailers to haul the horses from Dreams Found to the ranch here.

With summer coming, the mustangs would be able to be out in the pastures rather than have to be cooped up in the barn so much. Kahlo always preferred being outside too.

It was too soon to tell where her relationship with Matteo would lead. They'd experienced a major clash. Even though they seemed to have gotten past that, he wouldn't change overnight. What if she wanted to do something else he deemed unsafe? Would he challenge her again? She didn't intend to test him—mainly because she had no clue what she wanted to do yet—but she'd need to make sure he could accept her as she was before they could become any more serious.

He had to know he'd never have a domestic goddess in Dakota. She'd never be a great cook by any stretch of the imagination. Fortunately, Matteo's standards were pretty low; he liked whatever she fixed. Maybe she'd make him something special for supper tomorrow.

She went to the pantry and pulled out the box with the electric pressure cooker. His mama had bought it for him, telling him how quick and easy it would be to prepare his own meals, but he hadn't been interested. Dakota read over the instruction booklet, did a test to make sure she could assemble it correctly, and spent the next hour researching what to make in it. She watched several cooking videos until she found one for baby back ribs. Matteo would love those. The recipe seemed quick and easy, and she could let the pot do all the work while she hung out with the horses.

The sun called to her to enjoy the day now that she'd made that decision. She could go to the grocery tonight to get what she'd need for tomorrow's dinner.

Now what?

Maybe she'd take Kahlo out for a ride. The horse had warmed up to her, but still had her moments of skittishness. Dakota packed a sandwich and two bottles of water in case she didn't feel a need to hurry back. She just planned on having leftovers tonight, anyway.

No fun to cook for one.

After saddling and mounting the mare, she set out toward the mountains and the government lands. But she must have veered off the path she and Matteo usually took, because she found herself at the old miner's cabin that he'd talked about. Perfect time to explore.

Dismounting, she tied Kahlo to the porch railing. The structure looked sturdy enough, windows intact—including one pane in front that appeared to be modern—but, man, did this place ever need some TLC.

"Wait here, Kahlo. I'll be back in a bit." She deftly avoided a hole in the top step and crossed the porch to the only window in the front, wiping away some of the grime with her coat sleeve.

Dakota peeked inside; the place was a shambles. She wouldn't be surprised if a hundred rodents made their homes in there now, and who knows how many in the past. Still curious, she walked over to the door and tried the handle. The door budged a little bit, so she gave it a hard shove, and it opened a little more. It seemed to be warped or stuck, so she applied more force on the next try and stumbled inside.

Had Matteo left the cabin unlocked in case someone needed to find shelter? Not that she'd ever encountered hikers up here.

Dust motes danced in the rays of sunlight coming into the room from a side window she hadn't noticed from the front. Surveying the first floor, Dakota didn't see a lot of room for anything other than a rickety table and a small cot in the corner next to a potbellied stove. She glanced up to find a loft for sleeping but no ladder to get her up there.

She moved closer to the stone fireplace near the cot.

Gorgeous craftsmanship.

Her hand brushed across the cold stone, and she tried to imagine what it must have been like back in the day when the cabin had been lived in. A warm fire crackling in the hearth. Perhaps a hearty stew cooking in a three-legged pot to feed the miner after a hard day in the mine. Did he have a family or was he a loner? What kind of mining had been done here? With a name like Leadville, perhaps lead? Or had it been silver? Gold? Iron? Whatever, the industry had long since dried up, as far as she could tell. She decided a visit to the local historical society or museum would be in order so she could learn more about this place and whoever had lived here.

Dakota turned around and walked toward the side window, even dirtier on the outside than the front one she'd peered through a few minutes ago. Must get the brunt of the elements. She could barely see a thing, but it looked like an abstract painting of mountain peaks in the distance.

Stepping back, she looked at the little nook. A breakfast table would be perfect in this spot. She wondered why Matteo hadn't fixed up the charming place, but between getting a house and barn ready, working long days at the station and the forest service, and training for his skijoring festival, he probably hadn't had the time. Had he been the one to replace the pane in the front?

Perhaps he planned to do something with it later on. What fun it would be to give the place the loving touches it needed. What a shame to let it stand here neglected.

An idea struck her. She could invest her skijoring and bull-riding winnings into fixing the place up for Matteo. It would have to be a surprise, though, or he'd tell her to save her money. Rather than money, the place looked like it was more in need of time and elbow grease right now, both of which she could supply in spades.

Dakota's heart beat a little faster as she surveyed the room again, this time trying to think about how she'd decorate the place. She'd discovered a knack for restoration when she'd renovated her vintage Shasta camper/trailer, so this project excited her.

An image of her and Matteo wrapped in each other's arms, lying on a bearskin rug—or even a braided one—in front of the fireplace made her smile. It would take months to finish this place to that point, though.

Unless she decided to get a job or teach bronc riding. What else did she know how to do? She seemed to be losing the urge to resume the vagabond life. She had all she wanted right now with Matteo, his animals, and his friends who had welcomed her as their own too.

Maybe you're learning how to put down roots, cowgirl. Whoa, Nellie! Let's not rush things!

Her mind filling with decorating ideas she couldn't wait to put into action, she became anxious to get back to the house to gather some cleaning supplies and get started on that phase while Matteo was still on duty. She wanted to keep this a surprise for now.

Exiting the cabin, though, she noticed that the sun was no longer high above her and that she wouldn't have time to get down and back here today. *Darn.* She yanked the door closed with a slam so that it wouldn't blow open; the warped wood made it easy for it to catch and hold.

Kahlo nickered as if admonishing Dakota for deserting her so long.

"Sorry, girl. We'll finish our ride now."

Back in the saddle, she glanced in the direction that the side window faced and saw the Collegiates, as Matteo called them. What a majestic view to enjoy lunch or breakfast over. Remembering she'd brought her lunch, she decided she'd only need one bottle of water, and once she finished eating, she'd clean the grime off those windows. It would give her the sense of accomplishment and purpose she'd been longing for all day.

"Sorry, girl. Bear with me just a few more minutes, then we'll find you a stream for a drink." She tied Kahlo in a new spot, then Dakota sat on the porch to quickly down her sandwich and half a bottle of water.

Of course, she reminded herself, this wasn't her place nor was it her decision to make to renovate it. Would Matteo be appreciative or upset with her for meddling?

Dakota smiled. Only one way to find out. Grabbing the other water bottle from the saddlebag and wadding up her unused napkin, Dakota went to the side of the cabin, wet the paper, and began scrubbing the two lower windowpanes, the only ones she could reach without a ladder. The meager amounts of water and paper barely made a dent in the caked-on grime. She probably should have waited until she brought the truck up here and could haul lots of water. Next time Matteo was on duty, she'd do just that. She used the rest of the water in her own bottle too, because she wasn't all that thirsty and would be back at the house in an hour anyway.

Kahlo nickered again. The mare had been very patient with her today. Dakota gave up on the panes. Pocketing her empty bottles and trash in her coat, Dakota prepared to—

Kahlo screamed, and this time Dakota's heart skipped a beat. What had scared her? Dakota ran from the side of the cabin to find the horse fighting the rope tether. Looking around to see what the threat was, she didn't spy anything obvious. Her handgun was in the saddlebag, so she went to retrieve it.

"What's wrong, girl?" Dakota pocketed the pistol then rubbed Kahlo's neck in long strokes to calm her down while continuing to scan the woods surrounding the clearing. The snow had melted from the places where the sun had hit, but it lay deeper underneath the trees. Was something—someone—out there? The mare sometimes spooked over silly things, but Dakota never ignored a warning. Animals had a sixth sense about these things and could hear sounds humans couldn't detect.

Maybe they should start back down to the barn rather than go for that extended ride. Kahlo continued to dance around as if trying to unhitch herself from the porch post.

"It's okay, girl. We're leaving now."

Kahlo squealed more urgently, pawing the hard ground. When Dakota turned to survey the area again while simultaneously trying to calm her horse, another frightening scream filled the air.

"If you hear a woman screaming in the woods, head in the other direction. It's not a woman. It's a mountain lion."

Those words came to her in the voice she'd been hearing in her dreams—*Nana.* She couldn't see what had made the noise but didn't dismiss the warning.

"Easy, Kahlo," she said as she slowly approached so as not to spook the mare further. She hoped the horse would stay calm long enough for her to get down the mountain. "You have to trust me and cooperate, girl."

She unhitched the horse but held onto the reins as tightly as if they were a bull rope. The last thing she needed was for Kahlo to bolt and leave her stranded up here with that cat. Of course, Dakota could take refuge in the cabin, but her primary goal was to get both of them out of this dangerous situation safely.

Placing her left foot in the stirrup, Dakota mounted. The mountain lion hadn't shown its face and might not even be close, considering the way sound traveled, but she decided to gently nudge her heels into Kahlo's sides, rather than get her into a full gallop right away. Hopefully, the animal wouldn't start chasing them. Not that Dakota knew anything about how big cats reacted, but in the movies, people always seemed to try and move slowly to escape them.

Standing still wasn't an option either, so after they left the clearing and were back on the trail, she dug her heels into Kahlo's sides a little harder. That seemed to be all the permission Kahlo needed, because she tore off like a bronc out of the chute. Unfortunately, Dakota hadn't expected this extreme response, and even though she tried to maintain her grip on the reins, she lost control and flew off the mare's rump. Dakota's shoulders and head hit the ground hard, but her left boot remained hung up in the stirrups.

Damn it!

Kahlo began dragging her. Dazed from hitting her head, she shouted, "Whoa, Kahlo! Stop!" The friction against the seat of her Wrangler's burned, but not nearly as badly as the ribbing she'd take for getting bucked off an otherwise tame horse.

The cat let out another scream, closer this time. Kahlo took off running, dragging Dakota alongside. She twisted her body sideways to keep from hitting her head on the rocks that littered the trail. Extending her foot in a maneuver she'd learned from riding broncs, she managed to get her foot to slip out of her boot.

But no sooner had she released her foot than something crashed against her head. The impact had her seeing stars—until everything went black.

Matt ended his latest attempt to reach Dakota to say good night. They hadn't had connection issues since she switched phone carriers, and they always tried to talk before bedtime every day he worked.

The shift had been a busy one, so it was later than he'd normally call. When the tones dropped again, he knew he wouldn't be able to try phoning again for a while. He got into his turnout gear and jumped into the backseat of the truck as they headed out into the night for another vehicle accident, this one on the highway that ran by his ranch.

Matt's heart pounded as he feared finding Dakota involved on this run. Images from that nightmare he'd had a while back continued to haunt him. Had it been a glimpse into the future? He'd never been intuitive in the past. That was Franco's gift.

Matt's anxiety level increased with each mile as Engine 1 sped out of town. They passed his ranch in a blur; he'd been unable to make out whether Dakota's truck was parked in the lane. His sense of dread only grew worse.

Flames from the vehicle burning half a mile ahead of them lit the night sky.

Please don't let it be Dakota. Please, Papa, can you help her out of there if it's her?

As soon as they parked, Matt could see that, unless the occupant or occupants of that vehicle had escaped already, it would take a miracle for anyone to survive now.

Matt waited for the engine to come to a complete stop, then opened his door and ran over to see that it was an old pickup truck burning, but any identification of the vehicle was long since gone.

"Charge this line with foam!" his lieutenant ordered and Matt's muscle memory took over.

Holding the nozzle, he quickly knocked down the flames so he could inspect the interior. Matt saw the charred body that had fallen to its side. The flesh had melted off the face, burning any hair and making it impossible to tell what color it had been.

"Obvious death, Lieutenant."

Because the fire was out, his officer gave them okay to remove their masks; the smell of the body hit him immediately. Matt stumbled away to the side of the road where he bent over and threw up his dinner.

A few moments later, a hand on his shoulder brought his thoughts back to the scene. "What's going on, Matt?" His lieutenant's voice broke through the screaming in his head, repeating over and over that it couldn't be her. It just couldn't be her.

Without standing upright or facing the officer, Matt asked, "Any identification on the victim?"

"Too soon to tell. Any contents in the cab of the truck are gone, unless something survived in the glove box. The police are checking for a VIN now." After a pause, he added as if finally realizing what was upsetting Matt, "Ah, man, don't even go there. It can't be Dakota."

Matt stood and the two of them looked back at the smoking ruins of the pickup. "Could be her truck."

"That looks like a Dodge chassis. Doesn't she drive a Ford?"

Matt shook his head. "No. An old Dodge Ram." Squinting at the truck bed, its tailgate down, what looked like it might have been a haul of lumber and building supplies had been incinerated. Dakota wouldn't be needing lumber, so that was a hopeful sign, but he couldn't see enough from what was left of the burned-out vehicle to identify the model.

They'd have to wait for the coroner to arrive and take charge of the body, but Matt couldn't tear his gaze from the almost skeletal remains.

His throat tightened up, but he cleared it and blinked rapidly so as not to embarrass himself. "I tried to reach her by phone before we went on this run but got no answer." He didn't mention how many calls he'd made. He took enough ribbing from the guys for checking in with his girlfriend every night.

"You know how wonky cell service is out here." He clapped Matt on the shoulder, squeezing it reassuringly through his gear, and pulled him away from staring at the body any longer. "Come on. Let's get back to work. But since we go right by your ranch on the way back to town, we'll drive in briefly to let you see she's okay. I'm sure she's sound asleep."

Lieutenant's words let him take the first decent breath he'd had in the last hour. "Thanks. I appreciate that. Hope you don't catch any shit from some taxpayer driving by who thinks we're goofing off."

"Screw 'em. As it is, they don't pay us enough for all we do for them. But I can't have you worrying about Dakota all night. At the rate we're going, I don't expect this shift to end quietly, and I need you at one hundred percent for the rest of the shift."

Matt never let his personal life interfere with doing his job—not until tonight anyway. "Thanks, Lieutenant."

It took them another half hour to finish up and start back to the firehouse. The engineer slowed down, entered his lane, and drove toward the house. Matt was afraid to look, but the lieutenant calmed his nerves.

"See? There's her truck, parked right where it should be."

Relief flooded through him. *She's home.* Maybe she was just busy in the barn or somewhere and didn't have her phone with her when he'd called. The house was dark, so she probably was asleep. Still, he wanted to—

Before he could get out to go find her, the tones dropped again. *Damn it!*

"Sorry, Matt, but stop worrying about her. It wasn't Dakota in that truck tonight."

He nodded. "Yeah. That's a huge weight off my shoulders. Thanks for letting me check."

After Lieutenant gave the engineer instructions for the next scene, he made eye contact with Matt from the front seat. "You going to be okay now?"

Matt nodded. While he wanted nothing more than to wrap his arms around Dakota and hold her all night long, he'd have plenty of time for that after this hellacious shift was over in the morning.

Chapter Twenty-Eight

The pounding between her temples made Dakota groan as she slowly pushed herself into a seated position. A shiver passed through her from the damp ground. She took in her surroundings. What was she doing on the ground? Where the hell was she?

Then the memory of Kahlo throwing her off and racing away flooded back to her. Dakota wasn't sure how far she'd been dragged before freeing her foot from her boot.

Great. Now I only have one boot.

Was the other one anywhere nearby? A quick survey of the area didn't reveal it. How long had she lain here? No sign of the cabin. How far had they ridden before she'd been thrown?

All these questions hurt her brain, probably because she had no answers. And why would Kahlo throw—

Mountain lion!

Dakota searched for the predator in the nearby trees and bushes, but didn't see or hear anything. It was daylight still, although sunset would come within the next hour. She'd better start walking down the mountain, but no way could she make it to the house before dark. She hadn't bothered to bring her phone, because there'd be no point up here.

I sure will miss that flashlight feature in short order.

"Kahlo! You out there?" She called out in a loud whisper, not wanting to attract the cougar or any other predators that might be out there.

When she tried to stand up, her left ankle gave out. She looked down, and it had swollen to twice its size. *Damn it.* How was she going to get anywhere on a bum ankle?

The frigid air temperature made her shiver. Thank goodness she'd kept her coat on; the sun wouldn't be around much longer. Unfortunately, she'd lost her hat too when she'd been thrown off.

Maybe she should pack her ankle with snow from a nearby drift to ease the swelling, but the thought of making herself any colder didn't appeal in the least. She would need water, however. Dakota wondered if sucking on melted snow would provide the liquid she needed to survive but nixed that idea immediately. Something she'd read once told her that could lead to hypothermia.

She wished Kahlo would have stuck around to provide her with a little company, but the only sound she heard was the throaty peeping of a frog or toad. Matteo had identified the amphibian to her when they rode the trails up here, but she forgot its name.

Wait! Frogs and toads must mean there was a stream nearby. Water! The bottles she'd brought with her had been used to clean the windows at the cabin, but she'd tucked two empties along with other trash in her coat pockets. Her last sip had been before she left the cabin after lunch; she sure could use some right now.

Matteo would give her hell for not staying hydrated, but she'd welcome any form of contact with him at the moment, angry or not.

"I hope the mountain lion isn't still out there." Probably not, or she'd have been its dinner by now. But she had no way of knowing when it might come back.

Dakota reached into her coat pocket, relieved to find she still had her pistol. She'd loaded it before she set out today. With the safety on, it hadn't discharged when she hit the ground. She checked to be sure it was ready now, though, in case she needed to use it to protect herself. She'd never used it on another living creature before, but her survival might depend on it.

Stop feeling sorry for yourself and get going.

When the toad made another sound, she reluctantly began dragging herself in that direction, and now her pants were getting cold and wet. Even worse, her head throbbed with the blood pounding through it, but she needed to find water. She licked her parched lips in anticipation. The toad stopped peeping, but she was close enough to see the creek. Choosing a path that had more rocks than mud, she dragged herself closer until she could reach the water. Pulling the crushed bottles out of her pocket, she filled them and drank as much as she could stand before dipping them into the water and refilling each one to the brims. She doubted she'd make it back to this stream tonight, so the two bottles would have to do her.

Her fingers burned from the cold then started going numb. Too bad she hadn't worn riding gloves. The sun had dropped half of the distance to the mountain peaks now. She needed to get to a shelter before it got too dark to see where she was going. Her best bet would be to try and reach the cabin. She knew the direction and would at least be able to close the door on predators, even if there was no way of lighting a fire without the potential of burning the cabin down around her. That chimney had to be a mess after all the years of neglect.

She crawled some more looking for a nearby branch or something to fashion into a makeshift crutch. The first one she found was too rotted and broke when she tested it. She could use her pistol to shoot a branch off a tree, but what if she needed the bullets later on?

Remembering she had a pocketknife in her Wranglers, she wondered if it would cut through a live branch? The cowboy she'd dated until he went back to his ex-wife had taught her to carry the knife—said something about it being one of Gibbs' rules, whoever that was—although she hadn't really used it for more than cutting rope. Dakota spent the next few minutes scouting out her options, then found a rock to sit on, and drew the pocketknife out of her pocket to begin sawing at the strongest branch she'd found.

Progress was slow. At this rate, she'd be at it all night. She looked around and found a stone to use as a bludgeon. Maybe if she pounded on the knife, she'd make deeper cuts faster.

Whack!

It took a few more chops to see any progress, but she made quick work of the bark and soon the wood chips were flying. She'd managed to cut halfway through after about fifteen minutes and was able to bend the branch back and forth until she completely broke it off.

Yes!

The sun was turning pink. Not much sunlight left. Pulling herself onto her good foot, she leaned onto the crutch and started hobbling in the direction of the cabin. Good thing she'd become familiar with Matteo's property after all the time she'd spent up here riding.

I hope Matteo doesn't have to work overtime, and that he finds me quickly in the morning.

Problem was that he didn't know where she was. Her truck was still at the house, though, so he'd have to assume she'd be somewhere nearby. If Kahlo returned to the house and he saw her saddled and riderless, surely he'd figure out that she'd gone for a ride up here and there'd been an accident.

Thoughts of the horses going without their feed and clean stalls tonight made her heart ache. It would just be for the one night, though. Matteo would take care of them as soon as he realized they had been neglected.

She hated making them wait any longer, but Matteo would drop everything to find her if he thought she was in danger.

Dakota wasn't shivering too much yet; hopefully hypothermia wouldn't set in. Perhaps her exertions were helping to keep her warm. When the cabin clearing came into view, elation spread through her. Not much farther! Images haunted her of being back at the house tonight curled up by the fire, nursing her injured ankle and downing a beer.

Her head ached. Did she have a concussion like Jason had suffered after his skijoring accident? They'd told his parents he needed to stay awake, and they'd struggled to keep him conscious that night. She didn't have anyone to keep her awake, so she'd have to rely on herself.

Out of the blue, the big cat's scream split the air. *That was close!* Dakota ignored the jolts of pain in her ankle and leg as she hobbled as fast as possible while also looking over her shoulder to make sure the mountain lion wasn't about to pounce on her from behind.

Would it be able to pick up her scent or hear her breathing, and then find her? She had her pistol, even if the thought of killing an animal was abhorrent to her. If it tried to attack, Dakota would have no choice but to kill it, but maybe she could fire a warning shot and scare it away, if it came to that.

What a mess she'd gotten herself into. She tucked her head into the neck of her coat, pulled the collar flaps over her face, and moved as quickly as her bum ankle would allow.

Then she tripped over something and went sprawling to the ground.

Matteo, help! I need you!

As soon as his shift ended, Matt raced home and up the lane to the house and barn. After shutting off his truck, he ran into the house. "Dakota! Are you here?"

Silence.

He'd tried calling her again this morning but still no response. He checked the bedroom and bathroom, worried that she might have fallen or had a medical emergency.

No one here.

He looked for notes on the kitchen table.

Nothing.

Except her phone.

Where the hell did she go without her phone?

Outside again, he found her truck parked near the corral, so she might have used it to haul water or hay to the horses, but he didn't see any of the horses outside. From the racket he heard inside the barn, they sounded like they needed some attention.

Could she have fallen or been injured in there? Or had that asshole from her past tracked her down somehow? She'd taken every precaution when submitting her DNA test, but who knew these days?

Before he reached the barn door, movement in the pasture beyond the corral caught his eye. Kahlo grazed in the pasture just beyond the fence. Saddled.

What the…?

He whistled for the horse, but of course she ignored him and continued eating. No way would Dakota have left Kahlo out here with a saddle on. And for how long? He hadn't seen the horse last night when they'd stopped in briefly after the pickup-truck fire, but he'd been more focused on locating *her* truck and hadn't looked around before they'd been called to the next emergency.

He brought his hands to his mouth and used them as a makeshift megaphone. "Dakota!" No response.

Where are *you?*

Matt went inside the barn, thinking perhaps she'd saddled Kahlo then gone back in for something, but she wasn't there. The stalls were full of muck. Twinkle, Comet, and Van Gogh let him know that they wanted to eat and to have clean bedding. No one had been inside this morning, and probably not even last night.

Matt turned the horses loose in the pasture with Kahlo, checked the water level in the trough that they could drink out of from either the corral or the pasture, and spread some hay flakes in the field for them to eat.

"You'll have to wait until I get back before I can take care of everything else." He returned to the kitchen to get some carrots. Maybe he could bribe Kahlo to show him where she'd left Dakota. Back in the pasture, she accepted the carrots but shied away as soon as she finished them.

Fine. Be that way.

The skittish mare would probably like to be relieved of that saddle, but he couldn't help her if she wouldn't let him get close enough.

Matt jumped back into his truck to drive up to the government lands. Dakota liked to ride up there. Apparently, she'd run into some trouble while out there with Kahlo—yesterday? He wished it would have been this morning, though. Was she prepared to spend a night alone on the mountain? It might be spring, but the snow was still piled high up there and hypothermia would be an issue. There also were bears, rattlesnakes, and cougars she might encounter. Looked like something had spooked Kahlo if she'd thrown Dakota off and headed back toward the barn without her. Or had Dakota even been on the horse when the mare had headed for home?

I hope you have your handgun with you, Sweet Lady.

Matt grabbed his own gun out of the glove box of his truck and slipped it into his coat pocket. He had medic supplies in the backseat of the truck and loaded some bottled water and protein bars for a quick fix in case she hadn't had anything to eat or drink with her. She'd told him sometimes she packed a lunch and went up there, but he didn't know if she did that every time.

As he set out, he wondered if he should call in search and rescue or get an ambulance out here. He doubted Dakota would have ventured into new territory, afraid she might trespass onto private property.

Just to be on the safe side, he placed a call to 911 and reported the situation. She might need to be evacuated to a hospital if she had a serious injury. He wished they'd both had satellite phones, but it was too late to worry about that now. And too bad Jason was in school. He could have led crews up to the places the three of them liked to ride; he knew Matt's place and the federal lands as well as anyone.

In no time, Matt had gotten through the pasture gates and headed up the trail. He didn't see any sign of her in the open areas, but as he entered the woods, he came across her boot. *Damn.* She didn't need to be out in these frigid temperatures without both boots. Had she gotten hung up in the stirrup? Injured her leg or ankle? He stopped to retrieve the boot before driving farther up the mountain.

Every now and then he cut the engine and called out, "Dakota! Can you hear me?"

A breeze whipped up, and he wondered if she'd answered but her voice had been carried off on the wind in the opposite direction. He kept calling her name as he advanced closer to the forest lands, sticking to the trail she'd likely have ridden. The spring ruts made navigating in a truck difficult, but as he searched the snowbanks on either side of the trail, he saw no signs of a disturbance or footprints.

Matt came to the split that would lead to the federal lands or to the old miner's cabin. Would she have known to seek shelter at the cabin?

She'd never been inside as far as he knew, but he had pointed it out to her early on. He hoped she'd remembered and made use of it if she had been close enough.

He cupped his hands over his mouth, and yelled, "Dakota!" He listened again but still didn't hear anything.

Then he heard the scream of a cougar followed by a gunshot ripping through the air. The sound ricocheted, making it difficult to tell where it had come from. His heart stopped for several seconds, then pounded back to life. Who besides Dakota would have fired the weapon? Nobody had come up here to hike in the entire time he'd lived here, as far as he knew.

I have to go find Dakota. She needs me.

He grabbed his medic supplies and ran in the direction of the cabin, hoping that's where he'd find her.

"Don't make me shoot you. Go find something else to eat."

Dakota! She was alive!

He ran into a small clearing, still on his property not far from the cabin, and found a mountain lion slinking around Dakota.

"Go away!" she shouted. She leaned on a makeshift crutch, so she must have been injured, but otherwise she looked no worse for wear.

Matt pulled out this handgun and removed the safety. "Dakota, don't move. I'll take care of the cat."

Dakota shifted her focus to him, hopping on one foot while holding her left one a few inches off the ground, her leg bent at the knee. Her pistol wavered in front of her—not pointed toward the mountain lion but more at him.

Matt kept his gun trained on the cat. "Put down the pistol, Dakota, before you shoot me."

"Don't shoot Mabel. She's just hungry."

Mabel?

"You named the cougar?"

"I think she might be pregnant."

Great. All he needed was a passel of cougars up here.

"I've been trying to talk her into leaving, even fired a warning shot, but she's determined." Remembering the pistol in her hand, she lowered it at last. "Do you have anything she can eat?"

Had Dakota suffered a head injury? Was she delusional from a lack of water or food? "Dakota, it's a predator. We're not going to feed it, and we aren't going to let her feed on you or me, either. If she doesn't get lost, I'm going to have to shoot her to protect you."

Dakota glared at him, but he quickly turned his attention back to the cat, which seemed to have no intention of leaving. Usually, they picked on lone individuals, not two or more.

"Don't you dare shoot her, Matteo!"

Remembering something Tony had told him when they were hiking as teens, he holstered his handgun, raised his arms over his head, and waved them wildly while screaming. "Get out of here! Go on, get!" He made eye contact with the cougar, though, which might not have been wise. If he charged the cougar, could Matt scare it off? What if it had rabies and attacked him or Dakota? He didn't want to get too close because he'd need all his faculties to get Dakota off this mountain.

The cat turned back toward Dakota. The two exchanged some sort of silent communication, then the cougar turned and ran off in the direction of the federal lands.

Still unsure if the cat would return, he ran to Dakota. "Where are you hurt?"

"A bump on the head and a twisted ankle. At least I think it's just twisted. Kahlo got spooked by the mountain lion, and…" She glanced away as if embarrassed, "I took a tumble."

He cupped her face briefly, happy to prove to himself he wasn't imagining this moment. Then he began examining her head for bumps or cuts. "Where'd you hit your head?"

She pointed to a spot at the back right side. "There was a goose egg, but it's not too bad today. My ankle hurts like a mother, though."

"Did you lose consciousness?"

"For a while."

"Any idea how long?"

"Well, it was daylight when I got tossed off Kahlo and still daylight when I came to. But I didn't have my phone to check the time."

Hard to determine if she'd been out for more than five minutes, but the scans and exam at the hospital would determine if there'd been any major brain injury. She seemed to have her wits about her, though.

"Let me help you to my truck." He lifted her into his arms. "You can get rid of the crutch. I've got you."

"Are you kidding?" She clutched the crude implement to her chest. "It was a stroke of genius for me to cut that crutch using my pocket-knife. I'm keeping it as a souvenir."

She wanted to remember this hellacious experience? The woman never failed to surprise him. But he needed to get her to the hospital for a CT scan to make sure she didn't have any swelling or hemorrhaging of the brain. Not to mention evaluate that foot or ankle injury. Matt carried her back to where he'd left the truck.

"I had just decided to try and walk down the mountain, in case you didn't find me."

"Glad I got off work this morning." What if this had happened on his first shift day? "Where'd you spend the night?"

She didn't answer right away. Opening the passenger door to the truck, he set her down and grabbed a bottle of water out of the backseat. "Here, drink this."

"Got any food in there? I'm starving more than anything."

"Drink first. I'll get some protein bars." While she downed the water, he grabbed two bars and returned to her, handing her the first one. She still hadn't told him where she'd spent the night, but without both boots or the necessary equipment, she'd never have survived in the open.

"Were you outside all night?"

"Oh no! I managed to get back—I mean get to the cabin. Couldn't light a fire but managed to keep warm."

"How?"

She pointed to her injured foot. "After I got out of my wet clothes, I wrapped my lower body in a disgustingly dirty quilt I found and elevated my foot, then put my coat back on and made a little cocoon for myself inside it. It's amazing what conditions you can put up with when you have no choice."

Impressed with how calm she'd remained throughout, he asked, "Have you taken survival training?"

She laughed. "No, but I dated a guy once who was into that kinda stuff, and he told me some things over the months we were together."

Far from feeling jealous about an old boyfriend, Matt was grateful that she'd paid attention and been able to put the information to use when it mattered.

"We need to get you off this mountain and to the hospital." Matt knelt down beside her and checked her ankle, examining it as best he could. "Doesn't appear to be broken, but I'm more worried about a concussion."

"Oh, I'm fine. A little headache, that's all."

He stared up at her. "Which is one of the signs of a concussion." Of course, he'd expected to find her unconscious or dead, rather than nonchalant and mostly worried about eating.

"Let me get that ankle stabilized and wrapped. Might make it less painful when the truck hits the ruts." He took an Ace bandage from the emergency kit and wrapped her swollen foot as much as possible. At least there was no exposed skin now. He pulled a thermal blanket from the kit and wrapped it around her foot and ankle, which seemed to be the most exposed part of her body. Her missing boot would do her no good with swelling like that, though.

"Ready?"

"Definitely. I want to go home."

Home.

Did she think of his place as her home now? Or was it the concussion talking? Still, that simple word warmed him to the core.

"I can't wait to get in bed and sleep the rest of the day."

"I'm afraid that won't be possible, not right away at least. I'm sure half the county's emergency services will be waiting for us when we get off the mountain."

"You called 911? Why?"

Was she serious? "I didn't know what to expect when I found you or how long you've been injured or exposed to the elements. Sweet Lady, I've aged ten years since last night." He wouldn't even bring up the terror he'd experienced when he thought she might have perished in that truck fire last night.

"You started worrying last night? How'd you know?"

"We talk every night, remember?"

He'd leave it at that. No way would he tell her what had happened to make him worry she might have died in that pickup truck.

When he didn't get in the driver's seat right away, she said, "Okay, I'm ready when you are."

Anxious to get her warmed up, he put her improvised crutch in the backseat and closed the doors. He wanted to just hold her in his arms, so grateful that she'd survived relatively unscathed, but she wasn't out of the woods yet. Having her safe with him again was the best feeling ever, though.

Chapter Twenty-Nine

Dakota rested her head against the back of the seat, trying not to moan as her foot and other parts of her body reacted to the jolts the truck took on the way down the mountain.

"Sure glad you figured out where I was," she told him. "I didn't particularly like the idea of hobbling down this mountain. I'd still be at it tomorrow."

"No way would I have let you go that long. I would have called in some favors and come looking for you myself if I wasn't already off work."

As independent as she liked to think herself, no way would she be complaining about his being protective of her today. "I appreciate that." She held her hand out between them and he took it, giving hers a squeeze. Tears of exhaustion sprang to her eyes, but thankfully he couldn't see them. When he had to negotiate a rough patch, he put both hands on the wheel again.

They had barely made it through the first gate into the pasture before she heard a commotion and opened her eyes to see an ambulance with its lights flashing. She also saw half a dozen pickup trucks headed in their direction.

"I guess they gave up on waiting for me to get you off the mountain on my own." Matteo put the truck in park in front of the ambulance.

She had to laugh as she recognized the drivers getting out of their pickups as members of Matt's shift and others from the firehouse. "I can't believe they're out here right after your shift ended. They should be catching up on sleep."

"Not when one of our own is hurt or missing. That's not how we roll."

One of our own.

Just as they'd been there for Jason and his parents, now they'd come for her. Speaking of which, Darren, also off duty, approached the truck and opened the door while the ambulance crew pulled out the stretcher. He teased her about trying to outdo Jason's injuries from the festival.

"Go big or go home," she returned.

Matteo came around the truck and scooped her into his arms. He carried her over to the stretcher and gently laid her on it before leaning down to place a kiss on her lips. "I'll be right behind you. Be a good girl, and do what the doctor says."

She grinned. "You know I will." *Unless they tell me that I can't go home tonight, then all bets are off.*

She wished Matteo could come with her, but knew he'd be there to pick her up after her release. After she was loaded into the ambulance, one of the EMTs pressed on her ankle to assess the damage.

Sonofabitch! That hurt!

Dakota flinched and jerked her leg away from the pain but tried not to cry out. Glancing out the back of the ambulance, she saw Matteo cringe at her reaction. She hadn't intended to worry him again so soon after the bull ride.

On the ride to the hospital, Dakota bantered with the EMT, asking her why she'd gotten into the Emergency Medical Service.

"Being able to help people on their worst days is incredibly gratifying. Best job ever, although it's sometimes pretty stressful."

Dakota didn't think she'd be cut out for a medical profession. But what about the fire service? She was as strong as most men and in good physical condition. Matteo planned to take some additional EMT courses this fall and she'd been looking through the catalog he'd ordered from the college. Maybe she'd find something that suited her.

She definitely needed to find something to do if she was going to be hanging around Matteo's place for a while.

And after they'd weathered the recent storm in their relationship, she had every intention of doing so.

Ninety minutes later, Dakota waited in the examination room for the results of her ankle X-ray and head CT scan. She wished Matteo had been allowed to come back to wait with her, but they had said family only.

He is my family!

No sooner had she thought that than she heard his voice.

"Are you decent, Dakota?"

She saw his jeans and boots under the curtain and smiled as relief flooded through her. "Afraid so, cowboy fireman. But you're welcome to come in and change that status."

He opened the curtain and came inside, smiling. "Trying to get yourself kicked out of here already, Sweet Lady?"

She gave a shrug with her shoulder. "If that's what it'll take." He leaned down toward her face, and Dakota turned hers up to accept his kiss, sorry that it didn't last longer. She wanted to crawl into his lap and have him hold her but would have to wait until they were home again.

Home.

"I didn't think they'd ever let you back here."

"Sorry, but I just got here about fifteen minutes ago. I knew you'd be in good hands and needed to take care of the horses. Darren helped, but it took me a little while to catch Kahlo and remove her saddle."

She'd forgotten about the horse! "Is she okay?"

"Yeah. All the horses are fine. The only question I have is, how are you?"

"Anxious to leave. Waiting on results."

"Any verdict yet on the extent of your injuries?"

She shook her head, ignoring the pain the movement caused. "Waiting to see if my ankle is broken or sprained, and on the CT scan results.

"I brought your purse, figuring you'd need your insurance card and whatever else." He handed it to her and pulled a chair closer to the gurney. She wished there was room up here for him to join her.

"Oh, I found your lost boot while going after Kahlo."

"Great! I love those boots." She looked down at her swollen ankle. "Not that I'll be wearing the pair anytime soon."

"In any pain?"

"No. Not even a headache anymore." *Well, not much of one.*

Her phone pinged inside the purse, indicating an incoming email, but she'd check it later.

"Ms. Mathison?" They both turned toward the cubicle's entrance to see a white-coated woman standing there.

"Yes, doctor."

She entered and glanced at Matteo before addressing Dakota. "Who do you have with you today?"

"Matteo Giardano, my…" She wasn't sure how to introduce him. Her boyfriend? The man she lived with? A friend?

Matteo stood and extended his hand. "Dakota is staying with me. I'll be taking care of her when she's discharged." They shook hands, and the doctor smiled at him before turning toward her again.

"I'm glad to hear you'll have some help. I have the results of your X-ray. No fracture or tendon damage that I can see, but you'll want to follow up with an orthopedist in a few days to be sure it's healing properly. Sometimes hairline fractures don't show up right away."

"I've been in the rodeo long enough to know the drill, but I'm kind of new around here." She asked for a recommendation. Good thing she'd opted in for health insurance when it opened up to the self-employed, even if it sometimes took the place of food in her budget. Even so, this could get expensive if she needed a lot of follow-ups. "How about the scan?"

"Good news there too. No swelling, bleeding, or fractures. You're very lucky given how long you might have been unconscious. If you develop a severe headache, dizziness, balance issues, I want you to come back in so we can check further."

Dakota nodded. The doctor gave her a list of signs to watch for that she might have picked up a parasite drinking untreated water from the stream, but Dakota had worried more about becoming dehydrated. She'd deal with that problem if it arose.

The doctor promised to work on her discharge papers while she got ready to leave. Twenty minutes later, she was wheeled to the exit where Matteo had his truck waiting. He opened the passenger door and lifted her inside the cab.

She glanced down at her phone and saw the notification for the earlier email had come from the DNA testing company. Her heart beat wildly as she opened the message without saying anything to Matteo.

Dakota didn't want to say anything to Matteo yet but looked down at the map showing the various regions of origin that made up her genetic background. While interesting, that wasn't what she wanted to know. She quickly scrolled down to see what connections they'd found to other people.

Unfortunately, the closest matches were third and fourth cousins. *Damn it!*

Dakota's eyes burned. She'd placed all her hopes on finding a sibling or grandparents in the database, but now those dreams had been dashed. Her cheeks grew damp when she could no longer hold back the tears. A sniffle escaped.

Matteo squeezed her thigh. "Does something hurt? Do we need to go back to the hospital?"

Dakota shook her head, sending even more tears spilling down her cheeks. She wouldn't be crying if she wasn't so exhausted after trying to stay awake all night, even if she had dozed off a few times. Clearing her throat so that she could respond, she turned away from him, letting the phone rest on her lap. She cleared her throat. "Got my DNA results… No close matches."

"Oh, honey, I'm so sorry. I know how you anticipated finding some relatives."

Unable to hold it back any longer, a ragged sob broke free as she gave into her pity party. "I had such high expectations."

"Don't give up yet. I've been reading up on these things, and we can submit your results to some other databases to widen the net." She liked how he wanted to be a part of this journey with her. "And new people are joining these things all the time, so maybe there will be matches in the future."

His words lifted her spirits a bit. "You think so?"

"Absolutely! I know how much this means to you. We'll do everything we can to make your dream come true."

Later that night, Matt snuggled next to Dakota on the couch as they watched a movie. He couldn't stop touching her after he'd very nearly lost her on that mountain. He stroked her hair, so happy to have her home, safe and sound. Her ankle and foot were in a walking boot, propped on the coffee table. Getting her to stay off it, like the doctor ordered, would be a challenge, but Jason would be coming twice a day again on Matt's days at work. Hopefully, between the two guys, they'd be able to keep her off that sprained ankle.

"I'm not sure I can keep my eyes open," she mumbled. "Mind if I turn in early?"

"Sounds good. I couldn't even tell you what we're watching. Let's go to bed." He eased his arm out from behind her and stood, then helped her up.

"I'm going to hate showering with this boot."

"I can give you sponge baths."

She poked him in the side. "You are not giving me sponge baths. I'll figure it out." They laughed as they entered the bedroom. At least he'd managed to lighten her mood. After her bad news on the DNA test results, she hadn't smiled or laughed much today.

"It'll be nice to sleep in our bed tonight after a night in that old cabin."

"I'm just glad you found shelter to protect you from the elements and that cougar. That you were able to survive out there is a testament to how strong and resourceful you are, Sweet Lady." He helped her out of her blouse and skirt but when he offered to help her with the shower, she shook her head.

"Maybe in the morning. I just want to crawl into a real bed."

Matt grabbed the long john top she usually slept in and helped her into it, wanting to make sure she was warm enough. He'd caught her shivering at odd times throughout the day as if unable to warm up. But Matt would make sure she was warm, right here in his arms. Matt didn't want her far from his side.

They lay side by side in bed, her head cradled against his shoulder as she played with the hair on his chest.

"I've been thinking about what I want to do," she began.

"Do about what?"

"My future. I can't just sit around and help out here, but I'm not qualified for many other jobs. So I've been thinking about taking some classes at the college in Leadville."

Taking classes meant she'd be sticking around, at least if she attended them on the Leadville campus, which he assumed was her intention.

Matt smiled. "I think that's a great idea. What do you think you'll study?"

"I was looking over your catalog earlier while you were out with the horses, and a couple things appealed to me. Like Outdoor Industry."

"What's that?"

"It covers several areas, but action sports and avalanche science looked the most interesting to me. I'm not into retail or marketing stuff. I'd prefer to work outdoors."

"I think you'd be well suited for either of those." A degree usually took two years if going full-time. That pleased Matt a whole lot.

She remained quiet a while then finally continued, "The first responders and public safety program looked interesting too."

What kind of first responder? Cop? EMS? Firefighter?

His heart hammered so hard surely she could feel it against her fingertips. Knowing her penchant for thrill seeking, he was almost afraid to ask, but he didn't have to.

"I'm thinking about pursuing an associate's degree in fire science, but I'll have to find a part-time job first to pay for the tuition."

Fire science?

Okay, don't blow a gasket. Remember, Dakota's always going to be putting herself in harm's way. Whether it was for the thrill or she'd come into his life to test him, he wasn't sure. But where the hell had this notion come from?

"So you might want to be a firefighter?"

Dakota nodded. "I love the bond you and your brothers in the firehouse have. Might be time to get a woman in there." She shrugged. "Or perhaps I could work in fire prevention like you do with the forestry service. There are a number of options, and I'd need to do a lot of coursework before I'd have to decide whether to go to the Fire Academy or pursue some other avenue."

Fire prevention wasn't the only thing required of that job. He got called out for wildland fires on numerous occasions. With the way these fires had changed in recent years, he didn't want to have her out there—

He caught himself.

Not your choice.

Besides, maybe after taking a few classes, she'd change her mind and pursue something else.

"I know how much you want to find a new career path. I'll do anything I can to help. You might qualify for some tuition breaks."

She laughed. "I already saw that I can get the older student discount for being over twenty-three. I'll be like the class mom to some of these kids."

"I wouldn't go that far. Maybe a big sister."

"Well, thanks for that. Anyway, I'll apply for financial aid soon. After living with you since December, I already qualify as in-district but am hoping my post-office box address will qualify me as an in-state resident too, because that will make a huge dent in tuition."

"When do you plan to apply and start classes?"

"Not sure. Maybe in the fall. Then by the time the spring semester starts in January, I can claim I've lived in Colorado a year from the time I showed up here." She lifted her head and met his gaze. "Do you think that'll count? I did forward my mail here once I knew I wasn't going to be able to make it to the Pueblo Post Office to pick it up. So there's a paper trail."

"I'll vouch for you, if need be." Matt tried to look at the positives here—she was making long-term plans to at least stay in the area. "You know you have a home here for as long as you'd like."

Her face lit up. "Thanks, Matteo! I was afraid to ask, figuring I could find an apartment if you didn't want me here. Glad I haven't outstayed my welcome."

He lifted his head off the pillow and leaned forward to kiss her gently, not wanting to ignite any flames that would have to be extinguished to keep her from overexerting herself. "Never in a million years, Sweet Lady. I like having you here. And I'll support you in whatever direction you take with your education, job, or whatever."

"How'd I get so lucky that you and I met up again last year?"

He pulled her against his chest again and stroked her hair idly. "I'm the lucky one. You've made my life a thousand percent more worthwhile since you showed up here. I'm just glad you came to me when you needed someone."

"So am I."

And to make sure he would always be able to get in touch with her in an emergency, first thing in the morning, he was buying both of them satellite phones to carry with them into remote areas. He didn't want to go through another period of not being able to reach her when she needed him.

More than two weeks after Dakota's night alone on the mountain, Matt had just returned to the fire station after an extraction in a motor-vehicle accident when he glanced across the street and saw Dakota's blue truck parked in front of the Heritage Museum. She hadn't mentioned being on her way to town, but when she visited the station, she usually parked on Harrison. He hadn't heard any of the guys greeting her when they went inside the common area upstairs, though. Not seeing her inside her truck, he guessed she must be in the museum.

Matt smiled. Maybe she wanted to learn more about the community's history. She'd shown a lot of interest in local activities, including helping out with the festival last month. He liked seeing her putting down some roots here.

Maybe he—or Leadville—had grown on her.

He waited outside another fifteen minutes hoping to catch a glimpse of her, but when she didn't come out, he decided he'd better go upstairs and see what he could do to help prepare supper.

About ten minutes later, the door opened. "Hey, guys! How's it going?"

Dakota.

His heart beat differently at the sound of her voice and a grin came over his face—he was such a goner when it came to this woman. How would he survive when she moved on?

Don't think about that. She wants to stick around.

She walked over to Matt for a quick kiss, neither of them self-conscious about showing their affection for each other in front of the crew.

"Sit down and rest that ankle," he told her. "I saw your truck at the museum. Did you have a nice visit?"

"I did! I learned so much about Leadville's mining history."

"If you're interest in mining," Ackerman threw out, "there's a national museum a few blocks from here that'll tell you all about it."

"Wonderful! I'll check that out tomorrow."

"Why the interest in mining all the sudden?" Matt asked.

She sat at the bar stool and watched him as he resumed peeling potatoes. "No real reason. Maybe because I wanted to know more about the miner who lived in the cabin that helped save my life."

He stopped and looked up at her. "Thank God you took your handgun up there."

She rolled her eyes. "Of course. I wouldn't let a mountain lion or bear come anywhere near Kahlo or me."

Relieved, he went back to work prepping supper.

"Anyway, I also wanted to find out what was mined on your property and those federal lands, and maybe learn what happened to the miner when he gave up his claim."

Reaching for the carrots, Matt began peeling them. "The courthouse deeds might be of some help too." Matt gave her the name of the miner, in case she could find anything in the records. He was happy she'd found something to occupy her time.

She glanced at her watch. "It's still early enough that I might be able to do a little research before I head back out to the ranch. I think I'll start at the mining museum, though. They'll bring the dry names and dates to life."

He nodded but hated to see her go. "If you want to pick up a to-go meal at the café afterward, feel free to join us." He'd offer her some of their meal, but the crew frowned upon sharing the food they purchased by pooling their own money with friends or family members. Hell, they had three separate locked refrigerators, one for each shift, because they didn't like sharing with the other shifts, either.

"Thanks, but let me see how it goes at the museum first." She stood and came around the bar to give him a quick peck on the cheek. He couldn't wait to get off duty tomorrow and be in the same bed with her after supper.

The next day after finishing all the chores, Dakota curled up in bed to read the book she'd bought at the Heritage Museum yesterday.

Imagine that. Dakota Mathison reading in bed at night—and a local history book to boot. The old Dakota would either have been in a bar or conked out in bed sleeping off a bender after celebrating a day of bone-jarring saddle bronc rides.

Of course, if Matteo had been home, she'd have been talking with him—or making love, which had become a regular occurrence again now that her ankle was healing, although they had to get creative sometimes. Never a problem for the two of them. However, on nights like this when he wasn't home, she preferred to sleep in the spare bedroom. Being alone in Matteo's bed left her feeling lonely.

The wind howled outside as some kind of front must be passing through. She devoured half the book about the mining history of Leadville before her eyelids grew heavy. After jerking herself awake several times, she gave up, set the book on the nightstand, and stretched out, pulling the quilt up under her chin.

Her mind swirled with images of bygone days. Corseted women in long bustled dresses and frilly bonnets. Men with gun belts and at least one revolver resting against a hip. She wondered if the town did any reenactments or had pioneer days or anything like that. How much fun would it be to pull together the necessary wardrobe to participate in one with Matteo?

Eventually, sleep completely overtook her, and the scenes morphed into something more modern. A rustic ranch house in the middle of a dusty, desolate landscape but with yellow roses blooming near the unpainted picket fence. Mountains loomed on the horizon. The place seemed familiar, although Dakota couldn't place it.

A little red-haired girl played in the side yard.

A car drove up and a man got out. He scared her for some reason, and the little girl ran to hide at the back of the house, listening as he banged on the front door. An older woman shouted for him to go away, that Pumpkin didn't want anything to do with him. But the man wouldn't leave. He called out an unfamiliar name, one that seemed to be meant for the girl who was unsure whether she should remain in her hiding place or run to the shelter of her nana's arms.

Timidly, she walked up the back steps and into the kitchen. Nana *stood there in her apron next to the table where potatoes lay piled on the cutting board, half of them peeled.*

"Pumpkin, go to your room," Nana *said. She stared across the kitchen at the menacing man who had somehow gained entrance to the house. But to get to her room, she'd have to come dangerously close to him.*

"Pack your things, kid. You're coming with me."

No! *She didn't want to live with him again. He'd killed her mother in the wreck. The little girl's memories of that accident hurt too much, so she pushed them away.*

"Get out, Roger. The judge said she's mine to raise. Just go back to your own

kind and leave us alone. You've caused that girl enough grief."

"The kid's mine and you know it, old woman!" He rushed forward and back-handed Nana, who fell back against the counter before crumpling to the floor. The little girl tried to run to help her, but the man lunged and grabbed her by the arm, squeezing hard.

"Ow!" she howled, remembering that the arm had been broken in the accident. Looking down at Nana's lifeless body, she cried out as he lifted her off her feet. He'd killed Nana too! She screamed for her grandmother as he dragged her into the living room and out of the house.

"No! No! No! Don't want to leave Nana!"

"Shut up and get in the car." He opened the rear passenger door and threw her into the back seat. The little girl scrambled back up in time to watch as the only house in which she'd ever known love receded from her view.

The little girl wailed for her nana all the way down the long driveway, but he didn't stop the car.

"Keep up that racket and I'll give you something to cry about," he warned.

What more could he do to hurt her? He'd already ripped her away from her mother and now Nana, possibly killing the woman who meant the world to her.

A desperate cry spilled from her throat.

Dakota bolted up in the bed, sweat drenching her face. The quilt had been kicked off and lay bunched at the foot of the bed. Her gaze darted around the unfamiliar room to make sure the frightening man wasn't here. Not seeing anyone, her breathing began to even out and her racing heart slowed a bit as she remembered where she was.

But in that dream, she'd definitely identified as the little girl. She hadn't remembered any of that before, the trauma probably too much for her little mind to understand, but she had no doubt that this had been a memory, not a random nightmare borne out of her imagination.

That evil man had killed her nana.

Or so it seemed. She must have been about five or six at the time. Perhaps Nana had survived, but if so, where? Were there no relatives in the DNA database related to her? Well, perhaps those third or fourth cousins, but she wouldn't know where to begin in make connections that way.

She'd lived somewhere in the American West, at least at the time of the kidnapping, but that covered a lot of territory. Without knowing which state she'd been in or the name of the woman, Dakota couldn't fathom how hard it would be to locate her.

The man had called out to the little girl with a name Dakota couldn't remember now that she'd woken up.

Knowing the names of Nana and her younger self would have helped in the search for her identity. His name was Roger, but Dakota had no interest in finding him again.

Realistically, though, seeing how hard it was to learn anything about the miner who had staked his claim on Matteo's property—even though she knew his name—didn't make searching much easier. And nowadays, there were privacy laws that would hide more modern records, so she wouldn't expect things to be any easier when looking for someone for whom she had no name.

Still, Dakota became more determined than ever to do whatever she could to track down the woman with the gray-flecked ginger hair she'd called Nana in that memory.

As for the man, he was the one she'd been living with in Aspen Corners and all the other places he'd taken her to after kidnapping her from Nana's house. While he hadn't been physically abusive toward her in later years, perhaps he'd made good on his threats to *give her something to cry about* and she'd just repressed those memories and tried to obey him.

He'd told Nana she belonged to him, so was he her biological father and not a random kidnapper? She almost wished she'd been taken by a stranger, because this man's DNA could be linked to hers.

What if he found her again?

Chapter Thirty

On the first day of Matteo's shift the following week, Dakota nervously awaited the arrival of Mama and Paul. They'd texted them both last night saying they were coming down to take her out to lunch—without Matteo.

Mama had first mentioned wanting to do this when the family had taken her out for her Mother's Day earlier this month, but when no date had been set, Dakota forgot about it. Why the thought of going out with them while Matteo was at work made her nervous, she didn't know, but he thought it a great idea. Mama and Paul insisted they just wanted to get to know her better.

Why that made her feel a little insecure confused her. She'd created the Dakota Mathison persona not caring if people liked her or not, but Mama and Paul's opinion held more weight with her, just as Matteo's did.

Not that she wanted to take time for a get-acquainted meal right now. She'd planned on starting to clean up the miner's cabin while Matteo worked, now that her orthopedist had declared her ankle fully healed. But everyone in Matteo's family had been so kind to her and had treated her like one of them, she couldn't very well say no or that she was too busy.

The tires of their truck crunched on the lane outside the kitchen, and she went outside to greet them. Right on time, but Dakota expected no less. She opened the door and welcomed them into the house, offering them something to drink.

"I can wait until we get to the restaurant," Mama responded.

"Nothing for me, either, but thanks," Paul said.

Mama surveyed the room, her eyes opening wide as she took in the differences. "You've made some changes."

She didn't sound accusatory, just making an observation, but Dakota became worried. Was the woman upset that Dakota had been revamping this place Mama had originally decorated? Dakota didn't even think she'd made that many major changes. She wanted to save her money for the cabin renovation.

But she had painted the trim around the doors and windows turquoise, then gave it a bit of a distressed look the way she'd found on Pinterest. Last weekend, she'd added some rustic pieces like rusty horseshoes and antique blue mason jars she'd found in a nearby flea market. The jars reminded her of…well, she wasn't sure where she'd seen them before, but they made her feel good. She'd found some dead weeds outside, some with seed pods still attached, and filled the two jars with them. Matteo had said he liked the new look a lot.

Dakota chewed on the side of her lower lip, waiting for Mama's verdict. "I thought it would be nice to bring in some Western colors and themes, given Matteo's love of horses."

Mama walked farther into the room toward the couch. "I absolutely love it! Matteo made me stick to neutral colors when I decorated before he moved in last year."

Dakota relaxed. The woman's praise meant a lot to her.

Mama touched the Native American blanket Dakota had removed from her camper and draped over the rocker. Mostly black and red, it had bursts of turquoise in the center design that Dakota had loved since she'd found it a few years ago in Arizona while refurbishing her Shasta. And it went well with the other splashes of turquoise in the room.

"The colors on this blanket are perfect for this room. I don't know why my son liked to keep things so brown and dull before." She turned to Dakota. "Sweetie, you're a breath of fresh air."

Dakota laughed. "Honestly, I don't think Matteo notices things like decor, unless I shake things up with a drastic change."

"You might be right," Mama agreed.

"I probably wouldn't have, either, Angela," Paul said with a shrug before closing the gap with Mama. "It's probably a guy thing."

With this topic having run its course, the three decided to head to the restaurant. "You can ride with us, Dakota" Paul offered.

Twenty minutes later, Dakota sat across from the older couple, everyone looking over the menu.

"I'm looking forward to trying this filet mignon Matteo raves about," Mama commented while looking at the menu. "He's always loved his beef, unlike my other children. I couldn't afford to serve beef very often after Papa died, so I'm glad he's able to get his fill now."

"You kept them fed, clothed, and housed, hon," Paul said, stroking her hand as though to comfort her. "I've never heard any of them complain about your meals."

"Matteo loves your cooking! I wish mine was half that good."

"Angelina tells me you are coming along. If you've never really had a chance to cook much, how could you become a gourmet? And all five of my children were good kids. They helped me out so much during those lean years, never complaining. Especially Rafe, who gave up so much to assume the role of father figure for the younger children. He helped me a lot too, but I just feel guilty sometimes." As if self-conscious about sharing that, she smiled at Dakota. "Sorry about that. I don't normally indulge in a pity party."

"No apology necessary! But trust me, Matteo only has the fondest memories of his childhood. You don't know how much I envied him back in high school for all the love and support he had from his family."

Too late, she realized she'd revealed more than she'd intended to, but before anyone asked, she diverted the conversation back to Matteo. "In fact, he credits you and Rafe with steering him in a better direction than riding the rodeo circuit after college as he'd originally planned on doing."

Mama seemed surprised. Surely Matteo would have told her that at some point. Had Dakota spoken out of turn? This awkward lunch wasn't going well, after all. Thankfully, the server came, and they placed their orders.

After she left, Dakota tried to get their conversation back on safe ground. "I can attest that the rodeo can be exciting when you're young," Dakota added, still trying to light upon a safer thread of conversation, "but it's hard at this stage in life to look at all your championship buckles and realize you have no idea what you're going to do next."

"Have you decided to quit the rodeo for good?" Paul asked.

She nodded. "I think so—competition rodeo, anyway. I've been offered an opportunity to teach other women to ride broncs, but it's time to hang up my own spurs. My body can't withstand as much as it could when I was younger."

"Tell me about it," he said. "But you're young yet."

"I'm sure Matteo was happy to hear that," Mama added.

Dakota hoped Mama didn't think she implied that she and Matteo planned to stay together long-term. "Yeah, he was afraid I'd attempt to ride another bull someday."

Mama's eyes opened wide. "You think you might do that?"

"Oh, no! I really am done with bulls. Broncs too, for that matter. My new love is skijoring, which provides the rush of competition without as many risks."

"I wish you could convince Angela of that for me. Man, that looked like so much fun."

Mama gave him a pointed look before turning to Dakota again. "What do you want to do next?"

Dakota wasn't sure whether she should say anything but had no reason to lie to the woman or evade the question.

"I've been looking at starting college in the fall. Maybe joining the fire academy."

"Wow!" Mama's eyes opened wide. "A noble profession, for sure. How does Matteo feel about that?"

"I think he's learning that he needs to let me figure things out for myself, but how could he say it's too dangerous for me when he makes his living doing the same job?" Dakota turned to Paul, curious at what he'd think, given his own career choice.

"We need more women in our firehouses. I can't think of anybody who would be better suited than you, Dakota, given your athletic abilities." His words of encouragement and support warmed her heart. "Thanks, Paul. I appreciate the vote of confidence." She turned to Mama. "Yours too, Mama." She hadn't said anything about it not being a good idea for a woman to do, although the woman appeared to be more concerned about her son's feelings on the subject. "Of course, nothing's decided yet, and I'm a long way away from courses at the academy, if that's even my final choice of major."

"The associate degree is all that's required," Paul began, "and you can be taking fire academy courses simultaneously with the general education ones required. In two years, you could be hired on somewhere. But don't forget about finding volunteer opportunities in the meantime. Most fire departments—whether career or volunteer—are short-staffed these days."

Matteo volunteered with the forest service but she wondered if his firehouse ever needed students to help roll hoses or do any of the other tasks required after a fire. "Great idea. I'll talk with Matteo about that after I get some basic coursework under my belt."

"College doesn't start until August. Do you have any plans for the summer?" Mama asked.

"Actually, I'm about to start renovating the old miner's cabin on Matteo's place."

Mama's eyes lit up, "I love that place! It needs a loving hand to bring back the warmth that hasn't been there for some time."

Dakota had to laugh, respectfully, of course. "After learning more about the hard-knock life of miners, I'm not sure that life was as romantic as we like to make it, but I would like to make the place a cozy getaway." She gave an unapologetic shrug. "Who knows? Might be something for Matteo to remember me by."

Mama's eyes opened wider. "You aren't planning on leaving, are you?"

Oh boy. How to address the million-dollar question? "Not anytime soon, as long as I don't wear out my welcome. But I'm a realist and have learned not to get my hopes up too high about the future."

Mama and Paul exchanged a sad expression that confused her, but when Mama glanced at her again, she simply said, "Matteo is going to adore whatever touches you put on the place."

Dakota leaned forward as if anyone eavesdropping would care. "Please don't say anything about the cabin to Matteo, though. I want to surprise him."

Mama and Paul both nodded. "If you need help of any kind to make this happen, let us know," Mama offered. "That includes financial help, manual labor, or supplies—just ask and you've got it." She leaned closer. "We'd love to be in on your surprise."

Dakota couldn't believe her ears. With so much work needed in order to finish before she started classes—barely three months away—she'd accept all the help she could get. "I'd love to include you! I've been pricing the building materials and, while I shouldn't need to hire many contractors because surely zoning laws won't apply to the place, I doubt my savings will stretch far enough to finish it the way I'd like."

Already having second thoughts about involving them in what would be a monumental task, she added, "Before you decide, maybe I should take you up there after lunch to see what you think about its potential."

Mama didn't need to be asked twice. "I'd love to see it again!"

"It mostly needs elbow grease right now." She shared her plans over the next few minutes.

"I'm sure you can round up some free labor at the Leadville fire-house from guys on the other shifts," Paul suggested, "as long as you can swear them to secrecy."

"Oh, I'd hate to ask them to do more than they already do for their community. So many are stretched thin as it is with second jobs and families. Besides, the more people involved, the higher the risk of Matteo finding out."

"True. Well, if you'll accept my help once or twice a week when my days off coincide with Matt's days on duty, count me in" he offered.

"That's so sweet of you, Paul! I really appreciate that." Dakota couldn't believe how they'd jumped at helping without blinking an eye.

"I can help with cleaning," Mama began, "and when it comes time to decorate, we can check out some of the Leadville antique shops for local period pieces from that era. I even have my father's mining lamp that I'd love to put up there."

"I had no idea Matteo's grandfather was a miner," Dakota said. "He never said anything."

"He didn't really know him. My papa died before any of the kids were born. He'd immigrated from Italy late in life, before I was born."

Mama must know what a hard life mining had been, even though things had probably changed in the century since this old miner had worked his local claim.

"If we're all finished here, why don't we ride up there and take inventory before it gets dark?" Paul suggested. "I'm free tomorrow to help with the cleanup."

"So am I," Mama said.

"Ride horses up or take the truck?" Dakota asked.

"Horses would be fun, if it's not too much trouble" Mama said. "I haven't ridden Comet since I used to come down to spend time with Matteo before Paul and I married."

Paul called for the check, and Dakota thanked them for lunch. She couldn't wait to get back up there. Having others helping her would make quick work of the cleanup and she could move on to renovations.

"This is going to be so much fun!" Mama said.

After lunch, they returned to the ranch, saddled the three horses, and rode out to the cabin.

"It's so peaceful up here," Mama said.

"I can't wait to get to have lunch on the porch again and look at that incredible view." She pointed toward the Collegiates.

"I can't believe more of these windows weren't broken over the years."

"Probably held together by the dirt," Paul quipped.

Mama pointed at the newer pane in the front. "Matteo did fix this one so that the elements wouldn't do any more damage to the interior before he could work on the place." She turned to Dakota and smiled. "He's going to be so surprised."

Dakota hoped that he'd be happy about the surprise too.

"Let's go inside." Dakota shoved the door open and brought them in to have a look. "I don't see us digging a well or putting in plumbing or electricity up here. It's nice just being like the olden days."

"But you could get a composting toilet," Paul suggested, "and put in some solar panels to live off the grid with a few modern-day comforts."

She hadn't thought about that, although her limited funds hadn't really given her an opportunity to think about more than the bare minimum.

"That old mattress is probably teaming with all kinds of critters you don't want to meet up close," Mama said with a shudder.

"I'll bring the truck up tomorrow," Dakota said, "and load up the trash so I can get a better look at the place's bones." She glanced at the rickety table and twin bed frame. "The place can definitely use some new furniture." If she put in a bed, she'd want at least a double. She ran her finger along the bed frame. "We'll also bring up some cleaning supplies and start scrubbing before we get too much further."

"We'll make quick work of it." Mama said. "I hope I'm not stepping on your toes or butting in, though." She didn't seem to interject herself into her family's business unless worried about one of her adult children, as far as Dakota could tell.

"Not at all. I'm going to enjoy having some company up here. Besides, I'm not too proud to accept all offers to help," Dakota said jokingly.

Mama smiled. "Wonderful. I'll let you tell me where you need us."

"I'll be doing the heavy lifting," Paul insisted.

"Hey, I need to build up some upper-body strength to get ready for the fire academy, don't I?"

He shrugged. "Just don't overdo it or hurt yourself."

Paul must have that same protective gene that Matteo had.

But having them here to help would give Dakota a little breathing room and speed up the process. Maybe she could actually pull this off without Matteo finding out.

A glow from the setting sun warmed the room. "I guess we'd better head back to the house before it gets dark."

"Since Matteo's working tomorrow too," Mama said, "We'll head down early so we can spend the whole day up here."

"And I'll bring my toolbox."

"Good idea," Mama said. "I can use the tape measure to begin getting down some important figures."

"Sounds great!" Dakota hadn't thought that through yet. "Thanks so much!"

After they returned to the house and Mama and Paul left, Dakota pulled some sheets of paper from Matteo's printer and started making lists and sketches of what she envisioned for the cabin. Her eyes grew gritty and when she looked up at the kitchen clock, she saw it was past midnight. She'd better get to bed if they were going to tackle that cabin early tomorrow.

After Paul had told her about all the diseases rodents carry, Dakota was thankful to him for providing dust masks for the three of them. Dust and dirt flew in the air around her as she swept the floor of the cabin while Mama and Paul tackled cleaning the windows Dakota had attempted to do last month.

Wouldn't Matteo be surprised when she finally showed him what they'd done, but that would probably be months away. This project would definitely keep her busy until classes started. Finding a way to give back to Matteo after all he'd done for her since December made her smile. She couldn't remember when she'd ever had anyone in her life she'd wanted to please and thank before.

And tackling this project would fill her days while he was away at work. Then just before turning thirty-three, she would be focusing on college classes for the first time in her life.

She didn't know yet how far her winnings would go in this renovation, but Paul and Mama already said the toilet cost would be on them. Dakota wanted to get a fireplace insert, though, as soon as the chimney had been cleaned and inspected. It might require some repairs or a lining to make it safer, but that would all be on her budget and fairly quickly. She wanted to make that vision of her and Matteo making love in front of the fire a reality as early as possible.

Would she put in a cistern or just cart up their supply of water for drinking and washing? Paul assured her dry toilets didn't require any water source, so she didn't have to worry about that. She'd figure it all out.

"What do you think, Dakota? Any streaks?" Mama shouted at her through the closed window, although her voice probably came in through the cracks in the cabin's chinking without much impediment.

Dakota carried the broom over to the nook and looked out at the gorgeous view of the mountains Matteo loved so much. Her gaze went to Mama who had gotten down off the ladder Paul had been holding for her. "It's gorgeous! Just like I imagined!"

Excitement bubbled up inside her. Taking a step back, she imagined a small table in front of the window with one of the blue jars filled with wild or dried flowers and a blue checkered tablecloth. It was going to be so cozy.

Glancing up at the window again, she wondered if Paul would be able to work with the ones they had or if they'd have to replace them. The windows had been nailed shut, but she hoped they could keep the originals, although they might not be practical if they wanted to be comfortable up here on visits in the winter months.

Oh! She made a note to add some kind of shelter for the horses they'd ride up here in the winter. She wouldn't want them exposed to the elements but doubted a truck would make it up here in the winter months without massive snow clearing.

Funny, but more and more now, she pictured herself here with

Matteo. Perhaps the turning point for her had been realizing that he didn't want her to change into another persona; he accepted her just the way she was. Despite frustrating him with her desire to live life in the fast lane—something she'd probably continue to do forever—he hadn't argued when she'd told him she'd been thinking about going to the fire academy. He accepted her without trying to get her to conform to whatever the ideal woman should be, and that made it so much easier to love him.

She'd invented Dakota as a means of finding herself, and even though she might never know who she really was, Dakota was the closest she'd ever have to being whole. Even though she'd been misguided about who her people were, with the Giardanos and Leadville, she knew where she belonged.

And that's why what they think matters to you.

Before she had time to process that any further, Mama and Paul came back inside, putting their masks back on, and the three of them hauled out the filthy mattress and other items that had been home to countless mice over the decades. What needed burning, they piled into the truck, and the rest they dumped in the woods.

They worked for several more hours before taking a lunch break, tailgating a delicious meal of pasta salad and sandwiches off the back of Paul's truck and sitting along the porch of the cabin as they ate.

Mama regaled them with stories about her children's antics growing up, including some Dakota hadn't heard about before. "Tony and Matteo had quite a rivalry going in high school. I remember Matteo hid some asiago cheese between the mattress and box spring in Tony's bed once that went undetected for more than a week. Finally got to the point where we thought we'd have to fumigate the room before we found it and he confessed."

Mama shook her head before continuing. "Then Tony got him back with a small fish he'd caught in the river that runs through town. This was the summer before you arrived in Aspen Corners and before he had his horse. Tony hid the fish in one of the cowboy boots he'd been given for his birthday and it must have been in there a good five or six days before he discovered it. Ruined his boots, which probably accounted for him being so angry."

"A fish?" Dakota asked. "Does this have anything to do with his aversion to fish and seafood?"

Mama's eyes opened wider. "Come to think of it, you might be right. He never liked fish after that, but I was too busy to make the connection."

"All I can say, Mama, is you sure had your hands full with them."

Mama smiled. "I wouldn't change a thing. They survived and grew up to be of fine character." She paused then asked, "What made you want to fix this place up?"

Taken aback by the question, Dakota didn't really need long to think but felt a little embarrassed to put it into words. "I owe Matteo so much. He opened up his home to me when I was injured and exhausted from the world. And he's taught me a lot about myself. He took such good care of me, I wanted to give something back.

She laughed nervously as she brushed away a tear, not understanding why telling his mama this would make her cry. "When I won a little money at the Ski Joring Festival and again riding that bull in Grand Junction, I wanted to do something special to thank Matteo. But you know he'd never have accepted my money. Then I came upon this place and saw how he'd repaired that window." She pointed to the pane at the front of the cabin. "I decided right then to make the cleaning up and restoring of this cabin my gift to Matteo."

This time it was Mama's turn to wipe away a tear. "That's a wonderful, selfless thing to do, Dakota."

Dakota had never been selfless before in her life. But in her quest to try to be a better person and do more for others, she'd accept Mama's compliment proudly.

"Paul, I want to thank you for the idea of doing a DNA search," Dakota said.

He swallowed before responding. "You did one too?"

Dakota nodded. "I didn't have your luck in finding anyone, but I'll keep hoping that one day a close relative will submit theirs and there will be a match."

"Looking for anyone in particular?" Mama asked.

Dakota hadn't shared her past with anyone but Matteo, but Mama and Paul had always treated her like family. Why not confide in them?

"I have a lot of questions about my family of origin," she began. "I don't know who I really am." She went on to explain about the dreams she'd had and that she suspected she'd been kidnapped by the man she'd lived with until she ran away.

"I had no idea!" Mama squeezed her hand in comfort. "I'm so sorry you went through all that, and even sorrier I didn't know you needed help."

"How could you know? He kept us pretty much to ourselves."

Mama shook her head. "I never could understand why we never saw him at any of your 4-H activities."

"Oh, he didn't really like me doing things like that. I told him I was in tutoring after school and on the occasional weekends, or he wouldn't have let me out of the house."

Where had that information come from? She hadn't remembered it before. Who knew what else would pop into her mind when she least expected?

Mama stood up, setting down her plate, approaching Dakota who also stood thinking they were going to get back to work. Instead, Mama gave her a hug. "I've always felt a maternal connection to you, even when you were Alison, but I've never felt closer to you than I do right now."

Mama's words nearly gutted her. How could she recover and get back to work after this moment? Dakota hugged her back, feeling loved and accepted in a way she never had been since a child.

When they broke apart, Dakota cleared her throat. "That means a lot to me, Mama, because you are so important to me too."

They shared a silent moment before Paul said, as if uncomfortable with the emotions flowing, "Ladies, sun's going to be down in a few hours. We'd better finish this cleanup phase so you can start figuring out what you're going to do with those winnings, Dakota."

Grateful to be able to set the emotional stuff aside and get back to work, Dakota grinned at him. "Aye, aye, Captain!"

He growled. "Normally, I'd bust someone's chops for demoting me, but I'll take that title from you, dear girl."

Dakota gave him a quick hug too. If ever she could have had parents, she'd have wanted them to be just like Mama and Paul.

As they worked the rest of the afternoon, Dakota became lost in her thoughts. While this project was for Matteo, she couldn't separate herself from it yet. After spending a night in the shelter of these logs, the desire to restore and preserve it had grown doubly strong.

Yes, I'm going to leave my mark on this cabin, but I hope I'll get to make some wonderful memories here with Matteo too.

Chapter Thirty-One

A week later, Matteo and Dakota headed to Aspen Corners for a Memorial Day Saturday barbecue at Rafe's. Her heart pounded harder with each passing mile. Logically, she knew she wouldn't run into the man who had taken her away from Nana—Roger—but tell that to her body, which still harbored so many bad memories of that town.

Still, she hadn't said anything to Matteo when he'd asked her to come along. While she was with him, she wanted to be a part of this big, loving family, which meant there would be times when they went back to his childhood home where Rafe now lived.

She just wished it didn't have to be so soon.

"You're awfully quiet. Everything okay?"

She plastered a smile on her face and turned sideways toward him, but he kept his eyes on the road, so she didn't have to worry about giving anything away. On the other hand, perhaps she should let him in on her bout of nerves.

"This will be my first time back in the Corners since we graduated."

This time he did glance her way briefly before returning his focus to the highway ahead as he eased onto the shoulder. He parked the truck and took her hand. "God, Dakota. I didn't even think about that. You okay? We don't have to go if you'd rather not."

"We most certainly do! I'm not going to miss your family get-together just because I have some old ghost haunting me." Man, she hoped that asshole was a ghost by now.

Matteo seemed puzzled. "This isn't a tradition. We just thought it would be nice to get together, but maybe I should have thought it through and suggested we go to Angelina's instead."

"No! I didn't want to make a big deal about it, so I didn't say anything."

He seemed torn about continuing, then said, "If it helps, he left town soon after you did and I haven't seen him since."

That was encouraging. "Really?"

"Being unaware of what was going on with you and him, I actually kept hoping I'd see him because that would mean you were nearby again."

"That's about the sweetest thing I've ever heard." She leaned across the console to meet him for a kiss in which she tried to pour out how much she loved that he hadn't forgotten her the moment she disappeared.

He pulled away first, cupping the side of her face. "I mean it. We can go home and grill our own hot dogs and hamburgers. I don't want to stress you out."

She smiled. "Put the truck in gear, cowboy fireman, and let's go."

"Home?"

Wasn't he listening? "No! To your brother's. I'm ready to face my fears."

He gave her a lopsided grin. "I didn't think Dakota Mathison had any fears."

Oh, if you only knew. She might not fear bulls, broncs, or pregnant mountain lions, but she did have her demons.

"It's healthy to be afraid of some things, but this fear is completely illogical and I refuse to give it any strength."

His smile grew. "That's my girl. Heaven help anyone who tries to hurt you, because between you, me, my brothers, and in-laws, they wouldn't stand a chance."

He put the truck back into drive and they continued along the road and drove over Fremont Pass making their way to Breckenridge before heading south again to Aspen Corners. As the crow flies, Leadville and his hometown were probably only about thirty miles apart, but they had to drive twice that far because there were no roads directly connecting them.

Hoping to change the subject, Dakota spent the rest of the drive telling him she'd been accepted to the college for the fall semester.

"Classes start in mid-August. It will be here before I know it." With Mama and Paul providing some financial assistance on the cabin, she'd been able to set aside enough to cover her first semester's tuition. "And I applied for financial aid. I might be able to do some work study or get a job on or off-campus to help cover expenses."

"Let me know if you need anything. My place isn't in need of any work, and the Dreams Found Foundation is more than covering the costs for boarding their mustangs, even though I tried to tell them to keep the money."

The first fifteen mustangs had been transported to their ranch this past week. They'd separated three of them and put them in the corral to begin training them to the saddle, but the others were free to roam the pastureland for now. She enjoyed working with Matteo and the horses. A few were too wild to come anywhere near the food and water they'd set out for them, but she and Matteo were patient and would eventually win the mares over. For now, Luke and Ryder thought it best not to introduce stallions to the mix, and Dakota agreed that she didn't want to deal with the testosterone.

Matt's nerves were shot by the time they arrived at Rafe's. He'd been ready to give up on this whole thing and take Dakota home, but she'd insisted they go ahead. Was he making the right decision? Right now, she was in the kitchen with Mama and the other ladies. Every now and then, he'd peek through the window at them, and she'd be laughing or chatting and seemed to be getting along without any nerves or worries.

He wished he could say the same. This whole day had been planned out by him without telling anyone but Mama and Paul what was up, but still, he wanted everything to go smoothly.

Matt reached inside his pocket and rubbed the ring as if a lifesaving talisman. He'd worked out several scenarios in his head for how to pop the question. At first, the idea of proposing with his family surrounding them had sounded like a great idea, but now he started to worry what he'd do if she said *No*. He'd never hear the end of it from his brothers, and Angelina and Mama would just feel sorry for him.

Not to mention that he'd be devastated and the drive home with her would be beyond awkward.

Mama had tried to assure him after her visit last week that she didn't think Dakota would turn him down. How she could be so sure, Matt didn't know—some kind of woman's intuition maybe—but still he was a basket case now.

"Here," Rafe said, handing him an empty platter. "Quit pining for Dakota and make yourself useful." Matt held the platter as his brother loaded it with dogs, brats, and burgers. "Sounds like the wildland fire season is off to an early start. Have you been called out yet, Matt?"

"Not yet, but I'm on standby to head to the Idaho Panhandle for a couple of weeks if they need fresh crews."

"Be safe. Let's hope we don't have a repeat of the fire season a few years ago in Colorado."

Luke's wife Cassie had lost her cabin in that one, and Rafe and Tony had been on her mountain fighting that wildfire. Matt had been assigned to one of the fires elsewhere in the state that month.

When the last of the meat was on the dish, Rafe yelled over his shoulder, "Tony, tell the ladies we should have the rest of it off the grill in about fifteen minutes." Tony had been talking with Marc and Franco and excused himself to go inside. Everyone still jumped whenever Rafe gave them marching orders.

Two tables had been set up end to end in the backyard to make a table for the ten of them. Matt placed the heavy platter at one end and covered it with foil and a towel to keep it warm before returning to the patio. Rafe had already filled the grill with the same amount of meat that would be placed at the other end so that the dishes wouldn't have to be passed too far when they ate.

Man, I'll be eating good today.

Dakota came out carrying two large bowls of sides. She'd worn her Ski Joring Festival championship jacket today. Lately, she'd been getting chillier than she used to, even though the weather had been getting warmer every day.

"Hey, Sweet Lady, let me take one of those."

She laughed. "I think I can manage a couple of bowls, Matteo. Just show me where the pasta salads go."

He led her over to where he'd put the platter of meats and suggested that she put one on each table. They'd be dining family style, rather than buffet, so that way they could easily pass the bowls around.

Dakota did so, then wrapped her arms around him. "But I'd rather be holding you—even if I embarrass you too much in front of your brothers. I need a kiss."

Happy to oblige, he pulled her in closer and placed his lips on hers. A chorus of jeers and cheers broke out behind him, but he ignored them and kissed her harder.

When they finally separated, she giggled. "They're just jealous. Well, the single guys who were jeering are, at least."

"Let them be. You're all mine." *At least I hope you'll be.* Should he go down on one knee now, or wait until later as he'd originally planned? He breathed in and out in a short burst and decided to wait.

"How are you doing?"

"Your mama and the girls are so funny. I've been having a great time in the kitchen, although usually I'm more comfortable out by the grill with the guys."

No mention of her earlier nerves, until she added, "It's nice and secluded even from the neighbors back here."

"Not that you'd have to worry about any of them, either. They've lived in the same houses on either side of us all my life."

"Yeah, I was just having a moment of irrational fear earlier. I know he isn't around Aspen Corners anymore. As you said, he left soon after I did."

He kissed her on the forehead. "Good. I hate seeing you worried or stressed." *Or afraid.*

She laughed. "I'll try to postpone any worry until you have to help me get through my first assignments at the academy."

"Woman, if you decide to go that route, you'd better believe I'm going to put you through your paces a lot harder than most of your instructors might. I'll make sure you're ready to go out on the fire-ground when the time comes."

"I'm counting on that! You know I'll want to graduate as the best probie who ever worked in fire service."

He shook his head. "Everything's a competition with you, isn't it?"

"Pretty much," she agreed with an unapologetic grin.

Taking her hand, they walked back to the house to help carry out more of the sides. When everyone took their places at the tables, they wound up seated across from Paul and Mama.

"So, Dakota," Paul began, keeping his voice low so only she, Mama, and Matteo could hear, "I've been wondering if you've thought about uploading your DNA file to some of the other big databases?" He mentioned two companies to consider.

"I hadn't heard of those."

He explained how to go about it. She was afraid to get her hopes up again, but why not submit it anyway? "Thanks, Paul, but I might need some help figuring out how to do it."

"Anytime. Just let me know when you're ready."

She'd been trying to become more proficient at using Matteo's computer but had relied on her phone for most things until recently. In a few months, she'd have to start writing papers and doing homework on a computer, though, so she might as well use it for other things too.

Nothing more important than finding her people, even though Matteo's were quickly becoming her family of choice.

Matt could see the wheels turning in her head. What would happen when she did connect with family? Would she want to return to the life that had been stolen from her? Should he hold off proposing until after she was in a position to make that choice with all the facts lined up? They hadn't even talked about a future together involving marriage.

Maybe he was jumping ahead a little too fast.

He took a deep breath and let it out slowly. *Stay the course.*

After the meal and cleanup, a volleyball net was set up at the end of the backyard and, while she hadn't played since high-school gym classes, she picked it back up pretty quickly. She and Matteo were on the winning team, but she wasn't the only competitive one in the family. Rafe and Angelina were as well.

Mama called everyone back to the patio where she'd set up table with her fabulous *zuppa inglese*, Jordan almonds, and four bottles of chilled wine. Well, at least she hadn't given it away by having champagne or prosecco.

Dakota whispered to him, "Is this a special occasion or does she serve a trifle at every backyard barbecue?

"You know Mama," was Matt's only response.

"*Zuppa inglese* and Jordan almonds, Mama?" Franco asked. "What's the occasion?

"Since when do I need an occasion to serve my family a favorite dessert?"

Franco gave his mama a kiss on the cheek. "No complaints from me, Mama. It's always been a favorite of mine and Matteo's."

Dakota wasn't sure if she'd ever had one, but the layers of pound cake, fruit, and custard looked delicious. "I can't wait to try a piece."

"Matteo, why don't you do the honors and pour the wine."

"White or red?" he asked Dakota.

"You choose—whatever goes best with the cake."

"There's some rum sauce in it and a mix of chocolate and vanilla custard, so let's go with the red."

He then poured glasses of red or white as requested by his mama, Paul, Carmella, Angelina, Marc, and then came his brothers. She expected him to tell them to pour their own—but he didn't. They looked as surprised as Dakota. She'd seen this running gag play out at countless family dinners. What had changed this time to get Matteo to forego the ritual?

"A toast," Matteo said, lifting his glass and waiting for the others to do the same. "To my family. You have been here for me through thick and thin, and I hope I'll always be there for you too."

Everyone took a sip, then his gaze zeroed in on her. "Dakota, I hope you know that I consider you family too."

He smiled then set his glass down on the table with the cake and realization dawned a fraction of a second before he went down on one knee in front of her. *No way!*

Carmella took the glass from her hand before she spilled it all over Matteo from shaking so much.

"Dakota, you made me realize how lonely I'd been out on my ranch. My horses love you. My family loves you. My firehouse family loves you. My friends love you."

A chorus of affirmative responses came from those around her as tears filled her eyes and she held her hand to her mouth still in shock that this was happening.

"But most of all, Sweet Lady, I love you. And I hope and pray you will do me the honor of becoming my wife."

He pulled a ring from his pocket and waited for her to say something. Her mind went blank. How could she do anything but blubber right now?

She knelt in front of him, feeling awkward to be standing over him. "A thousand times, yes!"

The relief on his face confused her. Had he thought she might say no?

Matteo stood and helped her to her feet, wrapping his arms around her and kissing her to the cheers of everyone surrounding them with so much love.

"Don't forget to put the ring on my new sister's finger, Bro," Rafe teased.

Laughing, Matteo stepped back and took her hand. "Dakota, this is the ring Papa gave Mama when he asked her to marry him. Mama wanted me to give it to you because she loves you like a daughter, and, well, me as a son." She smiled as everyone around them laughed.

Matteo's nervousness was endearing and suddenly had her realizing why he'd forgotten to stiff his brothers on the wine pouring. She'd never seen him flustered before, but it only told her how important this occasion was to him.

He slipped the ring on her finger. It felt a little loose, but she wouldn't change it in any way. He kissed her again.

When they parted, she took a deep breath, trying to formulate words that would convey to him what he meant to her. "Matteo, you've given me the roots I never knew I wanted—or even needed. You've taken care of me when I was hurting—not just physically but emotionally. You've opened up a new world to me with your ranch, your community—" She stopped to take in the people surrounding them. "—not to mention an incredible family who've accepted me as if I was already one of them."

"You are," Carmella said.

She smiled at the woman who had helped her find one of her other new passions—skijoring. "I never pictured any one of you as being part of my future five months ago, and now all of you are—" her focus shifted back to Matteo, "thanks to Matteo."

She faced him again and kissed him before saying, "I love you, my cowboy fireman."

"We're going to have one helluva life together, Sweet Lady."

When she turned toward Mama, the woman had tears streaming down her face. Paul held her close against him with his arm around her as if he feared she might crumple to the ground.

Dakota went over to her and hugged her. "I'm honored that you would entrust me with something so precious."

"I hope it fits," Mama said," but you can have it resized if you need to."

Dakota smiled. "I meant your son, Mama. But I'll take care of your ring, too!"

Mama laughed as she took Dakota's hand and looked at the ring. "It's your ring now. You definitely need to have it downsized, but it looks beautiful on you." Dakota truly felt this woman was her mother now too. Meeting Dakota's gaze again, Mama said, "Welcome to the family, daughter."

Dakota hugged her even harder before turning to Paul and gave him one as well. He'd treated her like a dad would as well, even more so than he did Matteo and his siblings. She and Paul had been the odd ones out at first—Mama's grown kids didn't need another papa, after all. Since they'd met on Christmas Day, though, Paul had been there for her, encouraging her in everything she did.

"Paul, I want to thank you for everything." She didn't want to spoil the surprise about the cabin yet, and hoped he wouldn't spill the beans, either. But she had something she needed to say to them both. "I couldn't imagine what it meant to be someone's daughter until I met you and Mama."

He simply nodded and hugged her again, whispering, "Dear girl, you're the daughter I never had." That he felt the same way toward her sent fresh tears down Dakota's cheeks. She was beginning to feel like the whole family had asked her to marry them.

Oh my gosh, Lucy! This must be how you felt about Jack's family too!

On the drive home after several more hours of celebration with their family, Dakota remained on a high that far exceeded anything she'd ever felt before. She reached across the console to take Matteo's hand.

"Do you remember back on New Year's Eve when we were watching *While You Were Sleeping*?"

"Of course. I got my first kiss that night."

Dakota grinned. Was that all he remembered? "Well, I guess I never really told you why that movie meant so much to me."

"Oh, I think I've figured it out—family, right?"

Of course he'd understand. She nodded. "Earlier, after you proposed and Paul told me he thought of me as a daughter. Then your mama gave you her ring to propose with and everyone welcomed me to the family. Now I realize I have everything I ever dreamed of. But last

New Year's Eve, I had no clue what it would mean to be part of a big family like that. Italian to boot! I'm living Lucy's dream life now too."

He lifted her hand to his mouth and kissed the top of it. "My family is complete now with you in it. I never believed it was a coincidence that brought us together at that bar in Amarillo."

"Me, either. The Universe was making sure I knew how to find you when I needed you most—and on the cusp of figuring out that it was time to make some changes in my life if I ever wanted to go after a different future. Only what I got was so much better than anything I ever could have imagined, never having known how important family could be."

She now had little-girl memories of having been loved once, but even those had been too painful for her to remember. Now she was able to love someone back just as strongly for who she was.

"I'm going to love the hell out of growing old with you, Sweet Lady."

She giggled. "Even when I'm no longer a redhead?"

"I'll probably make you earn every silver strand you ever get, but nothing as fleeting as hair color is going to change the way I feel about you." He kissed her hand again.

"Your Mama told me that she and Paul had known you were going to propose when they came down to take me out to lunch."

"Yeah. She told me she wanted to find out something for herself, and told me she had, but wouldn't tell me what it was."

Dakota remembered something Mama had said out of earshot of Matteo after they'd enjoyed the cake and more wine. She couldn't really explain it to Matteo without spoiling the surprise of the cabin renovation, but perhaps she could say it without giving that away.

"Apparently, a project I'm working on for you convinced her I had only your happiness in mind." Selfless. After spending her entire adult life chasing after what she wanted for her own good, she'd probably never put anyone's needs or wants ahead of her own. But her desire to restore the cabin for Matteo, using what little savings she had and without any expectation of personal gain, had convinced Mama that she was the right woman for Matteo.

"Are you going to tell me what that something is?"

"Nope. It'll be a surprise. You'll find out soon enough."

"Well, I have one more surprise up my sleeve for you tonight."

How could she stand much more? "What's that?"

He pulled into the lane that led up to their house and the barn. "Rather than tell you, I'm going to show you. Sit there until I open your door—just this once, since I know how much you hate when I want to do that."

She shook her head but would indulge his traditional ways just this once. He came around the hood of the truck and opened her door, helping her down and giving her a kiss on the lips now that he wasn't driving.

Taking her by the hand, he led her toward the barn rather than the house. Inside, her gaze went straight to Kahlo's stall that had been decorated with a huge sign that read: "Welcome home, Mama."

Puzzled, she looked toward him, not sure what it meant. As she walked closer, she saw the poster had been signed *Kahlo.* Inside the stall, she saw that the horse's mane had been festooned with yellow and brown ribbons that reminded her of sunflowers, one of her favorites.

"She's mine?"

"Well, I don't think she'd accept me as her mama." Once again, her eyes filled with tears. She'd been an emotional wreck ever since the proposal, so why not one more crying jag?

She launched herself into his arms. "Thank you so much! I love her like she's my own already, but when did you deck her out like that? I said goodbye to her and the others just before we left."

"Did you notice anything missing outside?"

She tried to think what he might mean, but shook her head, having no clue.

"Darren and Annette were giving Jason the two-horse trailer today for his graduation gift. So while they were out here, I asked if Jason would mind doing the honors and braiding Kahlo's mane to make this even more special. I'd have asked Annette, but Kahlo's more comfortable with Jason."

She turned toward Kahlo again and let herself inside the stall, stroking her neck before giving her darling baby girl a kiss on the nose. "He did a fabulous job. Where'd he learn to do a French braid like that?"

"4-H."

She didn't remember doing horse braids in high school but hadn't had her own horse then.

"Actually," Matteo added, "from a girl in 4-H who's attending the same college as he is. I think they might be getting serious."

Ah. "Lucky boy." She hoped it would work out if it was meant to be. Dakota had lost so many years while chasing the wrong dreams—at least ones that didn't matter to her now—although everything that had happened to her before had served a purpose and brought her to this place and time.

To Kahlo, she said, "Girl, you and I have been through a lot together, but I'm so happy we found each other—" She turned toward Matteo and smiled. "And that we found your papa too."

He joined them, and surprisingly, Kahlo didn't try to get away from him. Animals could sense which humans were safe, even though it had taken Kahlo even longer than Dakota to figure out Matteo could be trusted.

"Should I take the braids out?"

He shook his head. "They'll be fine overnight. She doesn't make too much of a mess in her stall."

"Looks like they cleaned her stall while they were here too."

"Yeah, because that means I get to take you inside and show you just how much I love you, Sweet Lady."

Neither of them would be getting any sleep tonight.

Chapter Thirty-Two

Everything was happening so fast. Shortly after she and Matteo talked about when they wanted to get married, the two had compared calendars with his siblings and settled on July 11.

Mama had initially thought they meant of next year until they insisted they intended to get married next month. While that only gave them about six weeks to plan, neither of them saw any reason to wait. They wanted a simple ceremony here at the ranch with close family and friends. Nothing else mattered.

Unfortunately, within a week of their engagement, Matteo had been called away to Idaho to fight a fire with the forest service and would be gone for two weeks. She missed him terribly, but with so much going on, they wouldn't have had a lot of time to be with each other anyway.

The day after he'd left, Carmella and Angelina had taken her dress shopping, albeit in Western wear shops because she wasn't into the long, frilly dresses traditional brides wore. Paul had given her his credit card and told her to buy whatever she needed from head to toe.

At lunch in a tavern in Aspen Corners afterward, they introduced her to a family friend, Rico Donati, who owned the tavern and also ran a catering business. He said he'd love to take care of the food for Matt and Dakota's reception. She assured him the fare would be simple, just the way she and Matteo liked to eat.

Earlier today, she'd driven up to Breckenridge to visit Mama and Paul, and he'd helped her submit her DNA results to two more databases.

"You might get a hit soon," he'd cautioned. "I don't want you meeting up with anyone without having a family member there with you."

Dakota started to bristle at his assuming she couldn't handle it by herself because she was a woman, but she quickly curbed that knee-jerk reaction. Paul cared about her safety, but also her emotional well-being if things didn't work out. When you were part of a family, you let them be included in momentous events like this one.

I'm learning!

"Being rejected by them would be devastating. I've been dreaming about—and dreading—reconnecting with my birth family for so long."

"I know, which is why I don't want you to have to face it alone, especially if you have to drive afterward, assuming they're anywhere in the region."

"Would you come with me, Paul, if I schedule it on your day off, assuming I hear from anyone before Matteo returns?"

His eyes opened wider as if taken aback by her request. "I thought you might ask Angela or one of the boys."

"I'd like it a lot more if you could be there."

His eyes grew bright. "You know I'll always be there for you, Dakota. All you have to do is ask."

Imagine her surprise when the next morning she received an email from someone who connected with her at the first-cousin level. Dakota had been so busy; she hadn't had time to explore the new sites to see if she'd had any hits.

All day, she'd tried to decide how to respond, but decided to give the woman—named Cynthia, if she wasn't using a fictitious name too—her cell phone number. If she wasn't someone Dakota wanted in her life, she'd just change to a new phone.

When the phone rang within minutes of sending her reply, Dakota's heart jumped into her throat. The number on caller ID was the one Cynthia said she'd be calling from. Dakota wished Matteo was here to bolster her courage but answered the call anyway.

"Hello?"

"Hi! This is really weird, isn't it? I'm not sure how we're related, but I'm certain we are." The woman's bubbly voice went a mile a minute. Could she be related to someone that spirited? "Can you tell me your name and who your parents are so we can figure this relationship out?" Cynthia asked.

Well, nothing like making the call even more awkward. She still didn't know enough about this woman to know whether she could trust her and didn't want to give her a name yet. Even if she could.

"I'm afraid I can't. One reason I'm doing the DNA search is that I don't know my birth name."

"Were you adopted?"

She supposed that could be one way to avoid giving too many details right off the bat. "Yeah. Adopted." After all, she'd adopted her Dakota Mathison personality long ago.

"Oh." The woman sounded discouraged by the response. "I suppose it's possible you're who we're looking for, but I doubt he'd have adopted her out."

He? Was she talking about the man Nana had referred to in a recent dream as *Roger*?

Cynthia kept talking. "My grandmother has been looking for my cousin since she was kidnapped at the age of five."

Dakota's heart pounded so loudly she was afraid she'd miss something Cynthia said. "Can you tell me about your grandmother?"

"Oh, she's a pistol. Eighty-two years old and still bossing everyone around on her ranch up in Dickinson, North Dakota."

North *Dakota*? Could she have chosen her name because she'd remembered something about her childhood?

"Are you still there?" Cynthia asked.

"Yeah." Could this grandmother be Nana? But how could she be sure? "What's the name of the missing granddaughter?"

Dakota didn't know her own name yet, so the question was almost pointless unless something clicked when she heard it spoken again.

"Patryce O'Hare. I used to call you Treesee." In her mind, Dakota spelled it phonetically until Cynthia spelled out the nickname as T-R-I-C-E-E.

Unfortunately, neither of those names rang any bells with her. Was O'Hare Nana's surname or her bio dad's? Which family did Cynthia belong to?

"Of course, Nana just called her Pumpkin."

Dakota's hand shook so badly she dropped the phone.

As much as Dakota had wanted Matteo to be here with her when she met Nana and her cousin, the thought of waiting another week or more for him to return from Idaho was unbearable. Now certain that she'd connected with her precious Nana, she needed to see her in the flesh as soon as possible and had arranged to meet two days after the call.

"I really appreciate you coming with me, Paul—and for driving. I would have been too distracted to stay on the road."

"Don't mention it. Were you able to get ahold of Matt to let him know what's going on?"

She shook her head then answered aloud as Paul kept his eyes on I-70 driving them toward Denver where this reunion would take place. "He's probably sleeping every moment he can, and I hear communication can be difficult in those places, even with a sat phone."

"I'm sure it's not just the phone. He's got to be exhausted. They've been fighting that one hard."

Dakota couldn't wait for him to be home. She didn't like him going off for such long stretches. "Remind me not to sign up to fight fires with the forest service—state or federal." Imagine how infrequently they would be together if both of them were deployed, as Matteo called it, at the same time?

"You never know what type of service you'll want to be involved in, or what will be available to you. It's hard to stay at home when you have local fires, but it takes a special breed to go fight the fires in someone else's backyard."

Matteo was one of those special firefighters. She felt so proud of him in that moment, especially hearing the respect for what he was doing in Paul's voice.

"Here we are," Paul announced forty minutes later when he pulled into the steakhouse's parking lot.

Dakota had chosen a restaurant in Denver because the two women had flown into the Mile High City earlier today. She didn't want Nana to have to add a long drive to that, but keeping some distance between them and her new family made sense in case this all turned out to be some elaborate hoax.

But how could Cynthia know Nana called you Pumpkin?

Still, better to err on the safe side. She didn't want the evil from her past to come anywhere near the Giardano family.

She had told her cousin via email that she'd be wearing a cowboy hat and boots but had forgotten to ask about their attire. Dakota scanned the people seated to see if anyone seemed to be looking for her. They'd arrived a little early, not wanting to take any chances on I-70 traffic. No one seemed to be looking for anyone to join them, and the hostess said no one had been seated waiting on additional party members.

"Do you think they'll be here?" she asked Paul, suddenly feeling like this might not have been a good idea.

"We're early. Let's just have a seat over here while we wait."

Before she could even sit down, a tremulous voice asked, "Pumpkin?"

The voice transported Dakota back to the woman from the dreams she'd been having. Turning around, she found a silver-haired woman, about five-six—so much shorter than she remembered as a little girl. But her eyes! She'd recognize those green eyes anywhere, because they were the same eyes she stared at in the mirror every day.

Her throat closed up as tears blurred her vision. "Nana?"

The woman could have been in her late sixties, despite what Cynthia had said was her actual age. As Nana opened her arms wide, Dakota walked into her embrace without a qualm. She held on for dear life, sobbing as the woman clung to her as well, crooning unintelligible words as she patted her back. Dakota's ugly-crying sounds made it impossible to hear, but her heart made out words of comfort.

After an unknown amount of time, the tears slowed, but Dakota didn't want to let go for fear Nana would be yanked away from her life again.

"I've waited so long to see you again," Nana said, rubbing Dakota's back in long strokes. "Much too long."

Reluctantly, Dakota loosened her hold so she could take another look at her. "I didn't know. I would have tried to find you, but I didn't know who to look for."

Nana nodded in understanding.

The woman standing behind Nana cleared her throat. She too had tears streaming down her face. "Tricee, I can't believe we found you after all this time."

Had Dakota known this cousin as a child? They seemed to be fairly close in age, but she had no memories of playing with any children as a kid.

The need to connect had Dakota take the steps toward Cynthia with her open arms and the two younger women embraced, albeit more briefly. When they pulled apart, she took a few of Dakota's curls between her fingers and thumb.

"Just like Nana's. I remember you two both having that flaming red hair."

"I guess my genes are responsible for the redheads in recent generations," Nana said. "But my hair hasn't been that color for decades, Sunshine."

Sunshine. Dakota flashed back to a scene with her and a little blond-headed girl making mud pies in the front of the house she'd been taken from. "I think I remember you now." In her mind, Sunshine fit her personality.

Fresh tears spilled from Cynthia's eyes. "I am two years younger. You probably remember me as a little pest always wanting to do whatever you were doing."

"I'm sorry I have so few memories of my childhood."

Dakota's attention returned to her grandmother. If Nana had once had hair as red as hers, perhaps Dakota would have beautiful silver hair when she grew old too. She remembered what Matteo had said about giving her those silver hairs. God, she wished he could be here today to meet *her* family.

"I remembered your hair as red too, Nana. And that you loved to bake."

Nana's smile trembled. "I'd always hoped you'd remember something about me. You were so young when…"

"Why don't we get our table so we can continue to reminisce?" Sunshine asked, wrapping her arm in a protective manner around Nana, even though the woman was anything but frail.

Paul stepped forward, having stayed on the fringes during the opening moments of their reunion, and the other women looked at him with questions in their eyes.

"I'm so sorry! Let me introduce you to my fiancé's stepfather, Paul Janowski." The title seemed lame considering how she felt about him, but she hadn't really referred to him as anything other than Paul before, despite how close they were becoming.

He extended his hand first toward Nana. "It's a pleasure to meet you."

"Please, call me Arelene."

"Arelene it is. And I'm Paul." He shook Cynthia's hand as well. "I believe they have our table ready. I just didn't want to interrupt the reunion." He must have put their names in while the ladies were getting to know each other.

After they'd been seated at a table near the window and ordered their drinks, Dakota placed her hand over Nana's on the top of the table and held on because she needed the physical connection to last as long as possible.

Cynthia glanced at Nana before meeting Dakota's gaze again. "Hardly a day has gone by where she hasn't mentioned you, even after all these years."

Hearing that Nana hadn't forgotten her surprised her at first, but then she thought about how she'd remembered Matteo, so she could understand it better.

Nana leaned forward. "Now, fill us in on what's going on in your life. Starting with that ring and the fiancé you mentioned." She pointed to Dakota's engagement ring.

Dakota opened up, happy to tell them about her life. "I met the sweetest boy in high school—in Aspen Corners, near Breckenridge."

"High school sweethearts," Nana said with a wistful smile, pressing her free hand over her heart.

Dakota laughed. "Well, not exactly. We spent most of our time together in horse barns doing 4-H activities. I don't think he knew I was alive back then, although he seems to remember more about me than I thought he ever would."

"Don't you think for a minute he didn't notice you," Paul interjected. He explained to the ladies, "Angela, Matteo's mama and my wife, told me all Matteo talked about was Alison, the name she went by then."

Now it was Dakota's turn to be surprised. "He did?"

Paul crossed his heart. "Absolutely."

Wow. She had no clue. Realizing she was supposed to pick up the story again, she continued. "Last October, we reconnected after one of my rodeos in Texas."

"You're in the rodeo?" Cynthia asked.

"Well, I retired recently. However, I competed steadily for more than a decade until I got injured last December. I came to Matteo's ranch and, well, one thing led to another and," she held her hand up with her ring pointing outward.

"Matteo sounds hot." Hearing Nana refer to a guy as hot momentarily took Dakota by surprise, and then she laughed.

"Oh, he's hot all right. Not just figuratively—he's a firefighter. I know he's going to be disappointed that he couldn't be here to meet you, but he's actually fighting a wildland fire in Idaho right now."

A look of worry came across Cynthia's face and Dakota assured her he was an expert at what he did. Not that she didn't worry about him too.

"Do you have any photos?" Cynthia asked.

"Are you kidding?" Dakota pulled out her phone, opened her photo app, and swiped until she found one of her favorite recent pics.

Matteo sitting astride Twinkle in a close-up with the sun setting behind her casting a rosy hue on Matteo's face. She turned the phone toward Cynthia first, then Nana.

"Whoa, Nellie, if I were fifty years younger…" Nana smiled then winked at her. Dakota couldn't begin to count how many times she'd said the old-fashioned expression *Whoa, Nellie.* Had she picked it up from Nana all those years ago?

"You own a ranch?" Nana asked.

"Yeah." She still felt funny using the word *our* when talking about the ranch, but Matteo insisted it was hers too. "We have three horses and are fostering about fifteen wild mustangs for some friends."

"Cattle?"

"No, just horses."

"I've been in the beef industry my whole life. I raise Black Angus cross cattle." Was Nana disappointed that Dakota and Matteo weren't in the same business? She didn't remember anything about cattle, but she wouldn't have been actively involved in the farm operations at the age of five.

Wanting to change the subject, she held up the phone again. "Matteo's on one of our horses here—Twinkle Littlestar."

"Horses *and* a hot fiancé? Lucky you!"

"His whole family is wonderful. All the men in the family are with the fire service in some capacity, including one who is a paramedic. Paul, here, is a battalion chief. I can't wait for you to meet Matteo. Oh, and of course, you're invited to our wedding. We set the date for July 11."

"A wedding! You can bet your bottom dollar we'll both be there."

The server returned to take their orders and when he left, they discussed other members of the extended family, none of whom she remembered. Most of them were gone, so she would never have that opportunity now. But thank God, Nana and Cynthia were here and they were able to reunite.

The smile faded from Nana's face. "What do you remember of your childhood, Patryce?"

Would she ever get used to her birth name? It seemed rude to tell Nana to call her Dakota, though, so she let it go.

"Not a lot, I'm afraid. In fact, I only began remembering things about six months ago when I started to have vivid dreams about you and your ranch house."

"You remember me?" Nana asked, as if it surprised her.

"My memory comes back to me in bits and pieces. I remember you baking—but I assure you that gene did not pass down to me!" The two of shared the laugh after Dakota told them about her attempts at making a coffee cake on New Year's.

"I'll have to give you some lessons."

Dakota sobered. "A lot of what I remember is from the day the man took me away from you, Nana." She recounted what she remembered, her heart breaking a little as Nana wiped away a tear.

"We moved every few years; he changed our names and appearance every time. And he twisted and distorted the truth about my childhood, brainwashing me into believing all kinds of lies. I must have repressed most of the real memories because it became so confusing to reconcile one with the other. I'm hoping you can help fill me in on what really happened. Being a five-year-old at the time, my understanding was so limited."

Nana took a deep breath, staring Dakota in the eyes. "Your piece-of-shit bio dad—" she apologized to Paul for her language and continued, "did everything he could to destroy my family. He's responsible for your mother's death—"

"Drugs?" Dakota asked having heard stories about her mother being a drug addict.

Nana's eyes opened wider. "Is that what he told you?" Nana looked like she could spit nails. "That lying… Roger killed her, plain and simple. He was the only one with a drug problem."

The server came to deliver some jalapeño poppers Nana had ordered before she was able to continue. "He nearly killed you too. Do you remember anything about the accident?"

Flashes of memory of an injured arm and a car racing through the rain-soaked night came to her then flitted away as quickly as they came. "Not really. I know I hurt my arm, because I remember him hurting me when he yanked me out of your house. And I remember the screeching tires. The rain."

"He was speeding and lost control of the car. Your poor mother didn't stand a chance. And you had a concussion and a broken arm when they brought you to the hospital." Tears spilled down Nana's cheeks again. "You looked so fragile in that big hospital bed with bandages on your forehead and a cast on your arm."

"I have no memory of being in the hospital. Only the day he took me away from you."

"That was three months after the accident. If he hadn't knocked me out, I'd have grabbed my rifle and shot him."

Dakota almost smiled at the image of Nana going after the man who stole her childhood, but she sobered quickly. "I thought he'd killed you when I saw you lying there."

"I was up and on my feet before you two cleared the lane, but all I could do was call the sheriff. Unfortunately, they couldn't find you that day or in the months after."

"Honestly, I don't remember a lot in the time that passed between the kidnapping and my junior year in high school."

"When you met Matteo," Cynthia supplied, and Dakota nodded with a smile.

Nana wiped away a tear. "What's wrong, Nana?" Dakota asked.

It took her a few moments to compose herself. "I've worried about you every day for twenty-seven years. I prayed that you'd survive and even thrive wherever you were. When his sister told me Roger had died of a drug overdose nine years ago, I kept hoping you'd come back to us, but never heard from you."

She'd been looking over her shoulder all these years for no good reason. "I just didn't know who to search for—and didn't know he was dead until now."

"Good riddance. Eventually, I began to think I'd never see you again in this world, and yet I continued to look for you in every redhead

I came across." She used her napkin to dab away a tear.

"I'd rather not think about all the years we've lost," Dakota said. "The important thing is that we've found each other. We still have time to build a strong bond. Trust me, I know, based on the bonds I've formed with Matteo's family." She smiled at Paul.

"Dear girl, you've been a delight to welcome into the family."

"Knowing you've found a wonderful, loving family makes my heart sing," Nana said to her, then turned to Paul. "And I can't wait to meet the rest of the family to thank them for taking in my Pumpkin when she needed them."

Dakota stood and went around the table to Nana, bending over her as she wrapped her arms around her. "I'm so thankful we've finally been reunited." The two held each other a while and when they separated, Dakota went to her cousin to hug her again. "Thank you so much for contacting me after we had our DNA match. You're the hero in this whole thing."

"Now you're going to start me crying again," Cynthia said.

When Dakota heard the server delivering their plates to the table, she returned to her seat. Drawing a deep breath, she stared at them in turns, unable to take her eyes off these two women.

More family. Eat your heart out, Lucy.

How had she become so blessed?

After they began eating, Nana swallowed and asked, "I'm curious about the name you go by now. How did that one come about?"

"Actually, the name I used when I signed up with the DNA testing service isn't the name I go by. My rodeo name was Dakota Mathison, and when I ran away at seventeen, I kind of reinvented myself."

Nana's fork clanked onto her plate. Dakota glanced from one to the other, wondering what she'd said. Nana picked up her water glass and drained half of it before speaking.

"My last name is Masterson. Coupled with the similarity with Mathison and your choosing the name Dakota, which is where I live, I swear you were trying to drop some breadcrumbs for me to find you. Too bad I didn't follow the rodeo more closely."

Dakota hadn't known how close she was to Nana's name. She must have pulled it out of her subconscious but distorted the actual name.

"I just had no idea," Dakota admitted.

Nana patted her hand in comfort. "Well, you've found us now. That's all that matters."

"Yes, it totally is." Dakota wouldn't have to go through the rest of her life wondering where she'd come from or where she belonged. With Nana and Cynthia, she'd found the answer to her first question. And with Matteo, she had her answer to the second.

She'd hold off telling him about this reunion until he came home so he wouldn't have to think about anything but fighting the fire safely and returning to her.

Chapter Thirty-Three

Last night, he'd called Dakota to let her know that he should be leaving on schedule after Wednesday's shift ended. There was something in her voice that made him even more anxious to get home to her. The last two weeks away from Dakota had nearly killed him. Now he couldn't shake the feeling that she'd been keeping something from him, even though she'd insisted everything was okay with her, the family, and the horses. Nothing else mattered to him.

Maybe it was just the lag in reception on his new satellite phone, but it was better than no reception at all.

Bone-weary, he lay in his bedroll the morning of day thirteen of his deployment waiting for the call to load up the trucks and head back to work. He'd managed two hours of interrupted sleep at base camp, but today's backbreaking assignment would sap what little energy he had left in no time. That he'd even had the strength to call Dakota last night had been monumental. God, he missed her so bad.

He rolled onto his side and stared at the guy next to him whose snoring had kept Matt awake half the night. At least at the firehouse, he had his own room and could block out the noise of his fellow crew members. The other firefighters fell asleep as soon as their heads hit the ground. Matt could never sleep well anywhere but at home.

I can't wait to get into my own bed again—with Dakota.

The day after tomorrow, he'd hit the road for Leadville. He'd come to realize on this assignment that he was getting too old for this shit. He probably was the oldest firefighter here who wasn't with the command staff. But unlike Rafe, Matt had never aspired to climb the ranks in his department. He liked putting water on fire, although the guys on the ground didn't do that on a wildland fire. Mostly, they'd been digging trenches and setting backfires for the control line in their efforts to stop the advance of the fire. The hotshot and smokejumper crews took the brunt of the flames, but Matt enjoyed working at his firehouse too much to sign on for that kind of duty.

Besides, he'd never see Dakota during the fire season if he were on one of those crews.

"All right guys! Rolling out in five!"

Matt crawled out of his bedroll at the captain's order to move and donned his turnout gear. He packed some protein bars and bottles of water in his pockets in case they didn't get a lunch break. The truck would carry more supplies for the men and women working this detail.

"We're making progress in division four," Captain said. "Today should be the turning point, as long as the winds don't pick up."

Always a big *if.*

"We have a house structure in harm's way. We'll need to extend the control line to try and save it. Everyone's been evacuated, though, so let's not do anything that would put you or one of the crew at risk."

Within twenty minutes, they were back close to where they had stopped the night before to give everyone time to rest. He missed having the SCBA mask and cylinder he wore at home that would have kept him from breathing in the noxious fumes. His PPE consisted mainly of boots, gloves, fire shelter, goggles, a hard hat, and a Hot Shield flame-retardant face covering that protected his lower face.

Another good reason to consider retiring before it was too late to avoid some vicious lung disease or cancer from too many years of exposure to smoke and all the toxins emitted from burning and melting materials. He got screened every year for the top cancers firefighters face, but out here they had a lot less protection.

"Matt, get up that hill and give me a dot high, let that burn a little bit, and drop down here to give me a dot low," Captain ordered. "Then move in that direction and keep going."

"Sure thing, Captain."

Trudging up the hill with his drip torch, Matt set fire to a small area of fine fuel—grass, leaves and small plants—that would burn away and help create a firebreak to stop the forward progress in this sector of the wildfire.

When the blaze up top had taken off, Matt dropped down the hill. Lather, rinse, and repeat. He'd probably be at this task for most of the next twenty-four hours, although they'd likely relocate the crew once they'd either saved this structure or needed to abandon the operation.

Bulldozers worked on removing some of the fuel load nearby in the undergrowth of bushes and small trees. The beeping noises as they backed up before assaulting the target again and again would be something he'd hear in his sleep for weeks.

When a gust of wind blew flames at his face, Matt jumped back.

Shit. This couldn't be good.

Matt had gotten off duty with the forest service last night, but Dakota had told him to get a motel room and catch up on his sleep before he made the long drive home. She worried about how exhausted he'd sounded. If he didn't already have his truck, she'd have driven to Idaho to bring her man home. But he'd assured her he'd get some sleep and would be home tomorrow or maybe the day after.

Home. Matteo's ranch felt like hers now too. This was the first time she could remember having a place to call home. Even her stay at Nana's ranch had only been short-lived after the court granted Nana custody.

On her way back from the barn to the house, she stopped and glanced out at the pastureland where their horses raced through the fields along with the wild mustangs. Did the horses remember when they'd run in the wild? Even though it had been many years for Twinkle and Comet, they were having just as much fun as Kahlo and Van Gogh.

Dakota decided to pack up the truck and drive up to the cabin, rather than drag Kahlo away from her friends. When Matteo came home, she wouldn't be able to get up there again until the weekend when he went back on duty at the firehouse. So much work still needed to be done on the place before she could finally share it with him.

Suddenly, she noticed billowing black and gray smoke coming from the direction of the cabin. *No!*

Dakota ran into the kitchen to grab her keys and the sat phone. She bolted out of the house, got into the truck, and headed up the mountain. Her heart pounded so hard she became nauseous. All the work they'd done on the cabin could be wiped out in a matter of minutes. There might not be a darned thing she could do to save it. At the very least, she needed to try and get in there to retrieve the mining lantern Mama had entrusted her with. If it were lost in a fire, Dakota wouldn't be able to forgive herself.

After going through the last pasture gate and getting back in the truck, she floored the gas pedal and took the jarring road much faster than she should, but time was of the essence.

Had the fire been reported yet? She pulled out her phone and called 911. The lag was annoying, and she wasn't sure whether they understood who she was or where she was calling about, but she couldn't do anything more than that.

When she pulled into the clearing, she saw that the cabin was intact. Thank God! But the federal lands that provided a backdrop to the cabin were in flames. There wasn't much time!

Opening the door, she ran inside and grabbed the lantern and a framed photo of Matteo's grandfather that had been placed over the mantel. This was her family now too, and she felt it her responsibility to protect these precious family treasures. No way could she let them burn up in the fire.

She glanced around the cabin once more, seeing so much hard work and too many treasures to possibly rescue, but she had the most important ones now. Returning to the truck, thick, choking smoke assailed her, making her cough. The flames had doubled in size. What more could she do to protect the place?

After carefully placing the precious objects on the floorboard to keep them from falling off the seat, she grabbed an ax from the truck bed. Paul had told her which trees and bushes needed to be removed to give the cabin a buffer in case of fire, but they'd thought there was still plenty of time to finish. If they caught fire, the flames could easily transfer on the wind and destroy all the work they'd done up here. The thought of cutting healthy trees hadn't appealed to her before, but now it was paramount that she give this historic place a fighting chance. She'd just thought she had more time, although Cassie had told her she'd lost her original cabin in a June wildland fire.

Dakota had to do something. She couldn't just stand back and watch this cabin burn. Her efforts might be futile, but she cut down the bushes and small trees closest to the cabin. Then she dragged them far enough away not to be a threat any longer.

Coughing as the smoke grew thicker, she let tears of frustration stream down her face. All the work she, Paul, and Mama had done in the past few weeks was about to go up in flames. Now she wished she'd let Matteo in on what they were doing up there. He'd never get to see all the love they'd put into that place.

She worked feverishly, glancing toward the government lands every now and then to see if the flames were any closer. Right now, they seemed to be satisfied with the patch of land they devoured.

Please protect our cabin.

Suddenly, the wind picked up, blowing in her direction. She didn't think there was much more she could do now but hoped she'd done enough to spare the cabin.

Something roared into the clearing behind her, and she turned to find a familiar Leadville fire engine and Brush 1 pulling into the clearing. An answer to her prayer! She ran over to greet them when they pulled to a stop.

As two firefighters pulled hose, Darren got out of the driver's seat and glared at her.

"Darren, thank God you're here. I didn't know if my call went through."

"What the hell are you doing up here. Get off this mountain, Dakota. Now!"

"I wanted to try and save the cabin."

"I said get off this mountain. We don't know when the fire might cut off your escape. Go! Now!"

If she'd been trained already to help, she'd have argued and stayed, but at the moment she was only in the way. Dejected, she returned to her truck and started the harrowing drive back down the mountain. At least she had the family treasures with her.

She'd only made it through the first gate when a familiar truck approached. *Matteo?!*

He must have driven through the night. Why hadn't he listened to her? She pulled up beside him and got out of the truck, ready to give him a piece of her mind when he met her and grabbed her by the biceps. "What are you doing up here? Are you crazy?"

Her crazy?

Why was he yelling at her?

"Well?"

He wanted an answer? "I'm trying to save our cabin, that's what!"

His eyes narrowed, and he cocked his head in confusion. "That old thing? You're risking your life for a pile of logs?"

Dakota could spit nails at the callous way he'd characterized the cabin she'd been working so hard on.

"Go home. We'll talk later. I'm going up to see if I can help."

Waiting until he drove off, she turned the truck around and headed back up the mountain. Surely there was something she could do to help, even if all she did was continue working on the undergrowth around the cabin.

The engine truck didn't hold enough water to help with the fire on the federal lands, but the firefighters sprayed water on the cabin in an effort to keep it from burning. Several of them had helped her fix the interior up, so even though it didn't look worth saving on the outside yet, they knew what it meant to her.

Matteo had donned his gear and a chain saw and went to work clearing more of the brush she'd been working on earlier. Dakota grabbed her ax and went to the opposite side of the cabin to cut more trees, hoping Matteo didn't see that she was still up here.

The wind changed direction again and carried the smoke away from them now, thank goodness. She hated the smell. But she supposed she'd better get used to it if she was going to the fire academy.

"Damn it, Dakota! Where are you?"

Matteo bellowed for her, and she smiled. Nothing he could say at this point could piss her off. She'd helped save their cabin alongside Matteo and the men she hoped to work with one day.

Nothing will spoil my mood, not even a cranky fiancé.

Dakota came around the side of the cabin to the front with a smile plastered on her face, and her gaze zeroed in on Matteo. The crew was busy putting away the hose and packing up their tools. He came over to her and she thought he might grab her and yell at her again, but instead he stared at her in silence.

"Are you going to kiss me?"

"I ought to take you over my knee."

She teasingly looked over at the guys. "Why don't we save that for the privacy of our bedroom?"

He rolled his eyes then pulled her to him. "What am I going to do with you, Sweet Lady?"

"Kiss me?"

His lips pressed against hers and he did just that. She wrapped her arms around his neck and opened her mouth so he could deepen the kiss. When they finally separated, both were breathing hard, and not because of the smoke they'd encountered earlier.

"Looks like we dodged a bullet, and the cabin will be spared. But if you ever pull another stunt like this—"

"Matteo," she said warningly, "you do not want to finish that sentence."

Finally, he shook his head and grinned. "You came into my life like a wild, untamable fire. How could I possibly expect to suppress your spirit now?" He took her hand and led her to where their pickups were parked. "Head back to the house. The crews may need to stay a while, but I'll follow. We can talk when I get back."

When he reached the house, he found Dakota in the barn, and wrapped his arms around her, kissing her again. She held onto him even tighter. "I missed you," she said.

"Did I miss anything exciting—well, other than the fire?"

She grinned. "Actually, you did. I got a hit from one of the DNA databases, and I met her."

Her?

"The lady I kept seeing in my dreams—Nana."

Matt's eyes opened wider. "Already? That was fast."

She nodded. "I also met my first cousin who was my match from the database."

"How'd it go?" He hadn't been here to support her during this momentous occasion, which pissed him off, but he couldn't very well have asked her to wait on him for a reunion like that.

"Better than I ever could have dreamed. She's feisty, funny, runs a cattle ranch, and used to be a redhead too, so you'll get to see what I'm going to look like in fifty years."

"I'm going to love you no matter what your hair color is. Remember, you were a blonde when we first met."

"You weren't in love with me then."

"How can you be so sure?"

She cocked her head to consider his response, then smiled. "Anyway, Paul said I take after her, especially in my eyes and temperament."

He searched her eyes. "Paul went with you to meet your nana?"

"Didn't I tell you? Oh, I forgot! I didn't want to upset or worry you while you were on the fireground, but, yeah, he insisted that I not go to Denver alone. Good thing too. I wouldn't have been able to drive safely between the nerves heading there and the many thoughts swirling around my head on the way home."

He owed the man a beer next chance he got. The way Paul had taken Dakota under his wing and tried to be the father figure she'd missed out on with her bio dad made Matt ashamed that he'd once resented him for dating Mama. Paul had been there for Dakota when Matt hadn't been able to be, which meant the world to him. He'd also loved and cared for Mama since before the two had married.

"When do I get to meet them?"

"Three weeks—at the wedding," she said. "Well, they might arrive a few days before—they live in North Dakota. I think that must have been tucked away in my subconscious all those years until it came time for me to choose a name."

"Speaking of which, what's Nana's name?"

"Arelene Masterson. She spells it a little differently than the norm, but told me that's how her grandmother spelled it."

"What name were you born as?"

"Patryce." She didn't give a last name and he didn't ask, as it would have been the name of her kidnapper. "My cousin Cynthia, who's two years younger than me, called me Tricee. I don't have any memory of that, though."

Dakota patted him on the chest. "I need to get dinner started," she said. "Let's go inside." They held each other's hands as they walked into the house together. "What are we having?"

"Baby back ribs and baked potatoes."

"My favorite."

Before he'd deployed, she had been making ribs in that pot Mama bought for him on a weekly basis, but damn, he'd never grow tired of them.

After they'd finished the meal, he stood and cleared the table. He decided to do the dishes later and returned to her. Dakota stood and stepped into his arms. "Shower with me? I want to get the smell of smoke out of my hair."

"Better get used to it if you're going to be a hotshot firefighter."

She smiled. "I don't think my dream is to be a hotshot. I'll leave that to you."

"Actually, I was never on the hotshot crew and never wanted to be, but I think I'm ready to retire from the forest service. Those were the longest two weeks of my life. I don't want to be away from you that long."

"What if I decide to fight wildland fires?"

Was she seriously considering that? He hadn't given any thought to her doing anything but work out of a nearby fire station. Or was she testing him?

"Well, then, I guess I'll have to get used to being the one waiting for you to get home. Just promise me you won't do anything that might get you killed. Today you risked your life to save an old, dilapidated building when there wasn't anything in it worth saving."

Dakota opened her mouth as if to argue, then shut it.

"You're the most important thing to me, Sweet Lady."

She smiled and squeezed his butt cheeks. "Let's get that shower. And then get reacquainted. Best part of being apart all that time is the reunions when we come back together."

"You've got that right."

Chapter Thirty-Four

"You look so beautiful." Carmella smiled as she met Dakota's gaze in the cheval mirror.

"My brother is pacing like a caged animal," Angelina said, peeking out the window. She turned toward the other ladies in the bedroom. "It's probably time to put him out of his misery, although I've enjoyed watching him squirm since the rehearsal dinner last night." She smiled at Dakota. "I can't believe another of my confirmed-bachelor brothers is taking the plunge. I'm so happy he's taking it with you, Dakota, and I'm thrilled to have another sister."

She came over and air-kissed her so as not to smudge her makeup. Dakota pulled her into a hug, not the least bit concerned since she wore so little of the stuff.

Dakota had never had *any* siblings, which Nana had confirmed. "It means so much to me to have you both as my sisters now, and to gain four brothers too." In addition to Matteo's three brothers, Marc had also called her *sister* the night she and Matteo became engaged.

My family.

She'd always hoped to be part of one someday, and Matteo had brought her into a huge Italian one. Lucy's dream, indeed. Six months ago, when she'd watched *While You Were Sleeping* with Matteo, she never could have imagined this would become her own reality.

Today, her wedding day, she would be forever joined with Matteo.

My man.

Matteo had worn down all her defenses and had shown her what being part of a family and community meant—not just the benefits, but the responsibilities. Best of all, he'd given her unconditional love without demanding she conform or become someone she wasn't.

And she'd become a better person as a result. She'd stopped thinking the world revolved around her and had started thinking about others—Matteo, family, friends, and her community. She'd never be the same.

Dakota only hoped she could be the wife Matteo deserved, but her wandering days were over. Not that she wouldn't continue to compete—in skijoring and firefighting skills. She couldn't wait for classes to start, although she might have to postpone the more rigorous—

"Ready to ride?" Angelina asked, pulling her out of her musings.

Dakota smiled. "More than."

"Jason has braided Kahlo's mane to within an inch of her life," Megan said, smiling. "The ribbons are so pretty." She'd been quietly taking pictures all morning to the point that Dakota almost forgot she was there. "Kahlo's wearing them like she's the queen of the day."

"I thought she'd hate going to all that fuss again," Dakota said, "but I guess she knows how important today is for me and wants to look her best too." She gave Carmella and Angelina a mock-stern look. "Not sure I could have taken much more of you girls messing with my hair and makeup, though." But she grinned at them, not upset at all, even if she hardly recognized herself.

They looked so pretty in their lacy turquoise cowgirl dresses and embroidered boots.

A light knock sounded on the bedroom door. "Girls, I think they're ready for us!" Mama came in and stopped short as she took in Dakota and her outfit. "Oh, sweetie, you look gorgeous!"

"I feel gorgeous!" Just missing one thing. "Mama, I'd like you to put on the crowning glory." Dakota went to the dresser and picked up the white cowboy hat with the three sunflowers nestled in the netting at the back. The tulle spilled halfway down her back, her concession to wearing a veil today.

"I would love to, *figghia mia*."

"Mama, you'll have to translate for me. I'm taking Italian lessons online but haven't learned that phrase yet."

Mama's eyes swam with tears. "It means 'my daughter' in Sicilian. My nonna used to say that to me whenever we were together, because I didn't know my own mother."

Dakota had no idea she'd grown up motherless too—and now she'd surrounded herself with so many children and mothered Dakota, as well, with so much love and compassion. She wrapped her arms around Mama. "Sadly, that's something we share, but I'm so grateful to have you as my mama now."

When they pulled apart, they saw that Megan had captured the moment for them. "Megan," Mama began, "you're fast becoming the family photographer. I'm sure there will be more weddings and perhaps some christenings in your future."

Dakota's eyes grew wider. When Mama noticed, she smiled and patted her arm. "No, I'm not telling you to start on a family right away. There's plenty of time."

"Oh, okay, Mama." Dakota drew a deep breath and let it out.

Remembering that the ceremony couldn't start without them, Dakota pulled away. "We'll have years and years for hugs, but let's give Matteo a little breather and get out there before he passes out."

Everyone laughed, and Dakota sat on the chair in front of the mirror where she'd sat for what seemed like hours earlier having her hair and makeup done. She blinked away the tears so that she wouldn't miss watching the mama of her heart place the hat on her head, tilting it just so to give her a saucy look. She hoped Matteo didn't expect a blushing bride in a demure veil. If she could gallop on Kahlo down the aisle toward him, she would.

"Perfect!" Megan said as she snapped the photos. "Just lovely."

"I wish I had curls like yours," Angelina said as she gently patted the cascade of hair spilling out from under Dakota's hat.

"You and me both," Carmella lamented. "Mine's as straight as an arrow."

"You two don't know how lucky you are to have such thick, straight hair!" Dakota countered. She stood and took a deep breath. "Okay, let's do this!"

Matteo and their guests were gathered in the pasture behind the barn so that she could make her entrance the way she'd envisioned since they'd started planning their big day. She hadn't let Matteo know what to expect and in rehearsal last night, she'd simply walked down the aisle between the chairs on Paul's arm.

I can't wait to see Matteo's face!

She'd chosen a calf-length wedding dress rather than the traditional length, but the skirt was full enough that she could ride Kahlo sidesaddle and still keep most of her bare legs covered.

"Time to make my entrance." In front of the barn, she mounted Kahlo, crooking her knee over the horn. The girls adjusted her skirt so that it wasn't bunched up and she wasn't flashing anyone.

"Can't wait to show off my pearly-white boots, ladies." She'd been working them in for weeks, because she planned to dance in them at the reception without getting blisters. She'd fallen in love with these boots the minute she saw them while dress shopping in Aspen. A little prissy for a legit cowgirl, but what the heck? Angelina had gifted them to her and she couldn't say no. They'd grown on her.

Best of all, Matteo had a thing about seeing her dressed only in her boots, so she'd have fun wearing them and nothing else for him tonight.

Lots of surprises planned for later.

She'd worry about that later! Right now, the love of her life was waiting for her along with her new family and friends.

"Stop fidgeting," Franco said as he pinned the small sunflower boutonniere on Matt's lapel. His brother's agreeing to serve as his best man today meant the world to Matt. They'd become closer while working together at the Leadville firehouse until last year when Franco had moved away.

Matt took a breath, blew it out in his brother's face, but held still. He needed to blow off some steam somewhere. Being apart from Dakota since the rehearsal dinner last night had nearly killed him, especially knowing she wasn't that far away but he wasn't allowed to see or be with her.

Rafe had assured him over an hour ago that she was in the house getting ready, after spending the night at Angelina's with her grandmother, cousin, and the bridal party. He'd stayed here at the ranch with Mama, Paul, and his brothers.

At least he knew she'd be showing up for the ceremony, not that he really thought she might jilt him. Still, given her years of wanderlust, he'd entertained that "what if" scenario for the first half of his sleepless night. And the rest of the night, he'd worried about them being in an accident on the way back down here.

Rafe had come off duty this morning, but they'd scheduled the ceremony in the early afternoon, so everyone had been able to make it. While he'd been surrounded by family in the house, it wasn't the same as having Dakota here.

God, I miss her.

How would he handle it if she decided to sign up with the forest service after graduating from the fire academy? She sounded like she wanted to stick closer to home, but what if there weren't any job openings?

"Time to take our places, boys," Rafe said.

His eldest brother, dressed in his fire department's formal dress uniform despite everyone else being in Western wear, had gotten himself ordained by an online website just so that he could perform today's secular ceremony. An outdoor wedding at a ranch definitely wasn't going to be officiated by a Catholic priest. *Poor Mama.* Good thing Angelina had given Mama the traditional church ceremony she'd always dreamed of for each of her kids, because Matt and Tony sure hadn't. But at least she'd been invited to attend *this* son's wedding.

He glanced over at Tony, who was fiddling with his cowboy hat, not attire he was accustomed to. Franco, his best man, took his place between Matt and Tony.

Luke and Cassie had constructed a rustic backdrop shaped like a ranch-style gate from three aspen tree trunks they'd cut down on the mountain where Dakota and Matteo had gone on trail rides at Dreams Found Ranch. It had been decorated with a long white curtain draped over the cross branch, with sunflowers and other small white wildflowers and greenery at the juncture of the tree trunks in one corner near where Dakota would stand. A smaller setting of flowers and greenery hung partway down the trunk on the other side.

They didn't have designated seating for family and friends. Every seat had been taken by extended family and mutual friends, including Ryder, Luke, Cassie, Jason and his parents, some of the other guys from the firehouse and their families, and even Dolly from the café. Everyone who loved him and Dakota had joined them on their special day. And Megan was busy taking photos to record it all.

Nana stepped around the side of the barn just as "God Bless the Broken Road" began to play. She wore her cowboy hat, western blouse, and cowgirl skirt. He'd met Nana and Cynthia a few days ago and had hit it off great with them. Cynthia's husband had stayed behind to mind the ranch, but he and Dakota hoped to meet him someday soon.

Marc stood waiting with his elbow extended toward Nana. The two exchanged a few words, and she laughed at whatever he'd said. Then they grew a little more serious—both maintaining big smiles—and started down the aisle between the rows of chairs that had been set out this morning.

Before taking her seat, Nana winked at Matt. The woman had more spirit than he'd expected, and Matt could now see where Dakota's came from.

Marc returned to the back, and Matt's gaze became laser-focused on the area where Dakota would come out from—eventually. He couldn't wait to catch his first glimpse of his bride, but first Mama stepped around the barn and looked up at Marc. She bestowed her beautiful smile on him before resting her hand on the forearm he extended.

As they started toward the aisle, Mama's gaze zoomed in on Rafe, Franco, Tony, and finally Matt. He'd never seen her more radiant. She too had dressed in Western wear, hers deep blue. Mama took her seat in the row across from where Cynthia and Nana sat, and Marc left one chair open for Paul before taking his own seat. He and Angelina exchanged a warm smile, perhaps remembering their own wedding day.

Matt was grateful that Mama and Dakota got along so well. During his talk with Mama prior to proposing, Matt hadn't been sure how she'd feel about having a non-Italian daughter-in-law, but clearly, it didn't matter to her. She'd become a mother to Dakota just as if she'd birthed her. But he was glad their bond was purely from the heart!

Man, the weird things going through my head at a moment like this.

The music changed, and Matt's heart rhythm sped up. *Almost time.* He smiled, anticipating the first glimpse of his bride. When Carmella appeared from around the side of the barn next, he tried not to let his disappointment show. Apparently, he'd forgotten everything they'd gone over at rehearsal last night.

Her gaze zeroed in on Tony's face. Matt turned toward his brother, who looked at Carmella as if he hadn't seen her in a year.

I understand that feeling now.

Walking slowly down the aisle, Carmella held a single sunflower tied with a russet-colored ribbon. Next came Angelina, who carried a bouquet with three sunflowers to convey her role as matron of honor. She took her place beside Carmella.

A new song began to play: "Keeper of the Stars."

"Everyone stand, please, and welcome our bride," Rafe said.

All eyes became glued on the side of the barn, and Matt held his breath. Paul came out first holding a lead rope adorned with ribbons and flowers. Kahlo's ribbon-festooned head and mane came into view followed by the most beautiful woman in the world.

My cowgirl.

She wore a white cowboy hat and her dress appeared to be molded to her upper body, showing off her breasts. The neckline wasn't cut low enough for him, but he supposed brides liked to have a little modesty.

Matt shifted his focus to her face and caught her smiling as if she knew exactly where his thoughts had gone. They could read each other like a book now. He'd never felt as strong a connection with anyone before in his life.

As they walked behind the rows of chairs, he saw her hat had been decorated at the back with lots of puffy lace and sunflowers, her favorite flower. As they reached the start of the aisle, Matt caught a glimpse of pearl-colored boots. He'd been enjoying the hell out of them as Dakota wore them around the house breaking them in. They'd also look damned sexy on her after he removed that dress tonight.

Paul led Dakota and Kahlo down the aisle, closer and closer to Matt. He stepped forward to greet them, and when she was just a few feet away, Paul extended the lead to Matt but didn't release it.

"I'm delivering to you the love of your life, Matt," Paul said. "Be good to her, or you'll answer to me."

Matt raised his brows, then smiled. Without a doubt, not only Paul but everyone present today would be on his ass if he took a wrong step with this woman. Not that he ever would!

"Don't you worry, Paul. I'll cherish her until the day I die."

With a nod, Paul released the lead to him and moved across the aisle to sit beside Mama. Matt came around to Kahlo's left side. Dakota had worked hard to get the horse used to Paul and Ryder for today's ceremony. Matt stroked the mare's neck, thanking her for being so patient and for carrying his bride down the aisle to him.

Matt smiled up again at the beautiful cowgirl who'd said *yes* to him. The thought of spending the rest of his days with her humbled him greatly, and he had to swallow past the lump in his throat.

He lifted his arms to help her dismount. Once her boots were firmly on the ground, Angelina came forward to straighten her skirt, but Matt couldn't look away from his bride's sparkling emerald eyes.

"You're gorgeous," he whispered.

She blushed a little. "You clean up pretty good yourself, Matteo."

With a grin, he took Dakota's hand as Ryder led Kahlo off to the corral.

The couple took their places before Rafe who held a small booklet in his hand. Looked like Mama's prayer book. They'd shared copies of their vows with him ahead of time, in case either of them needed prompting. Rafe reminded them to face each other and join hands in front of the gathering.

"Family and friends," Rafe began, "we're gathered today to witness the joining in marriage of these two individuals who wish to begin their lives together. We're here to watch and celebrate with them as two hearts become one."

Damn, Bro! You're going to reduce me to tears if you keep this shit up.

Matt blinked his eyes, determined not to cry in front of Dakota. She gave his hand a comforting squeeze. *Busted.* He could never hide anything from her.

Matt missed some of what Rafe said next but picked it up again with, "Matteo, do you take Dakota to be your wife, to cherish in friendship and love today, tomorrow, and for as long as the two of you live, to trust and honor her, to love her faithfully through the best and the worst, whatever may come? If you ever have any doubt, to remember the love you feel for each other in this moment and the reason you came together today?"

Rafe's words hit him right in the gut. He'd never taken a more solemn vow, not even when he joined the fire service. But like that one, this one was easy to commit to.

"I do," Matt said loudly so all the world would know his intentions toward this woman.

"Dakota, do you take Matteo…" Rafe repeated the words for her, and hearing that "I do" as they stared into each other's eyes filled Matt with more love and joy than he'd known could exist. Thank God she'd come back into his life.

"If I could have the rings," Rafe said to Angelina and Franco, who both produced the rings they'd been holding onto for this moment and placed them on Rafe's open book.

"Before Dakota and Matteo exchange rings to seal their vows, they've prepared some special promises they'd like to share with each other now. Matteo…" Rafe prompted.

Matt swallowed, his mind a jumble right now with all the words he'd spent the past few days memorizing to say to his bride at this moment in the ceremony. *Blank.*

"Today, I marry…" Rafe prompted.

The words came back to him in an instant.

"Today, I marry my best friend." He cleared his throat so that he could get through the rest. "I'm so glad we found each other again and discovered how much we belong together. Dakota, I promise to be the best husband and friend I can be. I promise to be your champion and your advocate in all things and to encourage you in all your endeavors. I know we're a tiny part of a much bigger picture, and I will lend a helping hand to you and those around us. Together, we will meet each challenge we have to face and will strive to nurture goodness within each other and in our loved ones, our community, and our home. I will never take you for granted, Sweet Lady, because I know how blessed I am to have you in my life."

He brushed another tear off her cheek as the enormity of the responsibility and devotion he felt for her filled him. He'd carry those feelings with him the rest of his life.

Chapter Thirty-Five

Matteo looked so handsome dressed all in black from his cowboy hat to his Western suit coat with red piping, black Wranglers, and cowboy boots.

Seldom one to cry, Dakota couldn't hold back the tears today as she listened to Matteo's heartfelt words and promises. Her love for this man would never know any bounds. He'd already given her the world when he made her a part of his, but he'd also given her roots in their home and with their family and their community. Matteo reached up and brushed away the tear from her cheek, smiling with understanding because his own eyes were swimming a little bit.

"Dakota," Rafe prompted, "begin whenever you're ready."

She had taken a more lighthearted approach to her vows in places, and hoped he'd accept it in the spirit intended.

Here goes.

"Matteo, I haven't always believed in a higher power, but I know it wasn't a coincidence that we were brought back together last October in Amarillo. The moon and the stars aligned perfectly to bring us back together again on Christmas Eve, with a little help from an ornery bull."

He grinned for the first time ever at her mentioning a bull ride, probably because she'd promised not to get on another bull again as long as she lived.

"I can't promise to be any more domestic than you are," she grinned, "but with Angelina's, Mama's, and now Nana's guidance, I promise to learn how to follow a recipe and do my best to take turns in the kitchen at home and perhaps someday in the firehouse."

He'd been making strides in the kitchen as well, learning from the guys at the station.

Now that she'd calmed her nerves, Dakota grew more serious. "Matteo, you can count on me to be an equal partner—whether it's in the house, the barn, or anywhere else on the ranch."

She no longer recited from the script she'd written, but only Rafe would know that. These words came from deep in her heart.

"You have brought so much joy into my life, Matteo. I promise to work hard to bring even more into your life with everything I do and say."

Not that they wouldn't have their moments of misunderstandings and blowups, but he already knew that from their past history.

"I will delight in our adventures and persevere with you in any challenges we face. I will laugh with you in good times and console you when you're downhearted. And we will strive to come to mutual decisions that are best for both of us, as well as our family, friends, and community."

She glanced over at Nana who had tears streaming down her face, and then at Mama, who held onto Paul's hand, smiling through tears of her own.

Dakota returned her attention to her beloved groom. Being a part of a family and community like the ones Matteo had brought her into was the icing on the cake as far as she was concerned. She no longer had an urge to ramble around the countryside in search of whatever accolades or approval she could gain on the rodeo circuit. Her place was beside this man doing worthwhile things that made a difference in their world.

"Today is only the beginning of building our lives together. I will love and cherish you today, tomorrow, and forever, Matteo. I love you, my cowboy fireman."

Rafe didn't say anything, no doubt uncertain whether she had finished, until she gave him a nod and a smile.

"Matteo, if you'll take Dakota's ring." Rafe held out the open book and Matt picked up the smaller of the two gold rings. Then he took Dakota's left hand in his and positioned the ring at the tip of her third finger.

"With this ring, Dakota, we forge a new path on this adventure together called life. I love you now and always will. Please accept this ring as a token of my faithfulness and love."

"I will," she said through the frog in her throat. He slipped the ring onto her finger as the sun glinted off the gold, infusing light and love into this new phase in their life together. Carmella had told them about silicone rings, so they each had one of those as well for when they were doing anything remotely dangerous, but today was all about the traditional ones.

Next, Rafe held out the book to Dakota who picked up Matteo's ring and took his hand.

"Matteo, I give you this ring as a reminder of my love and faithfulness. Like these rings, our love is continuous and unbreakable."

"Matteo and Dakota," Rafe said, "today you have declared your wishes to be united in marriage in the presence of these witnesses and have pledged your love to each other. You have confirmed the same by declaring your vows, by joining hands, and by exchanging rings. Therefore, by the authority vested in me by the State of Colorado, I am pleased to pronounce you husband and wife."

Rafe paused and smiled down at them. "Matteo, I know you've been waiting for me to say this all day. You may kiss your bride."

Matt removed his hat and leaned closer to his beautiful, sexy wife. Using the hat as a shield from all those present except Rafe, he kissed her long and deep to the hoots and hollers of some of their friends and applause from the others. He heard Jason cheering them on and was fairly certain Nana's shouts of encouragement were the loudest.

I love that woman too.

Good thing, because she'd announced at dinner last night she was turning over the operation of her ranch to Cynthia and her husband, who already were heavily involved in running it. Nana planned to move to Leadville, at least for a while, so she could get to know Dakota better.

When his bride started to giggle—whether at Nana or the length of the kiss—Matt broke free and stared into her eyes.

"There's a lot more where that came from, Sweet Lady. Just wait until we're alone tonight."

"I can't wait."

Rafe cleared his throat. "We're not finished here yet." They looked toward his brother; even he couldn't hide a rare grin. He opened the prayer book and read:

May God keep you of one heart
in love with one another
for the rest of your days,
and may peace abide always in your home.

May you be blessed in your children,
have solace in your friends
and enjoy true peace with everyone.

Rafe looked up at them again. "Congratulations, Matt and Dakota. Now, turn and face your family and friends."

They did as instructed, clasping hands and smiling brightly. Matt donned his hat again.

"It is my honor to present to you Dakota and Matteo Giardano," Rafe announced.

When Matt had asked her if she wanted to keep her own name, trying to be a modern-thinking guy with his independent woman, Dakota said she'd never really had an emotional connection to the Mathison surname. She did identify as Dakota, though, more than Alison or Patryce, her birth name. So she'd told him she'd be proud to take on her new and final name—Dakota Giardano.

Man, I love the sound of that.

"We hope everyone can join the newlyweds under the tent on the side of the house for a reception and supper to follow immediately," Rafe announced.

Everyone stood clapping and cheering them on as they walked

down the makeshift aisle together. They ran around the side of the barn to get ahead of the crowd, and he pulled her inside so he could kiss her more thoroughly while they waited for the guests to make their way to the party tent.

He wasn't sure how long they were in there, but it must have been a while. Tony ducked his head through the door. "What are you two doing in here? We're ready for you." He closed the gap and clapped Matt on the back. "Welcome to the club, Bro."

Matt laughed. "I didn't think you and Angelina should be the only siblings enjoying wedded bliss any longer."

Tony turned to Dakota and opened his arms, and she walked into them. "Glad to have a new sister, Dakota." He pulled away and met her gaze. "And if this lug gives you any trouble, you just call Tony, and I'll kick his ass."

"I'm sure I can handle him myself, but thanks for the offer."

"Hey, which team are you on?" Matt asked her. He shook his head in mock chagrin, but he'd probably said something similar to Carmella after they'd announced their surprise marriage to the family two Christmas Eves ago.

"Ready to make your entrance?"

After Tony left, Matt figured he had time to kiss Dakota once more. Then they heard Franco's deep voice announcing, "Let's welcome Mr. and Mrs. Matteo Giardano to this party!"

Reluctantly, he parted lips with her. "I guess we can't hide in here any longer."

"The sooner we start the party, the sooner we start our wedding night."

"You going to tell me where we're going yet?"

She shook her head and answered, "Nope."

"Well, as long as you're there, I don't care where it is. Okay, let's do this."

They strolled into the tent to more hooting and hollering of their thirty or so guests. An intimate group, but all the important people in their lives were here, which was all that mattered.

Long tables and chairs had been set up under the tent to accommodate everyone. Each table had a blue mason jar filled with a sunflower and daisies. When Nana saw the jars, she told Dakota that the blue ones probably were more valuable because her generation threw out most of them. They'd never held a canning seal well.

Dakota smiled at that picture in her mind. Having Nana here had made this occasion so much more special. Cynthia too. She'd helped coordinate things because, apparently, she was quite the project manager.

The favors had been made to Mama's specifications—five Jordan almonds wrapped in tulle circles. When Dakota asked her why five, she explained that it's an indivisible number to symbolize the unity of husband and wife. Dakota loved the Italian traditions she was learning about, including the one that said a plate of Mama and Angelina's delicious cookies should be at each table.

Jason and his date came around to the guests, serving the prosciutto-wrapped cantaloupe Carmella had made. Pippa, Angelina's sous-chef, served an assortment of appetizers from the café. Rico's catering mostly consisted of making sure the steaks from Nana's ranch were prepared just the way Dakota had instructed and that the champagne flowed all night. His staff circulated the room with flutes of the bubbly now.

"Everyone take your seats," Franco announced after several toasts had been offered wishing happiness and long life to the bride and groom. "Rico's and Angelina's staff will start serving supper soon."

"Good," Matteo said to her. "I couldn't eat a bite this morning, but now I'm starving."

When Dakota had asked him what he wanted to eat at the reception, he'd immediately told her steak and potatoes. No surprise there, but she did surprise him by asking Rico to prepare the steaks in a unique way. Nana said it was popular in Medora, North Dakota, not far from her ranch.

After asking guests as they arrived to let him know how they wanted their steak cooked, Rico and his crew later fried the porterhouse steaks on brand-new pitchforks in three huge vats of oil.

Everyone helped to make the event special. Paul volunteered to roast fifty pounds of Idaho potatoes over the coals at the barbecue pit he'd constructed with cement blocks and a grate at the back of the house. Nana also insisted on making the special baked beans that Dakota had loved as a child. His brothers Tony and Franco were in charge of the Italian pasta salad and green salad, respectively. No fish or seafood in sight, just the way Matt wanted it.

But they were interrupted so many times while trying to eat that he didn't really get more than a few bites. Truth be told, Matt only had an appetite for his bride, but he'd have to be patient a few more hours. Then they could head out to wherever Dakota had chosen for their first night as a married couple. Didn't matter where to him, as long as she was with him.

The meal was followed by cutting the cake, which was served as dessert. Everything was happening so fast in some ways—and not fast enough in others.

They'd barely nibbled on a cookie or two when the next thing he knew, Franco returned to the mic. "It's time for the newlyweds' first dance, so gather around the dance floor, everyone."

A dance floor had been set down in the center of the tent. Matt took Dakota's hand to lead her to the edge of the dance floor where he left her. Then he crossed the floor to take his spot on the opposite side, just the way they'd rehearsed it. He'd never had so much fun dancing as he had practicing with her for this first dance.

Cody Johnson's "Ride With Me" started to play, and she lifted her skirt to swish at him as her gorgeous body began to sway to the beat.

Man, I could watch her dance all day.

Soon she began to close the gap between them, which was his cue to get moving toward her in a teasing, playful way, though they didn't touch each other yet. Her steamy gaze held so many promises—for tonight, tomorrow, and the rest of their lives.

Dakota and Matt circled around each other seductively until the moment Cody sang, *take my hand* for the first chorus. Matt wrapped his arm around her waist and brought her around to face him. Taking her hand in his, he led her into a two-stepping strut around the dance floor. Neither of them took their eyes off each other. At each subsequent chorus, he stopped to twirl her around to the cheers of their guests, then he'd wrap his arm around her again and they'd continue their dance.

At the mention of the gate opening and holding on tight, Dakota threw back her head and laughed. That damned bull ride had brought her to him, so he'd come to thank the cursed animal over time. But he didn't want Dakota anywhere near another bull as long as they lived, except maybe him. But that's not what she called him.

Her Italian stallion.

Her cowboy fireman.

Her man.

Dakota hated to have the song end, but Matteo gave her another deep kiss before leading her off the dance floor.

"Hold on, Matt," Franco announced. "Mama, Paul, would you join Dakota and Matteo on the dance floor?"

The older couple walked toward them. They'd done so much to make Dakota feel loved these past six months.

Mama gave Dakota a hug. "That was so much fun to watch. Love you, my daughter."

Tears stung Dakota's eyes. She'd never get used to having a mother's love again. Their bond would continue to grow over the years to come.

Mama turned to Matteo and Paul approached Dakota, giving her a hug and a kiss on the cheek. "Thank you for accepting me into your life," he told her. Like her, Paul was a newcomer to the family, but that probably made it easier for her accept him as a father figure, whereas Matteo and his siblings had grown up with a papa. Paul had given her advice, comfort, and had promised to be there for her no matter what.

"We're doing the next dance a little differently," Franco announced. "Mama and Matt will have their mother-son dance at the same time Paul and Dakota do their father-daughter one, both dancing to the same song."

She'd never heard of it being done this way until she'd found something about it when researching how daughters and stepfathers did their dance. To Dakota, her bond with Paul was an even closer one than that.

When Matteo had suggested each of them dance with their parent at the same time, she thought it sounded like the perfect idea. Mama and Paul had accepted her as their daughter, and Matteo said his dance with Mama would be an opportunity for him to show her how grateful he was to her for giving him life, raising him through good times and bad, and for accepting Dakota as her daughter.

Paul took her into his arms, and she smiled up at him. "I don't know how to thank you, Paul, for everything you've done for us."

"You just did. And you know the drill. Anything you ever need, just let Paul know."

She smiled up at him. What she didn't know was what song Mama and Paul had chosen for this dance, so when "My Wish," by Rascal Flatts began to play, tears came to her eyes immediately. How perfect.

Loved.

Not only had he been instrumental with her reuniting with Nana, but Paul and Mama had shown her unconditional love even before Matteo proposed. She glanced at Mama, who had tears in her eyes as she looked up adoringly at her son. She never showed favorites with her children or those they brought into the fold. Such a special person, and she'd accepted Dakota from the start, even as far back as high school.

When the song ended, Paul gave her another peck on the cheek. Before he could rejoin Mama, she placed a hand on his forearm. "Paul, you said I could ask anything."

He cocked his head but smiled. "I meant it too."

Dakota took a deep breath and blew it out, then asked, "Can I call you Papa?"

His eyes filled with tears, but he didn't do anything to dash them away when they began to stream down his cheek. He cleared his throat. "That would be my greatest honor next to being Angela's husband." She moved her hand to behind his neck and pulled him down to give him a kiss on the cheek.

He wrapped his arms around her. "Love you, dear girl."

"Love you too, Papa." She brushed away a tear of her own as he led her off the dance floor and back to Matteo.

"You okay?" he asked.

She smiled through her tears. "Never better." She'd tell him later what all the tears were about.

Then she'd probably create a few for Matteo as well.

Epilogue

Dakota couldn't believe how much fun everyone was having, including her and Matteo. As the three-hour reception began to wind down, she started going over the mental checklist of all they needed to do before heading off on their two-week honeymoon trip, starting with three nights at Glacier National Park. When she'd told him she'd wanted to go there and take a Red Bus tour on the Going-to-the-Sun Road over Logan Pass—just like her nana had done on her own honeymoon half a century earlier—he'd immediately booked them into the lodge at East Glacier.

From there, after turning in their rental car, they'd catch the Amtrak train west to Seattle where they'd hop on a seven-day cruise to Alaska. She'd never been on a cruise and Nana had insisted on giving that as her wedding gift. Mama and Paul sprang for the most expensive train ticket available, so they'd have their own bedroom and bath in a sleeping car. Then they'd fly home after a few days in Alaska.

Jason and Rafe had assured them that they'd take excellent care of all their horses while they were gone, with Luke and Ryder offering to be their backup, in case of emergency. She wasn't worried about leaving the ranch, but knew she'd be ready to return home too. They could go back to Alaska another time for a deeper exploration.

But first things first. Dakota couldn't wait to take Matteo up to the cabin for their first night as husband and wife. Ryder had loaned them a vintage buckboard and a horse trained to pull it. It had been parked out of sight at the side of the barn nobody had used today. Even before she rounded the barn, she could see it had been festooned with sunflowers and tulle. A quilt had been folded over the seat to protect their clothes. She wanted to make an entrance when she drove it around to the front of the tent to pick up her groom and load up their supplies.

She rounded the corner of the barn where the horse had been left hitched and tied by Ryder, only to find Franco near the back of the barn kissing someone. She smiled. Love was in the air! Mama would be thrilled if another wedding was in the works.

He didn't seem to be aware of her presence, and she didn't want to intrude on the moment, but the horse whinnied, and they stopped kissing and turned toward her before his partner ducked behind the barn.

Rico? Her eyes opened wider. She didn't even know the two were a thing—or to be honest, that Franco was gay.

"Oh! Sorry to interrupt, guys!"

The guilty expression on Franco's face caught her by surprise. Were the two keeping their relationship secret? Or was this thing between Franco and Rico something new?

Having competed in annual events run by the International Gay Rodeo Association for years now—an organization that had let her ride whatever she wanted over the years—she'd gotten to know a number of gay cowboys.

But Matteo hadn't mentioned anything about either of them being an item when she told him Rico was catering their event, other than that they'd been friends since high school, and that he'd been in Franco's class.

"Please, don't mind me." She'd feel equally awkward interrupting someone else's kiss. "I just came for the horse and buggy, then I'll get out of your hair. We're getting ready to head out."

Franco glanced behind her as if expecting someone to join her then ran his hand through his already mussed hair and started toward her. "Need any help?"

Seriously? But this might be a way to cut the tension. "Sure, that would be great."

She'd never seen Franco with horses, and his inexperience showed in how he held onto the harness rather than the bridle. "Thanks, Franco."

He stared at her a moment as if he wanted to say something else. "Listen, Dakota, about Rico."

"Nobody else should bother you if you want to pick up where you left off." She waggled her eyebrows the way the brothers often did when teasing each other.

But he seemed taken aback. She thought she heard Rico laughing from behind the barn, but he didn't come back out to join them.

Wait? Had she just happened upon a first kiss between the two? She smiled at him, thrilled to think their wedding day might have sparked a budding romance.

"I promise not to say a word until you two are ready to say something first."

Franco's facial features softened. "I appreciate that, Dakota. My little brother's one helluva lucky man."

"Oh no! *I'm* the lucky one. Not only did I gain a husband, but brothers like you and an entire family!"

She gave him a peck on the cheek before letting him help her into the seat and clicking her tongue to send the horse to the front of the barn toward the tent. Tin cans had been tied to the back of the buckboard and she turned around to look at Franco who shrugged. So that's what he and Rico had been doing back here. She shook her head and smiled.

As she came closer to the tent, her eyes scanned the crowd for her husband, and when their gazes met, he raised his eyebrows in question. Mama supervised Tony, Papa, and Rafe loading up their suitcases and a cooler into the back of the wagon.

"I'm not sure Leadville is equipped for a horse and buckboard."

"We aren't going into town," Dakota assured him.

He glanced toward the house. "Are you planning to circle around the barn or house to stage exit photos for Megan?"

"I'm sure she'll be taking photos, but we aren't *staging* our exit."

"I don't know how we'll get everyone to go home. Several told me they'd be staying overnight after having too much champagne."

The man certainly had a lot of questions and concerns about this!

"No worries. They can sleep in the house, the barn, or even on the dance floor. We won't be here, but I'm sure Mama will make sure everyone's taken care of."

He looked up at her. "Okay, I'm intrigued."

"I like keeping you guessing, cowboy fireman," she said as she took his hand to get down from the buckboard and hitched the reins to a post. "Let's say our goodbyes and get moving while the sun's still up."

After hugs and kisses with their family, they ran a gauntlet of friends and family members sending them off in a sea of thousands of bubbles. Dakota laughed, trying but failing to catch some. At the buckboard, he helped her up the step into the seat.

"Don't forget to toss the bouquet!" Angelina shouted.

"Oh, I did forget!" They weren't doing the traditional garter toss, either, which might have gotten a little risqué. But they would keep this wedding tradition. The eligible ladies gathered, and she turned her back to them, closed her eyes, and let the bouquet fly. When she turned around, she saw that Jason's girlfriend had caught it and blushed so sweetly as she smiled at the boy. A quick glance at Annette told Dakota that this mama wasn't ready to marry off her son, but hey, it was just a tradition, right?

"Jason sure seems sweet on her," she remarked to Matteo as he took his seat beside her. "They truly seem perfect together, don't they? Wish I'd been allowed to date you back in high school, Matteo. We missed a lot of years."

"Let's not look back. Hopefully, we still have plenty of years ahead of us and will pack a whole lot of living into every one we're given."

He leaned in to kiss her and they were reminded they weren't alone yet by the cheers from the wedding guests surrounding them. Laughing, he picked up the reins, then glanced her way. "I'm not sure I can take the lead here because I have no clue where we're going."

Dakota smiled. "I'll get us there." She took the reins and clicked her tongue to turn around in the driveway and head toward the large pasture.

"Aren't we headed the wrong way?"

"Trust me, cowboy fireman."

"Always." Matteo took off his hat and waved goodbye to the

crowd, then hid their faces once again as he turned her face toward his and kissed her soundly. The horse rode off to more cheers from their loved ones.

As they headed toward the government lands, Matteo peppered her with questions as he surveyed what was in the bed of the buckboard.

"I don't see any camping gear."

"Nope." She didn't want to give anything away.

"I suppose we could sleep in the back of the buckboard, but shouldn't we have brought some quilts and pillows?"

"We could, but we aren't, so we won't need them." She already had the bed made with a beautiful vintage quilt Mama had found for them. When he cocked his head in confusion, she grinned. "I plan to keep you guessing, cowboy fireman, until we're both old and gray."

He stared at her hair. "I'm going to enjoy the hell out of your ginger curls between now and then. And then I'll just have to get used to your silver curls."

The thought of growing old with Matteo made her heart sing. As she rounded the bend and the cabin came into sight, she pulled on the horse's reins.

"What the…?"

The cabin's porch had been decorated in tulle and sunflowers, the decorating theme of the day. She'd somehow veered them away from the cabin on their last two daily rides leading up to the wedding so as not to spoil her surprise.

"Welcome to our love nest, darlin'," she said with a smile.

"Are you sure about this? Nobody's been inside there since I bought the place."

She gave him a mysterious smile as she halted the horse in front of the front porch steps for them to unload.

"I like how you decorated the porch—and the buckboard."

"Thanks. I had some help from Angelina and Carmella yesterday afternoon."

Matteo stepped down first and secured the reins to the porch post and looked down at the porch steps.

"Hey, there aren't any broken boards anymore."

"Nope."

He gave her a puzzled expression and glanced toward the cabin window. Not that he could see anything inside because she'd kept the interior dark until she was ready to turn on the lanterns inside and show him all the work that had been done on the cabin.

"Wow, you washed the windows."

"Mm-hmm. With some help from Mama" Who'd done a whole lot more too.

Matteo helped her down, wrapping his arms around her waist and lowering her to the ground so that every inch of her rubbed against his hard body. "Sweetheart," he said, "I can tell I'm in for one helluva ride with you."

"Maybe several if you play your cards right tonight."

He laughed. "I meant life with you in general, but I do look forward to those rides too." He smacked her on the ass, and she couldn't wait to get into bed with him. But they had to take care of some chores before going inside.

"Let's set these things on the porch and get the horse settled for the night first." She'd always take care of her horses first!

Matteo looked around. "Where do you plan to board her for the night?"

Rather than tell him, she unhitched the horse from the buckboard and the post and led the mare around the back to the new lean-to shelter and small corral Paul—*Papa*—and some of the men from the firehouse had built for the horses. The mild July evening wouldn't be a problem for the horse if she stayed outside, as long as she had feed and water.

"I'm almost afraid to ask what else you plan to surprise me with tonight." He kissed her again, then they made sure the horse's needs were met before walking back around to the front porch.

"Am I right to guess we're going inside the cabin now?"

"Of course, silly. Where else would we sleep?"

At the door, she reached down and turned the doorknob. The door swung inward with barely a nudge.

"New door?"

Dakota laughed and shook her head. "New hinges. Now, if you'll carry me over the threshold, I have a few other surprises."

In fact, you're in for quite a few surprises tonight, husband of mine.

"Yes, ma'am."

He carried her into the room, but the waning daylight entering the room through the windows and door didn't show him much detail. The room smelled like lavender and strawberries. Not at all like it had smelled when he'd gone inside almost two years ago after buying the property.

Dakota turned his face toward hers and leaned in to kiss him, reminding him he was shirking his duties as groom. He kissed her back, his cock growing hard in anticipation of the night ahead of them.

She broke off the kiss first. "Set me down so I can turn on some lights, then I'll give you a tour."

At some point, he needed to take charge but right now, he had no clue what to expect or do. Slowly, letting her body press against him as he set her on her feet, he took her face in his hands for another kiss, but she broke this one off and went to the corner where a small table now stood. She lit a kerosene lantern and between his eyes beginning to adjust to the darkness and the growing flame of the lantern, he was able to make out more detail.

Dakota stared at him, apparently waiting for his reaction. Nothing could have prepared him for what he saw.

"Holy cow! Is this the same old cabin?"

"Well, yes and no. Same cabin, but completely new decor."

The interior had been transformed into a cozy place with a double bed on the opposite wall covered with a quilt. Next to the fireplace enough kindling and wood had been stacked to keep the fire burning all night.

Man, he couldn't wait to get his bride into that bed, but he had questions. Lots of questions. "Do you want to tell me what you've been up to?"

Dakota laughed. "Do I ever! I've been dying to tell you about it for months but didn't want to miss seeing the look on your face when you saw it for the first time. Come here."

He went closer to where she stood by a round table covered in an old-fashioned, light-blue checkered tablecloth tucked into the corner. "Look at the view before it's too dark."

He looked out at the Collegiates, still sporting some snowpack on the northern slopes. A vase with sunflowers—of course, it being her favorite flower—sat in a blue mason jar in the center of the table.

"We'll have a gorgeous view of the mountains over our breakfast table tomorrow." Assuming he'd be able to tear his eyes away from her. "Do you recognize this lantern?"

He studied it more closely. Looked familiar, but he shook his head.

"It belonged to Mama's papa. He worked in the mines and she thought this would be the perfect place for it, so she gave it to us."

"Wow. You're right. It used to sit in her bedroom in Aspen Corners. She never really explained the significance, unless I just wasn't paying attention."

"Remember the fire up here last month?"

"How could I forget?"

"I had left it up here already, so I mainly came up to rescue this lantern."

He scowled at her. "Woman, as precious as you might think this is to me and my family, nothing is more precious than you are. Don't you ever pull a stunt like that again."

She waved off his attempt at being stern and took his hand to pull him to the center of the room. Matt didn't see a speck of dust or any cobwebs like the ones that had been here before.

"If we decide to spend a lot of time up here, we can install solar panels and maybe have a small fridge."

They stood on a homemade red-and-black rag rug that filled the middle of the room, exuding warmth and welcome. Good thing it got chilly on this mountain, even in July, because his mind went straight to the thought of making love to her on that rug in front of the fire before their wedding night was over.

"You can't believe how difficult it was to pull off this renovation the past seven weeks," she continued when he didn't say anything. "I could only work up here the days you were on duty or deployed in Idaho, because I wanted to keep it a surprise."

"Wait. We were only engaged six weeks."

She nodded. "I know. I actually started on it before that. I planned to use my winnings from the Ski Joring Festival and riding Silverback. When your Mama and Paul came to take me to lunch and they heard what I wanted to do, they enthusiastically helped out. I never could have done as much as I did on my winnings alone, so I was so happy they wanted to help."

"Why would you want to spend your money on this place when you weren't even sure you'd stay?"

She grinned. "Oh, I think I knew I planned to stay, even if you didn't know yet you were going to ask me to. You might have had more trouble getting me to leave, actually."

"I never would have tried to do that. I've wanted you to stay since Christmas Eve, I think." He glanced around the little cabin again. A rough-hewn ladder was propped against the wall leading up to the loft, and the corner at the other end of the front of the cabin had been curtained off.

"What's back there?"

"A dry toilet, compliments of Paul."

He hadn't even thought about the necessity of having a place to go.

As they brought in the rest of their things from outside, he continued to marvel at what she'd accomplished. "How'd you do all this in such a short time? This took a lot of work!"

"Well, I had a lot of help from family and even a few guys from the firehouse who helped on their days off. Even Rafe came down a few times; he was a big help too."

Matt had noticed how the two of them often went off in quiet conversation over the past few weeks, but he just assumed they were making plans for the wedding ceremony.

"But I'll have you know that Mama and I held our own against all that testosterone and did our fair share of the heavy lifting. I still can't believe nobody let anything slip around you."

"Me too. God, I'm so proud of you, Sweet Lady!" He wrapped his arms around her and kissed her again. "Judging by what you did with this place, have you ever considered interior design and renovations?"

"One career at a time."

"Well, you've already made our ranch a real home and now you've given us this little getaway cabin for when we need one."

"It could come in handy," she said somewhat cryptically, but right now, he intended to make use of every moment they had before they left on their honeymoon. He lifted her into his arms and carried her the few steps to the bed.

"How strong is the bed?"

She giggled. "I think it can take anything we give it."

He dropped her on to the mattress and covered her with this body. When she winced, he eased off her.

"Everything okay?"

"Oh, I think my dress is just a little tight in the bodice."

Matt grinned. "I can take care of that. Turn over." She rolled onto her side, and he began undoing the tiny buttons. He needed both hands but finally had them all undone and pulled the top off her right shoulder, kissing her there. She scooted onto her back and helped him take it completely off, letting it rest at her waist. Her bare breasts must have swollen in the tight dress. Not that he was complaining.

He took her nipple into his mouth and sucked hard, but she gasped rather than moaned.

"Sorry. I thought you liked that."

"Oh I do, but…"

"Everything okay, Dakota?"

She nibbled her lower lip and his libido tanked. Was she sick or something?

"How do you feel about children, Matteo?"

"Love them. Keep waiting to hear I'm going to become an uncle, but Marc and Tony don't seem to be in any hurry." He bent down to give her a kiss, hoping to pick up where they'd left off. Didn't seem like anything serious if she was talking about…

He lifted his head and stared at her. "Why are you asking that at a time like this?"

"Well, unless one of them has a secret they haven't shared with us yet, I think we're going to beat them in that competition."

Matt swallowed hard. "You're pregnant?"

She nodded. "I only found out last week. I didn't even consider that was an option, even though I know we did slip up that time in the camper, but with so much going on and my periods always being crazy, it didn't occur to me to even check. But it showed up when I had my annual checkup. I decided I might as well surprise you, although my plan was to do so in the morning before we left."

He drew in a slow, deep breath, trying to process what she'd just told him. "I'm going to be a papa?"

"You're going to be an amazing papa."

After those words sank in, a slow smile spread across his face.

"I'm three months along."

He did the math in his head. "So, baby's due in January?"

She nodded. "The seventeenth. I should be good as new by the time the Ski Joring Festival rolls around next year."

He grinned and shook his head. "So you win the competition to give Mama her first grandchild and then turn around to make it two years in a row for the overall championship?"

"Oh no. I'll be competing in the Open next year. I'm going pro."

He sighed. "Promise me you'll at least take it easy and follow doctor's orders until after the baby's here. I don't want you pulling any dangerous stunts or falling off a horse or anything."

She narrowed her eyelids. "I won't be getting on any bulls, but you're not going to keep me off my horses, Matteo. Not unless my obstetrician grounds me, anyway."

"What about the bronc-riding school next month?"

"I'm the teacher, remember? I don't have to get on one myself."

"And the fire academy?"

"I'll put off declaring my major the first year and focus on the degree's classroom work first."

He better get used to the fact she wasn't going to slow down, back down, or let up.

"But there is one fire I intend to put out tonight." She pushed him off her and onto his back then lifted her skirt and straddled him. "I also plan to ride you, my cowboy fireman. I've been running around all day today without any underwear, and now I intend to get you out of your pants."

And she did just that!

Books by Kallypso Masters

Rescue Me Saga (Erotic Military Romance)

Kally has no intention of ending the *Rescue Me Saga* ever, but will continue to introduce spinoff series in the years to come. The following *Rescue Me Saga* titles are available in e-book and print formats on my website and at major booksellers:

Masters at Arms & Nobody's Angel (Combined Volume)

Nobody's Hero

Nobody's Perfect

Somebody's Angel

Nobody's Lost

Nobody's Dream

Somebody's Perfect

Rescue Me Saga Box Set Books 1-3 (e-book only)

Rescue Me Saga Box Set Books 4-6 and Western Dreams (e-book only)

Rescue Me Saga Extras (Erotic Romance)

This will be a series of hot, fun, short-story collections featuring beloved couples from the *Rescue Me Saga.*

Western Dreams (Rescue Me Saga Extras #1)

Wedding Dreams (Rescue Me Saga Extras #2)

Raging Fire Series (Steamy Firefighter Romance)

Angelina's brothers are getting their stories told now, beginning with *Tony: Slow Burn* **(Raging Fire #1)**. Book 2 is being serialized on Kally's Patreon fan page with *Matteo: Wild Fire*. Franco's and Rafe's stories will follow when ready, first in serial form then as complete novels and available wherever you buy books.

Roar (a *Rescue Me Saga* Erotic Romance Spin-off)

(Erotic Romance with Secondary Characters from the *Rescue Me Saga*. *Roar* provides a lead-in to the upcoming trilogy with Patrick's, Grant's, and Gunnar's stories.)

Bluegrass Spirits (Supernatural Contemporary Romance)

(Contemporary Romance...with a Haunting Twist)

Jesse's Hideout

Kate's Secret

kallypsomasters.com/books

About the Author

Kallypso Masters is a *USA Today* Bestselling Author with more than half-a-million copies of her books sold in e-book and paperback formats since August 2011. All her books feature alpha males, strong women, and happy endings because those are her favorite stories to read, but that doesn't mean they don't touch on tough life issues at times. Her original and best-known series—the Rescue Me Saga—features emotional, realistic adult Romance novels with characters healing from past traumas and PTSD, sometimes using unconventional methods (like BDSM).

Kally began publishing *TONY: Slow Burn* and *MATTEO: Wild Fire* her first two of four books in the Raging Fire series, as serials on her Patreon fan club page in spring 2019. Next up will be FRANCO (full title to be determined). From Patreon, the books undergo extensive edits and are then published as ebooks and paperbacks.

An eighth-generation Kentuckian, a few years ago Kally launched the ***Bluegrass Spirits*** series, supernatural Contemporary Romances set in some of her favorite places in her home state. *Jesse's Hideout* (Bluegrass Spirits #1) takes place in her dad's hometown and includes a recipe section with some of Kally's treasured family recipes, most of which are mentioned in the story. *Kate's Secret* (Bluegrass Spirits #2) takes place in Kentucky's horse country. Local flavor abounds in this series with more books planned in the future.

Kally has been living her own "happily ever after" with her husband of almost 40 years, known affectionately to her readers as Mr. Ray. They have two adult children and an adorable grandson, Erik, who was the model for the character Derek in *Jesse's Hideout* and Erik in *Kate's Secret.* (He insisted on having his real name used in the second one!)

Kally enjoys meeting readers wherever she travels and will continue to hold annual KallypsoCons in the United States and Canada as long as she's able. She also likes to cook (most days) and uses the hashtag #CookingAdventuresWithKally on Facebook. To keep up with future events, check out the Appearances or Kally's Events page on her website!

Keep in touch with Kally for updates and much more at
kallypsomasters.com/keep-in-touch

To contact or engage with Kally, go to:
Facebook (where almost all of her posts are public),
Facebook Author page,
Patreon Fan Club (for exclusive content/access and serialized stories),
TikTok (tiktok.com/@kallypsomasters)
InstaGram (instagram.com/kallypsomasters), and
Kally's Website (KallypsoMasters.com).

Always feel free to e-mail Kally at kallypsomasters@gmail.com, or write to her at
Kallypso Masters, PO Box 1183, Richmond, KY 40476-1183

Signed Books & Merch in the Kally Store!

Want to own merchandise or personalized, signed paperback copies of any or all of Kallypso Masters' books in the *Rescue Me Saga*, *Rescue Me Saga Extras*, *Bluegrass Spirits*, or the *Raging Fire* series? How about Kallypso Masters Ka-thunk! and and other promotional T-shirts, as well as swag items connected to her books? Kally ships internationally. To shop for these items and much more, go to kallypsomasters.com/kally_swag.

And you can also purchase any of Kally's e-books directly from her, too! Go here for a complete list of available titles. New releases will be published exclusively in Kally's Shop before being available on other retailer sites.
kallypsomasters.com/buy-direct

Roar (A Rescue Me Saga Spin-off)

A tragic accident left his beloved wife just beyond his reach, haunting Kristoffer Roar Larson for four years until a chance meeting with Pamela stirs feelings best kept buried. Her assertive alpha personality coupled with her desire to submit and serve fascinates him. Will he allow her presence to shine light once more into the dark corners of his life?

Dr. Pamela Jeffrey thrives on providing medical assistance to those in war-torn corners of the world until a health scare grounds her stateside. While pursuing her deepest secret desire, she encounters Kristoffer, who reluctantly agrees to help prepare her for a future Dom. The bond deepens between them as does her desire for him to be that man in her life, but Kristoffer cannot meet all of her needs. Can she be satisfied with what he can propose without regrets?

As the undeniable connection grows between them, feelings of betrayal take root. How can Pamela convince him he deserves another chance at love? Will Kristoffer be able to fully open himself to the ginger-haired sprite who makes him question everything he once believed? Or will he lose the woman teaching him to live again as surely as he lost the person who first taught him to love?

NOTE: While this book is a standalone, it includes secondary characters from the Rescue Me Saga, including Gunnar Larson, Patrick Gallagher, and V. Grant, and there is a scene in the Masters at Arms Club.

Reading Order for the *Rescue Me Saga & Extras*

kallypsomasters.com/books

Masters at Arms & Nobody's Angel (Combined Volume)

Nobody's Hero

Nobody's Perfect

Somebody's Angel

Nobody's Lost

Nobody's Dream

Western Dreams

Somebody's Perfect

Wedding Dreams

Reading Order for the *Raging Fire* Series

TONY: Slow Burn

MATTEO: Wild Fire

Reading Order for the *Bluegrass Spirits* Series
(Supernatural Contemporary Romances)

From the *USA Today* Best-Selling Author of the *Rescue Me Saga* comes a new Contemporary Romance series with supernatural elements set amidst the many flavors of Kentucky. In *Bluegrass Spirits*, Kallypso Masters distills love and happily ever afters—with a little matchmaking guidance from loved ones on the other side. While there will be updates about earlier couples in each subsequent story, each novel can be enjoyed on its own.

Jesse's Hideout

Kate's Secret

Made in USA - North Chelmsford, MA
1290907_9781941060391
11.18.2021 0855